Book 17 – THE OUTCAST
Graham McNeill

Book 18 – DELIVERANCE LOST
Gav Thorpe

Book 19 – KNOW NO FEAR
Dan Abnett

Book 20 – THE PRIMARCHS
edited by Christian Dunn

Book 21 – FEAR TO TREAD
James Swallow

Book 22 – SHADOWS OF TREACHERY
edited by Christian Dunn and Nick Kyme

Book 23 – ANGEL EXTERMINATUS
Graham McNeill

Book 24 – BETRAYER
Aaron Dembski-Bowden

Book 25 – MARK OF CALTH
edited by Laurie Goulding
(2013)

*Many of these titles are also available as abridged and unabridged audiobooks.
Order the full range of Horus Heresy novels and audiobooks from
www.blacklibrary.com*

Audio Dramas

THE DARK KING AND THE LIGHTNING TOWER
Graham McNeill and Dan Abnett

RAVEN'S FLIGHT
Gav Thorpe

GARRO: OATH OF MOMENT
James Swallow

GARRO: LEGION OF ONE
James Swallow

BUTCHER'S NAILS
Aaron Dembski-Bowden

GREY ANGEL
John French

GARRO: BURDEN OF DUTY
James Swallow

GARRO: SWORD OF TRUTH
James Swallow

THE SIGILLITE
Chris Wraight
(2013)

Download the full range of Horus Heresy audio dramas from
www.blacklibrary.com

Also available

THE SCRIPTS: VOLUME I
edited by Christian Dunn

THE HORUS HERESY™

Aaron Dembski-Bowden

BETRAYER

Blood for the Blood God

BLACK LIBRARY

*For my brother Barney.
In memory of the time we used gun turrets to shoot our
initials into the wall of an alien base.
And as an apology for that time I team-killed you with a plasma grenade.*

An accident, I swear.

A BLACK LIBRARY PUBLICATION

Hardback edition first published in 2012.
This edition published in 2013 by
Black Library,
Games Workshop Ltd.,
Willow Road,
Nottingham, NG7 2WS, UK.

10 9 8 7 6 5 4 3 2 1

Cover illustration by Neil Roberts.

© Games Workshop Limited 2013. All rights reserved.

Black Library, the Black Library logo, The Horus Heresy, The Horus Heresy logo, The Horus Heresy eye device, Space Marine Battles, the Space Marine Battles logo, Warhammer 40,000, the Warhammer 40,000 logo, Games Workshop, the Games Workshop logo and all associated brands, names, characters, illustrations and images from the Warhammer 40,000 universe are either ®, TM and/or © Games Workshop Ltd 2000-2013, variably registered in the UK and other countries around the world. All rights reserved.

A CIP record for this book is available from the British Library.

UK ISBN: 978 1 84970 388 8
US ISBN: 978 1 84970 389 5

No part of this publication may be reproduced, stored in a retrieval system, or transmitted in any form or by any means, electronic, mechanical, photocopying, recording or otherwise, without the prior permission of the publishers.

This is a work of fiction. All the characters and events portrayed in this book are fictional, and any resemblance to real people or incidents is purely coincidental.

See Black Library on the internet at

www.blacklibrary.com

Find out more about Games Workshop
and the world of Warhammer 40,000 at

www.games-workshop.com

Printed and bound by CPI Group (UK) Ltd, Croydon, CR0 4YY

THE HORUS HERESY
It is a time of legend.

The galaxy is in flames. The Emperor's glorious vision for humanity is in ruins. His favoured son, Horus, has turned from his father's light and embraced Chaos.

His armies, the mighty and redoubtable Space Marines, are locked in a brutal civil war. Once, these ultimate warriors fought side by side as brothers, protecting the galaxy and bringing mankind back into the Emperor's light.
Now they are divided.

Some remain loyal to the Emperor, whilst others have sided with the Warmaster. Pre-eminent amongst them, the leaders of their thousands-strong Legions are the primarchs. Magnificent, superhuman beings, they are the crowning achievement of the Emperor's genetic science. Thrust into battle against one another, victory is uncertain for either side.

Worlds are burning. At Isstvan V, Horus dealt a vicious blow and three loyal Legions were all but destroyed. War was begun, a conflict that will engulf all mankind in fire. Treachery and betrayal have usurped honour and nobility. Assassins lurk in every shadow. Armies are gathering.
All must choose a side or die.

Horus musters his armada, Terra itself the object of his wrath. Seated upon the Golden Throne, the Emperor waits for his wayward son to return. But his true enemy is Chaos, a primordial force that seeks to enslave mankind
to its capricious whims.

The screams of the innocent, the pleas of the righteous resound to the cruel laughter of Dark Gods. Suffering and damnation await all should the Emperor fail
and the war be lost.

The age of knowledge and enlightenment has ended.
The Age of Darkness has begun.

~ DRAMATIS PERSONAE ~

The Primarchs

WARMASTER HORUS LUPERCAL	Primarch of the Sons of Horus
ANGRON	Primarch of the World Eaters
LORGAR AURELIAN	Primarch of the Word Bearers
MAGNUS THE RED	Primarch of the Thousand Sons
ROBOUTE GUILLIMAN	Primarch of the Ultramarines

The XII Legion 'World Eaters'

VORIAS	Lectio Primus, Librarius Division
ESCA	Codicier, Librarius Division
KHÂRN	Captain, Eighth Company, and Equerry to Angron
KARGOS	'Bloodspitter', Apothecary, Eighth Company
JEDDEK	Standard bearer, Eighth Company
SKANE	Sergeant, Skane Destroyer squad, Eighth Company
GHARTE	Sergeant, Marakan Tactical squad, Eighth Company
DELVARUS	Centurion, Delvarus Triarii squad, 44th Company
LHORKE	'The First'; Dreadnought, Contemptor-pattern
NERAS	Dreadnought

The XVII Legion 'Word Bearers'

Argel Tal	Gal Vorbak, Commander of the Vakrah Jal
Erebus	First Chaplain, Dark Apostle of the Word
Eshramar	Vakrah Jal, Sergeant, Eshramar Immolation squad

The XIII Legion 'Ultramarines'

Orfeo Cassandar	Legatus of Armatura

Fleet Personnel

Lotara Sarrin	Flag-Captain of the XII Legion warship *Conqueror*
Ivar Tobin	First Officer of the XII Legion warship *Conqueror*
Feyd Hallerthan	Officer of the XII Legion warship *Conqueror*
Lehralla	Scrymistress of the XII Legion warship *Conqueror*
Kejic	Vox-master of the XII Legion warship *Conqueror*
The Blessed Lady	Confessor of the Word

The Martian Mechanicum

Vel-Kheredar	Archmagos Veneratus, representative of Kelbor-Hal

The Legio Audax 'Ember Wolves'

Venric Solostine	Princeps Ultima, and Princeps of the Command Titan *Syrgalah*
Toth Kol	Moderati Primus, Command Titan *Syrgalah*
Keeda Bly	Moderati Secundus, Command Titan *Syrgalah*
The Ninth	Mechanicum Adept, Command Titan *Syrgalah*
Audun Lyrac	Princeps Penultima

The Legio Lysanda 'Sentinels of the Edge'

Maxamillien Delantyr	Princeps, Titan *Ardentor*
Ellas Hyle	Moderati Primus, Titan *Ardentor*
Kei Adaras	Moderati Secundus, Titan *Ardentor*

Non-Imperial Personae

Tybaral Thal'kr	Praxuary, Imperial Magnate of Nuceria
Oshamay Evrel'Korshay	General of the Thal'kr Kin-Guard
Damon Prytanis	Perpetual

'Because we couldn't be trusted. The Emperor needed a weapon that would never obey its own desires before those of the Imperium. He needed a weapon that would never bite the hand that feeds. The World Eaters were not that weapon. We've all drawn blades purely for the sake of shedding blood, and we've all felt the exultation of winning a war that never even needed to happen. We are not the tame, reliable pets that the Emperor wanted. The Wolves obey, when we would not. The Wolves can be trusted, when we never could. They have a discipline we lack, because their passions are not aflame with the Butcher's Nails buzzing in the back of their skulls.

'The Wolves will always come to heel when called. In that regard, it is a mystery why they name themselves wolves. They are tame, collared by the Emperor, obeying his every whim. But a wolf doesn't behave that way. Only a dog does.

'That is why we are the Eaters of Worlds, and the War Hounds no longer.'

– Eighth Captain Khârn,
from his unpublished treatise *The Eighteen Legions*

PROLOGUE

Isstvan III

SKANE WAS THE one to find the body. He stood knee-deep in the dead, next to the wrecked hull of a Land Raider battle tank, his armour stained black by the sin of the weapons he wielded.

'Kargos,' he voxed. His voice was tinny, laden with static. One of the enemy had caught him in the throat during the battle, and it had jarred his augmetic vocal cords. They'd need retuning once he returned to the *Conqueror*.

'Kargos,' he said again, across the tomb-quiet vox-channel.

'What?' His brother's reply was also flawed by static, but from more traditional vox-corruption rather than a bionic trachea.

'Track my locator rune,' said Skane. 'Get over here.'

'I'm busy. Look around you, sergeant. You think you're the only one that needs my help at the moment?'

Skane didn't bother looking. He knew where he was and what he'd see – he was at the heart of it all, and the dead numbered in the thousands. Most here wore armour the green of shallow oceans, cracked and shattered by the treachery of their former kindred.

These were Horus's former Sons, betrayed by their brethren and slain for their disloyalty. Among their number, armour of bloodstained white stood out like pearls amongst seaweed. Too many World Eaters had fallen here, though victory was undeniable. The city was dead in every direction, reduced to ash and rubble.

A shadow fell across Skane, blocking out the weak sun as a Legio Audax Warhound passed with its rattle-clank stride, shaking the tortured ground. He lifted a hand to the war machine, receiving no acknowledgement beyond dull sunlight glinting on the Titan's ursus claw spear. It stalked onwards, splayed feet grinding ceramite and bone and twisted iron into the earth, its wolfish cockpit lowered as it hunted for life signs and scanner-scents among the dead and the dying.

Skane turned back to the ruined tank, kneeling by its front end where the minesweeper plough was decorated in scratches and gore. A body impaled on the dozer blade's spikes twitched in uneasy repose, its fingers still scraping in futility across the metal. Skane wasn't sure how the pinned warrior still lived, and doubted the trembling, bleeding figure would survive being pulled from the blade. Nevertheless, he spoke again.

'Kargos,' he said for the third time. It took the Apothecary several seconds to answer.

'I told you I'm busy. Fix your own damn throat, or shut up and wait until we're back aboard the ship.'

Skane disengaged the seals at the dying warrior's neck, lifting the helm free with a hiss of released air pressure. The revealed face was pale, bloodstained from the lips down, the eyes open and blind while the mouth worked in silent, wordless pain.

'I've found Khârn,' Skane voxed.

This time, there was no delay in Kargos's reply. 'I'm on my way.'

PART ONE
ARMATURA, THE WAR-WORLD

One year after the Isstvan V Massacre

I
Last Words

'Any who hear these words, I implore you to carry them across the Imperium. I am Vice Admiral Tion Konor Gallus of the Andarion Fleet, stationed in the Quintus Spread of Ultramar. My personnel clearance numericals are: three-three-Via-nine-one-K-O-L-five-one. We have come under intentional and malign attack by a fleet flying the colours of the Twelfth World Eaters Legion. Our escorts are already dead. Our remaining capital ships are suffering boarding actions. Most were destroyed outright. The Fulgentius Shipyards are lost to treachery. Get word t–

'Variano, they're still strangling this signal. I don't care how you do it, break through this jamming or I'll shoot you myself–

'This is Admiral Gallus of the Andarion Fleet. Get word to the muster at Calth. Get word to Lord Guilliman. We are betrayed. We are betrayed.'

– Admiral Tion Konor Gallus,
Aboard the Ultramarines battleship *Legate*, stationed at Latona

'Theodos to all remaining forces, maintain defensive formation above the arctic circle. Deny them bombardment until the astropathic cry is sent. Any unengaged support frigates in the seventeenth grid allocation, target the Word Bearers vessel identification: Deadsong. Kill it before it brings its lances to bear on the arctic bastion.

'All Aequitas *crew without sacrificial oaths, to the escape pods.*

'Theodos to the fleet: we're crippled and aflame, all non-essential crew abandoning ship. Disengage from any attempts to defend us. Repeat: disengage from any attempts to defend us. Use your guns elsewhere.

'How is this not working? Why are the astropaths silent?

'Put me through to the Deadsong. I don't care if they answer.

'I know you hear me, Seventeenth. We are your brothers. What madness has taken you? What mad–'

– Fleetmaster Gaius Theodos,
Aboard the Ultramarines warship *Aequitas*, stationed at Ulixis

'Still no word from the Calth muster. The signal may not even be reaching them.

'One of us has to get out of here alive…

'This is the flagship to the Azureus: break free by any means necessary. The Tears of Kyanos *and the* Immortal Patriarch *are to move in support, executing a Seven Rises Manoeuvre to take any and all punishment inbound for the Azureus. All escort squadrons, form up around the Azureus in a Deniquo interception pattern.* Igitur, *break off your attack and bring your guns to bear in the third grid to support the Azureus. I want you to peel that Twelfth ship off her tail. We'll only have one shot at this.*

'Azureus, *in the name of the Emperor and the Five Hundred Worlds, run and do not stop. Run to Armatura, and give my regards to Orfeo.'*

– Commander Krios Cassan
Captain of the Ultramarines warship *Vinculum Unitatis*, stationed at Espandor

ONE

The Archpriest and the Sorcerer
Armatura
Warpsong

THE PEREGRINUS BASILICA was an armoured fortress jutting from the flagship's spinal battlements, commanding a view of the warp above the entire spread of the warship *Fidelitas Lex* below. The cathedral itself would be a palace on any world, the size of a city sector in its own right, built in relative humility as a modest echo of the Imperial Palace on Terra.

Lorgar Aurelian was in the domed observatory atop the central spire. He stood calmly, this Lord of the Word Bearers, armoured but unarmed while his sons prepared for war on the hundreds of decks beneath his feet. The ship was alive with chanting and shrieking, yet Lorgar was at peace, watching the mists of madness crashing against the dome.

'Brother,' came a voice from behind.

Lorgar's features – pale, godlike and inked with golden scripture – dawned into a warm smile. Breaking the serenity of his heavenward vigil, he turned, his boots echoing on the mosaic deck as he did so. An image of his brother Magnus greeted him.

If Lorgar's skin was gold-inscribed marble, Magnus was an effigy of burnt copper. Both primarchs were reflections of their father, each of them made in the Emperor's image, but where Lorgar was like an aesthetically pleasing statue, etched with intricate runes and swirling mandalas, Magnus was more akin to a red-skinned heathen idol – a Sun God's avatar of the sort worshipped by primitive cultures in less-enlightened ages. His skin was the red of flayed muscles; his armour a suit of golden scales edged in ivory, and with a bronze helm crested with a lion's mane of bristling scarlet hair. A fist-sized gem of volcanic glass, carved as a black scarab, held his cloak over one shoulder. Lorgar couldn't be certain where his brother was in truth, but the projected essence standing before him was perfect in every detail.

'Magnus,' he said, still smiling. 'Tell me you've made your decision.'

As ever, Lorgar wore his emotions as openly as a soul could, and his genuine gratitude at his brother's arrival shone from his eyes. Even so, Magnus ignored his brother's words.

'I can hear your sons making ready for war,' he said instead.

Lorgar's smile didn't fade. 'A sound to chill the blood, isn't it? They've changed so much since Isstvan.'

'As have you,' said Magnus.

The Word Bearer's smile faltered at last and he looked back to the turbulent heavens. 'Strange. From Angron those same words come as a compliment, or as close to one as our brother could ever manage. From you, though, they seem more of a curse.'

Magnus shrugged.

'I wouldn't trust Angron if he swore to me that water was wet. Our brother is blind. Blind and lost.'

'You underestimate him,' said the Word Bearer. 'He too is changing. We all are. Ah, Magnus, you will see how my Word Bearers make war now. Even a handful of years ago, I'd never have imagined it…' Lorgar smiled once more, then shook his head. 'But you came to tell me of your decision, did you not? Please, brother. Speak it.'

The sorcerer gave a slight shake of his head. 'First tell me of Calth. The Great Ocean's tides crash at the edges of the Calth System,

Lorgar, and death emanates from the place in sickening waves.'

'Regrettable, but necessary.'

Magnus snorted, though Lorgar wasn't sure whether it was with amusement or derision. He turned to gaze back out to the roiling chaos of the warp, staring unblinkingly into its poisoned depths of manifest emotion.

'I'm glad you came,' he said at last. 'I've missed you.'

Magnus gave a low, rumbling chuckle. 'Am I to assume Angron does not offer the brotherly companionship you'd hoped for?'

Lorgar's radiant smile dawned for a third time, but he didn't reply.

Magnus came to stand next to his brother. The Crimson King's image gave off no scent, though his psychic projection made Lorgar's skin itch. No matter how strong the Word Bearer grew, merely standing close to Magnus was enough to set his teeth on edge. His taller sibling exuded a palpable force against the meat of his mind. Nothing physical. Nothing so unsubtle. This was the raw power of a soul, felt in the moment when psychic minds met.

'Where are we?' Magnus asked.

'Close to where we need to be,' Lorgar replied.

'So it is a secret?'

'A surprise, not a secret. There's a difference.'

Magnus hesitated. 'And where is Kor Phaeron? Where is Erebus?'

The Word Bearer tilted his head to regard his brother again. 'All that death you sensed at Calth? That is their work.'

Magnus grunted, noncommittal.

'The Legions are at war,' Lorgar pressed gently, 'and the galaxy burns. Accept it. End your seclusion in the Great Eye. Get back into the fight. You'll be part of Horus's plans, and won't need to ask me what's happening, or where, or why. You'll *know* where the playing pieces stand on the board. You'll be moving them yourself.'

This time Magnus was the one to break contact with his brother's sun-flecked eyes; eyes as divine as his smile.

'You've still not decided, have you?' Lorgar asked.

'I will. Before the end comes, at least.'

Lorgar did not press him further. Instead they just stood there, listening to the warp screaming against the observatory's warded glass and the Word Bearers continued chanting in the decks far below.

'Tell me something,' said Lorgar at last. 'Do you feel shame that Russ broke your back over his knee?'

'Aurelian.' Magnus used the name as a warning.

Lorgar waved a pacifying hand and changed the subject.

'You once warned me not to rely so heavily on Erebus and Kor Phaeron.'

'You're not gifted at following advice,' Magnus pointed out.

Lorgar laughed – a gentle exhalation through a smile. 'True, but you were right.'

'Of course,' said Magnus, then: 'Tell me of Argel Tal.' He made no attempt to hide the intensity of his interest.

'He is aboard the *Conqueror* as we speak, with his Vakrah Jal elite. Of my three closest sons, he alone remains devoted to my vision. And yet, brother, he is broken. As for the other two… I love them for their pride and ambition, yet the warp curdles around them, ripe with the sickness of their souls. They play their own games now. Erebus plays them at the behest of the gods. He is a slave, believing himself king. Kor Phaeron plays them for his own reasons.'

He paused, almost reticent to continue.

'And Ahriman, he is… similar?'

Magnus rested a hand on his brother's shoulder, causing no tangible sensation as he did so. The ethereal hand hovered against the parchment bound to Lorgar's armour.

'He is. A sickening thing for us to share in common, isn't it?'

Lorgar nodded and released a soft breath, not quite a sigh. 'I know I've been a coward, at times. For all my passion, my *zeal*, I faltered at the final hurdle. I should never have sent Argel Tal into the Eye before I entered myself. Of all things, I regret that the most. He has become a haunted creature, plagued by the ghost of a single life he failed to save. Worse, he's caught between what he was and what he is destined to become.'

The ghostly hand lifted. 'No fate is sealed, Lorgar. Change it while you still can.'

'I mean to do just that. He is the best and worst of my sons. The strongest and yet the most broken. I've learned a great deal from what the Pantheon has done to him.'

Magnus turned his face to the Great Ocean's tides breaking over the ship's Geller field. 'I dislike you referring to those sentient storms as a *pantheon*.'

Lorgar's sideward glance made his armour joints whirr. 'One word is as good as any, Magnus. And I cannot change the truth of what they are.'

'Words have power, Lorgar. I scarcely need to remind *you* of that.' The sorcerer grinned suddenly. 'And stop gawping at me, brother! Especially at my eye.'

His smile didn't quite rob his words of their hardness.

But Lorgar didn't obey. He stared openly at the constant metamorphosis of Magnus's visage: a warlord with a missing left eye, the wound sewn closed; a cyclops with one great orb in place of human eyes; a sorcerer with smooth flesh where a right eye had never existed.

When the Word Bearer finally spoke, his tone was completely devoid of the halting doubt that had marked his life for so many years before Isstvan V.

'It has always unnerved me how you look the most like Father.'

Magnus raised a scarred eyebrow. 'I? *You* were made to mirror him, Lorgar. Not I.'

'I did not mean physically.' Lorgar brushed a scriptured hand across his equally tattooed face. 'I'm speaking of your… facelessness. You are as powerful as him, and your face dances in the same way.'

It was Magnus's turn to chuckle. 'I am not as strong as our father. Would that I was.'

Lorgar waved it aside. 'Have any of us even seen your real face? Did you ever have two eyes?'

Magnus tilted his crowned head. 'Didn't you hear the story of how I tore the right eye from its socket in sacrifice for knowledge?' Magnus smiled. 'I like that one. It might be my favourite.'

'I've heard them all,' Lorgar replied, eager to learn more but letting the matter drop. He knew too well that his copper-skinned brother could not be tempted into spilling revelations when he didn't wish to. 'I need your counsel, Magnus.'

'It's yours, as always. Though I'll remind you what happened the last time you asked my advice, only to ignore it.'

The Word Bearer didn't laugh at the bitter jest; he didn't even smirk. 'You mean when I found that Father was lying to the entire Imperium and that the universe is not the godless place he insists it is? Yes, I have a vague recollection of those events.'

'That is one way of looking at it. Not the right way, of course.'

Lorgar shook his head. 'I have no wish, and no need, to debate such matters. What troubles me is something far closer to home. Watch, brother. This was last month, when we assaulted some meaningless Throne-loyal world that Angron couldn't just leave in peace. His World Eaters couldn't be recalled. They massacred the populace.'

He gestured with his empty hand, and a misty image formed before both brothers. Magnus recognised it at once: a figure, armed with two heavy, brutal axes, and armoured in the stylised bronze finery of a gladiator-king. The figure threw back its scarred head, roaring in silence to the sky. Cables thrashed from his skull as a mane of cybernetic dreadlocks. Most were plugged into the power feeds of his armour. As usual, several had torn free in the heat of battle.

'He's dying,' said Lorgar.

Magnus looked at the silent image of Angron facing down a charging Chimera transport. It struck him and ground to a halt. The primarch lifted it by the front ramming bars, flipping it onto its back. Its treads raced in futility the entire time.

'He looks in fine health to me.'

'No. He's dying. The implants are killing him.'

Magnus turned to Lorgar. 'So?'

'So.' The Word Bearer stared at the image. 'I'm going to save him.'

Magnus didn't ask how. He was silent a long moment, before cutting to the core. 'You have always been a fey creature, Lorgar. Sentiment guides you. You know the value of loyalty to those few who have been loyal to you. I admire that. Truly. But would the galaxy really miss Angron's tortured soul? Would his Legion even mourn his loss? Is his life really worth saving?' As his questions trailed away, Magnus turned his attention to the warp once more. He smiled.

'Something amuses you, brother?' asked Lorgar, his golden eyes glinting in the warp's hateful light.

The sorcerer nodded. 'I have just sensed where we are.'

THE FIDELITAS LEX burst into existence, ripping its way back to reality on shrieking engines. The wound that gave birth to it was a tear in space and time, pulsing in the darkness, bringing the impossibility of sound to the vacuum of space. A terrible screaming heralded the warship's arrival, and erratic, maddened laughter followed it through.

Kinetic generators along the warship's belly and backbone groaned as they woke, charging the nothingness around the *Lex*, bringing its void shields into being. Along its flanks and battlements, domes opened in a rattling ballet and blast shields lifted from gun ports as cannons juddered out into the void.

The arcane drives gifting the vessel with warp flight cycled down, relinquishing control of the ship to its physical engines. Deep in the vessel's armoured prow, a man with three eyes and a bloody cough surrendered control of the *Lex* back to the strategium, where hundreds of crew members were securing themselves into their thrones, bathed in the flashing lights of a battle stations alert.

Smaller ships ripped into reality behind the *Lex*, filling its wake with hungry iron children – all bladed, all battlemented. The escorts and destroyers burned their engines harder and hotter than the battleships, powering ahead to establish the first semblance of attack formation.

A shadow filled the wound, a reflection of the Word Bearers flagship. It shivered through into the material realm – a thing of crude, martial beauty, scorched and scarred from fighting at the heart of every battle it had ever seen. Just as the *Lex* had immediately readied for war, the *Conqueror* lit its shields and ran out its countless guns. Unlike the *Lex*, it didn't slow to allow its armada to take shape in formation. The flagship of the World Eaters pushed ahead, forcing lesser ships to drift aside from its gathering momentum.

'An ugly ship,' Magnus said, 'to match Angron's ugly soul.'

'You underestimate him,' Lorgar said again.

From the warded safety of the basilica, the Thousand Sons primarch watched the fleet manifesting above, below and in every direction besides. Ahead of them lay a world of pleasant skies, rocky grey continents and sparse, deep oceans turning in the lifegiving radiance of an ideal sun. A handful of small cities shone in the night, their cobweb of linked light forming the unmistakable image of civilisation: an image graven on the human mind ever since mankind's first voidnauts saw Old Earth from the cold comfort of low orbit.

'Armatura,' Magnus whispered. 'You cannot mean to do this.'

His brother continued to watch his fleet translating from the warp, and the utopian world hanging in space beyond them.

'The year's journey from Isstvan was more eventful than I'd anticipated. Angron and his Legion delayed us, pausing to murder world after world on their wrathful whims. Our brother's mutilated psyche makes planning anything something of a chore, but at last, here we are. The beginning of the end.'

'Where's the rest of your fleet?' Magnus asked, caution threading his tone.

Lorgar could now smell the salt of his brother's sweat and hear the muffled thunder of the sorcerer's heartbeat. Truly, the incarnated image of his brother was a masterpiece of psychic projection, becoming ever more *real* by the moment.

'Ulixis. Espandor. Latona. Elsewhere. They're killing their way across Ultramar, now Guilliman's sons are crippled at Calth. The Five Hundred Worlds have suddenly found themselves rather starved of protection. A shame, I'm sure you'll agree.'

Magnus didn't match his brother's smile. 'You can't attack Armatura with a fraction of your fleet.' The sorcerer narrowed his lone eye. 'There's some ploy you're holding back, some nasty little surprise hiding behind your words.'

'Yes,' Lorgar said. 'There is indeed.'

'You've foreseen all this,' Magnus accused him.

'A great deal of it. The gods whisper of what will come. They speak, and I hear them.'

Magnus's shadow stole over him in a slow spread. 'I told you, you shouldn't trust their whisperings.'

'I never said I trusted them, I said I could hear them. There's a subtle difference.' He laughed again, a sound ripe with honest amusement. 'Is there anyone you don't underestimate, Magnus? You've been here no more than a few minutes and already you've insulted both Angron and me several times.'

'Do you hate Guilliman this much?' Magnus asked suddenly. 'Do you despise him so much that crippling his Legion at Calth isn't enough? You've already won. Why must you reach out to annihilate his peaceful and prosperous empire?'

Lorgar's smile faded, but didn't die. The scripture inked across his face smoothed into neat rows once more. 'I don't hate him, brother. At one point, I was jealous of him. But that was fifty years ago, and I was a different man. I have since learned that the warp is a song, Magnus, a symphony, and I am the only one willing to play it. That's why we're here.'

Ahead of them, the World Eaters elements within the fleet began to diverge, to lose all sense of cohesion. Lorgar's irises were a soothing gold-brown, somewhere between the shades of amber and earth. He watched impassively, neither surprised nor annoyed. If anything, he seemed rather charmed by the disunity on display. By contrast, the Word Bearers ships sailed in smooth, effortless formation.

'The warp is *not* a song. I fear for your sanity, Lorgar.'

The entire basilica fell dark as they sailed beneath the curve of Pila, Armatura's lone moon. Spotted by the million lights of forge-fires and foundries, its smoggy bulk blocked the idyllic sun; a monument to human industry, eclipsing the light. Lorgar's divine features darkened in the spreading shadow.

'I imagine you do, Magnus, but you've always been gifted at criticising others for the sins you share with them so blithely.'

Magnus's smile was a snide, superior curl across his face. 'There's your overactive imagination at work once more.'

Lorgar stepped closer to the sorcerer, his once-warm eyes now colder than fool's gold. 'Tell me, brother, whose Legion is trapped in the Great Eye, devolving into maggots while the god of Change laughs into infinity? Tell me whose physical form was broken over Leman Russ's knee because he decided at the last moment that he wouldn't accept his punishment like an obedient son after all? You didn't commit to the fight, nor did you surrender and come to heel. Instead, you wasted your Legion and your life's work in half-hearted capitulation. You think *I* act in madness? Look to your own sins, hypocrite. And look to your *sons*, while there is still something left of them.'

He shook his head, taking joy in what he was saying. 'Mark my words, Magnus, if you do not act soon, your Legion and all that you worked so hard to create will be dust.'

'My Legion–' Magnus's face creased with rising anger '–was backed into a corner. My Thousand Sons died because of *your* treachery, because of the venom *you* whispered in Horus's ears to start this insanity. He calls it *his* rebellion, but we both know the first heart to turn traitor was the one beating in your chest.'

Lorgar laughed again, the sound one of unfeigned delight. 'See?

The blame always lies with one of us unworthy souls. Never with you for making the wrong compacts with the gods that you deny are even real!'

The parchments on Lorgar's armour flapped in the sudden wind of Magnus's ire. The Word Bearer stood unfazed, his serene smile boiling his brother's blood. The sorcerer's skin quivered, beetles writhing beneath it as witch-lightning danced across his coppery flesh. Magnus moved, his body forming from the air itself, shaped out of the poison behind reality's veil. Anger drove him into true incarnation.

'That is *enough*, Lorgar.'

Lorgar nodded. 'It is. I've no desire to trade insults. We've all made mistakes, it's how we deal with the aftermath that matters.' He gestured to the fleet around the flagship. The World Eaters vessels, as always, abandoned the armada's formation in favour of a more aggressive vanguard assault. In the year since Isstvan, Lorgar had slowly come to abandon any attempt at reining in the XII Legion's independent streak. They couldn't be collared, even for their own good.

'Watch,' he said.

'I'm not sure I want to watch two Legions die in the skies above Armatura.'

Lorgar didn't make eye contact. 'Trust me,' he said. 'For once, Magnus. Trust me. Both Legions will make planetfall in a matter of minutes.'

The Word Bearer closed his eyes and lifted his hands – a conductor before an orchestra in those tense, edged moments before the first note is struck.

'The warp *is* a song, brother. Let me play a verse for you.'

The word 'fleet' didn't quite do it justice. In truth, an armada thundered across the silent sky towards Armatura: dozens and dozens of vessels, yet a mere fraction of two Legions' strength.

Armatura turned in the heart of Guilliman's perfect empire.

Neither the crown jewel that Macragge claimed to be, nor the future capital Calth had threatened to become, Armatura matched both in importance, and vastly eclipsed them in population. If Ultramar was reduced to crude metaphor, Macragge beat as the heart of the astral kingdom, while Calth served as its soul – a sign of a bright future, now consigned to fire. Armatura was a war-world, feeding the other planets the way bone marrow feeds blood into the body. It fed the Legion with recruits; it fed the void with damaged warships reborn from its docks; it fed the Imperium with hope that the largest Legion would forever be the largest, and even if the XIII was reduced to a single warrior, as long as Armatura turned in the night, the Legion would live on.

Its close-orbit played home to immense shipyards, populated by thousands upon thousands of workers, servitors, archimechs, enginseers, serfs, thralls and technographers. It took an army of souls to breathe life back into the great warships of the Imperium, and here several million of them did their finest work. Orbital bastions of linked gantries and docking maws drifted above the placid world, crawling with insectile shuttles, lifters, loaders and tugs. Imperial warships limped here, scarred from the Great Crusade, and left months later in resurrected perfection.

Above and beyond the shipyard was the first concentric ring of void defences. Here, weaponised satellites and fire platforms bristled with turrets, alongside independent landing decks for fighter craft in lockdown.

Beyond those, the true defences began. Castles in the sky: great fortress-stations with their own racks of fighters and entire battlements given over to plasma batteries, laser broadsides and ship-killing lance arrays.

In highest orbit, the outer sphere of satellites was a three-dimensional spread of solar panels, clockwork engines and slaved servitor brains all connected to vast long-range weapons arrays.

Amidst that outermost sphere waited the Evocati fleet. While the Legion mustered at Calth, the XIII Legion's war-world could never be left undefended. The Evocati was comprised of several thousand Ultramarines drawn from a dozen Chapters, awarded the highest honour of all: overseeing the operations of Armatura and the training of new recruits, commanding an Imperial fleet to rival any other.

The vessels moved in a perfection of militaristic motion that even their enemies found beautiful to behold. As the Evocati rose into a defensive formation, the combined Word Bearers and World Eaters armada altered to compensate; a shifting dance across a battlefield no different from the rearrangement of regiments marching in ancient eras.

Battleships and cruisers, frigates and destroyers, all resplendent in XIII Legion blue, silver and gold, rising to defend the perfect empire.

'Do you hear it?' Lorgar asked, rapt in distraction. 'Do you?'

Magnus watched the first killing beams illuminating the *Conqueror*'s void shields, the impacts spreading with the greasy luminescence of oil on water. He sensed… something, as the fleet powered to its inevitable demise. A sensation not unlike the world itself holding its breath, the way Tizca's air was charged before a storm.

The Word Bearer tilted his head back, eyes closed as he let the flashing colours of the *Conqueror*'s shields dapple his face.

'Calth is the syncopated back-beat to the song. The rhythm beneath the rhyme. That much fire, that much misery, that much pain.' He smiled, his eyes still closed. 'Suffering has always fuelled the warp in random stains and stigmata. Now we learn the virtue of control. Can you hear it? Can you hear the pain stirring the tides? Can you hear the crash of those waves, Magnus? Can you hear how those black tides beat, a million hearts bursting out loud, as rhythmic as drums in the deep cold?'

He lifted his hands higher, gesturing with subtle relish, directing his invisible choir. 'The tides of the Sea of Souls can be altered by mortal hands, brother. Listen. *Listen.* We're reordering the warp itself, Magnus, changing it through pain. We're rewriting the song.'

Lorgar drew in a shivery breath as he continued. 'There, a ship burns in Latona's atmosphere, the cries of the doomed souls echoing into the empyrean. And there, a warship ploughs into the surface of Ulixis, digging its own grave, taking a hundred thousand souls shrieking into the afterlife. Do you hear them dying, Magnus? Do you hear the song shifting in time to their extinguished essences?'

He was laughing now, raising a hand to the heavens, weeping as he whispered.

'Every life. Every death. Every cry of pain across these burning worlds thins the veil between reality and the first-realm. Call it Hades or Hell, Jahannam, Naraka or the Underworld. Call it the warp... call it whatever you will. But I am bringing it forth onto the material plane. Calth was the genesis of the storm, Magnus. I will make an entire sub-sector suffer enough that the curtain falls and the Five Hundred Worlds drown in the warp.'

He turned at last, eyes aflame with psychic fervour. 'Tell me you feel it. Tell me you can hear the million, million daemons shrieking and baying, desperate to be born upon these burning worlds.'

Magnus felt it, as real as the wind he'd never again feel against his flesh. A pulling, a *tightening*, of the weave behind the physical universe. Far from the impassioned sensation his brother described, the sorcerer felt it with clinical distraction, no different from an equation written on parchment and begging to be solved. Lorgar, in his madness, was doing more than breaking the natural order. He was rewriting the code of the universe.

'You cannot kill Armatura,' Magnus said. 'You can shred the curtain between reality and unreality all you like, Lorgar. You can even call it a song, if you wish. Your life is still measured in minutes.'

The fleet began to dive in earnest above and around them. When the *Fidelitas Lex* took its first hit, the lights across its many decks flickered once, twice, then settled stable. Lorgar looked back to the black heavens.

'To break Armatura, we'll need a vessel to rival anything humanity has ever wrought.' He seemed thoughtful, a painting with unfocused eyes, brushing his fingertips over the scripture tattooed across his cheek. 'We had one, you know. Zadkiel's folly, the *Furious Abyss*.'

Magnus watched the combined fleet beginning to burn. 'And what happened to it?'

'Oh.' Lorgar shook his head, focus returning. 'It died days ago, close to the same moment Kor Phaeron struck at Calth. Its corpse is probably still a shadow in the skies above Macragge – a monument to the Word Bearers failure. Another inscription on Zadkiel's legacy of little idiocies. I told him he was a fool to attack Macragge, but he was so keen to bathe in glory, and all he ever heard were the whispers begging for revenge. I indulged him.'

'Why did you let him? Are your sons so disobedient?'

Lorgar laughed again, ignoring the ship shaking around him. 'Harsh words, from the primarch whose sons defy him in the grandest ways. Your Legion didn't bare their throats to the rampaging Wolves as you wished them to, did they?'

Magnus conceded that with a nod. 'Even so. Your fleet is dying, brother. What will you do without the *Furious Abyss*?'

Lorgar looked back to the embattled skies. 'This is what I meant when I said you underestimated us, Magnus. To you, this war is something shocking and new. Yet it is something I've been planning for half a century. I spent a quarter of the Great Crusade preparing for the moment when our father's sad cravings of eminent domain would end, and the true holy war would begin.'

The sorcerer swallowed, sensing the onrushing presence of *something* pressing against reality from the tumult of the warp. Something out there, about to make itself known.

'Ah! *Now* you hear the song,' Lorgar said. His laugh echoed around the basilica. 'You hear the rhythm at last! But we need more control. So we summon new instruments to enliven the chorus.'

Lorgar exhaled, gesturing to the deep void, past Armatura. Reality opened. Though Magnus's ethereal incarnation was immune to such weakness, instinct made him shield his eye. A warp-rift formed in space, far from both closing fleets. Something was coming through, something vast: a trident of dark metal immediately familiar to the sorcerer.

The ship grinding into reality was a reflection of the slain colossus Lorgar had spoken of. A city of monasteries and cathedrals rose from its back with the reverence of clawed hands sculpted to clutch at the stars. Where most Imperial battleships were spears of crenellated intent and iron-ridged might, this was a fortress in space, borne on the back of a great trident. The central tine served as the vessel's core: dense at the stern, encrusted with massive engines and tapering towards the prow, where it formed a pointed ram the size of lesser vessels. The trident's adjacent tines formed smaller blade-wings, each one barnacled with broadsides and cannon batteries.

If one were to clad the concept of *spite* in iron and set it sailing amongst the stars, it might approach the image of what burst back into the universe in that moment. It was, in every way, the *Furious Abyss* reborn.

'That,' Lorgar smiled, 'is the *Blessed Lady*.'

Magnus released an unnecessary breath, watching as a ship too vast to exist left the wound in the material universe. It easily eclipsed even the Gloriana-class flagships of the combined Legion fleet, and the warp's cloudy tendrils lashed at its spires, shrieking into the silence, seemingly reluctant to let the vessel back into reality.

'You built two,' the sorcerer breathed.

'Oh, no.' Lorgar didn't even open his eyes. He raised a hand to point into the void, where a second warp-slice ripped across the stars. 'I built three.'

TWO

Barely Human
Warriors and Crusaders
Broken Upon the Same Anvil

THE TWO WARRIORS were human only in the loosest sense. They'd been human children, but time, excruciating surgery and extensive gene-therapy had seen them grow along less natural paths.

There they stood, the sons of two worlds and two Legions, embodying the ideals and flaws of their birth worlds and bloodlines. More than any of their brethren, they exemplified their Legions' triumphs – and their fathers' sins.

The *Conqueror*'s primary hangar platform was already shivering with the first barrage from Armatura's guns. Flags and victory banners swayed in the false wind of the ship's shaking bones. Several of them were scorched, ragged standards pulled from the dead hands of Raven Guard and Salamanders on the killing fields of Isstvan V. Trophies to inspire the legionaries of the World Eaters in the final moments before they made planetfall.

The first warrior's ceramite armour plating was cast in the same white as clean marble, from churches that should never have been built. The suit's reinforced edges were the same blue as a winter sky back in the impious ages of Old Terra, before humanity burned the world's surface and drank the natural oceans dry. His skin was as pale as any consumptive, a legacy of the pain machine inside his skull. It pulsed even now, teasingly erratic, sending fire *tick-tocking* through the meat of his mind.

The helm he carried under his arm was a slant-eyed, snarling thing of red eye lenses and a Sarum-pattern mouth grille. An officer's crest of white horsehair rose, sharkfin-like, to mark him out from his men in the heat of battle. The etching on his shoulder guard, written in the mongrel tongue called Nagrakali, named him as *Khârn of the Eighth*.

A technological ballet was taking place around both warriors – an industrial performance of gunships and drop pods being craned and winched and towed into position. Khârn tried and failed to ignore the pain knifing through his head. When it became almost too much to bear, as it so often did, he pressed both hands to his face, digging armoured fingertips into his temples, seeking veins and pressure points. It occasionally helped.

Not this time, though.

He'd never prayed in his life, but he looked very much the part in that moment.

'The Nails?' his brother asked. The other warrior spoke in a voice made rancid by empathy. Khârn felt him rest a gauntleted hand on his shoulder, and moved away from the unwelcome grip.

'Don't touch me,' Khârn told him, as he'd told countless others, countless times. Being too near other people always gave him headaches.

The other warrior was long-used to Khârn's awkwardness. Colchisian runic lettering on his armour named him as *Argel Tal, Lord of the Chapter of Consecrated Iron*, and he was known to all as Khârn's brother by deed, not by blood. Standing in arterial crimson plating, edged by silver the same shade as pewter relics unearthed from an old tomb, Argel Tal's dusky skin spoke of birth on a world of sand and ever-present thirst. No pain machine crackled in his brain, for he was of the XVII Legion, not the XII. Instead, a faith he wished was untrue had left his soul deformed.

He spoke with two voices: the man he'd been, and the thing he was becoming. The latter underlaid his human voice in a bestial snarl – every word he spoke came out in both voices at once.

'Armatura,' his voices said. 'This world is suicide. The Armaturan Academy Guard. The Thirteenth's barracks-cities, for its initiates and Evocati overlords. The Titan Legio Lysanda. We're going to die down there, you know.'

Khârn wasn't sure he disagreed. He'd read the analytics and studied the reports. He'd led half a dozen briefings himself, outlining the expected resistance to other World Eaters centurions and sub-commanders.

And damn it, his skull ached today. The headache to end all headaches. Argel Tal always had this effect on him. The Word Bearer was as bad as Esca or Vorias.

'The numbers are exaggerated,' Khârn said with a pained grunt. A billion human soldiers. *A billion.* Not even counting Titans or Mechanicum skitarii. Not even considering the tank battalions stationed down there. Not even adding in the thousands of Ultramarines Evocati. The numbers had to be exaggerated, or they were all dead.

Argel Tal gave a bitter laugh. 'You don't actually believe that, do you?'

No. He didn't. The geo-conflict analytics came from Ultramar's own census archives. A handful of years out of date, certainly, but they were still facing a billion soldiers. Even if a tenth of them were teenage youths in the earliest stages of gene-implantation, there was no sense pretending this was going to be a bloodless triumph.

Khârn didn't answer. Even his eyes were starting to hurt now. The Nails were running hot. He looked back at the Dreadclaw assault pods – gifts from the Warmaster to suit the World Eaters way of warfare – being craned into place. Each of their hulls was a spiked and ridged testament to their lethal intent, a reflection of the vicious machine-spirits within. The number of 'accidents' due to Dreadclaw malfunction was on the wrong side of hilarious. Spiteful things, and that made them useful as often as it left them useless. Most Imperial commanders preferred to deploy using more reliable, less hateful machine-spirits.

Khârn liked them immensely. Not from any real affection, but from honest – and perhaps amused – sympathy. He liked them not out of admiration, but a sense of kinship. They'd never steered him or his men wrong.

Tech-priests moved between the raised pods, chanting and whispering last-minute invocations. A particularly spindly priest, walking on five stalk-like legs of burnished black iron, oversaw the preparations. His red robe stirred in the hangar's false wind, rippled by the shaking deck and the hot wash of gunship engines cycling up to launch.

'Archmagos,' Khârn greeted Vel-Kheredar, representative of Sacred Mars.

The robed cyborg turned three green eye lenses down towards them as it passed, speaking toneless greetings from a mouthless iron face. 'Centurion Khârn,' it said. 'Commander Argel Tal.'

The priest walked on, its eye lenses whirring and adjusting as it breathed a continual stream of orders in Martian binaric code. Soon enough, his calculated complaints were drowned out in the din. Was there anything louder than a warship's deployment hangar in the minutes before planetfall? Khârn had fought at the heart of cities that fell with less assault on the eardrums.

He turned to Argel Tal. 'This world would be suicide without the Abyss-class warships. With them? It might be easy. The Seventeenth Legion is too dour, brother.'

'Ah.' Argel Tal smiled. 'This again.'

Khârn wasn't jesting this time. 'You're right, Armatura will be suicide for skitarii and your levies of zealots. The rest of us will bleed as we always bleed.'

'I dislike the relish in your tone.'

He always did. Khârn gave a small smile. 'Do you fear death?'

'We are the Legiones Astartes,' said the Word Bearer. 'We know no fear.'

Khârn met his brother's eyes. His silence served to ask the question again.

'Yes,' said Argel Tal. 'I do. I've seen what waits for us on the other side.'

The sincerity in the other warrior's voice made Khârn shiver. 'We survived Isstvan III,' he said. 'We'll survive this.'

Argel Tal's features were very calm, almost aesthetic; the innocent face of a battlefield priest or a warrior-poet. Smiles didn't suit him – they depleted what dignified handsomeness remained to any Legiones Astartes warrior – yet he smiled often. Very few souls knew him well enough to see how false those smiles were. Khârn was one. His primarch was another. All the others were dead.

'*You* survived Isstvan III,' he said. 'I survived Isstvan V.' He hesitated, hardly blind to the pain-tics that were now making Khârn's face twitch in weak spasms. 'Be careful down there, Khârn.'

That really was too much. Khârn snorted before replying.

'Such warm words from a man with a devil in his heart.'

Argel Tal smiled again. Khârn loathed that smile, because this one *wasn't* false. It was the smile of a murderer, not a warrior. Fanatics smiled like that.

They walked the length of the hangar, watching over their warriors assembling before embarkation. While the Legions' differences were as distinct as night and day on the battlefield, they were no less stark beneath the harsh glare of emergency lighting.

The Word Bearers of the Vakrah Jal stood in neat, organised rows: blades sheathed, weapons deactivated, oath papers bolted to red armour plating. Several hundred soldiers, fresh from their months of training in the *Conqueror*'s gladiator pits and swearing their oaths of union with Khârn's own oversized Eighth Assault Company. As the two commanders passed, every Word Bearer went to one knee. They lowered their heads and chanted prayers drawn from the Word of Lorgar.

Khârn couldn't help but cringe. His skin crawled to hear such strange rhymes and benedictions vox-whispered by so many throats.

'I will never understand your Legion,' he told Argel Tal.

The Word Bearer watched his men and their reverences, their silver helms tilted down in contemplative repose, before looking over at Khârn's forces. Where the Word Bearers were a kneeling phalanx, the XII warriors were a disorganised mob – laughing, sharing last-minute taunts between squads, with the continuous background whine of chainblades being triggered in twitching fists.

Argel Tal raised a dark eyebrow as two World Eaters banged the foreheads of their helms together, with the unmistakable dull ring of ceramite on ceramite.

'And I will never understand yours,' he replied. His tone said it all.

'Understanding us is simple,' said Khârn. 'You just have to realise that there are some warriors who actually enjoy war. War, and the brotherhood that comes with it. I know that must be difficult for you to understand.' He gestured to the kneeling, praying Word Bearers. 'You come from a serious breed.'

Argel Tal muffled his answer in the emotionless mask of a crested, silver-faced helm.

'I've seen into the hell behind reality,' he said. 'It stole my sense of humour.'

Hard to argue with that.

'Good hunting,' Argel Tal told him.

The two commanders grasped each other's forearms. No lingering words; they simply clashed vambraces and went their separate ways.

Khârn's command squad waited in a shallow illusion of discipline. Esca loosened his wrists, cutting through the air with both of his blades. His psychic hood was an armoured half-dome over the back of his head, with its cables bonded to his temples. He was the only man in Eighth Company to lack the Butcher's Nails, and therefore the only man who didn't look on the edge of spitting in irritation or howling in impatience. Kargos, by comparison, was already helmed, checking the drills and bonesaws deployable from his narthecium gauntlet.

'I killed Harakal in the pits last night,' Kargos said. He drawled the words through the mouth grille of a Mark IV helmet. His accent was thick enough to be almost impenetrable. He came from the plains of Sethek, where the Imperial Gothic tongue was no more than a memory. Hypnotic implantation had given him mastery over other languages, but nothing could shake his accent free.

Khârn smiled, devoid of mirth. 'I liked Harakal.'

'Everyone liked Harakal. Didn't stop his head from rolling across the deck, though.' Kargos mimed the final blow in slow motion, sweeping a chainblade through Harakal's neck. The others could hear the grin in his voice. 'The look in his eyes was priceless, Khârn. Even you'd have laughed, you miserable bastard.'

Khârn doubted that. 'I heard you and Delvarus went to third blood.'

'Delvarus.' Kargos fairly spat the word. 'I'll get him, one day.'

'No,' Khârn shook his head. 'You won't. No one will.'

Kargos *tsked*. 'What do you say, Esca? Any prophecies for me? Will anyone ever beat that whoreson Delvarus in the pits?'

Esca shook his head, a refusal rather than a disagreement. 'You don't still assume I can see the future, do you?'

'No,' Kargos admitted. 'I was just trying to make you feel useful for once.'

Esca bowed. 'I appreciate your efforts, Apothecary.' He was scarred, even by Legiones Astartes standards. His face was a smeared mess of pebbled scar tissue – all part of the legacy of the Death Guard chainsword that had torn his features away on Isstvan III.

Isstvan III. Khârn remembered precious little of it. They told him he almost died that day.

'Angron is taking his time,' Kargos muttered. 'There's a war waiting for us.'

As if on cue, Esca coughed once. He tried to hide it, to bite it back, but all nearby caught the scent of blood flecking his gauntlet as he coughed into his hand. Darker, thicker blood ran in a slow trickle from his ear.

The World Eaters fell beneath a pall of sudden silence. All laughter ceased, all baiting quieted. They turned as one, falling into loose ranks as the western door rolled open on its grinding tracks.

The figure beyond moved in a hulking sway, its bronze armour stained by the stern stare of the hangar's illumination strips. Poets, remembrancers and war archivists often made a habit of drawing crude parallels between a battlefield's heroes and the false gods those heroes resembled. No such comparison ever worked for Angron the Conqueror, Lord of the XII Legion. His lethality defied comparison, for everything about him spoke of contrast.

His armour plating was layer upon layer of Mechanicum ingenuity crafted to resemble archaic gladiatorial worthlessness. His movements were feral, without any of the natural grace seen in the hunting cats stalking jungles of worlds still healthier than distant Terra. And if he could be called a god, he was a wounded one, scarred in flesh and mind. His over-muscled movements, coupled with the tidal grind of his armour joints, turned his stride into a lumbering threat. He could be swift, but only when the Nails hissed hot. Outside of battle, he was a ruined thing, a shadow of what could – and should – have been.

Khârn and the World Eaters stood straighter. This was their father, and he'd remade his sons in his image.

He breathed through the slit of his mouth, through the rows of replacement iron teeth whose tips almost touched. Mouth-breathing came naturally now; he was too used to his sinuses being clogged by fast-scabbing trickles from his bleeding brain.

'Sire,' Khârn greeted him, using the one honorific Angron tolerated with even a modicum of grace. He still rebuked those who fell back on traditional forms of address, but most of the time, he tolerated *sire*.

'I was on the bridge.' The primarch's voice was a guttural, sticky snarl. His teeth clacked together as his facial muscles twitched to the Nails' tune. 'I saw the Word Bearers new battleships. Each one is a rival to Dorn's precious *Phalanx*.'

As Angron turned to regard the Word Bearers in their orderly ranks, a nasty smile split his lips. He sensed their ardency, their efforts at propriety, and it amused him.

'You're smiling,' Khârn said, more a weary accusation than a question.

'It entertains me no end to see them masking the sickness inside their souls with such zeal.'

Khârn's men gave dutiful chuckles at their primarch's words. All but Esca, who'd retreated back from the ranks, back from Angron, and meditated in an attempt to stem his bleeding nose and ears.

'Lorgar has been planning this war for decades,' Angron said to his sons. 'The mere sight of those ships is evidence of that. Remember it, all of you. Remember it whenever you feel tempted to trust one of those serpents in red.'

The primarch's pupils were pinprick specks in the depths of his sickly eyes. A stalactite of saliva trickled its way down his scarred chin. Khârn merely inclined his head in acknowledgement of his lord's words. Arguing with Angron was never wise, even when it was necessary. Disagreeing with him now, when the Nails were so clearly singing in his skull, would be suicide. A great many World Eaters knew that from experience.

'Creature,' Angron growled. 'Creature, get over here.'

Somehow, his voice carried over the hangar's settling din, for Argel Tal crossed the deck to stand before the master of the XII Legion. The Word Bearer didn't bow. Argel Tal had learned the hard way that Angron loathed all signs of obsequious respect. Nothing irritated him more than polite submission. Only two things should prostrate themselves: frightened animals and dying men. Anything else was surrender, and no filthier word existed in any human tongue.

'Primarch Angron,' the Word Bearer greeted him with a neutral salute, fist over his primary heart. Khârn swallowed. He already knew where this was going.

'Creature,' the primarch said again. 'You have your orders?'

'I do.'

'Very well. Then be ready to execute them.'

Argel Tal saluted a second time, and started to turn away.

'Creature,' the primarch said a third time, smiling now. He enjoyed the way the insult tasted.

'Yes, sire?'

'I saw your lord's pretty warships lighting up the skies, just now. The *Trisagion* and the *Blessed Lady*, reaving their way through Armatura's defences. We owe this assault to them, eh?'

Argel Tal betrayed no response, merely waiting impassively, his silver faceplate staring with its crystal blue eye lenses. Khârn willed him to silence, to manage his composure. His brother may have been a Bearer of the Word, but Argel Tal had a XII Legion temper.

Angron's teeth clacked together again, in sympathy with another facial tic. 'The *Blessed Lady*,' he said. 'That name. She was your whore-priestess, was she not?'

'She was our Confessor.' The Word Bearer's armour joints gave a low thrum as he tilted his head and bunched his muscles. Angron didn't miss the telltale signs of rising aggression. He broke into a grin.

'Dead though, eh? Entombed on Lorgar's flagship. Is that the same shrine, or have you poor zealots been praying to more than one dead girl?'

A hesitation, this time. Argel Tal took a slow breath. 'It is her.'

'Is it true that fanatics pulled her bones from the coffin? They stole them as holy relics, like the heathens of old?'

Khârn watched Argel Tal's fingers flinch and curl. 'It is true,' the Word Bearer replied.

'Angron…' Khârn warned his father. Angron ignored him, as Khârn had known the primarch would. He was enjoying himself too much to heed any advice.

Khârn shook his head. *Here it comes.*

Angron's chuckle had all the charm and warmth of an avalanche. 'This is the same whore-priestess you failed to protect in life. Now you can't even guard her bones from human thieves. Lorgar must love you, creature. Why else would he stomach your failures?'

The Word Bearer spoke through clenched teeth. 'If my lord Lorgar finds fault with my service, he is free to offer punishment.' He was turning away now, regardless of the disrespect he offered. Angron baiting him was an old game, though this time it risked going further than ever before. 'And you, Broken One, are not fit to speak of the Blessed Lady.'

Angron's laugh was a wet landslide. 'Did you ever recover her bones, creature? Or are they still in the hands of your unwashed cultist slaves?'

Argel Tal, like all ranking Legiones Astartes commanders, had a personal armoury that would put any collector to shame, but now he carried two weapons sheathed across his back – his finest and favourite trophies. Both were crafted on Terra, in forges forbidden to all outside the Emperor's own inner sanctum. Both were genelocked, and could never be activated without the original owners' genetic imprints on the reactive palm grips along both blades' hafts. Argel Tal had broken that technological law, though he'd never shared how.

The first weapon was a guardian spear, with an ornate boltgun forming the tip, bonded to an underslung power blade. Its name, etched in acid-eaten lettering along the priceless blade, was Shahin-i Tarazu, and it was once the blade of Sythran Kelomenes Astaga Meren Virol Uhtred Mastaxa Cyrus Shenzu-Tai Diromar of the Legiones Custodes. It was the weapon that killed Xaphen of the Word Bearers, one year ago.

The second was a cousin to the spear – a two-handed sword forged in the same fires as Shahin-i Tarazu, and shaped by the same hands. Its crosspiece was an eagle of gold – the Emperor's Palatine Aquila – spreading its wings, and its blade also bore the weapon's name:

Iktinaetar. It was the blade of Aquillon of the Legiones Custodes – a warrior of many, many names earned in glorious service. It was the weapon that had murdered Cyrene, Confessor of the Word, an unarmed woman who'd lost the use of her eyes.

Brave, brave Custodians, thought Khârn. He had to wonder if they'd sung any victory songs after that battle.

Both weapons required two hands to wield with full skill. In battle, Argel Tal switched between them, moment by moment, foe by foe, using whichever served best.

In the hangar now, standing before Angron, he drew Iktinaetar. He pulled the blade in one smooth motion, and launched himself at the primarch. The stolen sword whined, the metal of its blade pure enough to sing as it cut the air.

Angron caught the Word Bearer in one fist, his fingers wrapping around the warrior's torso. It was over in a heartbeat. Argel Tal was hurled back before the blade could even come close to landing.

The primarch laughed, that same sound of sludge and gravel. 'Amusing as always. Back to your men, creature.'

But Argel Tal was no longer Argel Tal. He twisted in the air, disgustingly graceful, and struck the deck in a crouch. Huge and beautifully ugly black bat's wings rose from his shoulders. His silver faceplate was distorted in a snarling, wolfish maw of bent metal.

'Back to your men,' Angron told the thing again. He was already walking away.

This time, it obeyed. Argel Tal rose to his feet, the great wings folding back with the sound of wrenching metal, the helm smoothing over into emotionless Mark IV sterility.

Khârn sighed, purely theatrical, wanting the primarch to hear it. Angron's slice of a smirk tore a notch higher, and he did nothing but chuckle as he made his way to the nearest Dreadclaw.

'See you on the surface,' he said, and sealed himself away from his sons.

Khârn turned back to his men. 'You heard him. Squad by squad, into the pods. Armatura awaits.'

The World Eaters obeyed.

+He is no primarch,+ came Argel Tal's voice in Khârn's mind. The centurion's first instinct was to shudder. The Nails bit harder, hotter, in the wake of the psychic whisper; they hurt more every time. Khârn looked back to his brother, where Argel Tal was directing his own men into their own gunships and drop pods.

He is my primarch, Khârn replied, with no idea if Argel Tal could hear him. Sometimes the silent speech worked, sometimes it didn't.

+A primarch should be inspiring. Our genetics should react at the mere sight of them. Think of the moments you laid eyes on Horus, Dorn, or Magnus. I've seen Sanguinius and Russ with my own eyes, as well. Close enough to touch their armour. Think of when you stand before Lorgar: the awe and reverence that beats through your blood. The feeling of our genetic coding reacting to the pinnacle of the human process. I've never felt that instinctive respect for Angron, Khârn. Not once. He is a broken thing. Devastating, unrivalled in war, but broken.+

Khârn didn't answer because there was nothing to say. He boarded his drop pod, ascending the ramp and waiting for a robed Legion slave to secure his restraint harness.

+You feel it,+ Argel Tal said. +You feel it, too.+

In psychic silence, Khârn confessed something he'd never said outside his Legion.

Yes, we feel the same. The World Eaters, each and every one of us, knows what you know.

Argel Tal's voice was laced with cold, seething anger. +Why do you tolerate it?+

What can we do? Murder our own father? Did you destroy Lorgar when he led you into worshipping the Emperor? Or did you tolerate him in patience, hoping that eventually he'd find his way to equalling his brothers?

A pause. A long, long pause. Khârn took it as Argel Tal's capitulation and pushed on. *It's our shame to bear before the other Legions, brother. Angron was broken long before he ever reached us. Why do you think we let him beat the Nails into our heads? We hoped that by breaking ourselves on the same anvil, we'd finally feel unity with our father.*

There was nothing of mockery in the Word Bearer's reply. Only sympathy. Khârn's skin crawled. He'd have preferred mockery.

+It didn't work?+

The drop pod's sides closed in, armour plating locking to block all view of the hangar beyond. Khârn's last sight was of Argel Tal ascending the gang-ramp into a red XVII Legion gunship.

'No,' he muttered, as much to himself as to the distant Word Bearer. 'It didn't.'

THREE

**Lost to the Nails
Void War
Sacred Red, Faithless White**

THE ONE THING war stories always forgot was the dust. Khârn learned that early, and the lesson stayed with him through the years. Even two men kicking up sand in the gladiator pits was a distraction. Two armies of a few thousand souls on an open plain would turn the air thick enough to choke on. Scale it up again, and a few hundred thousand warriors locked in conflict would darken the sun for a day after the battle was done.

But the realities of pitched warfare rarely made it into the sagas. In all the stories he'd heard, especially those woeful diatribes from the remembrancers, battle was reduced to a handful of heroes going blade-to-blade in the sunlight, while their nameless lessers looked on in stupefied awe.

It took a great deal to make Khârn cringe, but war poetry never failed.

Two Legions fighting through a city was beyond anything else. Tank engines exhaled fumes in an oil-smelling smog. Gunships roared down on heat blurs and air washes, while those shot down fell from the sky to crash and roll across the ground as burning husks. Titans striding through the streets bled fire and smoke in equal measure – wounds that gouted pollution tenfold when one of the colossal war machines finally died.

The tens of thousands of soldiers grinding rockcrete and earth beneath their tread, and the last sighs of habitation towers bursting their dusty innards into the air as they came apart – they all added to the pall. Each spire that fell, every monument that toppled, every bunker that broke apart breathed a cloud of strangling ash in every direction.

Fighting in a ruined city was one thing, but fighting during a city's ruination was quite another. Visibility was a myth. It simply didn't exist.

In ages past, when bronze swords had formed the pinnacle of humanity's capacity to wage war against itself, mounted scouts tore through a battlefield's dust clouds to relay information and orders between officers whose regiments were blinded in the thick of it. That was another truth that rarely survived to make into the archives.

War had come a long, long way from those ancient days. Mankind's capacity to fight blind had not. Khârn's retinal display responded to his irritation, auto-cycling through vision filters. Thermal sight was a worthless smear of migraine colours when half the city was aflame. Tracking by echolocation auspex was unreliable with any atmospheric interference, and the dense clouds of particulate coupled with burning buildings all around most definitely counted as suboptimal conditions.

He didn't stop running. He had no idea where he was any more, but he didn't stop running. *When in doubt, move forward.* The old adage brought back his grin.

Khârn remembered the landing. The teeth-rattling descent in the Dreadclaw's dark confines, and the burst of sunlight that followed when the pod's doors blasted open. He remembered that first charge out into the city, pulling his weapons free, feeling the wasp-stings of lasgun fire failing to pierce his armour plating. They'd come down in a barracks district, amongst the entrenched battalions of Armaturan Academy Guard. Young warriors undergoing the process to become Ultramarines, alongside the hosts of uniformed, disciplined soldiers that were proud to serve the XIII Legion.

Damn Guilliman and his empire within an empire. Armatura, the war-world, was merely one globe in the Five Hundred Worlds. How did one man raise such vast armies? How did one Legion command such might?

He knew the answer, unwelcome as it was. Here was the gift of an unbroken primarch. Here was an unflawed genius at play, unburdened by a pain engine. While Lorgar wasted time with the mysteries of the aether and Angron tasted blood from his malfunctioning mind, Guilliman of the Ultramarines had reshaped an entire subsector into the Imperial ideal. Not even Horus had managed that.

A bolter shell had severed his irritated musing, crashing against his chestplate and throwing his stride into a ragged stagger. Khârn had roared without realising – an instinctive vocalisation of the pain drilling into the back of his head – and charged into the first platoon of Academy Guard holding the barricade at the road's end. Their Evocatus leader fought with an energised gladius, proving himself a swordsman of consummate skill. He lasted nine seconds before he collapsed, painting the avenue's stones red with his innards.

The city was still standing at that point. The dust hadn't had a chance to occlude everything under the sun.

THAT CHANGED SOON enough. Mere hours later and the cityscape was choking on its own breath. Now he'd lost Kargos and Esca and the others, and he was alone in a dying city, somewhere behind enemy lines. He remembered the Academy Guard breaking; remembered chasing them with spit thick on his tongue, crunching his axe into their fleeing backs, and the Nails ticking hotter, washing his vision red.

He remembered nothing more, until he'd come back to his senses a few minutes ago.

Shadows drifted from the smoke, becoming shapes, becoming warriors in armour the same blue as Terra's sky at sunrise. Khârn didn't slow down. He went through them in a roar of laughter and rending blades, saliva stringing between his teeth. His boots pounded across the rockcrete road.

'Lotara,' he voxed.

Her image pulsed into being, just her head and shoulders, in a crackling, distorted hololithic window to the right of his targeting array. As usual, her long hair was bound back in a ponytail to keep it from her face. Her features were in profile, with the imagifier attached to the side of her command throne.

'Khârn?' Her voice was a buzz, all quality savaged by the temperamental vox. It made a mess of her usual measured, spire-born eloquence. 'Are you smiling?'

'Give me the orbitals, flag-captain.'

'As you wish, not that there's anything to see. What are you doing down there, anyway? The city is drowning in dust. Even by your sloppy standards, this is a mess.'

Secondary image windows bloomed into being on both sides of his flickering retinal display. Each one showed the city from above, blanketed in clouds of choking smoke. Towers peeked from the very top of the ash cloud, but the cityscape itself was lost beyond hope.

'You should have let me bombard the city from orbit,' Lotara added. 'I'm sure the two Word Bearers king-ships would have loved to do the same. You never got to see the size of them, stuck in your little drop pod. Quite a sight.'

Khârn's smile was dangerously close to a sneer. 'You mock me and my men, flag-captain, but at least we know when our enemies are really dead. *We* finish the fight.'

He approached a dead tank, an idle and silent shape manifesting from the choking dust. His retinal display locked onto it, spilling out a screed of data he didn't need to see. Maximus-pattern armour was a technological marvel, but the autosenses took a great deal of tuning to meet a warrior's personal preferences. Khârn usually ignored most of what his armour tried to tell him. As if he cared what forge world had churned out any particular Rhino chassis. As if he cared about the density of the alloys making up its hull, and how they differed by point-one per cent from others.

A great XIII emblem marked the slain tank's sealed doors. He strained to hear anything within, but with the city falling down around him, that was always going to be a forlorn hope. Instead, he tapped the edge of his chainaxe against the vehicle's armour plating.

'Knock, knock.'

Silence answered from inside, no fun at all. Rather than climb the sloping sides, he vaulted up to its roof in a smooth leap. Both boots thudded on the top with a resonating clang. Any hope that a higher vantage point would help his vision was laughable, but he was willing to try anything.

He spared a glance back at the useless orbital imagery scrolling across his left eye lens. 'Intensifiers?' he prompted.

'I have servitors working on scrubbing the pict-feeds.' Lotara's image shook with something more than distortion. 'We're busy up here ourselves, you know.'

Khârn crouched by the sealed cupola. 'Very well. Enjoy your little skirmish in the void, flag-captain.'

She turned her head, grinning right into the imagifier. 'And you enjoy wading through the dirt, Khârn. Such an inelegant way to fight a war.' Her image blanked out, taking the useless orbital feeds with it.

Khârn was about to tear the cupola open when another rune blinked into life on his eye lenses. A name-rune.

'Skane?'

'Captain.' The reply was immediate, amidst a chorus of draconic howls. Engines. Turbines running too hot, for too long. The warrior's augmetic vocal chords didn't steal emotion from Skane's voice, but they did add a burbling, crackling quality to everything he said.

'You just came into vox-range. For the last seven minutes, the only contact I've had is with the ship.'

'Aye, it's all rather gone to spit down here,' Skane voxed back. 'Where are you?'

'I don't know.' A moment's pause. 'When we broke the Academy Guard, I was with the vanguard pursuing the survivors.'

'The Nails?' Skane asked.

'The Nails took,' Khârn admitted, knowing it would explain everything.

'Understood. We can't track you, our auspex is already dead.'

Of course it was. Of all his squads, it would be the Destroyers he made first contact with. The ones whose weapons annihilated the efficiency of their more temperamental equipment. Argel Tal often said that Fate had a vicious sense of humour. Khârn never doubted it for a second.

'Connect it to your armour. Leech power to amplify your locator rune for a moment.'

'That never works,' he muttered, but said, 'Aye, captain,' a little louder.

Khârn looked at the blue-painted hull beneath his boots. The Rhino was motionless, its engine silent, but the scanners might still be operational. It would certainly be easier than dealing with his Destroyers and their degraded tech–

Miracle of miracles, Skane's name-rune flared again, this time with translocation and distance data.

'Got you,' Skane voxed. Khârn was already running again.

LOTARA SARRIN HAD earned the *Conqueror*'s throne six years ago, just before her thirtieth birthday. Her promotion had made her one of the youngest flag-captains in the entire spread of the Emperor's expeditionary fleets, which in turn had made her a focus for scriveners and imagists inbound from Terra's remembrancer order. They'd plagued her, dogging her every step in the brief period Lord Angron had allowed their kind aboard the World Eaters flagship. When they'd been shipped back to Terra in shame, their work undone – in fact, barely even begun – the official notations recorded their departure as due to *'irreconcilable maladjustment to void wayfaring.'*

Spacesickness. That had been Khârn's idea, delivered with his usual sly, dry lack of a smile.

The real reason was simple enough: they'd annoyed Lotara Sarrin, therefore they'd annoyed Angron. The primarch had ignored them until the moment he heard Lotara's first complaint. They were banished back to Terra the next day. Khârn had been one of the warriors tasked with throwing them off the flagship, ignoring their shouted protests and the way they'd waved Imperial licences that supposedly gave them permission to remain. It had all been accomplished with an admirable – and, given the Legion in question, surprising – lack of bloodshed. If anything, the World Eaters were more amused than anything else.

Lotara's military record spoke in bland, archival terms – replete with neat, uninteresting servitors' handwriting – of exemplary bravery, steadfastness and patience, citing her frequent dealings and mediations with the primarch of the XII Legion. It also noted her many medals and decorations – none of which she ever wore outside of formal occasions, and most of which languished at the bottom of the wardrobe in her forever-untidy personal chambers.

Anyone reading this record would also find various notations of level-headedness, commendable tactical insight and a gift for logistics. All very orderly, all to be expected in a prominent captain.

The only citation she actually cared about was noted in the following terms: *'Awarded a unique distinction by the XII Legion for notable courage in the compliance of the worlds formerly claimed by the Ashul Stellar Principality.'*

She wore that commendation, loud and proud. The Blood Hand, a red handprint across the chest of her crisp white uniform, as if the raised throne of ornate filigreed brass didn't already mark her out from the three hundred other officers working in the strategium.

The *Conqueror*'s bridge was a hive of shouting voices, chattering servitors, and overseer officers calling from station to station. Lotara paid it no heed at all, content from the background noise that her crew was doing its job. She had eyes for nothing but the oculus viewscreen and the three-dimensional tactical display it generated. All the while, she kept a steady stream of orders relayed over her collar vox-mic, while drumming her fingertips on the armrests.

The void war was going well. She'd have known that with her eyes closed, given the unreal punishment both the Word Bearers kingships were delivering to the beleaguered world of Armatura, but it was far from a foregone conclusion.

The primarch was off-ship, fighting on the world below. She was free to minimise casualties as best she could, rather than send the fleet into yet another cruel assault purely to inflict maximum damage and deploy boarding pods, regardless of the cost in men and materiel. This degree of tactical subtlety was a rare treat. Harder, though. She was used to fighting dirty, like the Legion she served.

She'd not lied to Khârn – the surface war was a mess of unholy proportions. Lotara kept sparing glances to the pict-feeds showing the city drowning in its own dust. She'd been at the briefings weeks ago, when Angron had demanded to make planetfall on Armatura and break it from within. No surprise there. What had come as a surprise was the moment Lord Lorgar Aurelian of the Word Bearers nodded in agreement with the Eater of Worlds. The last year had seen them cut across the Imperium, reaving through the worlds in their way, despite Lorgar's protests to make full speed for Ultramar. Now they'd finally arrived in Ultramar's heart, all restraint seemed cast to the solar wind.

She spared another glance at the pict-feeds. This time, the city's images held her gaze. Lotara frowned.

'Intensify sectors eight and fifteen,' she ordered one of the servitors slaved to the orbital-scrye console.

'Compliance.'

She sucked a slow breath in through her teeth as she stared at the resolving images. 'They're bringing down buildings in quick succession,' she said. 'Look. Look at these barracks crumbling in neat order. That's not from the battle. Those buildings have to be rigged with charges. The Ultramarines are killing their own city to bury our Legion in the rubble.'

Ivar Tobin, her first officer, nodded to her assessment. 'So it seems, captain.'

'Get me Angron,' she said to him. 'Now.'

'Aye, ma'am.' He left her side to make her request a reality. Getting hold of the primarch while he was embattled would take no shortage of patience and resolve.

Lotara turned her attention back to the void war unfolding above Armatura. She called up a quad-screened pict-feed, hazed by distance, of one of the new Word Bearers king-ships. The thing was monstrous in its beauty, big enough to make her breath catch if she looked at it for too long. The human mind processed detail in stops and starts; it was only when a lesser cruiser's silhouette crossed the *Blessed Lady*'s battlements that the king-ship's size became apparent, and each time it did, Lotara felt her stomach lurch. The thing looked too big to be real.

Orbital wars were their own beasts, with their own methods and moments of madness. A war above a world tended to play out in much closer quarters than many stately, oddly-placid void engagements. Fighting it out in high orbit meant getting in your foe's face, and that suited Lotara just fine. She was used to it. The World Eaters liked to board their enemies' ships, and that almost always meant coming in close, no matter where the *Conqueror* fought.

'Why is that weapon platform not dead yet?' she asked, eyebrow raised. 'Chase the *Venator Vorena*, if you please. Pursue it into the fiftieth grid, with full broadsides on that platform as we pass.'

At only twenty-three, third officer Feyd Hallerthan was the youngest of the strategium's command crew. 'That will bring us dangerously close to the three cruisers holding off the *Lex*, captain,' he said.

She clicked her tongue – a habit of hers when she was on the verge of losing her temper. Feyd was wrong, because she could see the oncoming press of another Word Bearers cruiser and its frigate squadron would force the three Ultramarines cruisers to pull up and regroup for another attack run, unless they had a sudden hunger to be rammed or crippled by close-quarters rupture fire. Their sound tactical retreat would open up all the room she required. It took her all of half a second to discern this from the flickering dance of ship name-runes clustering and twisting on her tactical display.

She knew he had other ideas, and that they'd be acceptable enough. But Lotara knew her game better than anyone else.

'Look to the grid beneath the *Lex*, and the Word Bearers vessel rising in support. That's why you're wrong. The Ultramarines will pull up and away, before regrouping for a second run at the *Lex*.'

'I see it, ma'am. But if the–'

'As far as I'm concerned,' she interrupted with a smile, 'it's not my job to explain why my order overrules your ideas. You should perceive the reasons yourself. Now do as I say, lieutenant.'

Leftenant, she pronounced it, ever the spire-born.

He flinched, and the several tactical alternatives he'd been about to suggest shrivelled on his tongue. 'Aye, ma'am.'

Ivar Tobin – greying, stern, professional to his core – returned to her throne's side. 'The primarch has answered your vox-hails, ma'am.'

'Well, then. This is a day of many wonders.'

Lotara leaned back as the ship juddered around her, momentum dampeners straining against the tight turn. A couple of tapped keys on her armrest activated her personal hololith generator. Angron's image stood before her throne, towering tall, distorted and pale but undeniably the primarch. His axes dripped colourless blood, but the hololithic droplets ghosted away into nothing as soon as they hit the deck.

'What do you want, captain?' Pain tics flawed one side of his face, leaving the other slackened in a dull snarl. She knew better than to ask if he was in pain. Angron was always in pain.

'The casualty reports from the surface attack are looking rather unpleasant. What's going on down there?'

'The Evocati.' Angron's image distorted to the point of failure, then streamed back into grainy existence. 'And they have a Titan Legio as well. Sorry if we're not pacifying the world as quickly as you'd like, Lotara.'

'Don't be childish, my lord.'

'I am no one's lord, and I grow bored of telling you that. You're always very brave with me when I'm several thousand kilometres away, captain.'

'I know, sire.' She steepled her fingers, briefly distracted by the ship shaking around her again. The frigates passing their stern were targeting the *Conqueror*'s engine decks, to little effect.

'How's my ship?' Angron asked, spitting blood onto the rocky ground.

'*My ship* is fine,' she replied. 'How many Evocati are on the surface?'

The colossal figure grunted, lifting an axe in what might have been a god's shrug. 'A lot. All of them. I don't know.' He was looking away now, starting to scan the wrecked city over his shoulder. She didn't have long, he'd be lost to the Nails soon.

'The junctions in the capital, where the primary avenues meet; it looks like the Ultramarines have the buildings rigged to detonate. Be careful as you advance into the city, sire.'

'You worry too much, captain.'

She clicked her tongue again. 'Does it not seem perfectly reasonable, sire, that a war-world would be prepared for every eventuality when it comes to an invasion? At least consider advancing with the Word Bearers and sending scouts ahead to confirm what I'm seeing.'

'My brother's precious Bearers of the Word are hissing their insipid prayers as they march slowly down the streets. The war will be over before their bolters sing even once.'

She swallowed her temper as best she could. 'Do you at least want me to target the Titan Legio's foundries from up here?'

'I want you to leave me alone, captain.' Angron turned back to face her, his left eye twitching tightly closed in response to the spasms tugging at the corner of his lips. His unwilling smile bared one side of his implanted iron teeth. 'Shoot whatever you wish, but cease whining to me about it.'

Distance did nothing to steal any of the primarch's blunt, savage grandeur. He was a ruined, towering thing of pain-spasms and sutured flesh. Lotara had only ever seen two primarchs, but despite the legend that each was cast in the Emperor's image, Lorgar and Angron couldn't have looked less alike. The former had a face that belonged on antique coins, and a voice that made her think of warm honey. The latter was an angel's statue, desecrated by a hundred blades and left in the rain. Angron was ripped skin and roared oaths over a core of thick blood vessels and muscle meat.

Whatever aesthetic intention there'd been in his creation was long lost; time and war had seen to that. Had fate not intervened, perhaps Angron would have grown to be as beautiful as his brothers Lorgar, Sanguinius, or even Fulgrim – but fate was never a silent ally to anyone.

The primarch's distorted hololithic wavered as the ship took another barrage against its void shields.

'How's the void battle?' Angron asked. She knew he didn't want details, and knew his fragile, mutilated mind wouldn't hold onto them even if he tried. Grey blood was already trickling down his white chin. Another nosebleed.

'We're still here,' she said.

'Good. Stay that way.' As he turned his back on her, the image flickered once more and finally died.

'This isn't good,' she mused aloud. 'This isn't good at all.'

'Ma'am?' asked Tobin.

'Khârn's right about the primarch.' She turned her throne back to face the void war. 'He's getting worse.'

WITH RESTORED VOX, Khârn spent several painstaking minutes speaking with his sergeants, coordinating the movements of the few squads who weren't lost to the Nails. Precious few of them, as it happened.

Esca was immune to ever being *lost*. The Codicier's report was curt and clear; he knew full well Khârn preferred it that way. He had little to say, beyond the fact the fighting was fiercest at the avenue junctions. Ultramarines and Academy Guard resistance was at its strongest there, where they defended fortress-barracks brimming with defensive turrets.

Skane was still inbound, one of the few to keep his head in the battle, but Khârn found the Word Bearers before he found his brother.

A year's alliance thus far had reaped little tangible reward. The Legions had almost come to blows mere weeks ago – both their fleets hanging in deep space with guns rolled out and boarding pods racked into firing tubes. Beyond that aborted betrayal, halted only by Lorgar and Angron finding a xenos fleet to murder instead, interactions between the Legions were considered on the right side of cordial if warriors managed not to spit at each other in mission briefings.

A squad of Word Bearers stood in a half-circle around one of their battle tanks. Their chanting was an impassioned chorus, sounding disgustingly close to worship. It was in Colchisian, of course. The Word Bearers rarely deigned to speak Low Gothic, even around their brother Legion. Yet another bone of contention.

Their murmured prayers broke off as Khârn came closer.

'Captain,' one of them greeted him. Behind the sergeant, three Ultramarines were lashed in crucified ruin to the tank's hull. Iron spikes had been driven through the warriors' arms and chests, impaling them in place. All three legionaries of the XIII were still twitching, still struggling – even the one with a spike through his throat. It was hard not to admire such tenacity.

Khârn lifted his axe to gesture at the crucified Ultramarines. 'You truly have time for this desecration?' He kept the edge of condescension from his voice. Just.

The Word Bearers sergeant, clad in the crimson of his Legion's new livery, closed the holy book he'd been reading aloud to his men. The tome's pages met with a soft thump, and the book fell to hang on a short chain bound to the warrior's belt.

'It seems you have time to run off into the dust and get separated from your men, World Eater.'

Khârn felt the *tick-tick-tick* of the Butcher's Nails start again in the back of his brain. Misfiring signals from his skull made his fingertips tense, and he accidentally gunned his chainaxe's trigger, making the saw-teeth whine as they chewed air. The Word Bearers clutched their bolters tighter, but made no overt threat of their own.

'Watch your words,' Khârn warned. 'Get back into the fight, all of you. Victory is hardly guaranteed here.'

The sergeant, his faceplate silver against the red of his helm, looked back to the tortured Ultramarines for a moment.

'This is a sacred observance. We do not take orders from you, centurion.'

'And yet,' Khârn said, smiling behind his faceplate, 'this time, you will.'

The incoming whine of overburned jump pack engines punctuated his words. Skane was the first to land, hitting the ground running, skidding to a halt at his captain's side. The rest of his Destroyers came down in ragged order, weapons holstered, bandoliers of radiation grenades rattling against their armour.

'Is there a problem, captain?' Skane asked. The gritty, dusty wind clattered against his scorched ceramite. The only colour on his war plate was the leering red of his eye lenses. Beyond that, he and his brothers could have been shadows born from the ash – the ghosts of warriors slain in flame.

Khârn didn't answer. He kept staring at the Word Bearers sergeant. 'Back into the battle.'

Buildings fell in the distance, with the distinctive thunder of dying architecture. 'Yes, sir,' the Word Bearers officer said at last.

Khârn finally turned to Skane. 'Come with me.'

The Eighth Captain of the XII Legion left the Word Bearers by their Land Raider. His Destroyers followed.

'*Making friends, sir?*' Skane asked in Nagrakali, all guttural grunts.

'Speak Gothic,' replied Khârn. 'Make the effort to cooperate, even if the Word Bearers refuse to do the same.'

Skane's articulated collar gave a low whine as he turned to look at his captain. 'I wouldn't piss on a Word Bearer even if he was on fire. You think I care what toys they use to fly around in?'

'Just do as I ask, Skane.'

The Destroyer shrugged. 'Of course, sir.'

'Report,' Khârn prompted.

He could hear Skane's quiet chuckle behind the scorched faceplate. 'You're not going to like this, sir.'

Khârn resisted the urge to sigh. 'Where's Angron?'

'No one knows for certain. He was Lost to the Nails after we took the Krytica Junction half an hour ago. Delvarus was the last to report in; he says he saw the primarch eating some of the enemy dead.'

'Tell me that's a joke.'

Skane shrugged again.

Maybe Lotara was right. Maybe they should have just let her bombard Armatura into dust.

'Why is Delvarus down here?'

'It seems Lotara let him slip the leash. The flagship's hardly going to be boarded by anything worthwhile during that mess in the sky.'

Khârn waved the matter away. 'I need to get to the front line,' he said. 'Someone has to coordinate the assault with the Legio Audax. Damn it, I don't even know if we're winning.'

'I can answer that one for you, sir,' Skane replied. 'We're most definitely not winning.'

MAGNUS WATCHED THE warring heavens. Mostly, he watched the *Blessed Lady* and her twin sister, the *Trisagion*, making a mockery of Armatura's orbital arrays, dismantling one of the best-defended worlds in the Imperium with barrage after barrage from their howling, flashing weapon decks.

'You'll need those at Terra,' he said softly. Lorgar didn't answer. His brother hadn't answered anything in some time.

The ships' size and scale rendered all countermeasures obsolete. For the first hour, nothing could punch through their shields. Nothing even managed to scrape their skin. It took the combined firepower of a battle-station, two orbital defence platforms and a suicidal ramming from the Imperial warship *Steel Sky* to finally burst the *Blessed Lady*'s shields. She sailed on, oblivious to the thousands dying within one of the flaming monasteries on her back, for their agonies made no difference at all to a crew of half a million.

Lorgar knelt at the basilica's heart, head lowered in prayer. The mere sight of it made Magnus's skin crawl. Despite the aetheric nature of his new form, some instincts died hard.

'Lorgar,' he said. His brother's answer was to keep whispering his blasphemous, deluded devotions. '*Lorgar,*' Magnus growled.

The Word Bearer looked up, his inked face one of transcendent focus. He blinked then, for the first time in half an hour.

'Something is wrong.' Lorgar rose to his feet, boots sending cracks along the mosaic floor. He held out a hand towards one of the hundred bookshelves, and his crozius maul slashed across the cold air to land neatly in his right fist. 'We will speak soon. Farewell, Magnus.'

'Going to war, brother?' the sorcerer asked.

'I am needed on Armatura,' the Word Bearer replied.

'Ah. Don't you wish to talk me into the war? That is why you summoned me, is it not?'

Lorgar didn't look back. 'I know your decision, Magnus. You will stand with us at Terra. I was told this by the gods you insist aren't real.'

The sorcerer shook his head in dismissal. 'Tell me what demands your presence on the surface.'

Lorgar sealed his tri-horned helm in place, speaking before leaving the chamber.

'Angron is in trouble.'

FOUR

**Buried Alive
Communion
Valika Junction**

Serenity fled from him.

He clawed after it, raging against the futility of his own desperation. The taste of failure was already coating his tongue with familiar bitterness. He screamed skywards, wanting rainwater to wash the taste from his teeth. His scream ended dry.

He'd been so close to serenity that time. *So close.*

Yet it fled, hurling him back into the world of bleeding meat and bruised bone – a life where his violated skull pulsed fire around his body in rhythm with his racing heart.

He wished for something, anything, to ease the clockwork agony engine in his brain, mutilating his mind with its poison.

And he was weak. Weak and blind. He trembled in the dark, shivering and pained and inhaling the reek of his own blood. He couldn't see his hands before his face, but he felt how they bled.

Angron, said a voice.

Angron. The name meant nothing.

Angron. Angron. Angron. Several voices. Ten, maybe twenty. He wasn't sure. He roared a second time, bellowing for them to get out of his head.

I can't reach him, the strongest of the voices said. *The Nails have truly damaged his mind this time.*

I can't reach him, either, said another.

Then we have to risk Communion, said yet another.

The response was a silent wave of cold, cold repulsion, the psychic reflection of magnets refusing to bond.

No, one of the voices said in the wake of the nausea. *Esca, no.*

The strongest agreed. *We cannot countenance Communion again. Think of the losses last time, and how much weaker we will be without them.*

Then what? Do you trust Lord Aurelian?

An amusing notion.

Lorgar is powerful beyond our reckoning. He could reach Angron.

Lord Aurelian hasn't even made planetfall, and I am unwilling to trust him in a matter this delicate. We have to risk Communion. It must be us.

And if we don't?

The arguing voices fell silent. Their hesitation made him smile, though he wasn't sure why. Perhaps because it stank of indecision, and indecision stank of cowardice.

He's dying, the lead voice finally said. *This is one step beyond being lost to the Nails. He will never recover without our aid.*

Leave me be, he thought. Leave me be. Get out of my head.

Vorias... said one of the voices. *Give the order.*

Another long pause, another hesitation that reeked of fear. Cowardice wasn't the fear of death. Cowardice was having something to lose. What worth was a warrior who forged attachments to the impermanence of the world around him? Everything faded. Everything died. Everything decayed. Attachment was weakness.

The men behind these voices had something to lose, and it made them afraid. That made them weak.

Brothers, said the lead voice, reluctantly. *Join me in Communion.*

He turned from the irritating buzz the voices were becoming. His knuckles whitened and cracked as he clutched the drenched handles of his axes. When he opened his eyes, confronted by the utter blackness of his surroundings, he screamed through a mouthful of bloody froth and started digging. No surrender. No submission.

Despite no knowledge of who he was or why he was entombed, the kicking, thrashing part of his hind-brain focused on one thought. This wasn't the first time he'd been buried alive.

With no up, no down, there was only ahead or dead.

Khârn tasted his own blood – a rare and unwelcome flavour. The Ultramarine before him refused to die, and while he could sympathise with the warrior's will, he had enough to worry about already. The last thing he needed was the XIII dragging out their demise in a protracted last stand.

The wound in his side ached with an incessant pulse, throbbing in time with the beat of his heart. Pain nullifiers flooded his bloodstream from the intravenous injection ports at his wrists, close to his collarbone, and along his spine. Even so, warning runes flickered across his retinal display, in case he was somehow unaware of the blood haemorrhaging from the wound below his ribs.

The Evocatus moved in for another thrust, feinting and weaving, his footwork flawless on the rubble-strewn ground. Khârn stumbled back, blocking the gladius with his toothed axe rather than risk dodging on the unsteady rocks.

The warrior immediately riposted, coming in low with a second thrust. Khârn deflected it by slamming his fist into the Ultramarine's faceplate, sending the legionary reeling. It bought the World Eater enough time to bring his axe up again, as he *clanged* back to back with Kargos behind him.

'Captain,' his brother breathed. 'I'm having such a wonderful time.' He seemed to be grinning, but every World Eater in a

Sarum-pattern faceplate seemed to be grinning.

Around them was nothing but a chaos of crashing blades and cursing warriors. Blades against ceramite gave their distinctive dull toll, interspersed with the close-range bark of bolters. Flatlines played across Khârn's eye lenses as more and more of his men fell to XIII blades. Slain Academy Guard were slumped across the rocks and Khârn was treading upon their bodies as much as he scrambled across the uneven ground.

The Evocatus refusing to die bore the insignia of a sergeant. The warrior's cloak, once red, was stained with dust clinging to the blood and oil, scaled by encrusted dirt. A golden helm marked him as one of the honoured elite, those souls sworn to train successive generations of Ultramarines and send them forth into the Five Hundred Worlds. Khârn hated him for his stubborn tenacity as much as he admired him for it.

The Valika Junction wasn't supposed to be a chokepoint. They should have seen this coming. Another Legion – one not dancing to the tune of the Butcher's Nails in the back of their heads – would have seen it clearly, and that scraped Khârn's temper raw. The World Eaters had poured into it in a howling rush, jostling each other as they sprinted, chasing the fleeing Academy Guard in their filthy blue uniforms.

The Academy's towers detonated, and masses of falling rock came crashing down onto the avenues below. The roads had burst and crumbled, sinking into the earth. Hundreds of World Eaters gone in a handful of heartbeats, buried beneath a city district. The XIII had mined the avenues and rigged their own beautiful buildings for timed explosions, just as Lotara had warned. It was happening across the city, but the Nails stole caution, twisting it into the sick pleasure of joining a massacre.

Blood mattered, nothing more. Seeing the enemy break and flee invited howling laughter. The laughter lasted until the world exploded around the Legion's vanguard.

Khârn arrived late, after half of the squads here were already buried in the wreckage. The avenues were cut threads, strangled by the rubble of priceless marble. Here and there, the tracks of a World Eaters tank were visible at the very edges of the settled avalanche.

Sniper fire spat from the remaining rooftops and balconies above, lancing through World Eaters helms and dropping the warriors where they stood. Ultramarines gunships roared overhead, their engines laughing in crescendo to the staccato chuckles of their heavy bolters. They fired and fired, pouring their anger down onto the dying Eaters of Worlds. The Nails stole pain, gave him serenity, and lent him strength, but Khârn cursed them every time he went into battle. He cursed them now, as his senses rang with the dissonant chime of the countless flatlines.

He needed an aerial view. They couldn't keep fighting blind, with Ultramarines reinforcements pouring in from the east and west districts.

'Skane,' he breathed.

Skane was gone. Dead or too far away, Khârn wasn't sure which. Even Kargos, at his back a moment before, was gone to chase another foe.

Khârn turned, releasing the charge from his shaking plasma pistol. Bolts of corrosive fusion-fire splashed against the three uniformed humans scrambling towards him, incinerating them where they stood. He spun back in time to catch the Evocatus's descending blade, twisting it aside and levelling another kick to the Ultramarine's emblazoned chestplate. The wound in his side caught fire again, burning in the backwashed heat from his plasma shot. Through clenched teeth, Khârn howled to the strangled skies, up at the dust that blocked them from the fleet.

The vox was useless, lost to scrambled shrieks and taunting static. They had to get out of the Junction. They had to reach the primarch. There was no front line among the fallen buildings, only clusters of desperate, isolated bands of warriors.

His axe lodged in the Ultramarine's neck joint, finally dropping the Evocatus into the rubble. Khârn pulled the blade free on the third try, letting the whirring teeth cleanse themselves of blood. He was turning to seek another foe when he felt the first tingle of a teleportation flare itching at his gums.

For several seconds he stood there, turning slowly, trying to pinpoint the locus of arrival. Dust swirled around him, as the smallest rocks quivered and lifted from the destroyed ground. He saw, between duelling warriors in white and blue, where the flare would bloom and fade, bloom and fade, finding nowhere stable to lock. The uneven ground would murder a locus lock, as would the hundreds of moving bodies, and the interference from the dust.

'Lotara.' His voxed words melted together in a blur. 'Lotara, abort the teleportation at the Valika Junction. *Abort the teleportation at the Valika Junction.* We're fighting over cursed earth, there'll be no locus lock.'

Her image crackled back into life in the corner of his retinal display, briefly enough to deliver a single sentence.

'It's not us, Khârn.'

Her image distorted, vanished. He was left looking at data-spills and a leaping targeting reticule that couldn't ascertain which was the ripest kill in an ocean of enemy warriors.

A bolter shell cracked off his shoulder guard, the shell's kick sending him stumbling as shrapnel shattered across his helm. He fired back blind, leaving his plasma pistol starved as it recharged.

Argel Tal, you whoreson, where are you?

+Khârn?+ The voice was distant, weak, muffled by the Nails' beat.

Argel Tal? Brother, where are you? Bring the Bearers of the Word. We're being slaughtered here.

No answer. Nothing.

'Anyone,' he voxed. 'Anyone who can still hear me, anyone still alive, this is Khârn at the Valika Junction. I have the Eighth, Twentieth and Sixty-Seventh Companies with me. We need armour and air support, immediately.'

'Where are the Word Bearers?' one of his sergeants demanded. 'They're supposed to b–' Static ate the rest of the warrior's words, but he was right. The XVII swore to reinforce them at Valika. Khârn had led the briefings himself.

Other replies came in the form of howls and cheers. A Legion lost to the Nails. A Legion sprinting gleefully into a hundred ambushes. You couldn't collar the Eaters of Worlds.

The only voices that made sense in the aural melee all demanded to know the same thing.

'The primarch,' they called, over and over. 'Is it true? Is Angron dead?'

The entity called itself the Communion.

It rose above the Valika Junction, into the smoky sky. Nineteen threads pulled at it – nineteen bonds preventing it from soaring too high. The Communion turned in the air, staring down at the city beneath, where buildings toppled and men screamed in a world of dust and dreadful physicality.

Drawn by curiosity, the Communion drifted lower, watching the lives of the tiny creatures ending in minute flickers of sparking souls. Each death sent a sliver of mist rising from the broken shells of meat and iron. A warrior would fall, and the soul-flare would rise, hazy and indistinct. Each one shrieked, though some laughed between their screams.

The Communion drifted even lower, close to the ground now, running its clawed hand through the misty soul rising from the twitching corpse of a warrior in white. The soul parted, the way mist was broken by the breeze. The Communion laughed, delighted by such fragility.

The nineteen bindings pulled at it, shackling it tighter. An image formed in its consciousness – the image of a graven, bleeding god, lost in the dark.

Yes. The purpose. No time for these little games.

The Communion turned its focus onto the destroyed earth, and sank into the rubble.

Angron, *it called.* **Angron, hear me.**

* * *

He laughed in the blackness, the kind of laughter that spoke more of madness than mirth. He laughed as he dragged himself across the jagged rock, splitting his skin, unsure which way was up and which way was down. Blood beat behind his eyes, but that that could be from his wounds as much as from gravity. His laughter was little more than snarled wheezing. He'd struggled to draw breath in this airless dark for minutes, or hours, or days. He didn't know which. All was the same.

Trapped.

No. No, not that word. Even the thought of it set his hands shaking hard enough to almost lose the grip on his axes, and he needed them to dig. Not trapped, no. Not helpless. He wasn't trapped here in the dark, the epitome of dark, so thick and true he could taste it on his tongue. It seeped into his eyes when they were open – were they open? How could he tell? – and filled his mouth when he laughed.

The dark pressed against him, hungry and hot. *Alive*. That was the truth. It was alive. It lived, and wrapped him the way a burial shroud wrapped…

Angron, said a new voice.

He wasn't Angron. He was merely *He*: a creature of trembling hands, eyes that stung from grit, and laughter that had long-since died, replaced by a stammered wheeze that wasn't – *wasn't* – fear. He feared nothing. Not death, not the dark, not helplessness.

Angron, hear me.

He could feel his hands flayed raw, his fingers now sticks of wet meat fused to the handles of his axes by the glue of his own blood. Dragging himself through the rock was killing him, inch by inch, moment by moment. He was skinning himself alive. He didn't need to see to know that. The dark couldn't hide every truth.

The axes were dead, both of them. He knew that, too. Their toothless blades still broke rock, but they'd surely suffered past any ruination that could be repaired.

Angron.

But he wasn't Angron. He was…

…trapped.

Trapped in the Dark.

The shaking started, harder, heavier. He slavered with it, crawling faster, the stones carving into his muscles as he dragged himself over them, under them, through them.

Angron, you're crawling downwards, deeper into the earth.

No. That wasn't true.

He started screaming, venting his precious breath into the place between panic and rage. Blood sheeted from his mouth and nose. The pain engine in his skull *tick-tocked* into overdrive, knifing its needles deeper into the meat of his mind. He had to kill. He had to kill. He wasn't weak. He wasn't scared. He wasn't helpless.

'Kill,' he choked the words out, gagging on a mouthful of rock. 'Kill. Maim. Burn.'

Angron. Hear me. I am the Communion.

The anger – it wasn't fear, it wasn't panic – drowned in the wake of their words. He stopped shaking, stopped dragging himself through the rock.

'Who are you?'

The last nineteen still alive. I am the Communion. The only one who can reach you.

He tried to wipe his eyes clean of the clinging blood. It did little but smear it across his face.

'Who am I?'

You are Angron, Lord of the Twelfth Legion.

The calm suffused him now, easing his aching bones. He knew, without knowing how he knew, that it was artificial. The voices were doing something to him, to drown the anger-that-wasn't-fear.

I am counteracting the machine in your skull, by altering the chemicals flowing through your brain. I cannot maintain it for long, not with only nineteen of us left. Your mind is too different from baseline humanity. It resists any interference.

He tried to shake his head to clear it, but the crunching pressure of the rock all around denied him even that.

No. Lies. Lies, all of it.

'Who are you?' he spat this time.

I am the Communion.

Which meant nothing at all. 'If you have power to reach me, then free me.'

I cannot. I do not exist on this plane of being. I am the gestalt of nineteen psychic minds, nothing more. Nineteen minds separated by hundreds of kilometres, as the Legion marches to war across this world.

'Free me!' he said again.

You have to free yourself. You're digging downwards. The enemy mined the roads and collapsed the towers upon the vanguard of our army. You were over thirty metres beneath the ground when you woke. You're now closer to two hundred.

And bleeding. And weakening. And your axes are broken. Even your kind aren't immortal, sire.

He didn't believe a word of it. He didn't want to believe it. All the same, he relaxed his grip on the axes. He told himself it was to bide his time, rather than any relief from the agony in his head.

The thing called him 'sire'. That was interesting.

I am the meeting of minds, born of the last among your sons who still speak without speaking. I am the strength of the last nineteen that still live. I've silenced the Nails. You are yourself, for a few rare moments.

Try to remember all that came before. You are Angron, Lord of the Twelfth Legion, a son of the Emperor of Mankind. This is Ultrama–

No. Enough of the voice's whisperings.

He remembered standing in the dark.

He remembered standing in the dark, while his brothers and sisters died.

He remembered standing in the dark, while his brothers and sisters died, because he wasn't there to fight with th–

No. Not that, sire.

He remembered being blinded by his father's light. He remembered refusing to abandon his brothers and sisters, beneath a blue sky at high-sun, far from the city of Desh'ea. He remembered the mechanical thunder of absolute betrayal, when he was stolen from the death he'd so richly earned.

He remembered the cold moment of truth as he stood in the dark, his hurting eyes healing, that every day he breathed was an unwanted gift. He was walking another man's destiny now. His destiny was to be with the men and women who needed him, who called for him, who followed him into the mountains and died without him. A destiny denied.

He was Angron of Desh'ea. After that, nothing mattered. He'd listened to the others that begged him, that needed it all to matter. He'd played their games, living out another man's life. He'd led his fleets, he'd embraced his sons, he'd told himself that blood was thicker than water, and the Eaters of Worlds were the army he wanted and the horde he deserved. He'd sustained himself on lies, letting none see how he starved.

And he served in his cold-hearted father's empire, enduring the silent sneers of brothers he despised.

Yes, Angron. Angron the Conqueror. The Butcher. The Red Angel. All the things they'd made him into, after stealing his destiny as...

As what, sire?

He recoiled from the voice. It wasn't for them to know.

'Vorias.' He growled the name of his Legion's Lectio Primus.

Vorias is within me, sire. I am the Communion.

Angron wanted to spit. Filthy psykers. His Legion would be cleaner when the last of them finally died. Their whispers set the Nails ringing inside his skull like nothing else could. Already, he could feel blood sheeting from his nose.

'You've done what you wished to do. You reached me, now tell me which way to dig, and get out of my head.'

They did. They obeyed both demands. Angron spent several

gruelling, bleeding minutes twisting beneath the earth, before resuming his aching crawl. This time, bound for freedom and the light above. More importantly, bound for revenge.

Esca collapsed backwards, his armour thudding against the Rhino's hull. He slid to the ground in a slow hunch, ending the fall in an ungainly slump. Blood ran from his ears, his nose, his eyes, and none of this was anything new. It still hurt, it hurt every time, but even pain became mundane when it was a constant companion.

He could feel the Communion dying in the distance. The gestalt being they'd shaped with the union of their powers was crying out as it diminished, pained by the simple oblivion of each psyker withdrawing his mind and returning to individuality. Strange and unfortunate for the short-lived intelligence, but nothing else would have pierced the murk of Angron's broken psyche. The primarch's proto-Nails girded his mind from intrusion. No one knew why, or how, or if it was even intentional.

Esca crouched there, breathing through bloody teeth, too weak to even swallow. To force one's way into a primarch's mind was to swim blind through rockcrete. And the Nails… the Nails made torture into a nightmare. Angron's Nails were almost septic in their simplicity, clouding the warlord's brain from outside influence, turning his thoughts into untraceable, uncatchable ghosts. To even speak with him, mind to mind, took an event like the Communion, and an event like the Communion left the remaining World Eaters Librarians sickened and weak in the aftermath. Whatever went into the construction of Angron's cranial implants defied simple reverse engineering.

He finally managed to look up, at where his own brothers were judiciously ignoring him across the wrecked plaza. Esca stared into the dust, watching the white-clad sons of Angron duelling amongst the rubble, crashing blades against the silhouettes of Ultramarines who refused to give ground. Smaller shadows, the human soldiers of the Armaturan Wardens, fought in ever-retreating ranks, forming pockets of resistance with their quick-flashing lasrifles. Even through the dust-mist and the chemical stinks of burnt metal and tank engines, he could smell the fear-sweat decorating the humans' bodies.

A shadow blocked out the weak sun. A small shadow. He raised his head again, unaware he'd come close to passing out.

The stink of human skin hit him first. And then, the smell of blood. Thin mortal blood, unlaced by stimulants and unfiltered by enhanced organs. He couldn't make out the face or the features of the man's armour, but he didn't need to. It wasn't a legionary. The human wasn't on his side.

He lifted a hand. To kill the man? To ward off the coming execution? It didn't matter. Esca's hand shook in the air before him, the gravest and clearest confession of weakness. Betrayed by his own body.

+Vorias,+ he sent in silence, though that was worthless. Vorias was half a city away. +Khârn,+ he tried. +Kargos.+ They were both nearer. He couldn't see Khârn fighting in the chaos of the Valika Junction, but he could hear him shouting over the vox, demanding to abort a teleport lock.

Predictably, neither answered. They probably couldn't even hear him.

The human silhouette levelled a rifle, aiming at his head. Esca laughed, but it left his throat as a wet, wheezing chuckle – a man choking on his own bile.

'Why?' the man asked. 'Why did you betray us all?'

Esca's vision was swimming as he tried to focus his thoughts. He laughed again, just as weak. His hand was still trembling.

'*Answer me!*' the soldier cried. He pushed the rifle's muzzle against Esca's cheek.

The World Eater tried to answer, and instead vomited dark blood down the front of his armour.

A growl. A whine. Something flashing in the sun.

Blood, hot and too-human, painted Esca's face. The shadow fell, and another replaced it. This one came with the purring thrum of active armour.

'Esca,' said the new shadow. It carried a chainaxe, and its helm was crested. It smelled of war and hate and fire.

'Captain,' the Codicier replied in a raw whisper. 'My thanks.' He held out his shaking hand, needing to be helped up.

The other World Eater stepped back, as if threatened. Ah. Yes. Esca lowered his hand again.

'Forgive me, Khârn,' he managed to say.

'It's fine.' The warrior turned away. 'Now get up and finish this fight.'

Esca watched his captain moving back over the rubble. The Codicier stood almost a minute later, looking around for the weapons he'd dropped when he'd saved his primarch's life.

The Armaturan wore the dirty blue dress tunic of an Academy Guard officer, replete with gold ropes and silver frogging.

'Fff... for t-the Emp-peror.' The dying man stuttered the words from a ruined mouth. Blood streamed from his gums where his teeth had been until Khârn backhanded them down his throat only seconds before. Distracted, the World Eater dragged the struggling mortal into a headbutt, crashing his snarling faceplate into the man's forehead. Whatever bone remained whole after that blow, it wasn't enough to keep him alive. The Armaturan officer slumped to the ground, as dead as the city he'd failed to protect.

Khârn breathed in, inhaling the bloodstink painted across his faceplate. The Nails gave a pleased, warm pulse in response.

He looked skywards as the teleport locus fixed at last, ripping a conduit through the warp with a bang that blew out what few windows remained whole in a radius of several streets. The displaced air pressure was like a sonic boom of its own, blasting thirty metres above the battlefield. Khârn looked up when the airwave hit, feeling pebbles and grit clattering against his armour. Those closest to the airburst were thrown from their feet – World Eater, human and

Ultramarine alike. He was far enough away that it did little beyond scramble his retinal display for a few seconds.

A demigod in red and gold fell from the golden wound in the world's sky. A magnificent warrior-priest armoured in sacred crimson, each armour plate inscribed with runic mandalas and prayers written in Colchisian cuneiform. The oaths and scrolls bound to the dark ceramite caught the wind like wings of parchment, spreading as he fell. Khârn felt it then; he felt the instinctive sigh of submission, that skin-itching awe in the first moments that one stood in a primarch's presence.

Lorgar's ridged boots crunched down on the rubble, grinding the rocks to pebbles and dust. Sniper fire lanced the air at once, flaring with frustrated light as it impacted against the psychokinetic shield shimmering around the primarch's armour. Khârn shouted a warning, but Lorgar paid as much attention to the centurion's cry as he did to the incoming storm of fire that supposedly threatened his life. His attention was elsewhere, focused on the cursed earth lining the fallen avenue.

An Ultramarines gunship rattled overhead, rows of heavy bolters chattering and flashing in the dust-brought darkness. That got the primarch's attention. Lorgar turned in a measured, fluid arc, dragging Illuminarum's brutal maul-head across the ground before roaring as he hurled it skywards. The crozius spun in an energised blur, crashing into the cockpit's reinforced windshield with a shatter loud enough to be audible over the gunship's protesting jump jets. As the Thunderhawk banked away, Lorgar raised his hands towards it, fingers curling into claws. He gripped it, holding it in the air.

And he *pulled*.

The gunship's engines coughed black filth and shuddered in the sky. Lorgar *pulled* again, a prophet clawing wisdom from the heavens. The gunship fell, smashing into the broken avenue with an ear-aching crash of tormented metal, engines aflame, hull mangled.

The primarch ignored his lost crozius for the moment, and looked back at the rubble lining the wide avenue.

He said one word. Somehow, Khârn heard it distinctly, above everything else, though it was no more than a whisper.

'Brother.'

The Lord of the Word Bearers started hauling the rocks free and casting them away from the buried, collapsed road, with the same untouching ease as he'd pulled a gunship from the sky.

Skane came down, jump pack engines giving an ululating whine as he skidded to a halt next to Khârn. His black armour was painted white with the dust of the dying city.

'You're going to love this,' he said to his captain.

Khârn was unable to look away from Lorgar. 'Are you seeing what I'm seeing?' he asked Skane.

'This is even better, captain.' The Destroyer shook his head. 'Do you feel that?'

Once he paid heed, he couldn't help but feel it. The ground quivered, just faintly, but as regularly as a racing heart. The city shook not from its death, but from the footsteps of giants.

'Titan-tread,' said Khârn.

'I saw several coming through the dust,' Skane admitted. 'And none of them are on our side.'

FIVE

The Ember Queen
His Imperial Wisdom
They Cheer, My Princeps

THE HUNTRESS WENT by several names, some of which were affectionate, some of which were archival in nature, and some of which were curses as she cast her shadow over her foes.

In the various records kept by what remained of the 203rd Expeditionary Fleet, she was listed as *L-ADX-cd-MARS-Quintessence-[Necare Modification]-I-XII-002a-2/98: VS/TK/K*, which was hardly a name to strike terror into the enemy.

In the annals of the Dark Angels, she was known as the *Ember Queen*, remembered from the decades she'd served with the First Legion before finding herself sent with her sisters to fight alongside the Eaters of Worlds. A banner commemorating her victories with the Dark Angels had hung in the strategium of the Lion's flagship, *Invincible Reason*, only to be torn down when it was discovered that she had turned traitor.

To the troops who fought at her feet, she was more often known as *Jackal*, or *Howler*. Her cry always had her little brothers roaring in reply. To those who knew her best, those who guided her movements and formed the biological components of her brain, she was *Syrgalah*, First Huntress of the Ember Wolves.

The command Titan, as with every war machine in the Legio Audax, sourced her name in antiquity, taking it from the Himalazian dialects of proto-Gothic that still existed in scraps of lore from the lost ages of Ancient Terra. Long ago, when Terra had been Old Earth – when the skies were blue heavens instead of grey iron – entire cultures spread across the planet's largest continent. Now it was the site of the Imperial Palace, and echoes like *Syrgalah*'s name were all that remained of those near-forgotten souls.

Syrgalah moved forwards in a brutish hunch, her wolfish skull of iron-riveted ceramite angled down to stare along the road. Her weaponised arms tracked her gaze, panning left and right with each sweep of the cockpit sensor screens that served as her eyes. She stalked rather than walked, clawed feet crunching three-toed imprints into the rockcrete avenues, her gait making her lean side to side with every step.

A titanium plaque on the dense armour plating of her shin displayed the words *'If wolves have a queen, this is she'*, again in the Hindusian proto-Gothic that had given her a name. The Lion, Lord of the First Legion, had honoured her with the inscription decades ago. Years of war had left the plaque scratched, battered and warped, but the tech-priests always returned it to legibility. Who bestowed it upon her didn't matter. The sentiment was all.

In her armoured skull, the three command crew were strapped into their restraint thrones. Venric Solostine was eighty, but rejuvenat surgery kept him looking fifty, at the cusp of the second renaissance of handsomeness some men were lucky enough to enjoy. Silvering stubble marked his jawline, surrounding an easy and frequent smile. Connective neural cables ran from his temples and the back of his head, linking directly to his leather seat. He looked through *Syrgalah*'s cockpit-eyes, at the artillery tank grinding its gears to reverse back down the avenue. The vehicle's mounted cannon boomed with black smoke, and *Syrgalah*'s void shields lit up with the irritation of kinetic impact.

'That Vindicator needs to die,' Solostine said.

'Aye, sire,' Toth Kol called back from his throne. 'Pursuing.' The cockpit shook harder as the Warhound Titan started its lurching run. Grit rattled against its armour as it stalked through the dust clouds.

In the throne next to Toth, Keeda's face was cast in unhealthy amber light; the false fire from her flickering targeting display.

'I already have the shot, sire.'

In his command throne, Solostine pushed both his fists forwards, a slow and careful double-punch. Gears and hydraulics gave a heavy whine as *Syrgalah* mirrored his movement, its weaponised arms lifting and aiming in neural sympathy.

It was all the permission she needed; Keeda grinned and took the shot. *Syrgalah*'s left arm roared, the vulcan mega-bolters opening up with a deafening roar to obey the gunner's trigger finger. Spent shells rained onto the road in a monsoon of smoking scrap.

'Target destroyed,' Keeda said.

'The target is more than destroyed, my dear.' Solostine's approval murmured through the Titan, causing a shiver of pleasure through the old girl's iron bones.

Toth walked *Syrgalah* around the avenue's turn, marching into a side street. The Warhound gave the dead Vindicator a derisive kick as she passed by. The tank's hull, chewed through by Keeda's barrage, tumbled across the rockcrete road and into a wall.

'Moderati Primus?' Solostine called.

'Aye, sire?'

'The kick.' He was chuckling. 'A lovely touch. Auspex?'

Toth's bionic eyes refocused on the display monitor to his left. 'All formations holding within engagement parameters. Over half the Legio is embattled, the rest are moving up as planned. Loss ratio reported as one enemy engine for every one of ours.'

'Tolerable,' Solostine mused, 'but hardly exemplary, given the circumstances. The Legio Lysanda hardly outclasses us.'

Toth watched the road ahead. 'Lysanda fights in union with the Ultramarines.'

Solostine nodded. The implication need not be spoken clearer – the same thing happened every time the Legio Audax went to war. Where other Space Marine Legions would work in tactical conjunction with their Collegia Titanica forces, the World Eaters could never be trusted to keep their heads long enough to display such patience.

The Warhound lurched onwards, its rattling chassis plunging through the dust clouds strangling the city. They saw by auspex, moving towards mangled heat signatures and movement betrayed by wide-angle echolocation. Behind *Syrgalah*, the Warhounds *Maakri* and *Kalla* kept pace with their alpha. Their sombre armour plating showed the same abuses borne by the command Titan.

'Incoming message.' Toth was frowning. 'The flagship is filtering it as best she can. It's from the front line, to all outrider elements. They want us to converge on…' He pressed his bionic palm to the vox-input augmetically attached to his temple.

Solostine tapped his fingers on the armrest of his throne, effortlessly leaning into the roll and rock of the old Titan's tread.

'To converge on…?' the princeps asked. 'To converge on what? Don't tell me this will finally be the day the Twelfth Legion asks for our help.'

'Shit,' Toth said, releasing the curse in a slow breath. 'The transmission is from Eighth Captain Khârn. He's ordering all scout units back to the Valika Junction, and demanding immediate reinforcement.'

Solostine tutted at the swearing. 'A little dignity goes a long way, Moderati Kol.'

'My apologies, sire.'

'Forgiven.' Solostine was listening to the transmission himself, and his own smile dimmed. 'We'll have to fight across a quarter of the city to reach Valika. I… wait, wait. This can't be correct,' he said.

Keeda, without a link to the vox-net, finally looked away from her gunnery consoles. 'What is it?'

'Reports are coming in from half the junctions across the city,'

Solostine said. 'The worst is at Valika: Lysanda's engines are inbound. In addition, Lord Aurelian has made planetfall there.'

Keeda frowned, her orange glass targeting visor showing a continual scrolling data feed. 'Why can't that be correct?'

'Not that,' Solostine said. He keyed in a command to spread the vox-message to the cockpit's primary speakers. 'This.'

'...lost contact with the primarch, repeat, this is Khârn at Valika. We've lost contact with the primarch, reinforcements are–'

Keeda's frown went nowhere. 'The World Eaters always lose contact with the primarch. They lose contact with everyone, once... you know...' She tapped her fingers to her temple. 'The Nails take over.'

Solostine looked through the Titan's eyes, at the burning city beyond. 'Apparently, something is different, this time.'

Khârn screamed, not from rage nor from his wounds, but because he was still alive. The sound was one repeated a thousand, thousand times across the city by men pushed to their physical limits and beyond, yet given no respite. He screamed to override the pain of his own muscles, fighting against the lactic burning of an exhausted body flooded by combat stimulants. He screamed and laughed as he killed, and as his axe fell, and fell and fell.

He'd not lied to Argel Tal. Some warriors enjoyed war, and he was one of them. Not the crushing press itself, but the primal exultation of breaking the enemy ranks and the dizzying laughter that came with it; the prickling pleasure of breathing as others broke open and died. There was such depthless joy in survival.

But war-scribes had been getting their trade wrong since the very dawn of language. Some things simply couldn't be described, and war – true open war between clashing armies – was first among them. By the nature of perception, one man's wisdom would always be another man's lie.

Some tale-tellers focused on the moment-by-moment action and reaction of a warrior in the heat of the fight, describing the motions of mortality. Others focused on the atmosphere of the wider conflict, and the press of emotions on those involved within it.

The truth was both, and neither. Khârn knew it well.

No universal truth of battle existed. Sometimes he'd fought and never been able to recall a single axe-fall, nor the face of a single slain enemy, despite them crying out before his eyes for hours on end.

He'd also fought on battlefields where every contorted face clung to his memory for hours afterwards, and he remembered each and every nuanced tilt of his axe, as well as the exact tune it made shearing through armour and meat and bone.

Battle was a matter of endurance, the passing of time marked only by his own aching muscles and breathlessness. Front-line warfare – from the warbands of Ancient Terra to the grinding of vast hordes in the Great Crusade – was a war against the self. Skill meant nothing, while brotherhood and endurance meant everything. Every warrior in the 31st millennium who picked up a rifle, pistol or blade was duelling against their own reserves of courage, strength and endurance. They were duelling against their own brothers' and sisters' courage; their capacity to stand and hold the line.

After thirty thousand years, warfare had come full circle.

The sheer scale of humanity's conflicts disregarded the corrupt reliance on automation as seen in the Dark Age of Technology. Mankind was back down to swords beating against shields and men entrenched with their rifles, where the gods of myth were Titan war machines and Baneblade tanks.

In his calmer moments, Khârn felt honoured. He was living through a second age of legend, where the future's mythology was being written around him with each new victory. The World Eaters were the descendants of ancient phalanxes; the spiritual sons of shield-walls in lost kingdoms. They were echoes made manifest, conjured from battles that broke down into bronze-bladed duels between a thousand heroes, once formation was forgotten in the blood, the sweat, and the curses of two armies grinding.

They weren't soldiers, fighting in packs through conquered streets. They were warriors, drawing blades to fight in the moments where courage and endurance threatened to meet madness. Those moments never made it into the sagas.

But he saw no great art to warfare. At least, not beyond the momentary aesthetic pleasure inherent in a sight so unbelievable that it drowned the senses: a city aflame, perhaps, or an orbital pict-view of armies so colossal they blackened the very land over which they were killing each other.

And yet, he loved war. He loved the brotherhood, fighting side by side and back to back with warriors he'd die for, and who would die for him. He loved the momentary surge of life he felt each time a foe fell before his axe. And, as proud as any man without ever tainting himself by vainglory, he loved war because he had a gift for it.

The true strength of the Emperor's Space Marines was in their genetic coding. Not their strength, mighty though it was; not their discipline, for many lacked that virtue almost entirely; not in the armoured fist of their massed armour battalions, which in truth could be crewed by lesser men with little difference.

No, their strength was a testament to the Emperor's shrewd foresight for conflict, for he made warriors that could endure more than any other mortal. Secondary organs compensated when primary hearts and lungs grew tired. Wounds that would leave a man or woman stunned or crippled scarcely slowed a legionary at all. They were children harvested from a natural life, grown purely into creatures that were able to tolerate pain and damage beyond measure, and still keep going.

The Emperor, for all his supposed faults, understood war had come full circle. In his Imperial wisdom, he'd bred soldiers to win those ancient wars that would be fought again in the future.

So Khârn screamed. He screamed as he severed the head of a defiant, uniformed Academy Guardsman, and he screamed as he tore a female officer in half on the backswing. He screamed as he felt exhaustion that would cripple a human, and he pushed through it, again and again. An Ultramarine rose up before him, bolter and gladius ready. Khârn took the legionary's arm off with a chop, kicked his chestplate hard enough to send him sprawling, and looped a weapon chain around the wounded warrior's throat. He strangled the Ultramarine, embracing him from behind to throttle the life from him, roaring and howling and frothing all the while.

And the Nails sang. They pulsed hatred through his head, promising an end to the pain and never delivering.

Shadows darkened the day as enemy Titans passed, focusing their eardum-bursting weapons on the World Eaters battle tanks. The hammering crash of vulcan mega-bolters was loud enough to be Armatura's own heartbeat. Firesprays from discharging cannon arms lit up the dust in flashing hazes, their weak light backwashing to paint the Titans themselves as towering things of iron and shadow.

Khârn saw Lorgar's silhouette in the dust, hurling great rocks and slabs of fallen architecture aside with telekinetic fury. The primarch was digging deep, well below street level, leaving the air tense with a pall of psychic resonance sharp enough to breed migraines and toothaches among those nearby. Any Ultramarine descending into the hole died without Lorgar even sparing a glance; mirage-waves of kinetic pressure slammed into whole squads, hurling them away to die against the rocks. The human soldiers caught in those careless expulsions of force flew even further, pulping against the rubble where they landed. Lorgar kept digging.

A Warhound Titan, hunched and hungry, stomped its way through the dust cloud, bringing its weapons to bear on the primarch. Khârn drew breath to shout a warning, exhaling in wordless shock a second later.

Lorgar, his gauntlets rimed with psychic hoarfrost, lifted a chunk of broken masonry the size of a Rhino transport and hurled it across the avenue. Such was its speed that dust-waves parted in its wake. With the majestic toll of a ringing bell, it collided with the

Titan's armoured wolf-head cockpit, flattening the crew chamber and sending the Titan slowly, so slowly, toppling onto its side. The few World Eaters still sane enough to bear witness cried out with laughter and renewed their assault.

More Ultramarines poured into Valika, leading squads of human soldiers fresh from other fights. Others fell from the sky on growling jump packs. Still others dropped from gunships, descending through the dust on rappelling cables. Cobalt-blue tanks roamed inwards, grinding over the rubble, weapon mounts blazing.

'Where are our reinforcements?' Khârn demanded over the vox. 'Where are the bastard Word Bearers?'

Kargos and Skane fought with him, as did Esca and Jeddek. The Librarian threw himself into the fight, violet lightning dancing in blinding arcs between his axes. Jeddek was one of the oldest living Eaters of Worlds. He'd crusaded across the stars from the Legion's founding, long before they rediscovered the primarch's homeworld, or started recruiting from worlds beyond Terra. He held the Eighth Company's heraldic banner aloft, the great woven flag showing the fanged, 8-marked skull devouring a red, dead world.

Khârn fell back to stand with his banner bearer. 'What happened?' he shouted above the storm of sound.

Jeddek lifted the stump of his other arm. It ended at the elbow. 'The Ultramarines happened.'

Kargos crouched to reload his bolter. 'They're still happening, in case you haven't noticed.'

A bolt shell spat from the dust, crashing against Jeddek's chest and driving him to one knee. The banner wavered, dipping, falling.

Skane fired his pistols back, killing the hazy figure of an Ultramarine ascending the rubble slope towards them. 'You're avenged, Jeddek,' he voxed.

'I'm not dead yet,' the veteran growled. He hauled himself to his feet, raising the banner again. Blood marked the ruination of his chestplate. Khârn could see the hint of an organ quivering within the mess of cracked ceramite and sundered ribcage.

'Where is the cursed Seventeenth?' Kargos spat the words. 'Where are they?'

Skane – wasn't it always Skane? – voiced what was on their minds. 'Betrayal. They've left us to die in some great and holy joke, mark my words.'

Khârn looked at his chainaxe, toothless and warped from overuse. He looked at his plasma pistol, thirsting and weakened from overheating, venting pressurised steam in protest.

'They wouldn't abandon us.'

Skane grinned. 'You actually believe what you're saying? Tell them Lorgar is here, and then they'll come running.'

Khârn's answering smile was a bleak, thin thing indeed.

'This is Captain Khârn of the Twelfth Legion to any Word Bearers forces close to Valika. We're overrun, and need immediate reinforcement. Your primarch is here. Do you hear me, cowards? *Your primarch is here.*'

A reply crackled back at once, violated by vox-distortion. 'Confirm.'

Khârn laughed, sheathing his pistol and lifting a discarded Ultramarines bolter from the rubble.

'I'm looking at Lorgar as I speak, you cur. It's not just us you've abandoned here.'

'This is Torgal of the Word Bearers Seventh. Request for reinforcement acknowledged.'

Khârn cracked off a single shot with the stolen bolter. It burst an Academy Guardsman apart as he struggled to scramble over the rubble and into cover.

'What does *acknowledged* mean? Does it mean you're actually coming this time?'

The vox fell back to static.

'Cowards.' Skane was still grinning. He holstered both of his empty pistols and looked around for a weapon he could scavenge, coming up with a lightweight lasrifle, almost comically small in his armoured hands, complete with a human forearm still gripping it. After throwing the hand away, he still couldn't fit his finger in the trigger guard. Skane tossed the useless gun in the same direction as the severed hand. 'And tell them to bring ammunition,' he grunted.

More shadows became silhouettes, and the silhouettes became enemy soldiers emerging from the haze. The Armaturan Guard wore rebreathers to block out the dust. The Ultramarines led them in implacable, defiant dignity. More walkers – Warhounds – lurched out of the dust and into the desecrated plaza, blaring their warhorns as a wolf would howl.

'It's been an honour serving with you, sir.' Now Kargos was chuckling.

Khârn swallowed the acrid taste of his corrosive saliva. World Eaters humour – always the guilty, black laughter at the eye of the storm. He smiled back.

'Shut up, Kargos.'

The Warhound Titan *Ardentor* swung its weapon arms down, panning over the craters torn in the violated ground. Headlights on its muzzle cracked into life, carving this way and that, as the canine Titan snuffled the dirt for prey. Its void shields sparked with incidental fire from nearby World Eaters in the ruins, but with its energy barrier active, it stalked on in defiance of their meaningless gestures.

Another of the iron beasts bathed a nearby building in a spray of explosive vulcan fire, chewing through the stone to dice the legionaries within. Spent shells the size of a man's arm rained onto the road: hundreds of them in a clattering fall, spilling across the street.

Ardentor's horns blared as it crunched its first step down on the rubble slope. A cry of protest and a call to arms, all in one. Its vulcan bolters whined in throaty starvation, ammo-dry from hours of fighting without resupply. Secondary weapon mounts, good for little more than spitting at light infantry, chattered from its chin. Tracer fire slapped across the dusty ground, eating into the crater.

Princeps Maxamillien Delantyr leaned forwards in his throne, the attachment cables straining at his spine.

'I sense something down there. Maintain defensive fire.'

His Moderati Secundus emitted a binaric spurt of disagreement. 'Auspex still registers nothing.'

'Sighters confirmed this is the crater made by the enemy's psychic release event, whatever it was. There *is* something down there.' Delantyr scratched beneath his itching rebreather mask. 'Fire the primary plasma arm into the crater.'

'My princeps, we have no more than three unleashments remaining before reactor hypovolaemia.'

'We will rearm and recharge when Valika is cleansed, Kei. If our guns starve and our reactor goes thirsty, then I will grind these traitors beneath our feet. Now fire as commanded.'

'Aye, my princeps.'

As the helmeted moderati worked, bringing the right arm to bear, emergency lighting dimmed the cockpit into half-gloom.

'Core hypovolaemia threat,' crackled the tech-priest's emotionless tones from the plasma reactor chamber, housed in the armoured room behind the cockpit pod.

'I'm aware.' Delantyr forced a smile. 'Just give me one shot.'

'Accruing lethality,' called Moderati Kei. He rotated seven dials in quick succession, and squeezed his left trigger. 'Brace for unleashment.'

'All brace, all brace.'

The Warhound's heels locked tight as it fired, and a second sun was born at Valika.

Imperial plasma technology combined elemental gases to form the fire that licked across the skin of stars. In ancient ages, the process was better known as fusion – the ionising of hydrogen at a hundred million degrees – to recreate the heartbeat of a sun through human ingenuity. Cooking the plasma was half of the ritual. 'Unleashment' was the rest. Among the hallowed halls of the Legio Lysanda and the various Collegia Titanica, unleashment of their god-machines' plasma weaponry came with a wealth of prayers, invocations, benedictions, and the burning of a specific scent of incense.

The Warhound fired, its comet-tailed bolt of raw plasma contained within an engineered magnetic field to prevent the projectile's dissipation from the ionised atoms flying apart. Venting began at once, ghosts of coolant steam slashing from the relief ports along the Titan's weaponised arm.

The unleashment incinerated the dust, burning the air clear, and splashed a sun's core into the crater for the fraction of a second. The World Eaters caught at the blast's edges dissolved into bones and armour shards spilling through the air, eroding to powder, and then to nothingness.

In the crater's pit, Lorgar stood with his peaceful eyes raised to the staring Titan. Ash drifted away from his armour, the last remnants of the holy parchments bound to the ceramite. The air rippled with the force of his focus, and the kine-shield he kept raised with his outstretched hand. The ground by his boots, in a spread of several metres, was unharmed rock. Everything else was burned into sludged, black glass.

All three crew members leaned forwards in their thrones. Kei raised his targeting visor.

'What am I seeing?' he asked. 'It can't be.'

The Moderati Primus, Ellas, narrowed his eyes to squint. 'Is that...?'

'Fire, damn you!' Delantyr was yelling. 'Fire again!'

'Brace for–'

'*Just fire!*'

Lighting failed in the cockpit as power bled from the reactor. The tech-priest's voice snapped over the vox with uncharacteristic urgency.

'Core hypovolaemia threat,' he practically whined. 'And we aren't br–'

Ardentor fired again.

The discharge sent the Titan rocking back two steps, its splayed claw-feet crunching into the avenue to avoid falling. In the wake of its release, the weaponised arm hissed steam from its coolant vanes, like a forged blade quenched in water.

The lights reactivated. Kei's targeting visor came back online a moment later, and the control consoles followed.

'He must be dead,' Delantyr whispered. 'He has to be dead. We've killed a primarch. Walk us closer.'

The Warhound realigned, coming around to stare back down into the crater.

Kei's eyes flickered between the annihilation below and the pulsing chime of auspex contact. 'Inbound engines,' he said. 'Legio Audax. And gunships – declaration signatures marking them as Seventeenth.'

Delantyr spoke through clenched teeth. 'They're too late.'

The primarch of the Word Bearers had fallen. His armour, once red and engraved with scripture, was an ashen husk of charred plate. Cracked and weeping skin showed around the patchwork spread of bleeding burns. Not a patch of skin was left untouched. He didn't rise from his knees. He didn't lift his head. He did nothing at all.

'He's dead.' Ellas spoke softly.

'Fire again.' Delantyr breathed the words. 'Fire again.'

'You bled the core,' Kei replied. 'We're plasma-starved.'

'Fire the suppressing tracers. Three bursts.'

Ardentor's anti-infantry bolters spat their tracer fire at the prone primarch. The first burst chewed glass, spraying fragments everywhere. The second two punched home in the scorched armour, blasting the fallen Emperor's son onto his back – a vessel of cooked, punctured meat.

'We just killed a primarch.' Kei swallowed. 'We just *killed a primarch*.'

Delantyr's grin showed almost every tooth he had. 'Crush him. Leave them nothing to bury.'

Ardentor walked. Its backwards-jointed legs hammered down on the steaming, downsloping glass, breaking it underfoot as it staggered down into the crater. When it reached the primarch's body, Ellas raised the right claw-foot, and steered both control levers to slam the limb back down.

The Warhound shook, unbalanced with one leg in the air. Great gears in the war machine's knee and hip protested with rough, mechanical coughs.

'Get the leg down,' Delantyr ordered. 'Finish it.'

Ellas gave the control levers another wrenching shove. 'Something's obstructing us.'

Kei lifted his targeting visor again, looking out of the Warhound's left eye-windshield. He took a slow breath, and glanced back at his princeps.

'My princeps? The World Eaters in the ruins… They're cheering.'

THE BLEEDING DEMIGOD had torn his way through the ground, giving voice to his resurrection with a bellow nothing short of ursine. Gore sheeted him, painting him in dark, rich red wetness. He threw his axes away, ruined and never to be wielded again, and breathed freedom into his lungs. It smelled of melted glass and felt like sunburn.

'Lorgar.' He spat blood as he said the name, rising to his feet at last.

The Word Bearer lifted a scalded hand, not for aid, but in warning. Angron had no time to lift his mutilated brother, sprawled at his feet. The sun went dark, as dark as night falling in an instant.

He turned, raising his arms, and took a god-machine's weight on his shoulders.

Every muscle in his body locked tighter than the iron trying to crush him. Drool stringed through his metal teeth, skinned knuckles white as he defied the will of a Titan. He gave a bear's roar as the foot lowered another half-metre. Sinews crackled in his shoulders. His broken boots skidded back on the patch of unglassed rock; something cracked in his spine, something else cracked in his left knee. The compression of his bones sounded like twigs breaking underfoot, which was a vivid burst of imagination he didn't appreciate.

But he could hear his men cheering. He could hear them howling as they killed, and crying his name.

He blinked to clear away his sweat's greasy sting, and dug his boots into the ground. With a smile slitting across his broken-angel face, he shifted his slipping, blood-slick grip on the Titan's clawed foot, and started pushing back.

'Lorgar.' Angron spoke in something that wasn't quite a growl and wasn't quite a laugh. 'Get up. I can't hold this forever.'

SIX

**Ursus Claw
Respite
Gorechild**

Syrgalah limped into Valika, sparks spitting from its violated mechanisms, with its armour plating scarred by bolt shells and oil bleeding from ruptured cable-veins in its knees. Armatura wasn't kind to Scout-class Titans forced to fight on the front line.

Keeda and Toth both kept half an eye on their respective auspex consoles as *Syrgalah* stalked around the half-buried wreck of a World Eaters Land Raider. The junction was ripe with heat signatures, matching the hulking silhouettes of other Titans in the dusty murk. Toth read at least two Reavers at the junction's edge. The Legio Audax excelled in pack tactics to bring down bigger prey, but *Syrgalah* had arrived alone, and reinforcements were still inbound.

'We're outgunned,' he said, 'unless the rest of the Legio arrives before I finish this sentence.'

'Funny.' Keeda sighted an Ultramarines gunship in the dust cloud. 'I've got the shot,' she called back to Solostine.

His face was bloody; small-arms damage to the cockpit had hit him in the arm, but chemical pain nullifiers injected into his throat rather took the edge off that, yet allowed him to stay sharp.

'Fire at will,' the princeps replied. He indulged a moment's distraction to tongue a loose tooth. Must have happened when he cracked his head against the throne's side. It amused him to think that this was how the degeneration started, now they were so far gone from safe space and easy resupply. Rejuvenat surgery had replaced every tooth in his mouth with compound substitutes indiscernible from the real thing, but if he kept this up out here on the Galactic East, he'd have to consider the quicker, cheaper iron replacements favoured by the Twelfth Legion. He'd never met a single World Eater without at least one metal tooth jammed into his gums, and most sported whole sets from their time in the gladiatorial pits.

He felt the tremor of *Syrgalah*'s wrath as Keeda brought the gunship down in flames. Then he felt the tremor of something worse, something that stabbed little needles into the space between his vertebrae.

'Taking fire from behind,' he said. 'Bring us about.'

Toth turned them in a snarling lurch, and Keeda panned the vulcan arm in a whirling, fire-spraying arc. An enemy Predator tank rolled into view, spewing heavy bolter fire up at them.

Solostine hissed in empathic pain – sympathy wounds darkening his skin in stigmatic bruising, even as Keeda punctured the tank and left it a hollow, steaming shell.

'Do you hear that?' Toth interrupted Solostine's muttered praise.

'Tell me it's a resupply lander,' Keeda noted, tapping a display screen drowning in red runes. 'Our vulcan is starved.'

'It's not that,' Toth replied. He was holding a hand to his earpiece. 'It's this.'

He brought the hololithic generator between their pilots' thrones to life with a cranked lever.

The face that appeared in the air was female, in profile, her blue-white holofeatures speaking out of time with her crackling voice.

'*Ember Queen?*' she said.

'The lovely flag-captain.' Solostine inclined his head to the image. 'How goes the war in the heavens?'

Keeda occupied herself with the muzzle-bolters, one of many minor modifications their tech-priests had made in recent years. She hammered tracer fire through the dust at the blotchy shadows of Academy Guards fleeing from the turning tide.

'Walk us,' she whispered to Toth. He complied, letting Keeda chase the running soldiers, cutting them down.

The image of Captain Lotara Sarrin wavered. 'Venric? Contact is flawed. I can scarcely hear you. My scrying shows you at Valika.'

'Confirmed,' the princeps replied. 'With twenty engines inbound.'

'Can't see a damned thing, though,' muttered Keeda.

Sarrin turned her head, addressing an officer on her warship's bridge. Her voice was a hurried crackle when she returned.

'Listen to me, Venric. We're working through sighters on the ground, so I can't be much help, but you have to find the Lysanda Warhound *Ardentor*. Kill it. Kill it now.'

Toth and Keeda didn't need the order relayed. They started working their consoles, bringing *Syrgalah* into a limping run.

'Got her,' Keeda called.

Solostine tasted blood from the loose tooth. Not a good sign. 'Count on us, Lotara.'

She smiled. 'I always do, old man.'

Sweat rained from him.

Angron stood defiant, the weight of the world on his shoulders. He'd been braced against the Titan's claw for less than thirty beats of his heart. It felt like an age. It felt like two ages.

'Lorgar,' he said through teeth clenched hard enough to squeal. 'Get clear.'

The Word Bearer lifted an immolated hand. He couldn't speak, could scarcely move, but he added the dregs of his psychic push to his brother's strength. The raised hand trembled – where it wasn't cooked bloody, its burn-sores were weeping.

Angron knew plasma wounds well enough, and Lorgar was fortunate to still be alive. As he breathed in dust and oil fumes, panting against the weight, he managed to shake his head.

'*Now* you decide to be brave?' he growled, salivating in thick strings. 'Just get clear.'

Lorgar lowered his ruined hand, and started crawling.

'Finish it,' Delantyr yelled.

Ellas was trying. The servos in the knee and ankle were locked and unyielding, refusing to obey his controls. He couldn't lift the leg back up for a second try, either.

'Engine behind us,' Kei warned. 'An Audax engine.'

'Get the leg down!'

'My princeps–' Ellas started to object, but Kei interrupted, staring at his scanner.

'It's armed with… I can't even tell what that is. Something with magnetic accelerators, cycling up to charge. You need to turn us, fast.'

'I can't. The knee is–'

'Ellas,' Delantyr said, with sudden, cold calm. He had a service laspistol aimed at his steersman's head. '*Get us turned around.*'

Ellas felt gooseflesh rise on his skin. 'Aye, my princeps.'

Keeda sighted Ardentor in the crater and the surreal vision of the two bleeding primarchs mere moments from destruction. Lorgar was ravaged by burns, lying to the side. Angron stood beneath the Warhound's foot-claw, holding it up, braced against its final fall.

She knew the strength – in exact measurable power and force – in a Warhound's towering musculature, for she'd served Audax since childhood: first as a tech-menial and later as a member of two Titans' command crews. At fifteen, she'd been inducted into the slave maturation process to determine how well she'd acclimatise to cockpit interface and react in combat scenarios. At nineteen, she was weaponmistress aboard *Hanumaan*. At twenty-four, Princeps

Ultima Venric Solostine selected her for his own crew aboard the command Titan *Syrgalah*.

Her first operation as *Syrgalah*'s gunner had been referred to in Legio briefings as *Walk: CC00428al-0348.Hne*. History was already coming to call it the Isstvan Atrocity, when four Space Marine Legions purged their own ranks in the annihilated streets of Isstvan III's Choral City.

Valika was the first time she'd ever fired without permission.

The muzzle-bolters would do nothing, the vulcan arm was dry, but she had the last ace in her deck. Keeda had her spear, and her spear was forged to bring down the biggest prey.

The World Eaters claimed to be warriors, not soldiers. The Legio Audax, bound to the XII Legion for decades, claimed something similar. Their Titans weren't war machines. Their Titans were hunters.

She pulled back both unlocking levers, gripped her control sticks and fired the ursus claw. Magnetic coils in the Warhound's arm launched the spear, propelling it into the crater and sinking it home in *Ardentor*'s torso with a brutal crack of annihilated metal. Solostine gave a slow smile as he watched the Lysanda engine jerk with the impact.

'Beautiful shot, Moderati Bly.'

'My thanks, princeps. Magnetic bindings empowered.'

Ardentor rocked back and forth, its shoulder and cockpit holed through. The great impaling spear came active, magnetically sealing inside the lethal wound.

'Walk, Toth.'

'Aye, sire.'

The Audax Titan took three steps back from the crater's rim, pulling the harpoon cable taut. *Ardentor* toppled backwards, crashing onto the ground, its reactor-heart still active but its command crew destroyed in the impaling.

Syrgalah kept walking backwards, retracting its harpoon and dragging the downed Titan's corpse up the crater slope.

'Cut them loose,' said Solostine.

'Cutting them loose, sire.' Keeda deactivated the magnetic grapple on the harpoon's body and let the spear pull free of the mangled metal.

The hunter, *Syrgalah*, left its slain foe on the avenue and turned in search of other prey, as the cheering cries of World Eaters warriors crackled over the vox.

HE MOVED OVER to his brother, offering a skinned hand. The battle still raged above and around them, but incoming Word Bearers gunships and Audax Titans were finally pressing the Armaturan Guard back.

The two primarchs gripped wrists, and Angron pulled Lorgar to his feet. Apothecaries from both Legions were sprinting into the crater, voxing awed murmurs to the squads at their sides. Angron paid no heed. With the Titan's weight off his shoulders, he had more than a moment to glance at Lorgar. Half of the Word Bearer's face was sloughed almost to the bone, no different from wax trails down a half-spent candle.

'Are you dying?'

Lorgar grinned, with a ghastly cadaverous leer. 'I think I might be.'

'You look like you are.'

Lorgar's remaining eye fixed onto his brother's gaze. He was still grinning because the ruination of his face left him no choice in the matter.

'I sought to save you. To unearth you from that burial.'

Angron swallowed. He felt something in that moment – the uneasy threat of kinship. He sensed it, with one who was not one of his First Brothers, and felt suddenly unsure whether to retreat from it or embrace it. He'd always loathed Lorgar. Even seeing him fight after Isstvan, and how far he'd come from his years of cowardice, wasn't enough to build any real bond.

'Is that a lie?' he asked. 'You tried to dig me out?'

Lorgar's grin was a rigor mortis smirk of bloodstains and burned gums. 'You know it's the truth.'

'You weren't needed.'

Lorgar turned away. 'Be that as it may, I thank you, brother. Thank you for stopping the Titan.'

Another hesitation. For a moment, it seemed Angron would speak, but he said nothing.

Gunships were coming down around them now. The first Apothecary reached the primarchs; Angron dismissed him with a wave.

'Away with you, Bloodspitter.'

'But sire...'

'I said *away with you*.'

The World Eaters backed away. Khârn was among them, with his closest kindred.

Angron met Esca's eyes for a long, sterile moment, before nodding a grudging greeting. A thanks, perhaps. Of a sort. Esca returned it, though – as always – he kept his distance from the primarch.

Lorgar ceased his limping retreat to the closest Thunderhawk. He looked up at the dust-choked sky then turned his slagged face back to Angron.

'There are so many people dying on this world, right now, as we speak, and muse, and breathe. It's changing the song, brother. Every life ending in pain changes the tune. That's why we're here. That's why Ultramar must die slowly, in pain, rather than in the rush of quick fire. The tune must be pitch perfect.'

Angron felt naked without his axes. Already, distraction set in, sending him casting about for a temporary replacement.

'You babble, priest. Get back to the ships. We will speak when Armatura chokes beneath our Legions' boots.'

Lorgar didn't reply. Word Bearers flocked around him, chanting and praying, some of them falling to their knees in reverence. He didn't ignore them as Angron ignored his sons; Lorgar took the time to honour them, blessing their devotion with the touch of a hand on their helms, or pressing his bloody palm-print to their oath parchments. He honoured them in the ruins, baptising them with his own blood.

'Lorgar,' Angron called, as the Word Bearer reached the gunship. When his brother turned, the primarch of the World Eaters spat onto the blackened earth. 'Try not to die before I return.'

Lorgar gave his mutilated smile again, and ascended into the Thunderhawk.

Angron turned back to his sons, their armour spattered red on white, their faces and snarling helms staring in mute shock.

'Leave me,' he growled.

Khârn wouldn't let it lie. 'Sire…'

'Leave me, Khârn. Prattle at me later, when the Nails no longer sing.'

'No.'

The World Eaters turned to the Eighth Captain, several of them shuffling nervously. Above them, Word Bearers gunships drove the Ultramarines running from Valika, after the cost already had run to hundreds of XII Legion lives.

Angron, in truth, looked little better than Lorgar. Both were miserable with near-terminal wounds. The Eater of Worlds' armour was in fragments and his exposed skin was peeled raw from dragging himself from his rocky grave. Even weaponless and half-murdered, he could kill the half-dozen warriors before him without his heart rate increasing.

'You have something to say, captain?'

Khârn was implacable. His powerless plasma pistol and broken chainaxe were both sheathed. To occupy his hands, he pointed at the rising Thunderhawk carrying the primarch of the XVII Legion.

'Lord Aurelian tore rocks from the ground for almost half an hour to reach you, and slaughtered countless enemy warriors.'

Angron showed his shark's rows of iron teeth. 'And?'

'And you owe him thanks. His act was noble, despite his Legion's eternal cowardice, and he endured great horror to save you. I have never seen a warrior withstand such punishment, nor pull gunships from the sky by spite alone. This ingratitude is beneath you, sire. You are better than this.'

Kargos took an unsubtle step away from Khârn. Jeddek and Skane did the same. Khârn smiled coldly at their caution.

They'd expected anger. They'd expected to be sullenly ignored. What they hadn't expected was laughter. Angron shattered the tension with a low, rueful laugh.

'I'll bear that in mind, Khârn.' The primarch walked away, seeking a worthwhile weapon in the devastation that Valika Junction had become.

WITH THE PRIMARCH gone, Khârn sank to the ground. For a few moments, he was content to just breathe, surrendering to the aches that populated his body after hours of remorseless fighting. A legionary could fight for days – weeks if he had to – but a capacity to endure misery didn't offer complete immunity to mortal limitations.

And this, too, was a gesture repeated across the warring city. Soldiers stealing what rest they could – one of the realities of war that also never made it into the sagas. A Legion never fought alone; it marched with consistent trains of resupply and ammunition drops, or it halted and marched no further. Orbital assault played by the same rules. Once significant ground was taken, it was reinforced from above and served as a point for immediate resupply.

Khârn listened to the vox-chatter of World Eaters landers en route to Valika and other nearby junctions, bringing ammunition, grenades and replacement chainaxe teeth-tracks that the Legion had needed hours before. He could hear Word Bearers commanders, as well, somehow only just making it to link-up points after the World Eaters had taken a hammering at front lines across the city.

Retinal runes nagged him about the damage to his armour, but that could wait. They also nagged him about the fact that his wound had broken open again, despite his body's haemosealant capabilities. It was clotting as normal, to prevent blood loss, but kept re-tearing when he moved. He'd been bleeding on and off for over two hours. A human would have been dead in minutes.

'Your vital signs are singing a merry tune,' Kargos voxed. 'Let me take a look.'

'It just needs sealant,' Khârn replied. 'Leave it. It'll bide.'

Kargos crashed down next to his captain, unlocking his helmet and pulling it free. 'Armatura, eh? I'd rather have taken Calth. At least they had surprise on their side – almost enough to cancel out the enormous drag factor of fighting alongside these bastard Word Bearers.'

Despite himself, Khârn chuckled. Kargos had that effect on his brothers. The Apothecary wasn't done, though. 'I saw you strangle that Ultramarine Evocatus with your weapon chain. That was beautiful.'

Even seated, Khârn offered a theatrical, mocking bow. 'Not one of my more honourable duels.'

'I can't think of a single fight in Twelfth Legion history that could be described as honourable.'

Khârn hung his head, hoping against reason that the ceaseless pressure in the back of his mind would ease for just a few minutes. But the Nails wanted him up. They wanted him killing, or they'd bleach his brain of all other feeling.

'There was one,' he said. 'One honourable fight.'

'Ah.' Kargos grinned, showing metal teeth of his own. 'The Night of the Wolf doesn't count. We both know Russ will never have let that reach any Imperial records. Couldn't have his precious wardogs' defeat entered into the archives, could he? Not by us. Not by a worthless Legion with fire in their minds.'

Dust swirled around them both. Khârn breathed it in, tasting the char on the wind. The smell of a city ripped open to the bone.

'Any word of Argel Tal?' he asked.

'None. Perhaps it's good news. Perhaps he died, rather than choosing to abandon us.'

Khârn didn't chuckle that time. He did, however, feel a little guilty for his smile. The Nails rewrote his emotions, but they couldn't steal the joy from everything. Not yet, at least. He'd not worn them as long as some. He'd seen enough of the oldest veterans, like Jeddek, who felt nothing outside of slaughter. No smiles, no tears, no nothing. Dead-eyed glares and monotone murmurs, until they were turned loose on the enemy. Only then could they feel. Only then could they experience a palette of emotions beyond staring at everything and nothing with their faces twitching in pained distraction.

'A worthless Legion,' Khârn said. 'Do they still say that about us, I wonder.' It wasn't quite a question. And if it was, it wasn't one he expected an answer to.

Kargos spat onto the obsidian that served as earth in the wake of the plasma unleashments.

'That alpha Wolf you killed,' he said. 'The hero. I forget his name.'

Khârn felt the edge of his lips pulled in another smile. Two in as many minutes. How rare. When he spoke, he put on a thick, halting accent of elongated vowels and rough consonants.

'Aevalryff,' he almost growled, imitating the dead Wolf's voice. 'Baresark of *Tra*. Bearer of Serpentfang.' Khârn even beat a fist against his chestplate, as the Wolf had done.

Kargos grinned. 'That was it. So proud, he was! He died badly.'

'Everyone dies badly. We lead violent lives, and we die as we live.' Khârn rose to his feet, reaching for the helm he'd discarded moments ago. Kargos followed, replacing his helm at the same time.

'How are you so unscarred?' Kargos asked. 'It's uncanny. You still wear the face you were born with.' The Apothecary waved a hand over his own features, which – like most World Eaters' – was a map of thick stitching and overlapping scars.

'Skill.'

'Ha! If you say so.' Kargos started making his way to the closest pack of servitors, as supply crates and heavy armour were finally being unloaded from the gunships and landers. 'Khârn?' he called back. 'Centurion?'

Khârn walked to where an axe lay on the ground. Not his axe.

Not an axe that belonged to any legionary. It was a toothless relic, scratched and scraped and worn from too long carving rock rather than flesh.

'Khârn?' Kargos voxed again.

'A moment,' he replied. 'Give me a moment.'

He crouched to pick it up, but his fingers closed into a fist before they touched the black haft. Was this sacrilege? Was this sure to anger his volatile primarch?

Khârn clutched the haft and lifted the weapon with one hand. It was heavy, heavier than he'd been expecting, and would need both hands to swing with any artistry. But then, if he cared for artistry, he'd have been a swordsman.

'I've found Gorechild,' he said.

It was Skane's voice that crackled back. 'Don't,' he said. 'Sir, don't. You know his traditions.' Other voices joined in, all referring to the primarch's superstition of inherited weapons bringing ill luck. A gladiatorial conceit, from his homeworld.

'He threw it away for a reason,' voxed Esca. 'It's ruined, captain. It'll never function again.'

Khârn ignored his brothers' protests. He walked to the closest tech-priest, who was busy overseeing the distribution of fresh ammunition crates to World Eaters battle tanks.

'You. What's your name?'

The robed priest made a sound not entirely unlike a child screeching binaric code. Khârn held up a hand when he saw the priest lacked a mouth; a vocabulator replaced it, sutured in place, forming an eternal 'O' where the man's lips, teeth and a tongue had once been.

'Enough. Your name isn't important.' He hefted the toothless Gorechild, but pulled it back when the priest made to take it. 'This axe was toothed by the fangs of a mica-dragon. Do you recognise it?'

Again came a screech of code. Khârn assumed it meant yes – no Audax officer or minister could serve alongside the World Eaters and fail to have observed Gorefather and Gorechild at least once.

'I want this area excavated, the moment it's marked as secure. Find the chainsaw teeth to repair this axe. I imagine it will take days. I don't care, take as long as you need. Is that understood?'

The priest's eyes, still human, widened in alarm. He gave voice to another spurt of code, this one clearly a protest. Khârn blink-clicked a flashing icon in the upper left of his eye lens display, and waited for the translation runes to scroll across his vision.

'If it's not your area of jurisdiction, find someone in Audax I can rely on to do it.'

Another spurt. Another sighing wait for translation. The priest looked horrified, and the wide-mouthed speaker where his mouth should be only aided the impression.

'If it takes two hundred servitors and a week of painstaking engineering, then it takes two hundred servitors and a week of painstaking engineering.'

Another blurt, longer this time. Another pause as it translated.

'Khârn,' said the World Eater. 'Captain of the Eighth Company, most of whom are lying dead around us. Take note of that fact, when you excavate this junction. Treat their bodies with the necessary respect, until their gene-seed is harvested.'

The last screech was shortest of all. The priest bowed after vocalising it.

'After that,' Khârn confirmed, 'do with the corpses as you wish. Burn them or leave them to the carrion birds, for all I care.' He grinned, showing teeth which were still all natural. 'We aren't a sentimental Legion.'

SEVEN

No One Runs
Unauthorised Planetfall
Shield Wall

Lotara didn't mean to laugh, but she admired an enemy with a backbone. The War-Regent of Armatura was a captain in the Evocati, a silver-haired Ultramarines warrior with a regal sneer and eyes that suggested something hawkish in his blood and bearing. She liked him at once; he reminded her of her father, who was a spire-lord in his own right.

'That's very amusing,' she replied to the hololithic image, at the heart of her busy bridge. 'Considering your cities are overrun and your fleet is aflame.'

'I take it,' the Ultramarine said with kingly patience, 'that you're refusing to surrender?'

Lotara laughed again. 'I like you, Captain Orfeo. I hope you receive a quick death down there, for it would grieve me to know you suffered. To that end, I hope the World Eaters catch you before the Word Bearers. The latter tend to treat their prisoners rather unwholesomely.'

Disbelief, albeit polite and reserved, marked the soldier's face.

'What can you hope to achieve, Flag-Captain Sarrin? Armatura is but one world – one world among the Five Hundred. Calth may die and Armatura may wither, but how much damage can you hope to inflict? What is the purpose of your war?'

'My purpose here, my dear Evocatus, is to kill until my primarch tells me to stop killing.' Her tone was saccharine enough that several of her bridge officers found themselves smiling at her mockery of the Ultramarine. 'Look to the skies, Captain Orfeo. Your fleet lies in ruins. Their wreckage will shortly be raining upon your cities.'

No cutting retort. No bitter reply. He nodded once, as if dismissing a subordinate, and the hololithic image blinked out of being.

'And yet,' she said, turning her head to regard First Officer Ivar Tobin, 'he has a point.'

'Sympathy with the enemy, ma'am?' He raised an aristocratic eyebrow. 'An executable offence. I should draw my service pistol at once.'

She gave him a look. She gave him *the* look. 'I'm serious, Tobin.'

Sarrin keyed in a command on her throne's armrests. The primary oculus screen changed views, showing one of the Word Bearers king-ships slowly pulling up from Armatura's atmosphere. Just looking at it made her stomach lurch. Such furious, immense majesty. The *Blessed Lady* rose on thrusters, ramming through the wreckage of the destroyed Ultramarines fleet.

'Look at that,' she said. 'Tell me why, when Lorgar commands vessels like that, we even needed to make planetfall. One of those alone would have washed the surface with flame. And Lord Aurelian has two of them. That's not even counting the *Lex*, the *Conqueror*, and our armada.'

Tobin watched the vast ship in silence. Before speaking, he returned his attention to the strategium and its busy, bustling crew. With the void war winding down, the *Conqueror*'s bridge still buzzed with activity. Various stations were trying to piece together a full analysis of the battle, with losses and casualties; others were doing all they could to coordinate the nightmare on the surface.

Lotara, a void fighter far beyond any other in Tobin's experience, always joked that these were 'the little details'.

'You know my feelings on politics, ma'am.'

She had her boots up on one armrest now. 'Politics?' She gave a snort he sincerely doubted had come from her time in her home world's courts. 'This isn't politics. This is tactics, and you know it.'

'Be that as it may, ma'am, I feel supremely unqualified to comment.'

She shook her head with a smile. 'Coward. You're lucky I need you.'

'As you say, ma'am.'

Lotara turned at the sound of a proximity alarm. 'Details?' she asked.

'The Ultramarines vessel *Praetorian Trust* has powered up in the wreckage, ma'am.' Scrymistress Lehralla was a crippled thing, emaciated and legless, augmetically bound to the central auspex console. She turned to face Lotara, the cables stringing between her head and the ceiling machinery giving her a crown of serpents, like something from the old Grekan mythos. 'It seems to have powered down in the debris and played dead for several hours, drifting free of the battle.' Her voice was surprisingly gentle, and wholly human.

'Trust the Ultramarines to stick to the classics.' Lotara leaned forwards in her throne, watching the tactical hololithic. 'And trust us to fall for them.'

Tobin pursed his lips, watching the flickering red rune blink as it moved across the three-dimensional holo-map. 'They're running.'

'Like hell they are. No one runs from the *Conqueror*.' She gestured to the helmsmen. 'Chase at once. Order all other vessels to hold back, this one's ours.'

Tobin straightened his uniform as he kept watching the map. 'They'll be free to break into the warp in seven minutes.'

'They're sluggish and plasma-cold from hiding in silent running,' she replied. 'We'll catch them before their engines are even warm.'

'Four minutes, ma'am, if they wish to risk navigational flux from the debris field.'

Lotara was staring now, her eyes bright. The *Conqueror* shook as it breathed again, running hot and hard. 'We'll have them in three minutes, Ivar. Am I ever wrong?'

He cleared his throat, avoiding eye contact. 'There was the incident at New Kershal.'

Lotara held up a finger. 'Hush, now. We don't speak of New Kershal.' She grinned as she looked back to the oculus. 'Three minutes, you watch. Weaponmaster, ready the ursus claws.'

'Aye, ma'am,' came the reply, the only reply she ever wanted to hear when the sirens wailed.

Scrymistress Lehralla twisted in her life-support socket. She leaned over the hololthic projector table, her augmetic fingers manipulating the starfield image: rotating it, zooming, forcing focus.

'Ma'am, the Word Bearers king-ship *Trisagion* is also moving to engage.'

'Duly noted, scrymistress. Kejic?'

The vox-master looked up from his console. 'Ma'am?'

'Inform the *Trisagion* that this is our prey. They are to break off pursuit at once. Try to phrase it politely.'

As Kejic relayed the message in his crisp, clear tones, Lotara stared at the hololithic display, waiting for any sign the *Trisagion*'s rune was falling off pursuit. It blinked once, twice, and its projected vector turned aside.

'*Trisagion* reports that she's killing thrust and coming about,' Kejic confirmed.

'See?' Lotara said to Tobin. 'Look where manners gets you. All ahead full.'

The *Praetorian Truth* fled through the debris, and the *Conqueror* followed. Impact flares danced across both vessels' void shields as they ploughed through the junk field. *Praetorian Truth* fired her lances once, risking the threat of inertial drift and power drain by emitting a barrage of cutting beams to carve through the hull of a dead cruiser turning in space before them. They bisected the hulk, as neatly as any surgeon would incise flesh, and sailed clean through the dead ship's severed halves.

Lotara actually cheered in her throne. 'That was beautiful,' she said. 'Blood of the primarchs, what shooting. Convey my compliments to the enemy captain.'

Vox-master Kejic tried. 'No response, ma'am.'

'Oh, well. Ask for their surrender and cut space with a warning shot.'

The Gloriana-pattern *Conqueror*, outweighing the *Praetorian Truth* by several classes, spat an indifferent lob of lance fire after its prey. Everything went calculatedly wide.

The *Truth* kept running.

'No response, ma'am.'

'I don't know,' Lotara feigned a sigh. 'You try to be noble and you get nowhere.'

'Two minutes, captain,' said Tobin.

'Oh, do shut up,' she replied.

'And might I go on record as saying this is a most inefficient use of the boarding talons?'

'Your objection is noted and duly ignored, commander. The primarch and Khârn got to have their fun. Time for me to have mine.'

Ivar Tobin faced forwards again. No wonder the World Eaters liked her so much. She was one of them.

'Helm, how long?'

''Claws' range in twenty seconds.'

Lotara was never smug. She gave Tobin a glance, a slight raise of one eyebrow, but it wasn't the smug smile she might've gotten away with.

'Ma'am!' called several officers, the same moment a dozen others called, 'Mistress!'

She saw it herself. The *Praetorian Truth*, a spear of cobalt armour with bone-white spinal battlements, was coming about. It was actually coming about. Her skin crawled with unwanted admiration. The chase was over, and the prey had stolen her chance to pounce.

'Brave,' Tobin said quietly. Strange, how the atmosphere soured when the prey turned and showed its teeth. Always harder to kill a courageous enemy. Desperate ones? Cowardly ones? They fell with nothing but smiles on their killers' faces.

The ursus claws would be useless now. They were for catching fleeing foes, not engaging brave ones.

Lotara watched the smaller cruiser turning in the void, imagining the last speech its captain would be giving, as thousands of slaves ran out the warship's guns for the final fight.

'Kill them,' she said, softly, calmly. 'Just kill them.'

He led the remnants of three companies deeper into the city. The Armaturan Guard made them fight for every footstep, but Khârn's warriors were resupplied and reloaded, and no humans could be expected to stand against them. The mortals died, and those who didn't die added a handful of hours to their lives by running. They fell back in good order, disciplined to the last and defending every street in their city, but Khârn knew fleeing when he saw it. He chose to call it what it was, even when it wore tactics as a second skin.

This time, he countered snipers with gunships of his own, and answered Armaturan heavy armour with Land Raiders and Malcador battle tanks in the XII's battered blue and white. Sunset made little difference. Day was darkened by the dust, and night was brightened by the city's bones burning.

Gorechild was in guarded storage aboard his personal Thunderhawk, and he'd left the small army of servitors spreading across Valika Junction, beginning the painstaking excavation work with retasked loader-Sentinels. Heavier-duty mechanised lifters were on their way down from orbit. Rank had its advantages, once in a while. It was good for more than a helmet crest that marked you out to snipers and enemy champions with something to prove.

Time didn't pass in minutes or hours, but in broken barricades. Their howling, sprinting charges were backed by a percussion of booming tank guns and the enraged shriek of low-altitude thrusters.

He lost the last clutches of infrequent contact with the *Conqueror* sometime after the fifteenth road was reaved clean. Other vessels reported her lighting up the void with engine flare and chasing an Ultramarines cruiser making a last-gasp effort at flight. That was Lotara all over, and it didn't surprise him at all. She was denied the chance to bombard the surface; of course she'd leap at the first opportunity to do more than sit still and listen to the clicking count of the bridge's chronometer.

When they'd overrun the last roadblock, Khârn had found himself running alongside Esca, chasing the human soldiers side by side. The young Codicier spared him a glance and a nodded salute, before powering one of his force axes through a soldier's spine and hurling the body aside.

Khârn returned the nod, feeling the Nails sinking deeper into his thoughts. Even his skin itched at the other warrior's nearness and he felt his lips peeling back in an unwilling snarl. Grey danced at the edge of his vision, but he resisted the order to separate Esca yet again.

He noted the instinctive gap all other warriors left around the Librarian. Esca ran alone at the middle of the pack yet far from its heart. One of the last left in the World Eaters ignored, tawdry little Librarius Division.

Psykers. The Legion's first experiments in that regard hadn't been pleasant. Kargos was one of the surgeons first trained to implant Nails in legionaries' skulls, though he'd never beaten them into a psyker's brain, and wasn't responsible for the disasters that soon followed. What Khârn hadn't seen for himself, he'd heard from his Apothecary.

The first signs of unease came when implanted Librarians started causing their closest brothers to suffer blinding migraines and debilitating facial bleeds. No Librarian could stand in Angron's presence without enduring the same thing themselves; a reflection of what they inflicted on their brothers.

But the depths of the flaws became truly obvious in battle. Librarians gifted with the Nails lost the ability to control their psychic talents. One of them, a warrior attached to the 100th Company, had been lost to the Nails in his very first battle after implantation, and immolated three squads when he couldn't cease projecting witch-lightning from his eyes. Several others had just... burst. They combusted in flaming gore.

More and more died – none right away, but they never survived for long. In a single month, almost every Librarian had been fitted with the Nails. Mere weeks later, they started dying.

Optimism, albeit cautious, had reigned for a while. After the first deaths, the psychically trained legionaries had sought to master the Nails, to balance their sixth senses with the bionics now altering their brains' chemistry. A matter of willpower, they said, and their brothers had pretended not to notice the desperation in their eyes. Yes. A matter of willpower. It made sense.

But they kept dying. They died in battle, in storms of fire or lightning, or – in several incidents – by pulsing hateful pain through the Nails of nearby warriors and forcing their own kindred to suffer cerebrovascular blockages. Entire squads died of brain haemorrhages and strokes at their Codiciers' boots.

That settled it. Angron gave his psychic sons a choice between execution and the Nails' removal. The Legion learned, in those early years after their primarch's rediscovery, that they'd mutilated themselves in the image of a man without mercy. The Nails couldn't be removed; every World Eater knew it, for the Emperor's own technomages had failed to remove the primarch's implants. Even so, most Librarians submitted themselves for the attempt.

Every one of them died, without exception. With their rewired brains misfiring and enslaved to altered impulses, none of them died easy, and none of them died well.

Soon enough, the last Librarians were those who'd not yet

received Nails in a Legion now overcome by them. They eked out an isolated existence in the near-empty halls of their Librarius aboard the *Conqueror*.

One by one they, too, began to die. Not from malfunction or misuse, but because they were World Eaters, and World Eaters lived brief, violent lives. A hundred remained. Then fifty. Then twenty.

No one mourned them. In a Legion that prized the bonds of front-line brotherhood above all else, the silent brothers died alone – never forgotten, but always ignored. Their gene-seed rotted with their bodies, unharvested in case their genetic legacy resulted in the same curse infecting a second generation.

He watched Esca running ahead. A loyal brother. Quiet, for reasons obvious to anyone. Removed from true kinship, even with the Legion's utter refusal to heed – or even to acknowledge – the Edict of Nikaea. Obedience to that law simply blew beneath the World Eaters notice. By that juncture, their psychic kindred were an afterthought, scarcely worthy of consideration.

Esca was avoided by all others. But loyal. Did the last living Librarians deserve more from their brethren?

Khârn knew the answer would depend on who he asked. Angron would snort and ignore the question; just being near to one of them was agony for reasons no Apothecary had been able to discern.

Argel Tal would engage him in a good-natured debate over an army only being as strong as the weakest link in its chain, and the value of respecting sacrifice.

Kargos would screw his face up into something even less appealing than its usual stitched mess, and ask why Khârn even gave a damn.

Skane would give in to distraction, cleaning his weapons as they spoke, the yellow of his eyes betraying how radiation poisoning wasn't particularly useful for improving his attention span.

Each answer would be as annoying as the last.

Khârn cast it from his mind, relaying a steady stream of orders over the vox for his men to slow their advance and regroup. The dust was thick enough to choke on, but most of this district still stood tall. Great pillared buildings stared down onto the wide avenues, each one marked by statues cast in earth-dark bronze. Academies. Colleges. Colosseums. Watchtowers. Halls of debate. Armouries.

World Eaters gunships juddered overhead, their spotlights raking the ground, scouting ahead of the main forces. He had outriders on jetbikes, as well as recon teams ranging ahead, and for the last few hours they'd played the invasion out as any other Legion would. Rain, doubtless inspired by the atmospheric disturbance of thousands of vessels in low orbit and making planetfall runs to disgorge troops, lashed down in a tidal pour. It did nothing for the dust beyond turning the ground to clinging mud. It did, however, go some way to cleaning the World Eaters bloodstained armour.

A Storm Eagle, dense-bodied and hanging low above the next plaza, came apart in the sky. Khârn caught the garbled words of its pilot's last report before the gunship burst with a distance-delayed boom, sending engines and armour raining to the ground in fire.

'Ultramarines in the next plaza, then,' Kargos voxed. Khârn could hear his grin.

'All squads,' the captain said. 'Form up and be ready.'

The *Praetorian Truth* grew on the oculus. It grew, and its gun bays flashed as it bared its teeth.

The *Conqueror* shook in sympathy with its abused void shields. Mother-of-pearl light bled across space as the invisible kinetic energy field shimmered under the impacts. Away from Armatura, away from the tight-packed iron-sky chaos of two warring fleets, the engagement was much more traditional, at a range of thousands of kilometres. Even so, the *Conqueror* had been closing fast, and the *Praetorian Truth* was now eating up the distance by coming straight at its pursuer.

Ivar Tobin stood with his arms crossed over his uniformed chest, watching the oculus. 'They're game, ma'am. I'll give them that.'

Lotara didn't disagree. She gestured to her weaponmaster and his two dozen servitors and menials.

'Open fire.'

'Firing, captain.'

The *Conqueror* shook again. An initial volley spread radiance across the *Truth*'s shields. A second punctured them, discharging power into the nothingness of space, no different to fluid bursting from a blister.

The cutting began, at a cost in countless lives, as the flagship's lances knifed through unprotected battlements and spinal architecture. Fire breathed from the wounds, becoming mist in the dark, then becoming nothing at all.

'They're still closing,' Tobin noted. 'Looks like ramming speed.'

Lotara wasn't so certain. The *Truth* would be dead before it got the chance to collide, leaving her with other suspicions.

'Fire at will,' she ordered.

More than one lance beam went wide. The *Truth* was a heavy cruiser, but her captain and crew demanded the best from her. Lotara watched with an admiring smile as the vessel banked and rolled as fast as its bulk would allow. It drifted aside from the *Conqueror*'s long-range calculated spite, closing the distance in a steady drive.

'Ah,' said Lotara.

'Ma'am?'

She didn't reply. She waited. She waited until her lances had clawed and cut and cleaved through the *Truth*'s hull. She waited until the Ultramarines cruiser was a crumbling, flaming wreck on dying engines, struggling to hold itself together. Inertia kept bringing it closer.

'Here it comes,' she said. 'Any moment now.'

Kejic called from his station. 'Incoming hail from the *Praetorian Truth*.'

'Perfect timing.' She gestured her acceptance, a queen enthroned on black iron and brass. The voice that strained over the bridge speakers was human and wounded, and punctuated by the sounds of its ship detonating in the background.

'For the Emperor,' it said. 'Courage and honour!'

The link died. Lotara steepled her fingers beneath her chin, still watching the *Truth*'s death throes. She knew exactly what she was looking for, and she nodded to herself when she saw it. Airbursts along the *Truth*'s edges, but not the release of broadside weapons batteries. Oh, no. This was a Legiones Astartes vessel, after all.

'Western battlement turrets, form a contiguous firing solution. Interception spread.'

A servitor at the gunnery consoles blurted its lifeless response. 'Compliance.'

'Commander Tobin?' she asked.

'Captain?'

'Lock the ship down. Get Delvarus of the Triarii up here at once.'

It took him a couple of seconds to realise she was right. 'Aye, ma'am.'

As he moved away to give the necessary orders, she tapped a quick code into her throne's armrests and leaned back to get comfortable. The shipwide vox gave a three-tone alarm, preceding every captain's address.

'This is Captain Lotara Sarrin,' she addressed the tens of thousands of slaves, menials, officers and soldiers. 'All hands to your stations. Prepare to repel boarders.'

As a cautionary measure, surely pointless, she drew her sidearm and checked the power cell. Immaculate and charged, as always. On the oculus, the defensive turrets were spitting incendiary fire into the space between the vessels, but shooting down boarding pods was always an exercise in luck as much as skill.

'Captain?' Tobin called. Lotara wasn't sure she liked the note of unease in his voice. Nothing ever made Ivar Tobin uneasy. 'Captain?'

She holstered her laspistol. 'Commander.'

'Delvarus of the Triarii has been reported as making unauthorised planetfall.'

She sat straight at that. 'Pardon me?' she said, with a politeness and calm she most definitely didn't feel.

'Delvarus and the Triarii aren't on board, ma'am. From the reports, they made planetfall with the Legion and apparently "neglected" to inform command.'

Lotara took a breath. Could this Legion do nothing right?

'We're being boarded by what may well be an entire company of Ultramarines,' she pointed out, still with the same alien calm.

'I know, ma'am.'

The Triarii: five full companies of the World Eater's finest shipboard warriors, excelling in void warfare and boarding actions far beyond traditional Legion training. Five hundred of Angron's best, led by the Legion's undisputed pit champion, all of whom were vowed and bound to defend the flagship. It was their duty. Their honour-bound duty.

'This bloody Legion,' she said.

THE TWO ARMIES faced each other across the open plaza. Details were sparse through the dust, but Khârn could see their front rank standing still in funereal dignity. Bronze edges on their armour burned silver in the moonlight. Helmet crests wavered, but not from fear – from the wind's touch and the hammerfall of heavy rain.

Khârn stared at the front rank, hundreds of metres away, and the indistinct figures behind. Accursed dust.

As he watched, another gunship soared overhead. He activated his vox-link, speaking in a hurried slur.

'This is Khârn to gunship *Tyresius*, abort your–'

The gunship exploded. It blew into flaming scrap directly above a nearby memorial necropolis and crashed down, taking the marble building with it. Several World Eaters stared, several others chuckled. Most ignored it, in favour of watching the hazy ranks of the Ultramarines.

'I can't see a damn thing,' Skane said. 'How many do you think there are?'

'This has all the hallmarks of a last stand,' Khârn replied. 'We're not attacking without Titans.'

'Want me to make a weapons check?' Skane asked.

Khârn looked at the chainaxe in his hands; it was missing several teeth, but had a way to go before it was worthless. 'Do it. My thanks.'

He heard Skane making the rounds through the World Eaters loose ranks, checking the condition of blades, axes and supplies of ammunition. Another reality of war the sagas always missed.

Khârn kept watching the stalwart, unmoving ranks in the distance. More of his three companies' survivors were catching up now, thickening the World Eaters lines.

'Does anyone have an auspex still functioning in this dust?'

Several warriors gave noncommittal grunts. A few guessed at heat signatures of tanks among the heatwash of over a hundred Ultramarines, but no one had anything reliable to offer.

Khârn chose two squads to cut east and west respectively, reporting back on whatever they found.

More World Eaters caught up, with three rumbling Malcador battle tanks behind them. Chains rattled against the tanks' hulls, each one hung with dozens of legionary helms taken from the Isstvan Atrocity and the Dropsite Massacre.

He felt it, then. A subtle change in the atmosphere, not quite physical, but still undeniable. Chainblades started revving. Warriors started pacing, caged lions aching to hunt.

'Steady,' he voxed. 'All of you, steady.'

But he felt it, too. The Nails *tick-tocked* with little pushes of pain, demanding he *act, act, act*. He gunned his own chainaxe without intending to, lips falling into the familiar snarl.

'Steady,' he said again. And then, 'Esca.'

The Codicier came forwards. His brothers parted instinctively, several spitting on the floor before him, to ward off ill fortune. A superstitious habit taken from Angron's homeworld, and one that had resonated through the Legion.

Esca, unhelmed, had uncertainty writ plain across his features. 'Captain?'

Khârn swallowed back the rise of discomfort, which in turn was adding fuel to his anger.

'Can you use your powers to tell me what lies across from us in that plaza?'

Esca's surprise deepened. He blinked, and looked at his brothers around him. Khârn banged a fist against his own chestplate. 'Look at *me*, damn you. Answer me. Can you do it?'

The Codicier nodded. His eyes were slate grey, a rare colour on all of the World Eaters recruiting planets. 'Yes, sir.'

'Stand your ground, the rest of you.' Khârn leaned closer to Esca. Moving near him meant pushing against some unseen resistance, like walking underwater. 'Be swift,' Khârn warned. 'The Nails are singing.'

Esca knelt down, closing his eyes.

Khârn, and all the others, backed away to give him room for whatever he was doing.

'I don't suppose the Word Bearers would like to join us for this one?' Kargos ventured with an ugly smile.

Khârn had been listening to the other Legion's vox-traffic, flawed as it was by interference. 'They've got their own battles,' he said. 'They'll pr–'

'Vindicators.' Esca opened his eyes, rising to his feet.

All eyes turned to him.

'Vindicators,' he repeated, 'and other siege tanks – a battalion of them.'

The World Eaters looked to one another. Skane's back-mounted turbines started cycling up, while Kargos confronted Esca, face to face.

'They mean to shell us?'

The Codicier nodded. 'There's more. There's something near here. Something immense, and alive. Inhuman.'

'Where is it?' asked Skane.

'I can't tell.'

'*What* is it?' asked Kargos.

'I can't tell.'

The Destroyer and the Apothecary shared a glance, as if this only confirmed the Codicier's uselessness. Around them, the gathering World Eaters gunned their chainblades and started beating their weapons against their armour, prowling in loose packs, eager to run forwards and meet the enemy.

But Khârn's blood ran cold. He stared at the unyielding shadows of the distant Ultramarines in their phalanx.

'Something's wrong,' he said. 'All squads, fall back. Put distance between the tanks as well. The fleet can annihilate this plaza from orbit.'

His own men defied him, growling and arguing to the throaty whine of live chainaxes.

'Angron demanded no bombardment,' said Sergeant Gharte, his gaunt features unhelmed. 'The enemy must bleed, not burn.'

'We should charge,' Kargos insisted. Khârn saw the twitch in his brother's eyes, and the shine of saliva wetting the Apothecary's lips. 'Charge before they shell us!'

'This is the Nails talking,' Khârn said, but the words drowned in the cheer. They took up the Apothecary's cry, almost all of them, raising their axes to the occluded moon.

'Wait,' Khârn ordered. '*Wait.*'

But the first shell was falling. It struck far, far back along the avenue, not even touching the rearguard. It didn't matter that it missed. The World Eaters cried their rage at the filthy sky.

The second shell came no closer. The third did, though only barely. Loose debris clattered on the tanks' hulls, falling from the plume of soil and stone that shot into the air.

The sound of any Legion charging was earthbound thunder, something tempestuous chained to the ground rather than allowed to fly free where it belonged. Along with the roars rising from spit-flecked mouths and the aggrieved complaint of chainweapons chewing the air – when the World Eaters charged, the sound was close to tectonic.

Khârn was seven steps into the charge before he realised he'd been swept up in it. He stopped, looking back, seeing Esca standing alone. Even the Malcador tanks were rolling, engines belching smog, their turrets cranking around in readiness.

'Do not engage!' Khârn voxed to his men, trying in the face of futility. 'They're driving us forwards! They want us to charge!'

'Wait for Audax!' Esca joined his voice to his captain's. 'Wait for the Titans!'

The dust thinned as he ran, and Khârn saw just what they were charging.

Nothing in mankind's long history of warfare quite matched the sound of two Legions crashing together. Space Marine was never born to fight Space Marine, so betrayal had a tune all of its own. Not the metallic, bronze-banging din of the Ancient World, nor the chattering spit of automatic weapons in city streets that so blighted the age of humanity's first terrified steps into space. Ceramite hit ceramite with a cracked-bell *clang*, strangely dull, pervasively resonant, as if the sound itself responded to the wrongness of the act.

Khârn was in the front rank when the World Eaters met the Ultramarines. He watched the gold and blue Evocati vanguard brace their shields, clashing their edges together, forming an unbreakable wall of overlapping cobalt. Full-body boarding shields. These warriors were arrayed for tight-knit boarding actions, where protection mattered more than anything else. They stood behind their decorated pavises, clad in brutal suits of densely layered Mark III plate, pistols and swords held in their free fists.

Khârn's warriors had charged, in broken formation, a phalanx of the finest and most heavily armoured warriors in the Imperium. And he'd done it with the dregs of three disparate companies.

Break the wall. Nothing else mattered. Break the wall. Tear it down. If they couldn't break the wall, they'd be at the Ultramarines mercy and dead within minutes. It had to fall at the first charge.

He wasn't sure if he was thinking all this or shouting it. His men fired as they ran; gunfire clattered against the shield wall, leaving burn marks on the dark, sloping surfaces. He shouted for grenades, yelling in Nagrakali, but most of his men were already lost to the Nails.

The last thing he heard before the impact was the Ultramarines captain shouting a final order.

'*Ciringite frontem!*' he called in High Gothic. The shields lifted higher as the Ultramarines braced. The World Eaters roared loud enough to shake the sky.

When the lines met, they met with ceramite's unmistakable *clang* and a bodily crunch of weight levied against weight. World Eaters lashed out with whirring chainblades, thudding blunt against shields, or found themselves hurled from their feet by the press of their enemies' pavises slamming back as one. The Evocati were too closely packed. Every World Eater faced two Ultramarines. Khârn's overhead chop was blocked by one of his opponents, and he took a shield bash to the face from the other. He stumbled back, sprawling, cursing, screaming; bleeding inside his helmet.

The Nails punished him for trying to retain control by knifing into the soft meat of his brain.

Mere seconds after the lines met, the charge had faltered, broken and collapsed.

'*Contendite vestra sponte!*' cried the Ultramarines lord. His men shifted their weight, fighting back with their pistols and blades. The World Eaters still at the shield wall started dying in droves, cut down by enemies they couldn't reach.

Time slowed for Khârn in that moment. He found his focus stolen by eerie distraction – was this what Angron had felt on his homeworld? Was this what his doomed army of slaves and renegades had felt when they were being butchered by their masters' soldiers? When the outcast gladiator mob raised spears and swords against entire armies of shield-bearing warriors?

He rose. At least, he tried to. A bolt shell hammer-cracked into his shin, sending him stumbling again. Another tore his helm free, leaving his face stinging with bleeding burns, and giving him the taste of gunsmoke on his tongue. That flavour would never fade; he'd live the many centuries of his life never tasting anything else.

As he rose a second time, another bolt shell cracked against his pauldron, blasting fire and smoke into his face, and ripping the armour plating completely free. He didn't care. Slavering from the Nails' pain, he needed to kill to end the pressure inside his skull.

Staring with bloodshot eyes, a thick string of acidic drool hanging from his bared teeth, Khârn breathed two words at the advancing Ultramarines formation. They were the last two words he spoke before the Nails bit deep enough to take over. Anyone who had ever been faced with anger strong enough to steal reason knew that the *seeing red* spoken of by poets and scribes throughout history was no metaphor, but a literal staining of the sight.

He was no longer Khârn. Khârn, the identity built of a lifetime's memories and decisions, faded beneath the wash of red, red rage and frantic, berserk lethality.

Just two words.

'Our turn.'

EIGHT

Summons

A SHIP WAS never truly silent. One could never escape the steady hum of the drive engines, nor the muted echoes of distant bootsteps on other decks. Yet Lorgar prayed in silence; prayed through the pain of his wounds, while listening past the sounds of the ship for a deeper, sweeter song.

Something tugged at his thoughts. A presence, demanding his attention, as though his name were being called – barely heard – in another room.

The demigod-priest smiled at the sensation. Rather than ignore it, he turned towards it, questing for its source. It felt no different from chasing an old memory.

First, he saw the great, dark chamber, with its banners hanging from girder-rafters. Then he felt it, the cold against his skin, as if he were really standing there in the still air. His brother, one of the few he loved and who loved him in return, turned from the book he was reading on a raised plinth. Its thick cover slapped closed; neither brother was foolish enough to believe the peach-coloured leather binding was from a wholesome source.

'Lorgar,' said the brother in that far-off chamber.

The Word Bearer smiled – he smiled in his meditation chamber aboard the *Lex* above Armatura, and he smiled halfway across the galaxy – physically present in the former, a soul incarnated in the latter.

His brother looked like a god. No other word did the man justice. His armour was black chrome, a dark that suggested not only the absence of colour but the banishment of light, the way an eclipse swallows the sun. Many symbols covered its surfaces, the chief of which was the single, staring eye fashioned across the breastplate. That eye had once stared in lordly, but ignorant, invigilation. Now it glared, seeing all, black-veined by too many truths.

Above the breastplate, the face was bare, smiling, perfect in every dimension and detail, suffused with confidence. So beautiful. So very beautiful. Of all the primarchs, Lorgar's face most closely resembled a stable composite of their father's shifting features, but Horus was an avatar of an idealised version of the Emperor, perfected, iconic and completely devoid of the concerns of human existence. Or at least that was usually the case. Now, however, as Horus looked upon his brother, his sun-darkened features *were* deepened with the profoundest of concern.

'Lorgar?' he said again, as if unsure of the apparition standing before him.

'It is I,' the Word Bearer replied.

Horus stepped closer, as if he might reach out to touch his brother's ruined face. He hesitated, and lowered his hand.

'What happened?'

'Armatura. Angron looks little better. The difference is that he chose to keep fighting. I trust the war to my men.'

Unasked questions drifted in the air between them. In time, thought Lorgar. In time.

Horus gestured to the book on the plinth. 'I confess, I didn't expect this to work. To speak a man's name and have him appear before you? It reeks of black magic. The warp-flasks I can understand, but–'

'Black magic,' Lorgar smiled. He felt no pain here. Smiling was still something he was capable of. 'An amusing notion.' The Word Bearer walked to the book, an ephemeral hand above its closed pages. 'Have you read it all?'

'I have,' said the Warmaster. 'The binding is flayed skin. But whose?'

'Corpses. Corpses from Isstvan III. Very decadent,' Lorgar admitted, 'but the symbolism in such things is important.'

Horus gave a small shrug, the joints of his armour purring. 'Times have changed. It takes a great deal to turn my stomach, these days.' There was a pause, as he searched for the most fitting subject to speak of first. 'Magnus came to me, much as you do now.'

'I know. I see his decision in the skeins of fate, even if he still lacks the conviction to make it. In time, he will commit to us.'

'To us?' Something cold and black glittered in Horus's eyes. 'To me.'

'Very impressive. Very regal. Is this the voice you'll use when you take our father's throne?'

Lorgar smiled in the silence that followed his words. After a half-dozen heartbeats, Horus smiled, as well.

'What really happened?' Horus asked. 'Plasma?'

Lorgar waved a hand over his charred face. 'Plasma. A Warhound's plasma blastgun. Twice.'

Horus winced, an awed exhalation escaping his lips. 'You're lucky to be merely mutilated.'

Lorgar didn't reply to that. 'Why did you call my name, brother?'

'To see if I could. Nothing more, nothing less. How does your crusade fare in Ultramar?'

'Just as planned. Guilliman is crippled at Calth. Thirty other worlds already bleed, with our Legions divided and laying siege. Soon, another thirty will suffer the same. We are spreading pain onto the canvas and painting it into a landscape.'

'What of Calth?'

Lorgar paused again. The confession came without malice,

without any emotion at all. 'Kor Phaeron and Erebus are no doubt celebrating Calth as a triumph.'

'Then they won?'

Lorgar shrugged. 'They believe so. They gave birth to the Ruinstorm. It lacks the majesty of the Great Eye, or even the Maelstrom, but it's a beginning.'

Horus rested a hand on the skinbound book again. *'Why is it that you sound less than convinced of their triumph?'*

'One has to wonder how triumphant they really were, if their victory parade involves turning tail and fleeing from the Legion they supposedly crushed.'

Horus chuckled, conceding the point. After a short silence, he asked what Lorgar had been waiting for him to ask. The real reason he had summoned his brother.

'Will this work, Lorgar?' Horus smiled, but it was a melancholy thing, speaking of a vulnerability always suppressed before other souls. *'I cannot win this war without you and Angron. I cannot win it without your Legions.'*

It was Lorgar's turn to laugh. 'Spare me the false humility, Horus. Even if you lost every brother, every Legion, every ship and every soul serving you, you would still throw open the doors of Father's throne room and expect to win.'

But Horus wasn't smiling. *'Will it work?'* he asked again. *'Can you really drown Ultramar in the warp's tides, or is the blood of Guilliman's Legion the most we can hope for?'*

Lorgar walked the amphitheatre space of the *Vengeful Spirit*'s war room, known to the Sons of Horus as Lupercal's Court. He wasn't there, not really, yet his footsteps echoed all the same.

'You forced me to take Angron and the maddened fools he calls his sons. Now you question me, wondering if I will fail. When did you trade your trust in me for this undeserved doubt?'

'When you changed.' Horus said it simply. *'When you fought Corax, and left Isstvan V a different man, claiming to have defied destiny. When you teleported your warriors onto Fulgrim's ships and threatened his Legion with destruction because he was no longer himself. I traded trust for doubt when I was no longer certain just who you were, Lorgar Aurelian.'*

'I am the Archpriest of the Primordial Truth.' The Word Bearer's voice shook, just slightly. 'I am the Minister of Chaos Absolute.'

'Those are grand words, Lorgar. They mean little without results.'

Lorgar rounded on his brother. 'I am who I was born to be. You seek to punish me for no longer being the weakling, the lost one, the primarch with no purpose. Think back to Isstvan III, Horus. I heard that planet *die*, even thousands of systems away. Surely you spoke with your astropathic choirs, or the fleet's Navigators. That world's death-scream was louder, brighter, harsher than even the Astronomican.'

Lorgar lifted a hand, swirling his fingertips, forming an illusory sphere from white flame. It coalesced, forming a ghostly image of Terra. A lance of thin, utterly straight light beamed from the surface of the largest continent.

'The Blade of Hope. The Emperor's Blessing. Every Imperial vessel in the galaxy sails by that guiding light. Nothing else pierces the warp's restless tides. It's their only star to sail by, and for three beats of a human heart, you, Horus, caused enough pain on one world to eclipse the Emperor's own psychic beacon.'

He stepped closer to the Warmaster, fire in his eyes. 'Suffering, Horus. Do you understand? *Pain* and *terror* reflected from the material realm into the warp. The agonies of billions upon billions of mortals at the moment of death, poisoning the warp's song itself. You changed the tune, made the whole melody miss a note.'

He smiled, and while the smile was slow and serene, it still twisted his annihilated face. 'All pain passes the veil, manifesting as turmoil in the hell behind reality. Your deed sounded as a single drumbeat. I, brother, will compose a whole symphony. Doubt me all you wish. The worlds here are dying to torturous slowness, sending their protracted death-cries across the veil.'

Lorgar made a fist, clenching his teeth. 'I am *re-tuning* the warp.

Ripening it. I will project Erebus's Ruinstorm as a flood across the Five Hundred Worlds, pulling space apart by its seams.'

His snarling tirade came to an end and he lowered his gaze. 'Forgive me my passion, brother. But also trust me, please. I will sever Ultramar from the rest of the Imperium. I will take Guilliman out of the game.'

Horus had a gift for looking magnanimous no matter the moment. *'You have my trust.'* He leaned on the pulpit, as if the confession cost him. The Warmaster regarded his brother for a long moment. *'Will you heal? What have your Apoth–'*

'I will heal,' Lorgar interrupted. 'Through prayer and meditation, not the awkward fumbling of Legion Apothecaries.'

The Warmaster nodded, though Lorgar saw the doubt his brother sought to conceal. *'And what of Angron?'*

Lorgar raised a brow, scabbed over where his eyebrow had been. 'I have just realised what's happening here, brother. Am I one of your lackeys to stand at attention and report?'

Horus's laughter was unfeigned. *'Don't be petulant, Lorgar. We are planning to conquer a galaxy. Intelligence and logistics matter. Tell me of Angron.'*

Angron. There was a tale with a twist or two. The Word Bearer's wracked features blanked into a mask of neutrality. 'I will speak of Angron when I'm certain just what I can say.'

The Warmaster exhaled slowly, softly, a gesture to signify the erosion of his otherwise infinite patience.

Such theatrics, thought Lorgar.

'Brother,' said Horus. *'If you try to feed me excuses such as "the stars are not right", I will hunt you down and kill you myself. Then Guilliman's vengeance won't be a worry for you at all. Erebus once used that line of reasoning with me. It is fortunate that I was in good humour at the time.'*

Lorgar's eyes, the tawny colour of fox-fur, flickered with what may have been amusement. *The stars are not right.* That did sound like Erebus.

'Is something funny, Lorgar?'

'Many things, but nothing where Angron is concerned. Focus on your own half of the war, Horus. I will act in regard to Angron when I need to act.'

'Or when he forces your hand.'

Lorgar inclined his head – concurrence, not submission. 'Or then.'

'Is he going to die?' Horus fixed his gaze on his brother's. 'Answer me that at least.'

This time, Lorgar sighed. 'Yes. Most likely. I will do what I can, but the sickness within him runs deeper and truer than any of us ever knew. His Legion loathes him and emulates him in equal measure. He is getting worse, and they all see it. The implants drilled into his skull will be the death of him, that much is clear. Whatever archeotech was used in their fashioning, it was not made for a primarch's brain. They cannot be removed. They cannot be countered. But I am not entirely devoid of inspiration.'

Horus sensed that was as much as he was going to get. 'One last matter, then. What of Signus Prime?'

The Word Bearer was already fading. 'Signus Prime is your game, Horus. I have greater matters on my mind.'

'Greater matters?' Irritation marked the Warmaster's flawless features again. 'But Sanguinius…'

'Sanguinius will stand at Eternity Gate with tears in his eyes and acid in his heart, no matter what you and Erebus hope to accomplish at Signus Prime. Remember that, when your gambit there fails. Remember it when you face the Angel on the final day. Remember that I was the one who told you how it would really end.'

'What is a "greater matter" than the Angel, at this stage of the game?'

'Almost everything,' Lorgar's voice emerged from the cold air. 'Ultramar. Fulgrim. Guilliman. Wars we can actually win. There are only two among us who would stand in defiance of the Angel's wrath, Horus. Only two who would see him slain, once he fights with nothing left to lose. You are one. Angron is the other.'

Truth dawned behind the Warmaster's eyes. *'You've foreseen it. I hear it in your voice. And that's why you strive so hard to keep him alive.'*

The Word Bearer's voice softened, fading as his corporeal form had faded.

'Prophecy is a mistress with many minds, and should never be trusted with all one's heart. I seek to save Angron because he is my brother, Horus. There was a time when you'd have realised that and thought the same yourself. How soulless you sound now. Watch your thoughts, Warmaster, lest you find yourself hollowed out by your rising ambition.'

'*And you watch your tongue,* priest,' Horus snarled at the empty air.

Halfway across the galaxy, Lorgar opened his eyes, back in a body made of char-blackened meat.

And smiled.

NINE

**Awakening
Fury
Titan's Fall**

His first thought was that his targeting array was malfunctioning.

'My targeting array is malfunctioning,' he said. Except he said nothing, because nothing came out. Data, in jagged Nagrakali, rained down his red-glassed vision display. He read it, processed it, and because it made sense, he waited patiently.

While he waited, he watched the two humans before him. One of them was Lotara Sarrin. He liked Lotara. The Blood Hand marked her uniform, and it was a fine sight. He'd been there to see Khârn make the mark himself, after all the void-murder Sarrin had committed that fine day.

The other human was robed in red, hooded by an overhanging cowl, and possessed five rotating eye lenses instead of a face. In fairness, it could have been any number of tech-priests, but that didn't matter, as he liked none of them. He had an eidetic memory, as did all legionaries, so it wasn't that he forgot the priests' names. He just never bothered learning them.

He was cold, now that he was awake. A penetrating, heavy-rain kind of cold that sank into the pores and softened the bones. Not that it mattered. It wasn't like it would kill him. It wasn't like he could even shiver. No room for that in his coffin.

When he concentrated, shutting out the outside world, he could almost feel himself. The real himself: a naked, hobbled, foetal-curled corpse compacted into an adamantium shell. It might just be his imagination, though. Difficult to say for certain.

His vision shook, making the runes blue for a moment. Sound arrived with a blast, bathing him in the noise of a workshop at war. The crackle-sizzle of sparks and soldering. The rhythmic clang of forge hammers. The binaric burbles of robed half-men.

'My targeting array is malfunctioning,' he said. His voice was a mechanical rockslide.

'It shall be attended to,' the priest replied. He replied in binaric cant – a keening spill of ones and zeroes, but it was translated into Nagrakali and Low Gothic by the visor display.

'Captain Sarrin,' he said. He'd never been gifted at discerning human physical cues. Her eyes were narrowed. Her heartbeat was elevated. Her mouth was set in a thin, firm line that paled her lips. 'You are either angry or worried.'

'Both,' she replied. 'Lhorke, I need you to defend the ship.'

He hadn't refused, not that there was any chance he would. Lotara asked him to stand, to walk, to fight, and he would refuse her nothing. Nor would his brothers. All of them hungered to decorate their armour in blood once more. It had been too long – decades, for most of them. Decades when mercy dictated they'd be locked in dreamless sleep, but stasis was a lie of a word.

It was still possible to dream in stasis. Time didn't always freeze for the mind – only the body. The only thing to be locked into was the crippling mawkishness of one's own memories.

When he could walk. When he could breathe. When he could feel the kick of a bolter in his fist.

Lhorke shed his bleak musing the moment he pulled clear of

his restraint platform. The deck shook beneath his boots. *That* felt good. The tech-priests backing away before him as he opened his articulated, joint-grinding fists, and dry-fired the combi-bolters in his palms. That felt good, too.

'Load me,' he'd commanded them. They'd obeyed. And the truth was, having them obey his orders also felt very fine indeed. They'd loaded him as they'd finished waking his brothers.

His brothers listened to him in death, as they had in life. They were the first, yet he was the First, and while the emphasis was subtle – a single capital letter – the distinction was everything.

They were also the Wounded. The Failures. The ones who endured their handlers whispering binary code-words such as 'unstable' and 'volatile' and 'terminal degradation'.

That's why they weren't on the surface. That's why they were kept in stasis. They were the oldest, the first, before the techniques had been perfected.

Hellesek lacked one arm. His ironform was undergoing repair when he'd been reawakened, and he'd come online with a crushing power fist for a left arm, and the bizarre loss of temporary amputation on the right.

Krydal couldn't speak. His sarcophagus was bolted into his ironform, still damaged from his last battle, blessed and consecrated by holy oils but installed without his delicate vocabulator circuitry in place. No time for such things.

Neras was worst of all. He woke enraged, lost to the Nails, forever Lost even while he slumbered in stasis. Chains broke beneath his first heaving steps, and his roaring chainblades drowned out the sound of all other industry in the teeming workshop. The wiser tech-priests ran. The more devoted, or more foolish, tried to restrain him with electro-shock bindings – and, in one hilarious instance, a prayer to the Machine-God meant to invoke a sense of calm.

Lhorke had brought his Lost brother back. He achieved it by a volley of combi-bolter fire against the other Dreadnought's sarcophagus, to gain his attention, and then by beating him into submission with heavy fists. It was no contest at all. As the First, Lhorke was more than a sarcophagus bound to a war-body. His ironform was an avatar of the Machine-God. The Legion had honoured him, resurrecting him as a Contemptor.

Neras was still frantic, still fierce, but he'd come back from the precipice. He could function for now.

Thirteen of them, in all. Thirteen of the XII Legion's first Dreadnoughts – Lucifer and Deredeo-patterns, variously abandoned or intentionally forgotten, now standing in unique states of disrepair. They led the defence, as the only World Eaters on board.

World Eaters. Lhorke still felt an intruder to that name. He'd lived and died as a War Hound, in the decades before Angron, before they took the name Eaters of Worlds to honour the primarch's slain rebel army, the Eaters of Cities. He still displayed the old Legion scratch kill-markings on his ironform, and on his breastplate he bore the armoured wolf's head, collared by a chain around its throat.

War Hounds. That was his Legion. Not these furious, half-lobotomised madmen who abandoned all notions of honour when they lost themselves to berserker rage.

Even so, they were still his brothers. He couldn't hate them, but he could blame them. The rot started to creep in when they rediscovered the primarch from that worthless world he called home, and yet, the Legion could still have refused the Nails. They chose to emulate their gene-father, despite all it would clearly cost. They chose to tear open their skulls and let the poison be placed inside.

Angron had ordered it, but was that an excuse? Could the primarch have forced a hundred thousand warriors to bend to his will if they'd refused the mutilation of their minds? Lhorke had fallen in battle thirty years before the primarch's arrival. He'd been active day and night back then, before the mind's sluggishness began to take hold. It was difficult to remain awake after a few years. The mind, forced to exert itself to command the ironform, began to suffer the strain of isolation and claustrophobic confinement.

So he'd started submitting to the restful half-sleep of stasis. A few months, at first. Then it became a year for every year he remained awake. He needed more and more rest, to balance the exertion of mastering his ironform.

He'd never felt the kiss of the Nails in his brain pan, though. It was easy enough, given his circumstances: beating them into his corpse's skull came with significant risk, and he was a relic by any virtue of the word. They wouldn't risk him in the surgery, so he remained one of the few War Hounds among the rising ranks of the World Eaters.

But what was done was done. The old Legion and the new were bonded by blood, no matter how many disparate worlds the warriors had been drawn from over the decades. Kinship flowed between them, whether he willed it or not. Blood, as so many of their parent cultures had said, was thicker than water.

Lotara ordered the robed priestlings to upload a tactical feed of the Ultramarines boarding pod location points.

'The what?' Lhorke had asked. He turned from watching Neras undergoing the chanted Ritual of Reawakening, and looked down at Captain Sarrin's tiny, tiny figure.

'The Ultramarines,' she replied. 'The... Thirteenth Legion Astartes?' She looked worried, as if he'd forgotten who the XIII actually were.

Something rattled and clanked deep in his heavy metal guts. 'You want me to kill Ultramarines.'

'They boarded us!' she insisted.

Lhorke crouched down, his joints giving industrial-grade snarls as he did so. He brought his cranial input/output node, fashioned as an armoured helm, almost level with her face. A giant kneeling to address a child.

'Why did they board us?'

She was obviously worried now. 'Can't you fight other legionaries?'

Of course he could. He'd fought the Wolves, hadn't he? Sent them yelping back to their gunships after they came howling about the

Nails, after Angron had assumed command over the Legion. As long as he lived within this foetid, cold coffin, he'd never forget Angron and Russ fighting in the amber light of that alien sunset. The battlefield had reeked of their godly blood.

'What reason?' he replied to Lotara. '*Why* are we at war with the Ultramarines?'

'I... Because...' She'd trailed off. That's when she'd turned to a nearby priest, and ordered a further uploading of data.

They weren't at war with the Ultramarines. They were at war with half the Imperium. They were openly at war with the Emperor now, and they had been for over a year. Most of the time seemed to have been spent in warp transit, descending on unsuspecting worlds still blind to the unfolding war and massacring their populations wholesale.

Angron, he thought. The sheer bitterness of the conjured name made his corpse tremble in the amniotic fluid of his coffin-cradle. He felt his own withered limbs tense and twitch.

With that indecipherable dose of madness in mind, Lhorke had led his wounded and abandoned brothers back into battle.

Discipline won wars. Fury won fights.

Against the Ultramarines discipline, the only weapon that remained was fury. A fury beyond reason; a fury beyond containment. Fury so depthless it couldn't be countered, because those possessed by it cared nothing for their own lives.

When two warriors stood and fought, giving no ground, awareness of mortality couldn't be banished from even the most dutiful and courageous souls. Soldiers defended themselves to stay alive. Training and instinct forced their hands – they ducked, they dodged, they weaved and blocked and parried. On a conscious level, this was skill. It was finesse. On an unconscious level, it was the reaction of training and simple, instinctive awareness of mortality.

It was also the secret behind the World Eaters, how they won wars without the discipline so resplendent in other Legions. Fury won fights – win enough fights, and they'd still carry the war.

The Nails weren't implants as remembrancers and archeotechnicians understood the idea. The implants added nothing to a World Eater's brain. Instead, they stole from it. They bleached a warrior's mind of all reason, all caution, all mortality's instincts. The Nails rewarded rage with spurts of electrochemical pleasure, tingling synapses and deadening enjoyment of everything else. No better machine had ever been contrived to encourage warriors into pursuing the dubious peace found in absolute, careless, guiltless fury.

When Khârn hit the shield wall, he was barely Khârn any more. He was a shell of humanity stripped down to feverish rage, never thinking of defending himself, never responding to any threat of pain or danger. He ripped the boarding shield from his first foe's gauntlets, spraying spittle-froth into the warrior's faceplate as his axe cleaved down. He took blades and bolt shells against his armour without noticing, always attacking, always attacking, always attacking.

A warrior who wants to live has no defence against one who doesn't care if he dies. And Khârn, every warrior wants to live.

The primarch's words. Angron's quietly growled wisdom, in the hour before Khârn became the first to accept the Butcher's Nails in his brain.

'Blood for the primarch!' he screamed as he slaughtered the Ultra-marines, with his face painted red by dead men's insides. 'Skulls for the Twelfth Legion!'

Along the front line, where legionaries in bloodstained white met those in cobalt blue, the same performance played out a hundred times. World Eaters too wounded to charge dragged themselves across the ground, screaming their hate, axes and swords still revving in their hands.

Time meant nothing to the Nails-lost. Khârn sensed the escalation around him, the way a shark senses the ebb and flow of the tides without needing to really pay heed. In flashes of vision between the moving red-stained blurs of enemy limbs, he saw other warriors in white demolishing the Ultramarines ranks, as well as gunships brightening the sky on downturned thrusters. The headache-beams of lascannons lanced through the fighting crowds with resonant, waspish sounds, superheating the air around the growing hosts of warriors.

Titan-tread shivered the ground, their towering forms visible through the dust, fighting their own godlike wars above the herds of mere mortals around their ankles. When they deemed the ground battle worthy of their attention, the screaming, crashing hordes would die in great swathes, disintegrated in sunflame or swept clear by withering volleys of massed vulcan bolter fire. Here and there, the pressurised clatter-rattle of ursus claws loosed at larger foes. At one point, Khârn thought he saw the silhouette of a Warlord-class Titan dragged almost to its knees by four Audax Warhounds, pulled down by their harpooning grip. He had a heartbeat's span to see the great shadow kneeling, before the fight took him again.

He was close, now. Close enough to smell their breath when he tore their helms free and broke their faces open with his fists. Close enough to hear the crackle of their own vox-network ordering full retreat.

They wouldn't flee. The Ultramarines fought back to back in ever-diminishing circles, refusing to run. They wouldn't show their backs to the foe, and there was no way to retreat in good order, no matter what their commanders demanded.

'Khârn!' a voice cried above the battle. How it was magnified, the World Eater could only guess. He fought on in a frothing, panting fever, his hands numb from gripping the blood-slick axe haft. Everything existed in the flickering flurry of sword blades and shield edges and fists and boots and red-eyed bronze helms.

'Khârn!' came the voice again. 'Face me!'

He lashed out with his axe, its blade spraying sparks as it

skidded across an Ultramarine's breastplate. The teeth chewed and scraped, mangling the aquila emblazoned on the warrior's chest. Not the royal Palatine Aquila, the Emperor's own symbol borne among the Legions only by Fulgrim's sons. This was the worthless mark of Imperial dominance that any warrior was free to wear.

Khârn drew back for a second cleave. This time the spinning teeth bit into the legionary's throat, chewing the softer armour there and into the flesh beyond. When the body dropped, Khârn hacked a third time, took up the helm by its sergeant's wreath, and raised it in his fist as he screamed up at the choked sky.

A shadow eclipsed what pathetic light the moon tried to bring. It struck the ground hard enough to crack stone, manifesting behind the World Eater – a presence formed of blackness and blades.

He turned, lashing out.

Argel Tal smashed the blow aside with his golden two-handed sword. The axe sparked and splintered in Khârn's hands, falling to pieces as it met the Custodian sword.

'Are you insane, brother?' Argel Tal asked, his second, harsher voice dominating his human one.

The Word Bearer's armour was ridged by growths of dense, bleached bone forming the suggestion of an exoskeleton on the scarlet ceramite. His helm was crested by curving horns, and its silver faceplate warped into a wolfish maw. Veined bat's wings, formed from some unnatural blend of fleshmetal and scorched ceramite, rose in a living cloak from his shoulders. Something divine, fallen into sin: an angel as envisaged by daemons.

The sight of this creature was enough to pull Khârn back from the Nails' edge. Without his axe, he used the chains that bound his weapons, slashing left and right with the iron whips.

'*Where have you been?*' he managed to shout, through teeth sticky with blood and thick spit. The Nails pushed his muscles into action, wanting him to strike the Word Bearer. They promised him another pulse of pleasure if he would only betray his brother.

Argel Tal beat his wings, lifting off the ground long enough to deliver a kick to an Ultramarine's throat. He landed with his blade *en garde*, deflecting a bolt shell from the side.

'You weren't the only ones in trouble,' he replied. His human tone, lower and softer, was enriched with apology. The harsher voice, resonant and serpentine, spoke the same words at the same time, yet somehow implied amusement.

Khârn dragged a fallen gladius from the ground with one hand, and a chainsword with the other.

'Valika.' He spat the word, turning his focus to the fight. The brothers slammed back to back, duelling their foes at the heart of the battlefield. 'We needed you at Valika.'

Argel Tal's wings should have been a burden in close quarters, but in the heat of the moment they became weapons as true as his stolen blade. He wielded them as shields, rippling like sails in the wind, yet as durable as ceramite. Blades clanged aside from them, he beat them to throw his foes off-balance, slamming them into their helms and deflecting their thrusts. All the while, the Custodian sword rose and fell in his scarlet fists, reaping life.

The Word Bearer's reply was a breathless growl. 'Is this really the time?'

Khârn bit back a reply as the vox seeped with unwelcome words. 'This is Keeda Bly. *Syrgalah* down. Reinfor–'

'Can you help them?' he asked Argel Tal. Neither of them could see anything through the melee. Khârn stamped his boot down on a fallen warrior's throat, and asked again, uncaring of the desperation in his voice. The Legio Audax's command Titan was threatened. That took priority over all else. 'Can you help them?'

'I can try.' The Word Bearer pulled his sword from an Ultramarine's belly, twisting to rip the armour apart. Innards looped out in a slopping flood, and the Armaturan legionary still took another three swings before falling to his knees. These wretches took some effort to put down. 'You never really get used to killing your own kind,' Argel Tal breathed, and let the blade fall. The Ultramarine's head rolled clear.

'Stay alive,' he told Khârn, and launched skywards – wings beating, dust swirling.

TOTH WOKE HIMSELF with a moan, though it melted into a scream when the pain hit. He thrashed in his throne, inhaling the copper-smelling smoke filling the cockpit, dragging on the emergency release and yelling that it was jammed.

His thrashing cleared the smoke long enough to see that he was wrong. The release wasn't jammed, he just wasn't reaching it. The arm clawing for the emergency release lever ended at the elbow. Where his remaining organic forearm and hand had been, there was nothing but air and red ruin at the joint.

The sight actually stopped his screams. He looked at what was left of his arm in numb, amused horror.

'My arm's gone,' he said in a strangled whisper. 'My bloody arm's gone.'

He tried to reach with his other arm, but the distance was too great. His fingers curled uselessly in the air before the lever's shining iron handle. Shock and blood loss had him reeling, dizzy to the point of intoxication.

'Keeda. Keeda, I'm trapped in my throne. Keeda.' He rolled his head to the side, peering through the smoke. 'Keeda, my arm's gone.'

He was confronted by the sight of her backside in standard-issue grey overalls as she crouched on the control console, facing Solostine in the princeps's seat. He grinned drunkenly, though he'd never in his whole life felt an iota of attraction to her.

Toth's lolling head smacked against his headrest, against the iron edges where the support cushions had been before the crash. The entire cockpit was tilted halfway on its side, making it hard to keep his head up.

'Keeda,' he said to her backside. 'Keeda, I've lost a lot of blood.

I can't… I don't… Keeda. Keeda. I think my arm's on the floor. Keeda. Find it, Keeda. Please.'

She turned in the tight confines of the Warhound's cockpit, swore more viciously than Toth had ever heard her swear, and left Solostine in his throne. Toth couldn't really see through the smoke. The princeps looked asleep.

Keeda – who even under these dire circumstances was sick to death of Toth mumbling her name – reached to pull the emergency release by the steersman's throne. It clanked and clicked and gave a disappointing hiss. Nothing happened.

'Marvellous,' she said. 'Just lovely.' Her face was a soot-streaked mess. Toth watched her pull her service pistol, and dimly wondered why she would want to shoot him. She didn't, of course. With a soft-spoken apology to *Syrgalah*'s machine-spirit, she shot twice – destroying both magnetic couplings sealing the roof cupola closed.

'We're leaving,' she told Toth.

'We crashed,' he told her.

'We most certainly did.' She straddled his control panel, balancing precariously as she bound his severed arm in a tourniquet made from her sleeves.

At one point, she saw his arm on the floor by his boots. He'd guessed right, it was down there.

'Come on,' she said, as she started lifting him.

Shock was on her side; he was compliant, despite his ceaseless mumbling. 'Keeda,' he said again. 'What about the old man?'

'He's dead.' And she didn't have tears in her eyes. If she did, it was the smoke. Just the smoke.

'Keeda. He's not dead. Is he? Keeda?'

Good question. Unless you could live with half the avataric interface console rammed through your chest, he was most certainly dead.

'He's gone, Toth. Keep climbing.'

She was pushing him up through the cupola now, getting him

out first. 'If you say my name once more, you delirious bastard, I'll shoot you.'

Other hands reached in, frantic hands, grabbing at Toth's half-limp body and pulling him away from her. '*No!*' she screamed, and pulled back with one hand, scrabbling for her gun with the other.

'Be peaceful, Moderati Bly.' She knew that voice, its emotionless, vox-ish tone. 'It is me. Only me.'

She looked at the reaching hands, bionic in crude rendition of human musculature, yet strangely beautiful for that fact. Burnt scraps of red robe hung through the open cupola.

'Ninth?'

'Affirmative. It is me. The Ninth.'

'Have you got Toth?'

'A second and subsequent affirmative.'

'Keeda.' Toth was drooling in his rebreather, still mumbling. '*Keeeeeda…*'

'Hush,' she told him, not unkindly. 'Pull him up, Ninth.'

'A third and most welcome affirmation.' The tech-priest's augmetic arms heaved, cylinders and pistons and little gears tightening as he lifted Toth clear. She heard the moderati say *Keeda* yet again, followed by the Ninth muttering something about *exsanguination* and *the radial and ulnar arteries*.

Crouching by the slumped form of Princeps Solostine, she closed his eyes with a stroke of her fingers.

'Thank you,' she told him. A moment later, she was hauling herself up in Toth's wake.

The Ninth supported Toth, the former with his Martian red robes left in tatters, seeming naked without the shroud or the servo skulls that usually orbited him in antigravitational diligence. Most of his body was given over to articulated armour, unusually slender and carefully contoured compared to the dense plating of battlefield engineers. She'd had no idea his augmetics were so artful beneath the robe.

The Ninth, without his hood, revealed a shaven head marked by augmetic nodes, and a heavy visor in place of his eyes. A scarab of round iron replaced his vocal chords; from this tiny speaker came his tinny vox-voice. All else above the neck seemed human.

'The princeps?' he prompted.

'Gone.'

'There will be a grieving process, involving rituals both mournful and sincere. Come, Moderati Bly. We must get clear.'

Easier said than done. Keeda usually stood above the 'groundwork', where infantry duelled in *Syrgalah*'s shadow. Now *Syrgalah* had fallen, leaving her crew stranded in the thick of it. Warriors in white and blue battled and screamed around the toppled Titan. For several mute seconds, she wasn't even sure what to do, or where to run. The pistol in her hand was useless – a toy against any member of the Legiones Astartes.

'Moderati Bly–,' the Ninth began. The sentence ended in a smothered cry as the tech-priest was thrown forwards, nailed by a bolt shell in the back. Keeda saw him crawling on the ground, his legs severed, dragging himself to get back to her. No hope of that; she and Toth still stood atop the Warhound's grounded skull. She grabbed Toth before he could fall, pulling him close.

'*Traitors.*' The vox-voice was low and very, very sure of itself. She turned and fired at the Ultramarine below, her shots deflecting from his armour, leaving tiny, insipidly worthless burn marks where they managed to bite. He and three of his battle-brothers lifted their bolters. In the same second, a shadow danced above her.

It landed with a brutal crunch, eclipsing the light of the XIII Legion's muzzle flashes, and taking the worst of the gunfire in a storm of cracks and crashes against its scarlet ceramite. A figure. A thing. One of the Word Bearers, one of their maddened Gal Vorbak creatures. He pulled the two humans against his scorched armour, shielding them both, folding his bleeding wings around them.

'I am Argel Tal,' he said, in two voices through one throat. His face was a mask of canine metal, and the words were wet with the blood trickling from his fanged maw. 'Khârn asked me to keep you alive.'

Keeda had survived the death of her Titan, murdered by a Lysanda Reaver in black and white that killed them without looking twice. She'd survived the wracking pain of severance from *Syrgalah*'s great-hearted machine-spirit – a soul she adored and would willingly die to defend. She'd pulled her mutilated colleague free from imminent death and bidden her dead mentor farewell. She'd even fired hopelessly at soldiers sworn to kill her, whom she knew she could never have harmed.

But she only started screaming when a daemon embraced her and said he'd come to save her life.

TEN

The Ghenna Scouring
The War is Over
Endings

Lotara Sarrin had told him where to hunt. She'd uploaded nine separate boarding pod points of entry across the *Conqueror*'s port side, and the casualty reports over the vox did the rest. They were dealing with an estimated ninety Ultramarines, with a sub-analysis detailing projected casualties given crew density and armsmen response predictions at each impact point.

Lhorke stayed with Krydal and Neras, for they were the worst. They needed guidance, and orders to follow.

The other Wounded spread out, their stomping tread taking them across the ship. Lhorke and Captain Sarrin tasked them with leading the defence, though the vox was still alive with reports of Ultramarines massacring the human crew and the naval armsmen sent to hold their ground.

Bodies lined the walkways. If a veteran's guess was anything to go by, Lhorke considered the projected crew casualties on the wrong side of conservative. The Ultramarines invaders knew their lives would end on this ship, but that many warriors could easily tear the ship apart before they were brought down.

And they moved swiftly. Distasteful as it was, Lhorke was reduced to ordering armsman fire-teams to stand and be slaughtered in order to delay the Evocati squads for long enough that his Dreadnoughts might catch the boarders at all.

Still, the Space Marines were fragile enough, once they were in reach of his claws.

He paid almost no heed to the killing. What pulled at him most were the questions of this insane war against the Emperor and his empire. How had the Legion tolerated its own purge? How had they slaughtered their own brothers with impunity on Isstvan III? How could they betray their own blood? The War Hounds – and the World Eaters that followed after them – were a Legion founded upon brotherhood above all else. They taught it in the gladiatorial pits, bonding warriors from different worlds, chaining them together and forcing them to fight as pairs.

So how had it come to this?

Angron.

Angron and the Nails.

During the Great Crusade, the primarch's discovery had been a long time in coming. The War Hounds bore witness to other Legions uniting with their primarchs for the first time and were no strangers to disconsolate jealousy. Speculation was rife, from the muttered worry that their primarch might already be dead, to the hope he would be a warrior and general to rival Horus, Guilliman, Dorn or the Lion.

And then, on that foul backwater world, they finally found him. His first and most dubious honour was to be the one primarch to refuse the Emperor's benevolence and to turn his back on the Imperium's claims of conquest. Angron, master of his doomed slave army, cared nothing for a galaxy's worth of dreams and triumphs. He wished only to die with those rebels who'd escaped the gladiator pits with him. This ragged army of his brothers and sisters were holed up in the mountains with carrion birds and snow bears for company, waiting to starve or fall in battle – whichever death came first.

The Legion were told of his refusal. Their primarch had defied the Emperor.

The War Hounds didn't hate Angron for his choice. They worshipped him for it. What primarch better understood the bonds of brotherhood than one who turned his back on the Emperor, on the Imperium, on life itself – to die side by side with his kindred?

Yet the Emperor denied him the choice. Angron would lead a Legion in the Imperium's name whether he willed it or not.

Lhorke had been slumbering in the first of his necessary respites by the time they orbited Angron's worthless little world. They'd woken him, though. They'd woken all of the first ones in the weeks after Angron's arrival. The Legion had never known a more momentous event.

Gheer had been Legion Master, then. A good man, Gheer. An axeman to stand with the best of them. Uninspired around a planning table, admittedly, yet he'd managed to make bluntness into a virtue alongside brutality.

Dead the very night the primarch joined the Legion. Slain by their new father, in Angron's first uncontrollable, melancholic fury.

But in those earliest days, the Nails were a virtue. None of the newly-renamed World Eaters would face the fact their primarch carried a curse from the years on his homeworld. They focused on his prowess, on the strength and speed gifted to him by the archeotech implants, and when the primarch demanded his sons lie under the Techmarines' claws and the Apothecaries' knives, few had resisted the chance to share the same virtuous pain as their noble primarch.

Everything changed with the hammering of the Nails.

The World Eaters, once known for their brotherhood, became known first and foremost for their savagery. Reports began filtering back of excessive Legion casualties in tacticless displays of horde warfare, and Imperial Army forces pleading for assistance from other Legions when the World Eaters were the ones to answer the call. Planets surrendered rather than face the XII Legion in battle, but not all who surrendered were spared the war. The Nails dulled all other pleasures, until the heady bite of adrenaline was the only certain way to experience anything but the dimmest memory of emotion. Their rewired minds allowed no other pleasure beyond battle.

Worlds bled. Worlds burned. Worlds died.

The Emperor, it was said, had become... how had rumour put it? *Displeased.* What a word. So polite, considering the madness that followed in its wake.

Imperial records stated that two primarchs came to Angron, both claiming to have been sent by the Master of Mankind. The first arrived soon after Angron joined his Legion. The second wouldn't come until almost a century later. By then, it would be too late.

Russ was the first. He came, and he brought his Wolves. Already, they called themselves the Emperor's executioners. Had he been given the title? Doubts were everywhere, among the primarchs and their Legions most of all. Why the Space Wolves? Lhorke still recalled the arguments on everyone's lips. The Wolves lacked the Ultramarines numbers and Russ lacked the impartial wisdom of Guilliman. They lacked the Thousand Sons widespread gifts of sixth sense, and the Wolf King lacked the far-reaching knowledge of Magnus the Red. They lacked the ferocity of the World Eaters; the resilience of the Death Guard; and all but one of the twenty Legions lacked the grandeur, the reputation, and the victories of the Luna Wolves. More telling, every Legion but one lacked Horus, the First Primarch – suspected even then to be hailed one day as Heir to the Emperor.

But the truth twisted depending upon who told the tale. Russ lived the role as though it were his birthright. What mattered, in the shadow of that commitment? Nothing. Nothing at all.

They'd met at Malkoya, on the fields beyond the dead city of the same name. The World Eaters, battered and bleeding from Ghenna's compliance, formed ragged lines before the assembled Space

Wolves Legion. The primarchs stood before their hosts, armed and armoured – Angron awash with blood and carved up by fresh wounds; Leman Russ in resplendent plate the colour of the storms on his tempestuous homeworld.

Lhorke had stood with Angron, as had Khârn and the other captains. Even interred in his walking coffin, he'd been struck by the majesty of standing before Russ. Here was a being gene-coded to perfection: a reflection of humanity's beloved royal paragon. Russ bled authority without effort, and without the need for posture or pretence. In all ways, he should have been a barbarian – from the ragged blond hair to the frost-weathered skin that aged him far past his years. And yet, he inspired no mockery. He made barbarism a controlled trait, something noble to be understood and mastered, not a state of primitive regression. Leman Russ was the dynamism of a life free from civilisation's shackles. He was strength and purpose and heart, where all else was grey with the promise of inevitable stagnancy.

He wasn't a wolf because of how he fought and howled and bunched his men into packs. He was a wolf because of how he lived, forever echoing the vitality and honesty of the wildness at the heart of all life. It was said in smiling whispers that VI Legion genetic coding was tainted by canine blood. Lhorke believed it. Seeing Leman Russ made him yearn to breathe again, and feel anything beyond the cramped, cold-milk discomfort of his amniotic womb-tomb. Never had he felt more dead – not before, and not since.

The Wolf King hadn't come to debate or offer pleasantries. Nevertheless, Lhorke remembered the nod of respect offered by the primarch.

'Legion Master,' Russ had said.

Lhorke's ironform wasn't made for obeisance, but he lowered his chassis in an awkward bow.

'Great Wolf,' he'd replied. 'I am Legion Master no more.'

Russ had smiled, then. A crooked smile, offering the barest, whitest flash of his teeth. 'More's the pity. If you were, perhaps my presence would not be necessary.'

Angron spoke at last. Unlike Russ, he was savagery unrestrained by healthy dynamism. He brought no charismatic aura of life and passion. He was a god of war: broken, dangerous, and worst of all, unreliable. The Nails had forced his left eye to twitch open and closed in a madman's blink.

'Did he send you?' the Eater of Worlds asked.

Russ said nothing. His silence had Angron smiling, though it was an ugly slice of a thing, showing no joy.

'He didn't, did he? The Emperor and Horus sail the stars together without a care for any of this. You've come to punish me because you believe it's your place.'

In those early years, Angron carried his first axe, the precursor to all others. He called it Widowmaker. It would break this very day, never to be used again.

Russ carried Krakenmaw, his immense chainblade, toothed by some Fenrisian sea-devil from that blighted world's many myths. The wind toyed with his bedraggled hair, blowing strands of the golden mane across his face. Eyes the colour of melting ice never left the bloodshot orbs in Angron's cabled skull.

'Reports reach my ears, Angron. The words of commanders and captains who have suffered at your side. Soldiers forced to fight without orders, losing hundreds when mere dozens needed to die. Your own allies speak of the butchery done to them at your sons' hands. Report after report after report, witness after witness after witness. All of this comes to me, and I wonder, my brother: what am I to do?'

Two immense wolves circled the primarchs. Their fur was white, dusted by grey. One snarled, as wolves will always snarl when threatened, saliva-wet fangs on show, eyes sharp and ears low. The other merely paced, content to watch the speaking godlings, its dark eyes catching the light of the setting sun. The calmer beast came within Russ's reach, and the warlord dragged armoured fingers through its thick coat.

'I am not your lackey to judge,' Angron stated. The cybernetic cables forming technological dreadlocks tensed as he clenched his iron teeth. 'And you have no authority over me. Over any of us.'

Russ smiled again. 'And yet, here I am.'

'To do what? To commit to a war that will see both our Legions in ruins?' Angron wiped a wounded hand over his face, as if the simple gesture could clean away the pain. 'Leave. Leave before this becomes something you regret.'

The wind was picking up, now. Lhorke felt it as a dull whisper against his ironform, but it tore at the banners raised above the Space Wolf ranks.

Russ spoke again, pale eyes unwavering. 'The surgery must end, Angron. The Emperor himself wills that it be so. The massacres end here and now, as well. Look what you have done to this world.'

'Cleansed it.'

'Butchered it. Reaved it. Ghenna is scoured of all life. Is this a deed you want listed beneath your name when statues rise to celebrate the Great Crusade?'

Angron cared nothing for statues, and said so plainly.

Russ shook his head. 'You cannot sail the stars in this frenzy purely because you're too damaged to learn the art of war. The implant surgery must be reversed. Your sons will submit to mine for a return to Terra. Once we reach the Palace, everything will be done to remove these parasitic engines from your men's minds.'

Despite the twitches, Angron's tortured eyes were wide in genuine surprise. 'You think you have any authority over me? You think you can threaten me and expect to walk away?'

'I think there's a good chance of it, aye.'

Angron grinned, though it was an anguished thing. 'And if you die?'

The wind pulled at Russ's wolfskin cloak. 'Lorgar wrote something several years ago that has nourished my thoughts each day and night since he shared it with me.'

The World Eater snorted, showing just what he thought of his pious, scrivener brother's musings, but Russ was unfazed.

'*It is not enough that corruption is recognised,*' Russ quoted. '*It must be opposed. It is not enough that ignorance is acknowledged. It must be defied. Win or lose, what matters is making a stand for the virtues we will bequeath to the human race. When this galaxy is finally ours, we'll hold a worthless prize if we plant the last aquila, on the last day, on the last world, having led humanity into moral darkness.*'

Angron listened, but cared little. Even then, he was a stubborn creature, taking spiteful pride in his own isolation.

'Lorgar wages war with a quill,' he said, 'but the galaxy will not be brought to heel by crude philosophy. Your ideals are meaningless.'

'Ideals are what we fight for, brother.' There was something colder in Russ's tone, then. A decision had been made, frosting his voice.

Angron had laughed, the sound rich and true. 'Such pretty lies! We fight for the same reasons men have always fought: for land, for resources, for wealth and for bodies to feed into the grinders of industry. We fight to silence anyone that dares draw breath and whisper a different opinion from ours. We fight because the Emperor wants every world in his hands. All he knows is slavery, painted in the inoffensive cloak of *compliance*. The very notion of freedom is a horror to him.'

'Traitor,' Russ hissed.

Angron stood tall, still grinning. 'Do we give choices to those we slaughter? A true choice? Or do we broadcast that they must throw their weapons into the fires of peace and bow down, faces pushed into the mud like beggars, thanking us for the culture we force upon them? We offer them compliance or we offer them death. How am I a traitor, wolfling? I fight as you fight, as loyal as you are. I do the tyrant's bidding.'

'We offer them freedom.' Russ spoke through clenched teeth, the moon bright in his eyes. 'You are mutilating your own sons and stealing their minds – now you preach of the Emperor's tyranny? Are you lost so far in your delusions?'

Angron's smile faltered, fading away. His face seemed slack, his eyes staring past Russ. Defeat was etched upon features still twitching in pain.

'You are free, Leman Russ of Fenris, because your freedom matches the Emperor's will. For each time I wage war against worlds that threaten the Imperium's advance, there comes another time when I am told to conquer peaceful worlds that wish only to be left alone. I am told to destroy whole civilisations and call it liberation. I am told to demand millions of men and women from these new worlds, to make them take up arms in the Emperor's hordes, and I am told to call this a *tithe*, or *recruitment*, because we are too scared of the truth. We refuse to call it *slavery*.'

'Angron…' Russ snarled.

'Be silent! You have given your threats, dog. Now hear *me*. Listen to another hound barking, for once.'

'Then speak,' Russ had said, as if permission were his to give.

'I am loyal, the same as you. I am told to bathe my Legion in the blood of innocents and sinners alike, and I do it, because it is all that's left for me in this life. I do these things, and I *enjoy* them, not because we are moral, or right – or loving souls seeking to enlighten a dark universe – but because all I feel are the Butcher's Nails hammered into my brain. I serve because of this "mutilation". Without it? Well, perhaps I might be a more moral man, like you claim to be. A virtuous man, eh? Perhaps I might ascend the steps of our father's palace and take the slaving bastard's head.'

Both Legions tensed. Thousands and thousands of warriors clutched bolters and chainweapons tighter. Lhorke had even taken a step back, his joints loud in the sudden silence.

Russ felt no such hesitation. He drew his blade and launched at Angron, only to be met with the World Eater's axe blocking the blow. The brothers breathed hatred into each other's faces.

'You are lost,' Russ growled. 'You gelded, black-hearted *heretic*.'

'I am merely honest, brother. In all but this you are no different from me.'

'If you cannot see the chasm between savagery and ferocity, then you are hopelessly gone, Angron.'

The World Eater threw Russ back, sending the Wolf King staggering. 'Then I am gone. But we both know the day will never dawn that you can best me in combat.'

For several seconds, the primarchs stared at each other.

Lhorke never saw who fired the first shot. In the decades to come, the World Eaters claimed it came from the Wolves' lines, and the Wolves claimed the same of the XII Legion. He had his suspicions, but what was hindsight in the face of catastrophe? Without either primarch giving an order, two Legions fought.

The Night of the Wolf, they'd called it in the years since. Imperial archives referred to it as the Ghenna Scouring, omitting the moment the World Eaters and Space Wolves drew blood. A source of pride for both Legions, and a source of secret shame. Both claimed victory. Both feared they'd actually lost.

LHORKE HAD BEEN forced to slumber increasingly often in the following decades, easing the pressure on his caged brain and withered form, but his awakenings were frequent enough to perceive Angron's deterioration through the years. Slow and subtle as the alterations were, the primarch still couldn't hide them. In truth, he may not have even been trying.

Each time Lhorke rose to walk the *Conqueror*'s decks and join his brothers in their Great Crusade, he could see the primarch suffering the bite of those hateful implants. The Nails' afflictions struck harder, more frequently, and their pain lingered longer.

Worse, it was spreading across the Legion. The legionaries' brains were almost human compared to the primarch's transcendent physiology, and the erosion of their self-control was accordingly quicker. Lhorke watched it with a curious mix of detachment and guilty compassion, noting another notch on their descent each time he awoke. Concentration seemed a chore for them, over long periods of time. They laughed less and relied increasingly on

Legion serfs to maintain their armour. Attention spans shortened, wandered, forever looking to the next war.

Still, the brotherhood remained strong at the Legion's heart, and there was the test that truly mattered. World Eaters were still chained together in the fighting pits and duelled to the cheers of their brothers. They entered without armour, naked but for loincloths to show they feared no wound, and to prove every warrior would fight on equal ground.

For especially deserving legionaries, the XII even opened its pits to those born of other bloodlines. Sigismund of the VII paired with Delvarus of the Triarii, and the two of them won every fight they entered – always to first blood, never lasting more than half a minute. No one could keep up with them. No one even came close.

Amit of the Blood Angels paired with Kargos, and few ever wished to come up against the Flesh Tearer and the Bloodspitter. They were known for always fighting past first blood, third blood and into *sanguis extremis*. No dirty trick seemed beyond them, and every one of their matches was a death bout.

And then there was Argel Tal. Lhorke had first seen the Word Bearer in the pits, paired with Khârn. From the very first moment they were chained together and stepped into the chamber, ringed by howling gladiators looking on, Lhorke knew the two of them would lose more than they ever won. Khârn was an indifferent competitor and found few World Eaters willing to stand with him. Lhorke could tell right away that in Argel Tal, he'd found a kindred spirit, silently laughing at the same joke.

Regardless of the lethal grace they so plainly shared, and the effortless brotherhood that bonded them, neither took sparring seriously. They saw no honour in the pits; merely distraction and amusement. When they fell in defeat – which they did almost every time – it was always without rancour, despite the fiercely competitive nature of the duelling taking place in the *Conqueror*'s iron bowels.

Sigismund once knocked Khârn to the deck in seven short

seconds; the same moment Delvarus scored first blood on Argel Tal's bare chest. Enduring the jeers and laughter of their comrades, the World Eater and Word Bearer had crashed their manacled wrists together in a Legiones Astartes battle-sign of mutual respect, and did the same with their opponents. The traditional salute of a good fight, fairly won.

'You're useless,' Delvarus had said, a smile on his mouth but not in his eyes.

'I am,' Argel Tal admitted, 'when my life isn't on the line.' He spoke in Nagrakali, the World Eaters' bastardised tongue. When a Legion was born of three dozen worlds, they needed a new language to share. Argel Tal spoke it with a curious softness, almost scholarly in his tones.

Delvarus had grinned. 'That's Khârn's excuse, as well.'

'True enough. But Khârn is your primarch's equerry and his name is known throughout the Legions. Delvarus is a name shouted here and here alone.'

'Are you implying something, Word Bearer?'

Argel Tal's dark eyes shone in the murk. 'I thought I was directly stating it, but yes, you could say "implying" if you prefer.'

Delvarus was one of the few World Eaters not to shave his head. The discomfort of hair in his helm was irrelevant; he'd never cut his long black locks. In the pits, he wore it loose, and as he re-tied it in the wake of Argel Tal's words, he looked between the Word Bearer and Khârn.

'A death bout, then. Sanguis extremis.'

Both Khârn and Sigismund objected. The Black Knight refused on issues of honour, for the sin of slaying a cousin from another Legion, while Khârn had shaken his head, running his fingers along the edge of his toothless duelling axe.

'It would be wrong to deprive the Triarii of their captain. Best take your anger elsewhere, Delvarus.'

Lhorke's concerns had been eased by the display, as they always were when he saw the pit-fights still forming the core of the

Legion's bonds. But on the battlefield, the World Eaters were a changed force. Russ's warning went unheeded. More and more, Angron would stalk from tactical briefings before any decisions were made, never citing the pains in his head but never needing to. His sons weren't blind. Besides, they felt the same pain, forever growing like a cancer in their skulls. From a Legion once as concerned with logistics as any other, the XII was soon hurling men at enemy strongholds without thought of civilian casualties, let alone their own lives. They advanced ahead of their marked resupply points, outpacing their heavy armour, and caring nothing for how bitterly expensive each victory became, so long as the blood flowed.

'Legion Master.'

His former title dragged him back from futile reverie. Lhorke had to crouch to make it through the corridor arch into the next chamber where the lesser Dreadnoughts waited. Neras had vox-blurted his name.

'Do you hear that?' Neras boomed from his ironform's vocalisers. A squat, proud model ironform, rather than bearing its coffin on the front, Neras's frontal armour was formed into an ornate helm with a T-shaped visor. Either side, murals of his victories were acid-etched into his sloping armour plating.

'I hear it,' Lhorke replied. Bootsteps, in the hallway ahead. Too heavy to be human.

He looked briefly at his massive metal fists, as if he were still alive and carried a bolter to reload. The huge gauntlets were bloodstained, with silvery grey metal showing beneath the remaining flecks of paint. He'd never killed an Ultramarine before this evening. Now he'd killed four himself, while the other wounded amassed their own tallies.

They powered up with a thought, marred only by the slightest time delay between his desire and their activation. Wreathed in shimmering, humming energy fields, the blood smears flash-fried to his weaponised hands bubbled and dissolved away.

'Get to the bridge,' he declared. 'I will deal with these dregs and make my way to the primary engineering deck. Hold the strategium until my arrival. Now go, in the name of the Emp–'

Neras's chassis gave a grinding gear-slip of a sound. Laughter, of a kind. 'Old habits,' the Dreadnought growled.

'Go.' Lhorke demanded.

The dead men separated at last, walking through corridors as familiar to Lhorke as anything in life. This ship – back in the age it bore the name *Adamant Resolve* – had been his to command.

'They're safe.'

The draconic shadow appeared by Khârn's side again, its golden blade burning the air in wide, buzzing arcs. Wherever the sword cut, the air held the sea-salt smell of ozone.

'Where?' the World Eater asked. Above them, the avian shriek of single-man Gyrfalcon fighters split the sky. Around them, the World Eaters and Ultramarines still killed each other, trading exhausted blows. Sweat painted Khârn's face, stinging his eyes, and he could feel the clumsy ache in his leaden limbs. The ground was lousy with the dead and the dying, making all footwork treacherous. Every warrior kept sliding on the blood-slick ceramite of the corpses beneath their boots.

'They're safe, damn you. I got them to my Fellblade.' Argel Tal pulled his wings close with a crack like cloth sails catching wind. Khârn caught a split-second glance of them snapping tight to the Word Bearer's back, both of the daemonic limbs ragged and bloody.

'Khârn!' he heard his name cried out above the chaos.

Endure. Survive. Fight. He lashed out with his weapons, thrusting into unprotected joints, battering other blades aside if that was what it took.

'Khârn!' the voice shouted again. '*Face me, coward!*'

Argel Tal laughed. 'Someone knows you're here.'

'More fighting, less jesting.' The World Eater backhanded one of his opponents away, but he staggered as his boot came down on a dead World Eater's sloping pauldron. Unbalanced, he was easy prey – a sloppy parry snapped his chainsword halfway along its length, tracked teeth scattering like gambler's dice. His opponent shield-bashed him back against Argel Tal, stumbling both of them.

The Word Bearer beat his wings to turn in a blur, his relic blade catching the blow meant to end Khârn's life. Ultramarine and Gal Vorbak pushed against each other, energised blades grinding, raining sparks in an incandescent spray. The deadlock lasted a moment, no more, before Argel Tal's greater strength started pushing the Evocatus back. His boots squealed over the stone as he tried to stand his ground.

Argel Tal's eye lenses flared an unhealthy, crystal blue. Sick heat throbbed from his armour, emanating a plague victim's final fever, and he spoke three words in a tongue that spilled into Khârn's ears and scraped letters of fire behind his eyes.

'Eshek'ra mughkal krikathaa.'

The Ultramarine's fists opened, letting his sword fall. Before the warrior could offer any reaction or emotion at all, his helmeted head tumbled clear. Argel Tal booted the headless corpse in the chest, sending it to the ground with its brothers where it belonged.

Khârn felt blood trickling from his nose. 'What was that language?'

'I told him to drop his sword.'

'That isn't what I asked, brother.'

Argel Tal risked leaving himself defenceless, offering his hand to help Khârn rise. The World Eater fired from the ground, plasma blasting a hole through another Ultramarine's chest. As the warrior fell, the axe he'd been raising to strike Argel Tal from behind clattered to the floor.

'A child's error,' Khârn chided his brother, scrambling to his feet without taking the hand. His breath was sawing in and out of his body. 'Focus.'

'*Khârn!*' came the shout again.

The centurion swore in Nagrakali. 'Who is shouting that?' he added in Gothic.

It was Argel Tal who answered. He aimed his golden blade deeper into the melee, where a cloaked and crested Ultramarines officer was carving his way towards them. He didn't need his warriors to part the sea of enemies. He came in an unpretentious stride, crested helm bowed, a power sword in one hand, a gladius in the other. Khârn watched him disembowel one of Skane's Destroyers with a sweep of his sword, while ramming the gladius home in another World Eater's throat. Both blades slashed back from the dying warriors' bodies in perfect order, only to catch an incoming axe strike, deflecting it rather than block it. The World Eater pulled back for another swing, only to be parried a second time. He jerked back as the captain's gladius sheathed itself in his belly, struggling free just in time for the sword to ram through his chest.

Even amidst the storm, Khârn breathed in slow awe. Perfect grace. Perfect fluidity. Perfect economy of movement and balance and application of strength.

He had to kill him. What a trophy that helm would make.

'He's mine,' Khârn said. 'He is *mine*.'

The captain couldn't have heard, but he levelled his stabbing sword at Khârn all the same, marking his foe. '*Khârn!*' he shouted again, vox-amplified by the muzzled Mark IV helm.

'I think you might be his.' Argel Tal was grinning, teeth white in his dusky face.

'You take his honour guards,' said Khârn.

The Word Bearer looked at the spearmen flanking their captain. Each of them bore a helm crested with a white horsehair tail. 'There are four of them.'

'There are indeed.' Khârn kicked up a fallen chainsword from the ground, stealing the bloodstained blade from one of his dead brothers. 'So I wish you luck.'

He heard Argel Tal's wings spread with another cloth-sail crack, but he was already sprinting ahead. Ultramarines parted before him, weapons raised in defence as they backed away, funnelling his charge towards the Evocati captain. By contrast, World Eaters still hurled themselves at the swordsman, only to be cut down and kicked aside with shameful ease. As he ran, Khârn imagined the officer's contempt etched clear across his face beneath the blue helmet.

The Nails gave a pleased pulse as his adrenaline flowed fresh, the feeling as soothing as ice on a burn.

'Khârn.' A hazy pict-feed flared into life at the edge of his retinal display. 'Khârn, the *Conqueror* is back in orbit, but we're still–'

'Not now, Lotara.'

'But–'

An irritated thought was all it took to kill her image and lock the signal out. There were other Legion officers, damn her. Officers not up to their throats in enemy heroes. She could harass them instead.

He knew that was the Nails talking. He didn't care.

The Evocatus threw back his dust-darkened white cloak, casting it to the ground. His honour guards intercepted the World Eaters still seeking to reach their captain, cleaving them apart with blows from their halberds. Petty envy burned within Khârn that moment. Their unity of movement, their disciplined teamwork – when the World Eaters charged, they fell into barely bound packs, relying on ferocity and individual strength over any tactical cohesion. This was like looking at what might have been – and what once was – without the Nails.

Argel Tal landed at the heart of the honour guard quartet, wielding both spear and blade in fists that should have only been able to hold one or the other. No human could move as he moved; no legionary could, either. He melted away from every cut and chop and thrust that should have ended his life, reality itself rippling around him as he moved faster than mortal muscles could follow. The fluidity went past grace and into something almost boneless.

Khârn could hear his brother's blended voices mocking the warriors, but couldn't make out the words. It didn't sound like the harsh, alien tongue he'd used before, for which Khârn was bemusedly grateful. That was his last thought before he reached the officer.

They met blade to blade, long enough for him to see the faint impression of eyes behind the captain's coloured lenses.

'Orfeo,' the Ultramarine breathed. 'Legatus of Armatura. Now you know the name of the warrior who will end your pathetic legend.'

'Horus,' Khârn replied. 'Warmaster of the Imperium. Now you know the name of the next Emperor.'

They disengaged, throwing their weight against their joined blades to come apart cleanly. Both warriors were exhausted from hours of battle, and aware the eyes of their nearby kindred were beginning to fall upon their every movement. Breathless and aching, they brought their weapons up once more, no longer part of the wider battle at all.

The former Legion Master crouched beneath the archway as he entered the bridge. His walk had fallen into a halting limp, dragging the seized burden of one locked limb. Bolters still thudded, which boded ill, and everywhere he looked the deck was brutalised by scattered corpses and the aftermath of fragmentation grenades. If they lived through this – and he was no longer certain they would – the ship would need drydocking for overhaul.

Familiar figures were visible through the gunfight. Krydal was a one-armed wreck, gored by massed bolter fire and slumped at the base of Lotara Sarrin's raised throne. Neras was down and twice as dead, the entire left side of his ironform melted to waxy slag by a vicious shot from a vape-gun.

Lotara herself was defying the protective wishes of her personal guard, crouched behind the tertiary weapons console and firing back at the Ultramarines holding the rear of the chamber. Her armsmen guards wore full suits of matt-red carapace armour with rebreathers and rangefinder goggles, and they crouched with her, ringing her with the fiercest loyalty. Lhorke saw her elbow one of them away when he sought to pull her back into cover. She didn't even stop firing.

Of the several hundred crew that populated the strategium, at least three-quarters were dead or close enough not to matter.

Lhorke knew it upon first glance, even without his scrolling auspex-scan feed telling him *Deceased... Deceased... Deceased...* with tracking flickers on every corpse in the room.

The Ultramarines turned away from the abundance of easy prey, sighting Lhorke down their gun barrels as he entered the chamber. Four of them remained, holding the balcony at the strategium's rear, and of these last four, two were down and crippled, firing from where they lay. Even prone, they used their bodies as shields for their brothers crouching behind them.

The body of one other, already slain by massed shotgun and lasfire, lay by the command throne, risen above the charnel house of mortal corpses. Lhorke suspected he'd died inflicting casualties of a hundred to one in this nest of easy murder; butchery to do any legionary proud.

He ignored the cheers from the surviving bridge crew as he started his leaning, limping run. The bridge itself shook beneath his tread, ceiling spotlights shattering to rain glass shards on his etched armour plating. Lotara's cheer was harder to ignore – he heard her swearing in gutter Nagrakali: '*Get these dog-screwing whoresons off my ship!*'

Bolt shells burst against his atomantic shield. A roiling bolt of plasma splashed over it, briefly lighting the energy screen with oily, refracted luminescence, only to dissipate into painless steam. Lhorke took their onslaught head-on, striding up the stairs, joints whirring out a grind-song despite the limp, as he pushed his ironform to move faster, faster.

His shield burst at point-blank range. It died with a final, gasping surge, sending worms of discharging electricity crawling across the power pack mounted on his back. It meant nothing. It meant less than nothing.

He crushed the first crawling Ultramarine beneath his massive foot, crumbling the warrior's ceramite into mangled metal panels and smearing the pulped biological remains across the deck. Bolts clattered against his armour, decorating him in scorch marks, scrambling the delicate circuits of his retinal display yet not quite blanking his vision. Scratches. Flesh wounds, for want of a better term. Lhorke reached for the next two warriors, the combi-bolters in his fists opening up with nasty chatters even as he lunged to smash the enemies aside. He caught them both and started squeezing.

The Ultramarine in his left fist was dead before he clutched him, holed through by the combi-bolter volley. He shook the fresh corpse regardless, its limbs and neck breaking, before it was hurled across the bridge to crash along the deck.

The one in his right hand took several seconds to die, fighting and shouting in fruitless defiance against the slow-closing fingers. With a final meaty crunch, the warrior fell limp and gushed blood from a ruptured body. Lhorke hurled the organic detritus in the same direction as the last.

'You,' he said to the last Ultramarine. A more patient, sonorous threat had never been uttered on the *Conqueror*'s bridge.

The warrior was scrambling back, unable to run with the injuries to his knee and belly. Defiant to the very end, he raised his plasma gun. The magnetic coils glowed, then brightened, then went phosphorous.

Lhorke tore it from the warrior's hand, compressing his iron claws and scrapping the priceless weapon without a thought. Its gathering power erupted in a torrent of liquid blue-white fire, eating into the Dreadnought's arm. Retinal temperature gauges spiked to the accompaniment of warning runes. Lhorke looked through them, reaching down to clutch the Ultramarine's leg as the warrior crawled away.

A twist, a rotation of his wrist servos, and the legionary's spine crackled into worthless bone pebbles. Lhorke tossed the paralysed wretch away, towards a crowd of bridge crew armed with service pistols and unsheathed knives. They descended in a pack, finishing what the Dreadnought had begun.

He heard the Ultramarine scream, but only once. From the pain of being carved apart, rather than fear. Very admirable indeed.

Lhorke walked past the central auspex array table, where a legless young woman, surgically implanted to the scanner machinery around her, was shivering on her augmetic suspension cables. Her eyes were wide, unseeing. How she still lived after being at the eye of the firefight storm, he could only guess. The wires and leads linking her head to the ceiling rattled as she trembled with shock. He almost reached out a hand to comfort her, before recalling just what he was now. Dead men entombed in towering bodies of oil-bleeding iron were not, by and large, a comfort to victims of trauma.

He passed her, limping to where Lotara was rising from cover with her overprotective armsmen.

'Captain Sarrin.'

'Lhorke.' She wiped her forehead with her sleeve, craning her neck to look up at him. She scarcely reached his thigh.

'These were the last.'

'Thank you, Legion Master.'

He almost said *I need to rest*, but caught the slip before it left his speaker grille. 'I will submit myself for repairs,' he said instead, then hesitated. 'With your permission.'

She nodded, seeing the eerie calmness of devastation's aftermath taking hold of her bridge. Somehow, it was worse than the gunfight.

'I have some work to do here.' As if just recalling, she cleared her throat and asked, 'How many of your brothers still walk the decks?'

He performed a vox-relayed calculation, citing vital signs uploaded to his retinal feed. 'Three,' he said. 'Including myself.'

Something like guilt paled her skin. 'Thank you, Lhorke. Convey my thanks to them, as well.'

He bowed – a gesture that didn't come naturally to the Contemptor-class ironform, nor to the warrior bound within this one – and left the bridge in her hands.

DISTRACTION WAS A warrior's worst enemy. More than once, Khârn's gaze snapped to the wealth of inscriptions on Orfeo's armour, unintentionally reading a detail or two. The captain had fought in more campaigns across the Eastern Fringe than Khârn was even aware had taken place. No wonder the XIII claimed five hundred planets as their kingdom.

You couldn't parry a power blade with a chainsword; doing it once was pushing your luck, doing it twice was asking to be disarmed. The energy corona around the former would break the latter apart. Chainblades parried poorly at the best of times, always with the risk of losing teeth if struck at the wrong angle.

The disadvantage of chainsword and gladius would have had Khârn on the defensive, but the ground was thick with corpses and unclaimed weapons. Barely twenty heartbeats had passed before he managed to steal a fallen Ultramarine's power sword. He grinned as he thumbed the activation rune, blinking away the sweat stewing his eyes. Lightning snaked along the silver steel, rippling from the generator in the hilt and dissolving the dusty blood that had dirtied the blade.

They met again, each of them forced to fight as their weapons allowed. Orfeo led with his long sword, cleaving in a series of arcing chops, while using his gladius *main-gauche* to parry more than thrust. As a stabbing weapon, it was worthless without a kill-plunge to the belly.

Khârn had the advantage of reach with his two longer blades, but his chainsword was a fragile boon at best, useless against the captain's reinforced ceramite and already spitting teeth from deflecting the shortsword's infrequent lunges. It was almost amusing how every other warrior avoided them both now, making room for the fight between their commanders. Energy flared each time the two power swords clashed. Khârn lost track of time, focusing everything he had on the battle before him.

'That isn't an axe,' Orfeo laughed at one point. He parried another of Khârn's cuts, and the World Eater heard the smile in the other warrior's voice. 'Look at you with that blade. Always trying the edge. However did you earn your reputation, Khârn? Who trained you to fight as though all foes were lumber to be chopped?'

Khârn lashed back with three cuts, as quick as his burning muscles would allow. Each one *clanged* as it was blocked and turned aside.

'Lhorke,' he said. 'Legion Master of the War Hounds.'

Their blades locked again, and Khârn found himself glad of the moment's respite. He tried to catch his breath, but Orfeo disengaged with a flourishing spin, launching immediately into another barrage of blows.

'Lhorke is dead,' Orfeo voxed from his helm's grille. 'Lhorke died on Jeracau.'

Khârn was backing up now, his footwork fumbling on the tide of corpses beneath his boots. How long had he been fighting? It could have been hours, and he'd believe any man that told him so.

'You run from me, World Eater? The great Khârn, fleeing from a fight?'

The Nails replied before Khârn could. They stabbed into his skull, pulling at the nerves in his brain, sending electrical fire through the blood vessels. He screamed to vent pain, charging in to swing at the advancing Ultramarine. He cut high. Orfeo parried, and cleaved low.

Fresh agony danced a line down Khârn's side, adding a second carving along the wound he'd taken earlier that day. With a grunt, he staggered in a halting spin, bringing his blades down in time to turn back a thrust that would have cored him from spine to belly.

A kick to Orfeo's thigh forced the swordsman to stumble, but Khârn swore as he missed the sweet spot to break the knee. Nevertheless, he took what ease he could get, moving back and casting the defanged chainsword aside. In its absence, he clutched the power blade tighter.

'I was never much of a swordsman.' He tried to say it through a smile, showing no pain, but the Nails turned it into a rictus, pulling at one side of his mouth in quick twitches.

'Brother,' came two voices at once. Khârn dared a glance away from Orfeo.

Argel Tal drew close, wings folding, his spined and calcified armour creaking. Whatever beast lived inside his heart, it made itself known, warping the silver-faced helm to the visage of a flayed skull, then Khârn's own features, then those of Argel Tal himself, giving him a death mask of his own features cast in silver.

More World Eaters closed in, jackal-packs of them, tilting their heads or watching in mute silence. Orfeo seemed not to notice.

'Look around you, captain,' Khârn said quietly, and with gentle respect.

Orfeo did, turning slowly, faced with an army of ragged, bloody XII legionaries standing knee-deep in the blue and white dead. Behind them, scarlet Word Bearers crouched among the corpses and brandished silver knives. Orfeo saw them digging through the fallen, chanting in Colchisian as they cast prophecies in entrails, or leashed war totems together from Ultramarines' carcasses. Wounded survivors were already being dragged for crucifixion against XVII Legion tanks.

'The war is over,' said Argel Tal.

Orfeo turned back to the Legion commanders. 'Do you say so?'

Argel Tal gestured to the lone champion. 'I believe the scene speaks for itself.'

The Ultramarine nodded. 'Then I accept your surrender,' he said.

The World Eaters shared a low laugh.

Orfeo wasn't finished. 'Tell me why you came to this world.'

'To kill it,' replied Khârn.

'To make it suffer,' Argel Tal amended. 'To make the cries of Armatura's population pierce the veil and enrich the warp. It is all part of a great chorus, playing out across your kingdom of Ultramar.'

Orfeo's officer crest wavered as he shook his head. 'Madness.'

'To the ignorant,' Argel Tal allowed. He spoke softly, never threatening, almost regretful. 'But you will shortly see what lies on the Other Side. Your screams will add to the song, as your spirit boils away to oblivion in the Sea of Souls.'

'Madness,' Orfeo said again.

'Your brothers spoke of courage,' interrupted Khârn. 'Courage and honour.'

'And you speak of knowing no fear,' Argel Tal added, his words blending with Khârn's. 'Yet Macraggian poetry has always felt foul on the tongue.'

Orfeo looked between the ragged form of Khârn and the vicious thing Argel Tal had become. He pulled his helm free, breathed in the choking reek of his burning world, and lifted his gladius for the last time. It hissed as Khârn's blood baked on the live blade.

'Enough talk, traitors. Come, learn the price of setting foot on the Five Hundred Worlds. Live or die, it will spare me from your preaching.'

Argel Tal stepped forwards, but Khârn warned him back.

'Let me finish this.'

But nearby legionaries were shoved aside by a taller, bulkier figure approaching. The primarch was lacerated by a hundred wounds he did not feel.

'No,' Angron breathed through sticky teeth. 'Let me.'

ELEVEN

The End of Armatura
Triarii
Homecoming

'I WILL REMEMBER these screams until my dying day.'

The toneless quality of Argel Tal's voices suggested neither disgust nor pleasure, but a perspective detached from both. If anything, he sounded weary.

The Word Bearer was himself again, the silver death-mask gone, his wings melted back into the ceramite of his armour. One moment he'd walked with Khârn through the dead and the dying in what his Legion whisperingly revered as his 'divine form'. The next, Khârn had been walking alongside his brother as he knew him before Isstvan.

Just how and when the Change took hold of the Word Bearer was something Khârn couldn't quite grasp. Sometimes it seemed slow, sometimes it happened in the span of a blink. Sometimes it was subtle, other times overt enough that there seemed little left of the warrior Khârn admired beneath the slavering thing in Argel Tal's armour.

The Word Bearer removed his helm, closing his pale eyes for a moment and breathing in the taste of the charred air. It smelled of victory, but that was a laughable truth. Victory and defeat smelled the same – it never mattered which side's tanks were burning and whose blood had flowed. Death still assaulted the same senses in the same ways.

The screaming continued unabated. Khârn had been the first to turn his back on their source, and to his surprise, Argel Tal had been the second. Now they walked together, taking the names of the slain, recording them for the necrologists.

'Your men do worse,' Khârn pointed out. He gestured as they made their way through the plaza, where the two Legions were dealing with the distasteful duty of finishing the fight. The World Eaters were mercy-killing any survivors among their fallen foes. The Word Bearers were dragging injured Ultramarines towards scarlet tanks and gunships, to be taken back into orbit and dealt with away from prying eyes. Arguments over the choicest wounded were breaking out between the warriors in white and those in red, but the presence of their commanders restored a semblance of discipline.

'Worse is a matter of perspective,' Argel Tal replied.

Captain Orfeo's screams rose above the combined cries and moans of all the other Ultramarines currently being mutilated and sawn apart by XVII Legion knives.

Khârn looked over a gladius he'd acquired from amongst the dead. 'Why does that one warrior's agony distress you, given what your men are doing here? Why is it that his fate leaves you sneering?'

'You will not like the answer, brother,' said Argel Tal, recording the name of another fallen Word Bearer as he did. 'Don't make me speak it.'

'Speak it, anyway. For the sake of the next time we're chained together in the pits.'

'Deal with him first.' Argel Tal gestured to a fallen World Eater, clad in the colours of a sergeant. 'Blood of the True, is that Gharte?'

Khârn moved to the corpse, atop a loose mound of three Ultramarines. Damn it. It *was* Gharte.

Khârn crouched by the body, lifting the sergeant's head in his hands and gently turning the helm this way and that. He had no idea where his own helmet was. He'd been breathing in the gritty air for so long that, despite the genetic enhancements done to his respiration, Armatura's taste was a smoky itch in the back of his throat.

'Captain,' the wounded warrior voxed. 'I can't move.'

Gharte had no legs below his mid-thighs – Khârn couldn't begin to guess where they were in this sea of mangled corpses – and his chest was a ruin of violated breastbone and ceramite.

'Bide,' he said, lowering the warrior's helm. 'Kargos will come.'

The warrior gripped Khârn's collar with weak fingers. 'The Nails are aflame, even now.' He coughed something wet into his helm. 'How can that be? I'm dying, and they still sing? What do they want from me?'

'Bide,' Khârn said again, though he knew it was useless.

'Just give me the Peace.' The warrior sank back to the ground. 'Seventy years of serving the Butcher and his Nails is long enough.'

Khârn wished he'd not heard those words. Discomfort danced its tingling way down his backbone.

'You served well, Gharte.' Khârn disengaged the seals at the warrior's throat, lifting the helm clear. There wasn't much left of the sergeant's face. Something must have reflected in Khârn's expression, for Gharte made his devastated face into something like a grin.

'That bad, eh?' he asked. His gurgling laughter became another cough.

Khârn's reply was solemn obedience. He held the gladius above Gharte's left eye, its point a finger's breadth above the dilated pupil.

'Any last words?'

'Aye. Piss on Angron's grave when he finally lies dead.'

Khârn wished he'd not heard those words, either.

He rammed the blade down, with the sound of dry twigs

breaking beneath a boot, and the faintest *clink* of the point striking the stone under Gharte's head.

He rose after it, hearing Argel Tal speaking to another of the fallen.

'Greetings,' the Word Bearer said, pressing a boot onto an Ultramarine's chestplate. The warrior clawed useless scrapes against Argel Tal's leg. 'Even in death, you still fight. So defiant, Evocatus? You should have worn Dorn's yellow.'

Khârn drew nearer. 'I'll end him.'

'No.'

The World Eater shook his head at Argel Tal's refusal. 'How can you hold such a depth of hatred for this Legion? Their backs are broken. They suffer as the Ravens and Salamanders suffered on the killing fields. Isn't that enough? Is your sore pride still not avenged?'

'Hate them?' Argel Tal looked up, confusion slowly giving way to humour. 'That's what you think? Why would I hate the Ultramarines, Khârn?'

'Monarchia. Your humiliation, kneeling before Guilliman.'

Argel Tal's eyes glittered in amusement. Khârn was less sure of his words with each passing second.

'Do you hate the Wolves,' Argel Tal asked, 'for descending upon you?'

'That's different.' The World Eater bared his teeth. 'We weren't humiliated. The Wolves didn't win.'

'No? I heard a different tale. I heard it was Russ who howled in triumph when dawn brought the Night of the Wolf to an end.'

'Lies.' Khârn barked a nasty laugh. 'Lies and slander.'

They regarded each other a moment, before Argel Tal cracked the ghost of a smile. 'Thousands of the Legion detested the Ultramarines. Lorgar ordered many of us to gather when we were already en route to Calth. I, and the others who would become commanders and apostles among the Vakrah Jal. He wanted our counsel on what to do with those among the Legion he no longer trusted. Our Legion culled its ranks in a trickle down the decades, but nothing like the Isstvan Atrocity that Angron is so proud of. Lorgar knew loyalty within the Word Bearers was never in doubt. *Competence* was a different matter.'

Even Khârn was ignoring the struggling Ultramarine now. He was silent as Argel Tal continued.

'Lord Aurelian asked what we should do with the warriors he felt were no longer reliable. Those whose hatred burned brighter than their sense. Tens of thousands of them, Khârn. Whole companies. Whole *Chapters*. Their rage was no longer pure.'

'You killed them?'

'Not directly. We gave them the mission they craved. They sailed with Erebus and Kor Phaeron, to martyr themselves in glory.'

'You can't be serious,' said Khârn.

'As serious as the wasteland this world has become. Your Legion was purged on Isstvan III, brother. Mine was purged at Calth.'

'But we've had word from Calth. The Seventeenth won. *You* won.'

'Victory is a matter of perspective.' He scowled at Khârn's expression. 'I don't understand why treachery is so unpalatable to you. You have no sense of honour to offend. You took part in the annihilation of a quarter of your own Legion-brothers, now you act affronted we allow ours to kill themselves in a sacred crusade.'

The Word Bearer looked down at the Ultramarine he was pinning to the churned earth. 'I don't hate the Thirteenth Legion, Khârn. The *Emperor* forced us to our knees, not Guilliman. Here and now, their suffering is symbolic and serves a higher purpose. Nothing more, nothing less.'

Khârn watched the fallen Space Marine scratching at Argel Tal's greaves. 'This torture is childish. What will one man's pain add to the song?'

'Everything,' Argel Tal sounded distant, staring down at the cobalt-clad warrior. 'Each moment of agony is a note in the melody.'

'Enough preaching, brother. Save the mysticism for those in your Legion's red. Just kill the poor wretch.'

He expected a weary sigh and a grudging refusal. Instead, Argel

Tal drew his spear. The Word Bearer's grip on its haft was enough to quicken the blade, generating the aura of killing lightning. With a simple downward thrust, he planted the halberd through the Ultramarine's chest.

The warrior quivered and fell still, giving one last jerk when his killer wrenched the spear free.

'Mercy suits you,' Khârn told Argel Tal. 'Slaughter is one thing, torture is another. Leave that to your Chaplains.'

'Mercy is for the weak,' the Word Bearer replied.

'Then what does it make you, when I've witnessed you being merciful?'

Argel Tal scratched at the dark skin of his cheek. Stubble was growing there in a faint black shadow. He looked ever more like the desertborn boy-turned-warrior.

'I have never pretended to be anything but weak, Khârn. I don't enjoy war, yet I fight. I don't relish torture, yet I inflict it. I don't revere the gods, yet I serve their holy purpose. Humanity's weakest souls will always cling to the words *"I was just following orders"*. They cower behind those words, making a virtue of their own weakness, lionising brutality over nobility. I know that when I die, I'll have lived my whole life shrouded by that same excuse.'

Khârn swallowed. 'So will I. So will any Space Marine.'

Argel Tal looked at him, as if that proved his point.

They moved on, eyes raking the ground in casual discontent. Neither relished this task, but both refused to leave it solely to their men. Neither officer would give orders they weren't prepared to carry out themselves.

As they walked and murdered with mercy, Khârn watched the Word Bearers at work. Historically, the Legions rarely indulged in taking prisoners, but here was another excess of the new age. In contrast to their ascetic reputation, the Word Bearers now embraced every opportunity to herd the wounded into their cargo holds. A prisoner had a thousand uses beyond mere servitude in the slave decks.

Warriors of the XVII wrote parchment transcriptions of the *Book of Lorgar* in the blood of captured enemies. They decorated their armour with trinkets of scrimshawed bone and flayed skin. Cloaks of human leather were commonplace, many of which also served as fine tableaus for illuminated scripture. Horns of brass, bronze and ivory rose from the legionaries' helms, cutting stark shadows against the candlelit walls aboard their voidships.

As Khârn drew breath to speak again, Orfeo's distant screams reached a crescendo. He saw Argel Tal cringe.

'What's wrong with you?'

'Your primarch is insane,' replied the Word Bearer. 'Worse, he's dying.'

Khârn stopped walking. 'What?'

Several legionaries turned to watch their officers. Argel Tal kept walking, knowing Khârn would follow. Sure enough, he was right.

'Angron is killing that captain so horrifically because a mechanical parasite is stunting the function of his brain. My Legion inflicts suffering because pain serves a metaphysical purpose. It pleases the Pantheon. It shows devotion and invites their favour. Suffering is sacred to them. Pain is prayer.'

Khârn listened, eyes narrowed at the irrelevancy. 'Angron is not dying,' he said.

'You don't need me to tell you that he is. You've said yourself, he's getting worse. What, pray tell, is the logical conclusion at the end of that degeneration?'

'Has Lorgar told you this?'

'Lorgar tells me almost nothing anymore. He's distracted by the great song. He hears it more clearly than he hears any of our voices, even when we stand next to him.'

The World Eater narrowed his eyes again. 'Do *you* hear it?'

'The warp's tune? No. I hear Cyrene when I sleep. She dies every night in my dreams, but I never hear the holy hymn. That gift is my primarch's alone. He shared it with me once, letting me sense a fragment of what he hears. The music underlying reality. The sound made by every soul that is now and that ever was.'

For once, Khârn felt no inclination to draw back from such superstitious talk. 'And what was it like?'

Argel Tal took a slow breath. 'Like Orfeo sounds now. Only worse.'

Khârn didn't look back the way they'd come. Orfeo's screams still echoed over the battlefield.

The Word Bearer spoke on, his voice more sibilant than deep; more daemon than man. Liquid silver began to bubble in the sockets where his eyes had been.

'The warp around this world is boiling, Khârn. The amount of suffering taking place across its cities is enough to draw the Four gods' eyes. And how many other worlds in Ultramar share this fate? How many more, before we call our crusade complete? This isn't conjecture, nor is it blind faith. Soon we will push the surviving population into skinning pits and then heap them onto funeral pyres while they still breathe. The true Pantheon will watch, and smile, and bless us for our devotion. All that suffering, Khârn. All that pain.'

Khârn halted to ram his gladius through the neck of a crawling Ultramarine. 'So you keep saying, but the heavens *aren't* burning in a warp storm.'

'Not yet.' Argel Tal's eyes still shimmered, mercury-wet.

'I am weary of your Legion claiming sadism as a holy virtue.'

Something in Khârn's voice made Argel Tal glance over at him. The silver dried, hardened, and flaked away. His own eyes looked back at Khârn.

'Don't mock me,' the Word Bearer said. 'I didn't *ask* for this to be the underlying Truth to existence. I take no pleasure in offering agony in worship to gods that cannot be ignored and yet do not deserve to exist. But life isn't what we wish it to be. Or do you actually *want* that neural implant squatting like a spider upon the cobwebbing blood vessels of your brain?'

They stared at one another for a long moment, until both broke into low chuckles. The tension dissipated, as simple as that. It had always been this way between them, since they'd found themselves knocked onto the deck within seconds of their first pit-fight. Their Legions couldn't be more different, but they shared a bleak amusement at being carried along by the storm.

Argel Tal gently kicked a downed Ultramarine and moved on when the body remained a corpse.

'Sometimes I ask myself how we reached this point,' he said. 'Fighting ignorance and slavery with genocide. We can either live in delusion and darkness, or become something we hate. My nights are haunted by the shrieking of a blind girl I failed to save, and a warrior with a mechanical parasite in his skull and the daemon wrapped around my soul are my closest brothers.' He smiled wearily. 'We're definitely on the wrong side, Khârn.'

'How can you say that?'

'Because both sides are wrong.'

Captain Sarrin met them on the deck. They'd wanted to come up with *Syrgalah*, riding in the salvage ship with her wounded form rather than coming ahead on a personnel shuttle. But a summons was a summons.

Lotara intercepted them as they disembarked, practically running to the gang-ramp. Servitors and cowled Mechanicum adepts moved aside for her, recognising her from her uniform, or the Blood Hand on her chest. World Eaters were spilling from their gunships elsewhere in a stomping tide of filthy ceramite. The hangar smelled of fyceline and the chalky scent of urban ruin.

'Keeda,' she said. 'Tell me the reports are wrong.'

Keeda still wore her crew overalls, with her visored helmet clipped to the side of her belt. She supported Toth, whose head was bandaged in clean linen.

'Captain.' Toth gave an awkward salute. The brash manufactory sounds of the *Conqueror*'s hangar were already playing havoc with his sore skull. The heatwashes from engines powering down didn't help, either.

'Just tell me,' Lotara said.

'He's dead,' admitted Keeda. '*Syrgalah* is down. The old man died with her.'

Lotara covered her mouth with both hands. Not given to dramatic displays of emotion, she still needed a moment to catch her breath.

'Moderati Bly,' said a voice from behind her. 'Moderati Kol. I'll take your report at once.'

The three of them turned to the speaker. He was short, rounded by sloth, with a widow's peak of dark hair thinning above two bionic eyes. His machine eyes clicked and whirred as they refocused, looking between the two crew members. He favoured Lotara with a slightly more respectful 'Captain', followed by a crisp salute.

'Princeps Penultima,' Lotara greeted him in return.

'Penultima no longer. Remember to update your archives, captain. With the passing of Venric Solostine, I am Princeps Ultima of Legio Audax.'

'What you are, Audun, is an officious little shit grabbing for the old man's rank pins before his bones are even cold.'

The portly Titan officer stood straighter. 'We all mourn the loss of Princeps Solostine, flag-captain. I will let your emotional outburst pass unrecorded, but please address me with the respect due my rank in the future.'

Lotara was already ignoring him, her eyes on Keeda and Toth. 'I'm glad you made it off that bloody rock. Will *Syrgalah* walk again?'

'I think so,' said Keeda.

'She's in a bad way,' Toth confessed.

'So are you.' Lotara forced a smile. 'Good luck with the *Ember Queen*. I'll make sure she's brought up with all honours, and granted priority docking.'

Audun Lyrac cleared his throat. 'Whether she walks again or not depends on salvageability.'

Keeda went pale. Toth grunted something obscene. Lotara rounded on the new lord of the Legio Audax, but her words were drowned out by the howling engines of an incoming Stormcrow gunship. Its forward-swept wings cast a vulture's shadow on the deck.

'...my ship,' Lotara finished over the quieting engines. 'Is that clear?'

'Uh, perfectly, ma'am.' Audun drummed his thick fingers on his uniformed belly. He'd heard maybe one word in ten, but it didn't pay to push the flag-captain's temper.

Lotara looked pointedly at the two Titan crew members. 'I want complete copies of your reports. If I don't get them, I'll know why.'

Toth nodded, and Keeda smiled. 'Aye, ma'am.'

'Good. Now go to the apothecarion and get Toth patched up.' She stepped back, making way for them. Just as she turned to begin the long journey back to the bridge, she noticed just who was leaving the Stormcrow. The warrior's crested helm marked him out above his brethren, but she'd have known him purely from the bronze versions of the XII Legion symbol on both of his shoulder guards.

She watched him as he descended the gang-ramp into the hangar, his walk assured, his grace undeniable, his arrogance unbounded. He spoke to his companions, ignoring the human serfs and hangar crew going about their business around him.

Very calmly, Lotara Sarrin drew her laspistol, took aim, and shot a World Eaters captain in the face.

His head snapped back from the las-beam's impact, and she had a momentary flush of pleasure at scoring a truly wicked shot, before the World Eaters circled their captain and raised their bolters, aiming across the crowded hangar deck.

There was, very distinctly, just long enough for Lotara to think *they won't shoot,* before they shot. She saw the flare of muzzle flashes as their guns kicked in their fists. Time didn't slow down as she'd been led to believe by the war-sagas. She barely had time to blink before the bolts detonated in the air not six metres from her face, spraying her with burning, stinging shrapnel.

Serfs and thralls were scattering with the same haste as cockroaches fleeing a sudden light. She stood dumbstruck for one of the first times in her life, unsure why she was still alive, yet more annoyed they'd dared to shoot her aboard her own ship.

Another World Eater moved to stand by her side, his hand raised to ward off further attack from the captain's bodyguards. He spoke a single word, soft and low.

'Enough.'

The others weren't listening, and the captain wasn't dead. He came to his feet, storming towards her at the head of nine of his brothers. A meteor hammer rattled loose on its chain, hanging from his right fist.

'You puling little whore,' he snarled down at her. 'How dare you?' He pulled the weapon back, activating its spiked head, meaning to wipe her from the face of the deck. Lotara spat at his boots, but the World Eater at her side took another step forwards, preventing the two of them from coming to blows.

'I said *enough*.' He kept his hand raised, warning them back. 'Stand down, Delvarus.'

The Triarii captain turned his grim-faced helm towards the Codicier, eye lenses gleaming. 'You have no authority over me, Esca. The bitch shot me. Get out of my way.'

'That,' Esca replied patiently, 'will not be happening. Move away.'

The other Triarii pulled steel, as another three World Eaters came to stand by Lotara. She looked up at them, each of them a full head and a half taller than her. All three wore Destroyers' black.

'Problem, captain?' said the sergeant, in a voice laced by vox-corruption.

Delvarus pointed at the mortal woman in the middle of the towering pack of legionaries. 'She–'

'I wasn't asking you, Captain Delvarus. I was asking Captain Sarrin.' He looked down at her, his empty grenade bandolier *clanking* against his chestplate.

'Nothing I can't handle, Skane. But you're welcome to stay anyway.'

More Triarii were arriving to swell the ranks of those around

Delvarus. The captain's cloak was ruined from the surface war, but he imperiously cast its ragged remnants over one shoulder.

'This doesn't concern either of you,' he said. 'Sergeant, Codicier, you're dismissed.'

They ignored him. Lotara spat on his boots again. 'You abandoned the ship, Delvarus. That's dereliction of duty. Every life we lost in that boarding action is blood on your hands.'

He laughed down at her. 'You were *boarded*? When I left the ship, the fight was a foregone conclusion. How did you manage to get boarded, Lotara?'

She smiled, the sweetest knife of a smile. 'Would you prefer I took this to the primarch?'

'Aye, perhaps I would. You think he'll even care? He barely knows who he is, any more. Dereliction of duty may be a grave threat to an Ultramarine, but we're a little more grounded in the realities of war. Now get out of my face, girl. I'll let this insult pass once. Try it again, and I'll give your skull to my artificers as a pot for night soil.'

More legionaries gathered on both sides. 'This looks entertaining,' said Kargos, moving next to Skane. 'Have we missed something?'

'She shot me,' Delvarus said.

Kargos snorted, sounding suspiciously like a snigger. There was a similar bark of vox-chuckling from Skane's augmetic throat.

'Well, I'm sure you deserved it,' the Apothecary said.

'You aren't funny, Kargos.'

Kargos was still grinning, iron teeth on show. 'Maybe not, but you are. Getting shot on your own hangar deck? I only wish we still had remembrancers around to record that in your archives of personal heroism.'

Delvarus gave a snort of derision and turned away. 'I'm done with this idiocy.'

'Stand your ground, soldier.'

The Triarii captain halted, and turned with a feline and somehow amused slowness, to regard the woman who'd addressed him.

'What is it, Lotara?'

'You will address me as *Captain Sarrin*. And you are confined to your arming chamber until I say otherwise. Discipline exists even if you consider yourself above it, Delvarus.'

'Enough, girl. You're still alive. The ship's still in one piece.'

She stepped from the protection of Skane, Esca and Kargos, until she was right before the Triarii, staring up at him with narrowed eyes. Her head reached his chestplate. Barely.

'We lost over two thousand crew to the Thirteenth Legion's bolters, you stupid whoreson. The Ultramarines knew where to board us, and where to strike. *Two thousand men and women dead* because you wanted to chase glory down there in the dust. Not slave-deck dregs and war fodder, Delvarus. Trained, vital crew from the command and primary enginarium decks. We sustained enough internal damage over several systems that the *Conqueror* won't function fully until she's been drydocked for a month or more. Am I making myself clear, you arrogant swine? You have your orders. Now get out of my sight.'

For a moment, it looked as though he'd refuse. In the end, Delvarus inclined his head in a nod, saluted her with a fist over his heart, and led his men away.

'I'm going back to the bridge,' she told Esca. 'Thank you for doing… whatever it is you did. With the bolt shells, I mean.'

The Librarian bowed, his ravaged and restitched face in its usual hideous calm. 'Hunt well, captain.'

She looked around the battle-damaged crowd of World Eaters around her, with their weapons in their hands. How many people had died with a scene just like this as the last thing they ever saw?

'Thank you, all of you.' They each nodded, only dispersing once she walked away.

On one of the gantries overlooking the hangar deck, a figure three times the height of a legionary stood in contemplative silence, still the way only statues and corpses can be, for he was a little of both. He watched and learned, and in knowing, he began to plan.

Perhaps sensing something, the Codicier Esca turned and looked up at the secondary loading platform, where Lhorke stood alone. He raised a hand in greeting to the former Legion Master.

Lhorke returned it, raising his iron fist.

FOR A TIME, the Chaplain lay in the gloom, recovering from the trauma of transit. His abiding memory was of a sun's death, shrieking its radiation across the void, painting a whole world with poison. Despite the chill bathing his body, the thought brought forth a sense of contentment. It was good to serve. It was even better to serve well.

He lay there, with his heartbeat serving as a metronome for the passing of time. When the shakes abated, he rose to his feet, casting cursory glances over his undamaged armour. Even his parchment scrolls were intact. An omen?

Yes. Surely.

A good omen.

The grilled deck *clanked* beneath his boots as he made his way through the arched halls of the *Fidelitas Lex*. The first menials he saw were two slaves in Legion tunics, whispering in an alcove, sharing smuggled power packs. The trivialities of mortal life and the human communities aboard the warship meant nothing to him. Even so, he was polite and reserved. The application of violence to reach one's ends should be used as a scalpel, not a bludgeon.

They heard his armour, his bootsteps, and tried to run. He stopped them with his measured, considerate voice. No sense harming them. All he needed was the date.

'Wait,' he asked them. 'What is the flagship's chronometric count?'

They told him, and he felt the press of tension ebbing. Calth was no more than a week ago. Good. Very good.

It was evidently their turn to speak, for the two cowering slaves abased themselves, praying to him as the messenger of the gods. One of them risked a beating by touching the holy Word inked onto parchment and bound to the Dark Apostle's armour.

He let them live unharmed. He even blessed them in the names of the Four, and wished them long and faithful lives.

'Thank you, great one,' whispered the first.

'May the gods bless you,' the second wept. 'My Lord Erebus.'

TWELVE

A Legion's Leaders
My Brother, My Enemy
Salt the Earth

THE FOUR GATHERED together in the Peregrinus Basilica, with the three coming straight from Armatura to join the one who had prayed among the stars. The fleet drifted above them, spreading out in high orbit now the battle was over. Debris littered the void, still a danger to navigation, and the armada's captains pulled their vessels back to avoid collisions with the graveyard of Ultramarines hulks.

Lorgar was out of his armour, clad in a hooded red robe – a simple garment, woven from the silk of Colchisian desert worms, sporting no decoration or embellishment. The priests from before the tempestuous faith wars of Lorgar's homeworld had worn something similar. The hood was raised, leaving his features in soft shadow.

Angron, Khârn and Argel Tal still wore their battle armour – each suit emitting the unhealthy crackles and fuzzes of abused servos. The knee joint of the primarch's bronze gladiatorial wargear sparked when he put weight on it. Khârn's white armour was stained grey by dust and dirt, with frequent splotches of gore marking the ceramite in placidly hypnotic dappling. Argel Tal's armour bore the same bruises, though the holy scarlet hid the damage far better. He kept moving his arm, bending the elbow with a nasty grind of fibre-bundle cabling, to keep the joint from seizing.

The formality seen so often in other Legions was absent, here. On a golden plaque by the chamber's black iron altar, Colchisian runes stated in elegant script: *'Here all stand equal beneath the gaze of the gods.'*

Lorgar passed among the bookshelves, letting his fingers stroke over the spines of the leatherbound books in their neat rows.

Argel Tal and Khârn shared a look; Lorgar's hand was pale skin turned golden by runic tattoos once more. No sign of the plasma burns marked his flesh.

'Twenty-six worlds have fallen,' said the Bearer of the Word to his brother, his son, his nephew. 'Armatura was one of the last. The others, it seems, can be accounted as the warp delaying our fleets. But the numbers begin to reach us now and this is where we stand. Twenty-six worlds slain, their populations butchered, their pain manifesting as prayer in the Empyrean.'

Angron glanced up, his bloodshot eyes not soothed by the dark, nor by the slow dance of the two Legions' ships above.

'What of Calth?'

'Calth makes twenty-seven,' Lorgar amended.

'No.' The World Eater's struggle to concentrate was like a war being waged across his ruined face. A war fought in twitches and tics and slow, low growls. 'No, I mean the storm. You said there was a warp storm at Calth. It isn't spreading like you promised.'

Lorgar continued reading the books' spines as he walked. 'The song hasn't yet reached its crescendo, but clearly the analogy is lost on you. Imagine instead that all of this slaughter as a monument. A pyramid. It won't be complete until the capstone is placed. Only then will it point to the stars.'

Angron grunted in annoyance. Khârn sighed.

'Fine, fine,' Lorgar chuckled. 'In terms a child would understand? Everything we do here reverberates through the warp, but a veil still divides our realities. A ritualised supplication will release the energies we are harnessing, opening the way for the warp to spill through into the material realm. At Calth, Erebus and Kor Phaeron killed a sun to serve as their ritual's capstone. When enough of the Five Hundred Worlds burn, I will fashion a capstone of my own. But it must be much, much grander than the slow death of Calth.'

He held up a healed finger, silencing their questions before they could be voiced. 'Don't ask what, for I don't yet know. A death of monumentally symbolic importance, most likely.'

Angron grinned at the idea. 'How casually you speak of destruction now. Horus would be proud.'

Lorgar's reply was a polite smile.

'What next, my lord?' asked Argel Tal. His dual voices behaved strangely in the cathedral. The near-human voice, resonant and low, echoed around the chamber. The daemon's purring hiss did not.

'We divide the fleet again. Once we've recovered our forces and materiel from the surface of Armatura, and once the population's remains are consecrated according to the patterns of the Pantheon, we will move on to the next world. But we will no longer need this armada. The *Blessed Lady* and the *Trisagion* are fleets unto themselves and no world in all of Ultramar is defended like Armatura. With the war-world dead, we are free to move in smaller fleets.'

'And then?' Angron pushed.

'And then, my brother, we will simply do it all over again.'

The World Eater clacked his teeth, biting the air. 'With your kingships and our two Legions, we could simply kill Macragge.'

'True,' Lorgar conceded. 'Though I'd ask why that would even matter. The XIII recruits from everywhere across the Five Hundred Worlds. Macragge's death would be meaningless symbolism. There's also the matter of Guilliman himself. He already sails the stars in pursuit of us, you know. My astropathic choir sings of Calth's retribution, riding the warp's wind.'

Khârn finally spoke up. 'Killing Macragge will do nothing. It is merely one world among the Five Hundred.

'But it's a symbol,' said Argel Tal. 'I agree with Lord Angron. We should annihilate Macragge next.'

'It's a waste of time,' Khârn replied. 'A symbol of what? What will its death prove that Calth and Armatura have not? Calth was a symbol of hope for the future – Armatura was their most heavily defended bastion-world for training and recruitment. We've proved any point we needed to make, and smashed any symbols that matter. If we need to kill populated worlds, then so be it. We have thirty fleets laying waste to Ultramar, let's not exalt Macragge as anything more than a distant globe of uninspiring rock.'

Angron looked back to Lorgar, a sliver of drool marking the edge of his mouth. 'Just cast your damn spell,' he told his brother. 'Shroud Ultramar in the chaos you promised. Spread the storm and be done with this foolish magic.'

Lorgar winced. 'If you ever say the words *spell* or *magic* in my presence again, Angron, I may have to kill you for unforgivable ignorance. We are dealing with the metaphysics that underpin reality – the very foundations of creation – not the capering of fools conjuring coins from behind children's ears.'

The World Eaters primarch pulled a book from the closest shelf and fanned the pages, not reading a word. 'We are dealing,' he said flatly, 'with foolish mysticism.'

Lorgar's irritated smile was visible beneath his hood. 'Listen and learn.'

He spoke a single word, scarcely more than a whisper, but it threw Angron and the others from their feet with a hurricane-blast of wind. Three bookshelves exploded, quite literally blasting apart in a storm of splintered wood and powdered parchment. Khârn managed to arrest his skidding tumble by jamming his fingertips between two marble flagstones. Argel Tal and Angron crashed past him, their armour shedding sparks as they scraped over the cream-coloured stone.

The wind from nowhere vanished as suddenly as it arrived. Khârn was first to his feet.

'I-I know that tongue,' he said to Lorgar.

'I doubt that, Khârn,' replied the primarch with surprising gentleness.

'Argel Tal spoke it,' he said, 'on Armatura.'

'Ah. Then you do know something of its power.' Lorgar waited until his brother and son rejoined them from across the chamber. 'That, my brother, is what I mean. Reality obeys certain laws. Gravity. Electromagnetism. The nuclear forces. Cause and effect. If I breathe in, my body converts air into life, unless I am too weak or diseased for the process to continue. There are millions of laws that are unknown to all but the most enlightened. Magnus knows many more than even I, but I have learned enough. It is not *magic*.' He fairly sneered the word. 'It is manipulation of the infinite potential that is the source of *all* realities. A blending of components from the universe of flesh and blood and the divine realm of pure aether and emotion.'

Angron was silent several moments, his brutal face troubled.

'That noise you made,' he said finally. 'That "word". What was it?'

'It is for the best that I do not speak it again,' said Lorgar, smiling sardonically. 'The books I just destroyed were very valuable, and I'd rather not lose more of them.'

Seeing his brother's expression, Lorgar's smile became more sincere. 'Some words and sounds shake the foundations of reality. For example, the concept and sound of a hundred and one blind men choking and gasping as they all drown at the same time serves as the name of a certain daemonic princeling. Compressing that noise and its meaning into a single sound can be enough to draw that entity's attention and render it easier to summon. The word I just spoke was… similar. I see the question in your eyes, and yes, I can teach you this tongue.'

Khârn spoke without meaning to. 'That's how you've healed yourself.'

Lorgar nodded, though he didn't pull the hood back. 'It is. The pain, however, was indescribable. Were I mortal in the usual sense I'd be dead from the attempt alone. Reknitting skin and muscle meat is easy enough in principle, but everything comes at a price.'

Lorgar took the tome from Angron and placed it back on one of the surviving bookshelves.

'We are about to be interrupted.'

They all turned as the great double doors opened. The figure that entered wore the ashen black of the XVII Legion's Chaplains and carried a silver crozius in one hand. His helm was held in the crook of his other arm, leaving his scholarly, solemn features bare. Helmetless, he couldn't entirely hide his surprise when he saw who stood with his primarch.

'My lord,' said the newcomer, bowing deeply to Lorgar.

'Erebus.' Lorgar beckoned him closer. 'The suffering of Calth's sun and the millions who died on the world itself rings through the warp. The secret song heralded your deeds.'

'I am pleased, lord.' Erebus offered Angron a respectful bow; Khârn and Argel Tal received glances and nods. 'Calth succeeded beyond all expectation.'

Lorgar bared a thin crescent of porcelain-white teeth in a subtle smile. 'Success *beyond* expectation? Truly? Then I would ask, if this is the case, why does the warp's melody not sing of such an outcome?'

Erebus's stern eyes flickered to the others gathered by his primarch. 'We should speak, my lord.'

'We *are* speaking, Erebus.'

Again, the flickered glance. 'Alone, sire. What we speak of may not be for... the uninitiated.'

Lorgar smiled, the expression as paternal and patient as any living soul had ever been and could ever be. 'Just speak, First Chaplain.'

They all saw it. The moment Erebus stood straighter, guarding himself, sensing something was wrong. Angron grinned at the warrior-priest's discomfort. Khârn and Argel Tal stood in resolute silence.

'The Ruinstorm is born,' Erebus stated.

'Yes,' replied Lorgar. 'But tell me of this grand success you spoke of. And where is your ship, Erebus? Where is *Destiny's Hand*?' Lorgar looked heavenwards, where the fleet lay at rest in the black sky. 'Strange that I cannot see it.'

Erebus smiled, his thin lips paling as they pressed together. 'I believe she sails with Kor Phaeron and the *Infidus Imperator*.'

'Of course. And Kor Phaeron no doubt orbits Calth in victory, yes? He has sacrificed my brother Guilliman to the Pantheon, has he not?'

'Sire–'

'Calm, Erebus. I only wish to share this moment of triumph with you. So. Calth has fallen, the Ultramarines are finished and Guilliman is dead. That was, after all, the expectation of success that you claim to have exceeded. So you are to be commended. I've been worried that you'd failed to kill my brother, lost half the fleet I granted you to an Ultramarines counter-attack, and abandoned tens of thousands of my sons and mortal servants on Calth's irradiated surface while you fled into the Maelstrom.'

Erebus swallowed and said nothing.

'But that would be leaving them to die,' Lorgar continued. 'Never to be reinforced. Never to be recovered. All those Gal Vorbak who spent months of their lives fasting, praying, scarring their flesh in preparation for a chance to taste the Divine Blood… They'd be lost, wouldn't they?'

Angron was chuckling now, taking a leering amusement in the whole scene.

'Sire…' Erebus began.

Lorgar raised a hand. 'I don't blame you, Erebus. Have no fear. You achieved the base level of success that was required of you.'

'My lord, Kor Phaeron calls for reinforcement.'

The primarch turned his head away, the silk cloth of his hood rippling gently. It took several moments for Khârn to realise Lorgar was laughing.

'Reinforcement,' he chuckled. 'The very idea.'

'The Ultramarines are pursuing our survivors.'

Lorgar returned his gaze to his son's rigid face.

'I'm sure they are. That's what happens when you run away – your enemies give chase. He is dreaming if he believes I'll whore ships and lives away to save him from a fate he worked so hard to earn. When next you speak with him, convey my regards and inform him that my lack of sympathy is the price of his failure. You're dismissed now, Erebus.'

'Sire,' Erebus said for the third time, bolstering his resolve. 'We still have much to discuss. What of Signus Prime?'

'That name again.' Lorgar's gold-flecked eyes narrowed. 'I care nothing for Signus Prime. It is a fool's errand.'

Erebus's solemn confidence reasserted itself in his half-smile. 'The Warmaster and I are confident–'

'Erebus,' Lorgar interrupted with a sigh. 'You will not kill the Angel. You will not enlighten his Legion. Do you think you know my own brother better than I?'

The Chaplain showed no emotion at all, his austere mask firmly in place. 'Lord, I have walked the paths of the Ten Thousand Futures. I have seen destinies unfolding where the Angel falls, and others where he fights at our side. If we can engineer events to play out according to those paths…'

Lorgar's hood shifted as he shook his head. 'You aren't listening, Erebus.'

'I do nothing *but* listen. I hear the gods as clearly as you do, Aurelian. Or did you forget that?' He spoke the words softly, even kindly, but they rang out across the basilica with the force of a hammer blow.

Argel Tal tensed, feeling his lips peeling back from his lengthening teeth. Ceramite wrenched and squealed as ridged rune-carved bones started pushing through the surface of his armour. Great bat's wings of blue-veined scarlet fleshmetal rose from his shoulder blades, dripping blood-sweat onto the white stone floor.

'You!' he snarled in two voices, the daemon's hiss in clear dominance. 'You *dare?*'

Lorgar sighed and raised a hand.

'No. Argel Tal, Raum, both of you, stay your wrath. Please.'

Wings flexing silently, the lord of the Gal Vorbak glared at Erebus for several heartbeats. Another ugly chuckle from Angron broke the tension.

'As you command, sire,' Argel Tal replied at last, his voices in uneasy balance. The Change receded with the same protestation of cold metal reshaped against its will.

'I will not argue with you, Erebus. I know you, Kor Phaeron and your old friend Calas Typhon cling to your belief that you were enlightened before all others, and are therefore uniquely placed to steer Fate itself. But I will give you this last coin of advice, to take or leave as you will. You *will not* enlighten Sanguinius.'

Lorgar passed a hand through the air before him. An image of a haloed warrior, garbed in blood-bright armour and framed with magnificent wings of the most pristine white, shimmered into existence.

'Look at him and what do you see? An angel. *The* Angel. In a universe that the Emperor claims is godless – in an Imperium where our civilisation's wisest and greatest have dismantled all the trappings of religion – Sanguinius is an icon of something that should not exist, glorious and supernatural. My brother knows this. He feels it. He's too intelligent, too *soulful*, not to.'

Lorgar lowered his head, the shadow of his hood darkening his features down to his chin.

'The Emperor, for all his *many* flaws, knows his sons well. Horus was chosen as Warmaster because he is the best of us. In Horus, all things are found in balance, and yet every facet is raised to excellence. Sanguinius is similar. His virtues eclipse the rest of us, for which of us could match his grace, his compassion, or his understanding of the human condition? And yet our brother is unbalanced. Profoundly so. He represents both the very best *and* the very worst of what it is to be a primarch. He is the noblest of us but also the most fearful; a glorious creature enslaved by insecurities.'

Lorgar gestured again and the glowing image of Sanguinius vanished.

'Oh yes, the Angel is righteous and he is strong and he is beautiful in practically every way. But he has a cancerous weakness in his heart – a weakness known to only a few of us. Sanguinius is loyal to our father out of perfect love and perfect nobility, and if that were all, he might still be turned or killed as you so desire, my son. But what you fail to consider is that he is also loyal out of perfect fear. He fears the reason he has wings. He fears what they might represent. He fears something went terribly wrong during his creation and he fears the effects this may have upon his own gene-sons.'

Angron watched Lorgar with undisguised fascination, the Nail-induced fire in his skull momentarily forgotten. Erebus maintained a resolute silence.

'The insecurity that binds Sanguinius to the Emperor, perhaps more so than any other of our father's sons, is that he believes he has the most to prove.'

Lorgar looked down to the smooth, gold-inked skin of his hands and exhaled softly. 'And yet, in comparison with the rest of us, that simply is not the case.'

With eyes that glinted from beneath his hood, the lord of the Word Bearers returned his gaze to Erebus. 'Listen to me now, if never before. You and Kor Phaeron are investing too heavily in fools' gambits. I know Kor Phaeron sought to illuminate Guilliman rather than slay him as ordered. His failure echoed through the warp: a discordant note in an already less-than-perfect performance. And I know that in making his clumsy attempt at conversion, he lost his chance to land the killing blow. History will repeat itself. Committing everything to Signus Prime will leave you no more victorious than Kor Phaeron at Calth. It is too late to change that now, but then, I've warned you of this before. Now go.'

The Chaplain stood stunned, his face a facade of dignified shock. He bowed low at last, and asked permission to leave.

'Of course,' said Lorgar softly.

Erebus turned to go but was halted by the rumbling sneer of Angron's voice.

'The timing of your arrival was fortuitous, *priest*.' The Eater of Worlds almost spat the word. 'Just in time to miss the fighting. Tell me, are all your prayers and little treacheries making you more preacher than warrior?'

Erebus walked from the chamber without further comment. Angron watched him leave, his metal teeth glinting in a vicious smile. As the doors closed, Lorgar turned to Argel Tal, meeting his eyes.

'My son. My truest son.'

'Father?'

'Erebus will make you an offer soon. I see it in his eyes, and I hear it in his heart, though the details are beyond my ken. Refuse him. No matter the temptation; no matter what redemption his offer might seem to bring – you *must* refuse him.'

'I will, lord.'

Lorgar smiled, golden and benevolent. 'I know you will. Now, back to your duties, my friends. We must make ready to burn this world and move on to the next.'

KHÂRN PICKED HIS way through the mess of the *Conqueror*'s bridge. The bodies had been cleared and the stains scrubbed away, but he could still smell their burst flesh, their spilled blood and the refuse-stink of their emptied guts. Death lingered aboard a ship, despite the best efforts of any air-filtration vents. Cables dangled and sparked from the ceiling. Entire banks of screens and consoles were smoking lumps of metal. Las-burns and bullet-holes riddled the floor and walls, punctuated by the deeper craters of bolter fire. These were rarer, for the Ultramarines had been spoiled for choice when it came to targets.

Lotara was in her throne, above the madness, and Khârn had never seen her so angry. There was something almost predatory in the way she projected her temper as a cold seethe. She didn't need to say anything. She didn't even need to scowl. Her mood was apparent from the ice in her eyes and the way she sat back in her throne, staring, staring, staring.

Khârn halted in his careful tracks when he saw Lhorke standing vigil behind her throne. He ascended the stairs, paying respects to the Dreadnought before the captain.

'Legion Master,' he said, and felt the strangest compulsion to kneel. *Too long spent with the Word Bearers*, he told himself. 'You walk.'

'The captain woke me.'

'I heard about Delvarus and the Triarii.' He glanced to Lotara, who was watching him. 'Things have changed since you last walked among us, sir.'

The Contemptor gave a resonant *clunk-clunk* of servos locking tight. It sounded like an expression of distaste, though Khârn wasn't sure how.

'So I see. You've been busy, Khârn.'

This wasn't the warm-hearted reunion of brother-officers that Khârn had expected. He looked to Lotara.

'Angron is on his way. He asks you to be ready to bombard the planet in twelve hours.'

She leaned forwards in her throne, eyes wide. 'Is that a joke? After all this, you want me to do what I should've done at the very start?'

He didn't feel like going into the metaphysical details of pain resonance and the spiritual reflection of emotional torment. It wasn't that he didn't understand it; it was that he wasn't sure he believed any of it.

'Lorgar's orders.' He was too weary to even smile. 'The world bleeds, and all remaining life has gone to ground. He wants to burn them for the sin of cowardice.' *And to squeeze out the last trickles of suffering*, he thought.

'Khârn...' She looked at him, helpless fury in her eyes. 'What are we doing here? What kind of war is this?'

He didn't have an answer for her. Nothing tangible, at least.

'The new kind,' he said.

She wasn't placated. 'A mad kind. Everything has gone wrong since Isstvan III. Since we sided with Horus.'

Khârn looked between the captain and the Contemptor, but said nothing.

The bridge's port-side doors didn't grind open on heavy tracks any more, they'd been removed from the wall and taken away for repair. Angron entered with a dusty-looking tech-priest behind him. The robed adept had his hands clasped together in his sleeves as he trailed after the primarch, almost cringing away from the World Eater's muscled bulk.

'Khârn,' Angron growled across the debris-strewn chamber. 'This red-robe has been hunting for you.'

The primarch left the bowing priest at the violated doors and made his way through the mess that his bridge had become. He gave a short, throaty bark of a laugh at the devastation.

'How did this happen?'

Lotara rose from her throne, looking down at Angron from the raised central dais. 'Delvarus and the Triarii made unauthorised planetfall to join the surface attack. We were boarded in their absence.'

Angron walked over to where Lehralla dangled from her cables, bound to the auspex console. With a gentleness none of his brothers would have believed he possessed, he rested a massive hand on her shoulder.

'You are not hurt?'

The crippled young woman, surgically implanted onto the table, raked her filthy hair back from her face.

'No, sire,' she replied, utterly undaunted by the demigod before her.

Angron gave an ugly grin and looked back over the bridge. 'And where is Delvarus now?'

'I confined him to his quarters.'

Clearly amused, the primarch gave a short bark of laughter. 'I like that.' He started ascending the dais, facing Lhorke. The Contemptor towered above even the primarch, but nothing – living or dead – could ever make Angron seem small. 'Lhorke of the War Hounds.'

'Angron of the World Eaters.'

'You look good, old warrior. Still in the outdated colours though, eh?' Angron rapped his knuckles against the Dreadnought's ironform where the collared wolf stood proud. In instinctive reaction to his discomfort at being touched, Lhorke's combi-bolters reloaded with twin metallic rattles.

'Do I owe you thanks for defending my ship?' the primarch asked.

'I did little. Your gratitude should go to the other first Dreadnoughts, and the two thousand and seventy-one souls that lost their lives in repelling the assault.'

Angron lifted a scab-knuckled hand to his temple, feeling the dull return of pain. '*Hnnh*. You're still a miserable bastard, Lhorke.'

'I died. A little too late to change now.' The Dreadnought forced its ironform into a grinding bow, this one to Lotara, and made its way down the wide steps. 'I must go. I require maintenance.'

Angron felt the deck shivering beneath the Contemptor's tread. He remembered with a keen rush just how it felt to fight such a creation. The Isstvan campaign had been such an educational experience.

'Captain,' he said. 'In twelve hours, we'll bomb Armatura into memory. Salt the earth, Lotara.'

She looked at him as she reclined in her throne, boots thumping on one armrest.

'As you wish.'

PART TWO
NUCERIA, THE HOMEWORLD

Three days after the Siege of Armatura

THIRTEEN

Bones

ARGEL TAL ALWAYS went alone when he visited her tomb. His bootsteps echoed around the arching chamber, thrown back by the gothic walls with their spines of stone. Life-size statues of the honoured fallen watched him pass by, their wrought-iron faces staring out into the candle-lit half-dark. He knew each of them by name. Several of them were friends and brothers, lost to misfortune or martyrdom.

He passed one such monument, raised to remember *'Xaphen of the Gal Vorbak, Chaplain of the Chapter of the Serrated Sun'.* The warrior-priest stood with one boot resting on the cracked chestplate of a sculpted Raven Guard, raising a crozius maul to the sky. The Chaplain's head was lowered, not staring at the legionary he'd killed, but turned to the side with an air of contemplation. In this recreation of dark metal artistry, Xaphen looked almost soulful in regret, which amused Argel Tal no end each time he saw it. His brother had been many things in life, but regretful wasn't one of them. No more zealous creature had ever worn the

Legion's scarlet. Xaphen had even enjoyed Isstvan, considering it a test of faith. A test he'd relished and passed, according to his own exacting standards.

The plaque beneath his name read, in jagged Colchisian cuneiform: *He walked in the realm where gods and mortals meet.*

Argel Tal reached out as he passed, gently touching his knuckles to his dead brother's breastplate.

He repeated the gesture several more times as he passed the statues of Gal Vorbak butchered on Isstvan V. The *first* Gal Vorbak: the warriors with daemons in their hearts because they mutilated their souls on the first treacherous steps into Hell. Not like the thin-blooded daemon-hosts that he had bred for Lorgar in the years since. They were Gal Vorbak in name and blood, but not in spirit. They'd not walked the Pilgrimage. They came to their power with no comprehension of what it cost to earn.

When he finally reached her tomb, he crouched before her graven image. Where many other statues were cast in the patina-green of copper or the clean sheen of wrought-iron, she was embodied in pure marble. Her eyes were hidden behind the blindfold she'd only rarely worn, preferring to simply keep her eyes closed once she adapted to sightless life. She stood without the strident, ardent poses displayed by the hundreds of fallen Word Bearers memorialised in the great hall. Instead, she remained a frail, slender thing, dove-white in the gloom, one small hand outstretched to offer comfort to whomever rested before her.

Cyrene Valantion, the plaque read, *Confessor of the Word. Martyred by the Emperor's own guardians, for the sin of seeing the truth.*

Even on her plinth, she wasn't as tall as Argel Tal's full height. His fingertips stroked over her marble hair with the softest brush of ceramite over stone. Not a loving touch, nor a longing one. If anything, it was apologetic.

As he always did when he visited her, he drew the sword that ended her life – the sword he carried now as his own. And as always, he felt the hot rush of temptation to just break it over his knee and leave it behind. He resisted, for the pain of bearing this blade was a lesson in itself.

The Hall of Anamnesis – called the Hall of Hindsight by disloyal slaves when no Word Bearers were nearby to overhear – housed the bones of almost a thousand Legion heroes, deep in the core of *Fidelitas Lex*. Only one statue stood above a defiled stone coffin, and it belonged to the only human interred among nine hundred legionaries.

They'd taken her bones. Cultists, fanatics, call them what you will; they'd stolen their way into the hall, seizing her bones and claiming her as a saint of the Pantheon. 'The first martyr', they called her. Her name was a sainted whisper among the Word Bearers fleet's vast human population, for the dubious honour of being the first human slain by the Emperor's minions for praying to the Pantheon.

As if it were that simple. He rose to his feet, eyes never leaving the statue of the slain girl.

Argel Tal would never forget her final words. He thought of them often. Not the unfinished letter he found when she was already three days dead, but the very last words to leave her bloody lips. *What have they done to you?*

She said it with a smile, the weak smile of a girl who knew she was dying. Her hands had fallen from his helm's faceplate, leaving smears of blood where she'd been touching the daemonic mask his face had become.

What have they done to you?

Who did she mean? The gods? The primarchs, in their desperate civil war? His own brothers?

What have they done to you?

Thoughts of Cyrene stirred the beast within. Raum, the second soul inside his body, awakened with a bestial twitch.

Hunt?

It spoke in a snake's licking whisper, the words caressing Argel Tal's mind.

No. I am at her tomb. We hunted for days on Armatura. Is your hunger never sated?

Raum's derision was weaker than its irritation. **You are so maudlin, brother. Wake me when blood must flow.**

He felt the presence curling upon itself, shrinking again. But not slumbering, despite what the daemon claimed. Raum was content to lie in silence, watching through Argel Tal's eyes.

The two of them remained as they were for another few minutes. When Argel Tal heard footsteps, Raum uncoiled again in a dangerous writhe, suddenly on edge.

Someone comes. The Word Bearer felt the daemon reaching out beyond the boundaries of his skull, a hound sniffing for a scent. ***Ah. It is the Deceiver.***

'Hello, Erebus,' Argel Tal said. He didn't turn around.

'My boy,' came the voice from behind. 'It is good to see you.'

He is lying.

I know.

He fears you will cast him away, as the Lorgar-Father did.

I know, Raum. I know.

Erebus stood next to him, joining his vigil over the statue of the martyred girl. 'What happened on Armatura?' The First Chaplain's voice was composed, somehow cold without being hostile. 'The World Eaters have reported devastating losses, and I hear many of them baying for our Legion's blood. What went wrong?'

Argel Tal thumbed his tired eyes. 'What always goes wrong with the World Eaters? They charged ahead too far, too fast. The Ultramarines and Armaturan Guard forces that sought to flank us instead spilled into the gap between the two Legions, taking the opportunity to divide and conquer. The World Eaters pushed on into a hundred ambushes, while we were locked in a slow advance against the other half of the city's armies. By the time we broke through, let us just say that Twelfth Legion tempers had prevailed.'

'Khârn's report speaks ill of our Legion.'

'Of course it does, we failed to reinforce our allies. My report will speak ill of the World Eaters for pushing ahead without us. We are hardly going to praise each other for a perfect crusade.' Argel Tal finally turned to Erebus, his dusky features showing a slight smile. 'What happened at Calth, master? How did you fail so catastrophically?'

Erebus turned to look at the statue of a Word Bearers captain, fallen at Isstvan V. 'We gave birth to the warp storm that will sever Ultramar from the entire Imperium. A feat of such aetheric significance that we had to murder a sun to ignite the ritual. How is that failure?'

The daemon in Argel Tal's body crept its way through his bloodstream, making his veins burn.

He knows he failed. Shame bleeds from him, the way warm skin steams in cold air.

'Guilliman lives,' Argel Tal replied to Erebus. 'You abandoned how many thousands on Calth? And your fleet was scattered. You can forgive Lord Aurelian for seeing both sides of the coin.'

Erebus, ever solemn, walked around Cyrene's statue. 'In almost every future, you die at Terra.'

To that, Argel Tal only grinned. 'I know. And there will be no grander place to be on the last day.'

Erebus raised a thin eyebrow. 'You accept that fate?'

'The primarch has seen it in the warp's tides. He claims it's merely one possible outcome, but it matches what Raum tells me. I'm destined to die in the shadow of great wings.'

It's true, brother. We die in the shadow of great wings.

I know. I believe you.

Argel Tal gestured to the statue. 'Why did you come? To see the Confessor?'

'To see you, my boy.' Erebus wore his monkish robes rather than his battle armour. The red silks fell in a long, regal flow, like a cardinal's attire from one of Ancient Terra's many eras of false faith.

'Enough of the *"my boy"*, master. Those days are done.'

'You wear armour,' Erebus pointed out. 'Even here.'

The lord of the Gal Vorbak nodded. 'I can no longer remove it. It's part of me, like scales or hide.'

He sensed rather than saw Erebus's smile. 'Fascinating,' the Chaplain said.

'It happened after Armatura. I don't know why.'

'Fascinating,' Erebus repeated.

We should kill him, breathed Raum.

How sad that it's actually tempting.

A bronze chain secured a great skinbound tome to Argel Tal's waist. 'You should read this.' Argel Tal unhooked the book, offering it to his former mentor.

'The *Book of Lorgar*.' Erebus made no move to take it. 'I've read it. I transcribed many of its pages myself.'

'No.' Argel Tal kept holding it out. 'This is the version he shared with the other primarchs. This is *his* writing, his philosophy down in ink. Not yours, not Kor Phaeron's, not the mere dictations of the gods. The true *Book of Lorgar*, the scripture that will inform the Legion for millennia to come. He calls it the *Testamentum Veritas*.'

Erebus took the book in both hands, but didn't open it. 'You have such faith in him.'

'You speak as though you don't.'

'I have less faith in the Emperor's sons each time I cross paths with them. For all their claims of being perfection incarnate, they are also humanity's flaws writ large. Look at Horus. The galaxy burns from his ambition, not because I arranged to have him cut by an envenomed blade. The latter merely hastened the former. And look at Russ. The purity and savagery of a wolf, yet he begs at the Emperor's boots, crying out for an alpha to lead him.'

Argel Tal had no patience for an argument over the merits and flaws of the Eighteen Sires, especially not in this sacred place. He let silence voice his disapproval for him.

'Very well,' Erebus conceded. 'I wanted to speak with you because I need your help.'

Argel Tal didn't take his eyes from the statue. 'Then speak.'

'As I said before Lorgar, I've walked the Ten Thousand Futures. In many of them, if events play out along those paths, we will lose at Terra. Horus falls and his loyal Legions are broken upon the Imperial anvil. We are not merely exiled, Argel Tal. We are torn whole from the annals of the Imperium. Our names become legend, then myth, then forgotten in full.'

The Gal Vorbak listened, as did the daemon inside him. Erebus spoke on, his scholar's eyes looking over Cyrene's clean marble likeness. 'From the beginning, we've guided Lorgar, Mortarion, Fulgrim, Horus and the others. A coven of articulate, intelligent souls within the Legions, at the primarchs' sides, guiding their movements and decisions. Calas Typhon stands for the Death Guard, even without their Librarius. Fabius's vision of perfection ensnared Fulgrim's imagination and caught the Emperor's Children. We've played to their pride, as well as their fears. But now, when we should be pulling together, Lorgar is slipping loose.'

Argel Tal shook his head. 'And you want me to steer him back? The primarch is his own man, Erebus. He's stronger since Isstvan. End your craven need to control him and simply be proud he's become who he was born to be.'

Erebus sensed his former pupil's reticence, and reshaped his argument.

'Nothing so crude,' the Chaplain said. 'But we must... guide him. That's all. In all the futures where we lose, Lorgar was allowed to manipulate events to his own desires. That is why we must bring Sanguinius to his knees at Signus Prime, no matter what our father believes. We lose the war in many of the futures where the Angel reaches Terra.'

For the first time he could ever recall, Argel Tal was brutally, utterly honest with the man who'd trained him for so many years.

'I don't care. I am no schemer, and I trust Lorgar's vision far above yours.'

'But we have to forge events in accordance with–'

'*We said we don't care.*' Argel Tal's eyes burned molten silver.

Raum's eyes. 'We came here to pray, Deceiver. You are fouling the sanctity of this place with your forked tongue.'

'Deceiver?'

The silver faded. 'It is what Raum calls you,' Argel Tal admitted.

'I see. Then I shall trouble you no further, my boy.' Erebus made to leave, but hesitated at the last moment. He dared to touch Argel Tal's shoulder; the warrior and the daemon within the officer allowed it. 'I will do what I must to engineer events as I see fit, for I will not lose the war for humanity's soul because others are too blind to see the light. I only wished you at my side, Argel Tal.'

Argel Tal's eye lenses – the blue of Colchisian skies – met his former master's. 'It's always death, with you. Who needs to die this time? Whose death will set fate along the path you choose?'

'Many lives will have to end before we raise Horus's flag over the battlements of Terra. Almost all of them fight for the other side.'

'Almost. Not all.'

Erebus took a breath, as if unwilling to burden his Legion-brother with an unwelcome truth. 'Not all, no.'

Argel Tal's lip curled. 'It's Khârn.' The words weren't a question. 'That's why you came to me. Khârn will foul your plans somewhere down the pathways of fate, and you want him dead.'

Erebus didn't answer, which was an answer in itself.

The silence was broken by the creaking squeals of protesting ceramite and the wet crunches of bone scraping through flesh. Gnarled, overly-knuckled fingers lengthened, unsheathing long black talons as they did. Argel Tal's faceplate distorted into the canine maw his men had come to know as Raum's face, before melting into Argel Tal's own silver deathmask, hearkening back to the entombed Faero-kings from the myths of the oldest empires.

Erebus carried himself as one of the most composed, calm souls in all the Eighteen Legions. He knew secrets that he believed were known to no others, and had presided over the enlightenment of genetic demigods. Yet even he backed away from Argel Tal's possessed form. Dark mist, cinnamon-sweet with the reek of decaying flesh, rose from the warrior's black-veined gargoyle wings.

'Argel Tal,' Erebus began.

'Be silent! Your prophecies are poison. We are sick of others whispering about the future. At least Lorgar doesn't demand we dance to fate's tune.'

'But I bring a warning.'

'You bring lies and schemes and treachery!'

Argel Tal roared, lashing out with his claw. Erebus barely managed to parry with his crozius, moving back as he deflected the blow. The daemon-thing's talons crashed into another Word Bearer's statue and wrenched it from its pedestal to crash across the stone floor.

Erebus clutched his crozius tighter. 'Boy,' he said. 'Enough of this.'

'Do we look like we have any wish to betray Khârn? He is the last flesh-and-blood brother we trust. He is the last to never fail us, and the last we have never failed. Xaphen lies dead; you are a viper; Aquillon fell to murder. Only Khârn still stands. With us, he holds the two Legions together. With us, he keeps the primarchs from killing one another.'

The thing that had been Argel Tal took a step closer. 'Go from us. We hunger, and there is no finer wine on the tongue than Legion-blood; no finer taste than the salt-meat of Legion-flesh.'

Erebus took another step back, but no fear played across his features. There was only awe.

'You have become a walking monument to the Pantheon's divinity. How far you've come from the day I took you from your family.'

'We have become the Truth. We warned you to go. Now go.'

Erebus didn't lift his crozius again, he merely held up a hand to warn the daemon-thing from coming closer. 'I would not ask you to shed Khârn's blood. I know you never would, you've been brothers for too long, over too many compliances. That's not why I came.'

Argel Tal stood where he was, his armoured shoulders rising and falling in rhythm to his heavy, inhuman breathing.

'We are listening.'

'Khârn will fall before the war's ending. I have foreseen it many times. It will be down to you, Argel Tal, to fight at his side. You are the only one who can keep him alive.'

The monstrous figure grunted, barking a wad of ichor-saliva onto the floor. 'Nothing can kill Khârn.'

'There speaks a brother's loyalty.' Erebus risked harnessing his crozius on his back, moving slowly so as not to draw the creature's ire. 'I am telling you the truth, son.'

The silver deathmask warped into an expression of rippling mercury torment. *'We are no longer your son.'*

'No. Forgive me, an old habit come to the fore.' Erebus lifted a hand again. 'I am telling you how to save your brother. Have I ever done you wrong? Where does this anger come from?'

It came from within, and from without. It came from the daemon in his heart, sending spite through his bloodstream. It came from rage at the way Kor Phaeron and Erebus treated the primarch. It came from irritation at the way both of them smirked knowingly and claimed to know everything about everything.

Argel Tal bit back his rage, swallowing it hard and whole. Raum scratched pain along his bones, wanting to kill, kill, kill, but that was nothing new. The daemon loathed the First Chaplain on some instinctive, unearthly level. Erebus had always revolted him, the way nocturnal creatures despised the sun.

'The anger is Raum's,' Argel Tal said, though it was his as well. 'Say what you wish to say.'

'You can save Khârn. The vision is difficult to interpret, for the future stretches out not like a path, but a cobweb, every decision threading out to a million other possibilities. But I can tell you this for certain: Khârn dies at sunrise on a world of grey skies. In every future I have seen, he dies as dawn lightens the heavens. And he dies with a blade in his back.'

'Who wields it?'

'Someone that hates him. All I sense is the murderer's emotion, not his face.'

Argel Tal settled, gently prising Raum's grip from control over the body they shared. It was the mental equivalent of flexing one's muscles after waking from a long slumber. Already bored and sensing no prey to toy with, the daemon allowed it with only ill-tempered muttering.

This is the offer your godling father warned you of?

So it would seem. *Everything he gives comes with a cost.*

You should have let me kill him.

Argel Tal smiled. *Probably.*

'What amuses you?' Erebus asked. 'I hear that soft laugh of yours.'

'Everything amuses me, of late. I will bear your warning in mind, master. Thank you.'

'You still call me *Master*. Those days are as long gone as the others, surely.'

'A bad habit, no different from yours.' With the burning in his veins beginning to ease, Argel Tal turned back to Cyrene's statue. He picked up his sword from the ground, unsure when it had slipped from his grip. During the Change, most likely.

'Let me tell you of Calth,' Erebus said. 'Hear my words, and judge for yourself whether I failed or not.'

Argel Tal listened in silence as Erebus told the whole tale. The ambush at the fleetyards. Burning ships raining wreckage down onto the world below. The poisoning of Calth's sun. The birth of the kaleidoscopic Ruinstorm, a cancer just waiting to spread across healthy space.

Argel Tal waited until the very end, though in truth he heard very little after the first half. His mind was afire with one grave possibility that he didn't dare call hope. Erebus trailed off at last, his explanation done.

'Did we fail?' he asked. The confidence in his voice suggested he considered his case made to perfection.

'Torgaddon,' Argel Tal replied. 'You used his flesh in that ritual. You summoned a dead man's soul.'

Erebus nodded. 'Kor Phaeron first learned of the rite, through his own prayers. We–'

'It doesn't matter how.' Argel Tal's eye lenses burned with inner light. 'You brought him back.'

The Chaplain nodded, seeming to know, in his limitless patience, just where this was going.

'I did.'

He lies, Argel Tal. He lies to us both.

No. Not in this.

You think a mortal spirit can return unscarred from the Sea of Souls?

What matters, Raum, is that they can return at all.

Argel Tal ignored the snarling protests of the beast within. He gestured at the statue with the blade that had killed the girl herself.

'Bring her back.'

Erebus breathed slowly, not making eye contact. 'For you, my son. I will.'

FOURTEEN

**Reassignment
Unsanctioned
Forge Fires**

KEEDA WASN'T ASHAMED for weeping when she first saw *Syrgalah*'s wreckage. The Warhound had been pulled from its recovery sarcophagus by the ceiling cranes, broken and still smoking from its wounds. One-armed, unable to stand upon her two crippled legs, with every metre of armour plating corroded, *Syrgalah*'s head hung slack on a neck too ruined to bear the cockpit's weight.

No, that hadn't been easy to watch. It was better now, but not by much. At least she was standing.

The Ember Queen was held up by solid gantries either side of her, regaining her stature despite her injuries – all part of the Machine Cult's belief in restoring the Titan's warrior-soul by treating it with dignity as much as through technological engineering. So she stood among her sisters, one of ninety surviving Warhounds in the dark colours of the Ember Wolves. Yet she was far, far from whole.

Eight tech-priests worked on her joints, supported by servitor teams flocking in packs behind them. *Syrgalah*'s metal skin crawled with humans, cyborgs and lobotomised slaves, as well as a number of drifting servo-skulls scanning whatever mechanism they were told to scan at any given moment.

Toth was with her, his new arm not yet coated by synthetic skin, its iron bones bare from the elbow down. It wasn't taking well. Angry red veins showed along his bicep, perhaps the first signs of infection. He kept testing it, making his new fingers curl into a fist every few seconds. Clearly it still hurt, if his wincing was anything to go by.

One of the red-robed priests approached them, his features masked entirely by his hood. His spindly secondary arms folded close to his shoulders as he drew near.

'Moderati Bly. Moderati Kol.' His voice was a vox-ish drone, devoid of emotion, that could easily have belonged to any tech-priest either of them had met.

'Ninth?' Keeda asked.

He responded by pulling his hood back, revealing his shaven head, the nodal implants at his temples, and the visor across his eyes.

'Affirmative. It is me, the Ninth.'

'How are the repairs going?' Toth asked.

The Ninth's throat-speaker buzzed. 'They proceed as you see them. No visual deception is occurring.'

Keeda smiled for the first time since they'd been brought down by that damn Reaver and its lucky shooting.

'What Moderati Kol means, is when will *Syrgalah* be ready to walk again?'

The Ninth turned his visored eyes to Toth. 'Then why did he not simply phrase his inquiry using those precise words?'

Toth's new arm tightened again. He made a fist. 'Just answer her, Ninth. My head hurts enough as it is.'

'Very well. L-ADX-cd-MARS-Quintessence-[Necare Modification]-I-XII-002a-2/98: VS/TK/K will be ready to walk in the next engagement, providing fleet rumour holds no incorrectness. The estimated planetfall of twenty-seven days hence allows our technicians significant time to see the repairs completed.'

Toth looked at the Titan. Sparks danced from her joints as cutting and welding tools did their work in servitors' mono-tasked hands. 'A month?'

'She is *Syrgalah*,' the Ninth said. 'She has of course been prioritised above all other considerations. The Archmagos Veneratus himself is operating on her.'

The Mechanicum overseer hove into view as if summoned. Slender, many-jointed limbs sprouted from a circular generator implanted between his shoulder blades. He needed no gantry or platform for support; his stick-insect limbs magnetically sealed to *Syrgalah*'s armour plating and allowed him to climb the Titan as he desired. They *click-clanked, click-clanked* as Vel-Kheredar made his way down the Warhound's left side. Even when he made it to the deck, he refused the use of his own legs, letting the spider-limbs take his emaciated weight as he stalked over to the small group.

Three green eye lenses – none of them of uniform size, and none of them exactly where a human's eyes should be – looked down from the darkness of his hood.

'Moderati Bly and Moderati Kol.'

'Archmagos,' both said, as they bowed. The Ninth practically prostrated himself, which drew the Archmagos's attention in a whisper of hood-silk and a whirr of eye lenses.

'Eralaskesian Thyle Maraldi, Ninth of that Name.'

The Ninth rose. 'My master?'

'To your duties.'

'At once, my master.' The Ninth bowed and, with a final glance to his fellow crew members, made his way back to where he worked, on the joints of *Syrgalah*'s mangled foot-claws. They heard him muttering and redirecting the cutting lasers of his floating servo-skulls.

Toth looked awkward at his companion's dismissal. Keeda looked annoyed. 'Has the Ninth displeased you, Archmagos?'

The Martian lord lost half a metre in height as his spidery legs vented air pressure from their multiple gear-filled knees. He was still taller than any legionary, but lacked their bulky width. Keeda felt the tri-eye lenses focusing on her, revolving and whirring, clicking as they captured picts for future reference.

'From available context, it is apparent you refer to Eralaskesian Thyle Maraldi, Ninth of that Name. And you refer to his dismissal as suppositional evidence of my displeasure. Perhaps, you reason, I perceive him as requiring to continue work at once to fulfil a certain quota of effort or achievement in the reparation of the Titan you call *Syrgalah*.'

Toth and Keeda shared a look. His was accusatory, that she'd started this. Hers was apologetic, for the same reason.

'Forget I spoke, Archmagos.'

'An impossibility. My neural structure prevents erosion of recorded data.' His eye lenses refocused again. 'To answer – and indeed, to allay – what I perceive as your fears, I will state: no. The Ninth has not displeased me. He was ordered to return to work because he commands his team of menials more adeptly than many others on the reparation crew, and his presence is required for the most complicated procedures currently taking place.'

The Archmagos emitted a blurt of vox-casted noise, the sound like a kicked beehive. 'I would venture that in addition to his expertise, he also works to greater skill because of an unfortunate emotional investment in the god-machine itself. To use your parlance, he *cares*.'

Keeda frowned. 'Is it unfortunate, if it makes him work harder?'

'Emotion inevitably leads to intellectual compromise and, therefore, to weakness. But now is not an appropriate juncture to partake in an exchange of the subtleties in Martian positivistic philosophy. Tell me: now you have conversed with Princeps Ultima Lyrac regarding your reassignment, have you reached a final decision? The records require updating and we await the choices both of you must make.'

'*What?*' said Keeda and Toth at the same time.

'Reassignment?' Toth stammered. 'That can't be.'

'Ah.' The tech-priest lord rose higher on his insectile legs again. 'A sudden event has demanded my immediate attention elsewhere. Be well, moderati.' He turned to escape, skittering away.

'Wait, please!' Keeda called. For a wonder, the robed figure actually waited. 'There's no sudden event, lord. You're a terrible liar,' she told him.

'I am more skilled at obfuscation in binaric cant,' the Archmagos admitted. 'Nevertheless, this is a matter for the Princeps Ultima to discuss with you both. I supposed incorrectly, and offer apology for the errors made in this dialogic-exchange.'

Toth wasn't listening. 'Reassignment? That fat son of a bitch.'

'Where is the princeps?' Keeda asked.

'Aboard *Syrgalah*. I shall have him summoned.'

She nodded. 'My thanks, Archmagos Veneratus.'

'Your thanks are not necessary. My primary subroutine is to facilitate exchanges between the Mechanicum's myriad elements. A moment, if you please.'

Toth and Keeda waited together, cursing between them. It took less than a minute for Audun Lyrac to emerge from the Titan's insides, clambering down a ladder to reach the deck. He ran an oily hand through his thinning hair.

'Greetings to you both,' he said, offering a salute.

Keeda and Toth returned it. In truth, she was taken aback to see that he'd been working aboard *Syrgalah*. His face was beaded with perspiration and his sleeves were rolled up to reveal grime marking his skin.

'Reassignment?' Toth snarled at his superior officer. 'Let's get straight to business. You're throwing us off the command crew?'

Keeda felt her anger diminish a little at the sight of Audun blinking in surprise. He didn't seem smug or pugnacious, just startled. The princeps bristled, standing straighter and pulling the creases from his uniform.

'I do not answer to you, Moderati Kol.'

'This time you do.' It was all Toth could do not to pull his laspistol and riddle the man with burn-holes. 'I've given seven years of my life to *Syrgalah*, and sixteen to Audax. I'm the best steersman in the Legio, and Keeda's the best gunner. Why are you doing this? Because of my arm? Because you're trying to piss all over the old man's legacy and make your own name?'

'That's enough.' Audun narrowed his round eyes, inflecting his voice with as much cold threat as he could muster. Keeda found it surprisingly effective. 'If you wished to refuse the honour,' Audun said quietly, 'you had only to say so.'

Keeda had a sudden sinking feeling. Something didn't feel right.

'The *honour?*' Toth fairly spat the word. 'Are you drunk?'

Audun rolled his sleeves down and rebuttoned them at the wrists. 'Very well. I will offer the ranks to other officers.' He shook his head, not just unnerved at the confrontation but a little disgusted, too. 'Was this necessary? A simple refusal would have been enough.'

Keeda, silent so far, felt her sinking feeling give a sudden lurch. 'What ranks?' she asked.

Audun blinked again. 'Have you even read the offers? I transloaded them to your quarters' communication occuli this morning, with the request you seek me out as soon as you'd decided.'

'We heard...' Toth trailed off.

'So that's a *No* then. You haven't read the offers.'

Keeda swore softly. 'You weren't demoting us. You were giving us our own Titans.'

Audun Lyrac looked at her like she was the basest breed of idiot. 'Of course I wasn't demoting you. Your records are beyond exemplary, and we have eleven Titans lacking commanders after the engagements in Armatura's cities. Your promotions didn't even need consideration.'

Toth cleared his throat. 'We thought–'

'I know what you *thought*, Moderati Kol. It may surprise you to learn that while I don't have Solostine's impressive battle-record, I am not a preening fool incapable of making good decisions. I've been managing promotions and reassignments for twenty years while the old man devoted his entire focus to fighting. Who do you think had you both assigned to *Syrgalah* in the first place? When Venric asked for a new steersman, I advised him to choose you, Toth. When he needed a new gunner, I suggested you, Keeda.'

Both officers stood in awkward silence, taking the reprimand as it came.

'Did you assume I was petty enough to throw you back into the menial ranks purely because we had a disagreeable first meeting?'

'Uh,' said Keeda.

'Well,' said Toth.

Audun sighed. 'Go read the damn offers, both of you. If you wish to take command of *Darahma* and *Seddah*, then the Titans are yours. If you refuse, despite your clear lack of faith in me, I would welcome you serving as *Syrgalah*'s command crew when she walks again. And she *will* walk again, I promise you that. Her honour is Audax's honour.'

With that, he waited for their salutes, and turned back to the Titan.

Keeda and Toth watched their princeps rejoining the hive of activity swarming over *Syrgalah*'s red and black skin.

'Not our proudest moment,' Toth confessed, making his new hand into another fist.

Keeda nodded. 'Not our cleverest, either.'

THE SHIP THROBBED in transit, its engines running hot. It managed to hold itself together in the warp for now, but the Ultramarines had done their work well. At random intervals, with almost no warning, the flagship would come screaming back into realspace, trailing aethereal fire and mad laughter. Each time, the *Fidelitas Lex* would rip its way back to reality a moment later to guard the *Conqueror* while it revived its warp-engines.

Of their respective fleets, there was no sign. The primarchs had divided their Legions and warships yet again, sending more forces deeper into Ultramar to prey upon Imperial worlds while the XIII

Legion was crippled at Calth. Both flagships had abandoned the need for anything but the meagrest escort squadrons, in favour of sailing alongside the *Trisagion*.

Lotara made her way to the Audaxica, through the wide avenue of the *Conqueror*'s central spinal corridor. A rat, stunted and black-furred, scuttled by her boots before disappearing through the iron grillework on the deck. She tutted.

'Why do all Imperial vessels house colonies of rats? The *Conqueror* was built in orbit, and has never once landed on even a single world. Do we take crates of vermin on board when we dock for supplies?'

Behind her, Lhorke stomped on in noisy silence. He'd been awake several days now, and though he couldn't yet sense the telltale weariness of extended activity, the headaches had already started. Whatever remained of his tortured husk in this armoured shell, it was beginning to suffer from the lack of rest.

They reached the massive, dense double doors that led into the Audaxica. Heavily-augmented Mechanicum skitarii stood watch at the sealed portal, though the group parted before her. Or did they move aside for Lhorke? Difficult to say for sure; they certainly couldn't help themselves staring at the Contemptor.

Lotara braced herself as the Audaxica's doors rumbled open. She knew what was coming, yet the dragon's breath heat still hit her hard enough to rock her back on her heels. The char-scent of molten metal pushed at her, thick as treacle in her throat. The air was practically resinous with forge-smell.

The Audaxica itself was a chamber of monumental scale, wide enough to walk a pack of Titans abreast and tall enough that the arched ceiling was a dark blue, with its millions of etchings and carvings too distant to make out unaided. Colossal ground elevators transported Titans from the Audaxica to the Legio's planetfall hangar below.

Every one of Audax's Titans was a variant on the Warhound-pattern, bulkier from additional armour and each bearing a stylised head of dark metal resembling a jackal or a wolf baring its teeth.

Lotara watched one of them rattle its way past in a gracelessly threatening hunch, splayed feet-claws crashing on the deck.

As the Titan cleared her field of vision, her gaze settled upon the motionless form of *Syrgalah*. She noted the showers of sparks streaming from its joints. Repairs were clearly under way. She even caught sight of Keeda and Toth pitching in, both of them up crew ladders, working on the cockpit's interior.

Vel-Kheredar descended when she approached, his secondary limbs clicking against the Warhound's armour, then across the deck. He brushed by Lotara without so much as a glance, coming to a halt before Lhorke.

'Such an ironform,' he vox-blurted, stalking in a circle around the Dreadnought. 'Oh my, yes.' Without asking permission, the techpriest pressed his augmented hands to the Contemptor's chestplate, where the symbol of the War Hounds still stood proud. 'I can almost feel the life within.'

Lhorke tolerated this in silence. Lotara wasn't certain how it was possible for a war machine to look irritated, but the evidence was right before her eyes.

Vel-Kheredar's burnished hands smoothed over the Dreadnought's head, cradling the oversized metal helm with its precious cargo of sensor nodes and visual auspex and pict-finders, linked to the foetal corpse curled up deeper within.

'We fashion them with heads,' Vel-Kheredar was saying, 'to focus their awareness forwards. It helps create an impression within the corpse's neurological sensory input/output that it is still alive, for it sees just as it saw in life: from a human perspective. Taller, though. Oh, yes. Much taller.'

Only then did he look down at Lotara. 'How is the revenant pilot performing, Captain Sarrin? This unit is functioning within acceptable parameters, yes?'

It was 'the unit' that answered. Lhorke took a step back, joints giving heavy grind-snarls.

'Get away from me, priest.'

Vel-Kheredar gave a droning vox-laugh, surprisingly human given his extensive cybernetic reconstruction.

'Still such a temper, Legion Master.'

Lhorke's answer was to reload his combi-bolters in twin, slow cranks. Vel-Kheredar's tri-eye lenses rotated in some nameless and doubtlessly blunted emotion. He turned to Lotara, adjusting his height by lowering himself through venting pressure from his five stalk-legs. He was now the height of a legionary, rather than the towering Contemptor.

'It is my supposition that you are here in answer to my request for a dialogic-exchange.'

Lotara, who was trying not to smile at Lhorke's irritation, nodded to the Archmagos. Sweat was already painting her face from the haze of the *Audaxica*'s industry.

'Do you have somewhere we can speak away from the heat?'

'But of course. Come.'

He led them to a wide section of the floor marked by waspish hazard striping, and flipped open a compartment on the back of his mechanical forearm to reveal numerous telecommand dials. Vel-Kheredar pushed an activation rune and twisted one of the dials three notches. The deck gave an immediate shudder, juddering as the platform sank through the floor and into the steel-smelling darkness between decks.

Down.

Down, down. The relief from the forge-heat was immediate enough to make Lotara sigh.

Lhorke's shoulder-mounted searchlight cracked into life, daggering through the black. Lotara winced when it beamed over her face. Vel-Kheredar merely refocused his eye lenses. The platform kept shuddering beneath them.

'My ship,' she said, 'to coin a phrase, took a beating. What repairs can you make whilst we're in transit?'

'Anything that needs to be done, Captain Sarrin. It is *my* ship as well.'

She felt herself smiling. On Mars, this man – or whatever was left of the man within the augmetics – was a wealthy Machine Lord, owning a subterranean forge-city of several million souls all heeding his will and working towards his experimental vision. Here, in the deepest black of Ultima Segmentum, he was a much more amiable soul than his lofty position within the Machine Cult might suggest.

'Is that some of the unfortunate affection you're always criticising your lessers for?'

He fixed her with his triple eye lenses. 'I don't know. I criticise them for so many things.'

'Did you just make a joke, Archmagos?'

'I made the attempt. Auditory analysis notes the tonal resonance of your voice as being negatively disposed since you entered the Audaxica. I sought to defuse your discomfort through the application of humour.'

'Very funny,' she lied. 'Is there word from Mars?'

'None,' he replied. Not that fear was within his palette of emotion, but he did harbour *concern* for Sacred Mars, surely blockaded by Rogal Dorn in the wake of Horus's rebellion. His city beneath the holy red sands could withstand orbital bombardment, but the internecine unrest would be a factor to consider. The whole world was likely at war by now. 'None at all.'

They emerged into the harsher glare of strip lighting, descending from the primary muster hangar's ceiling towards the deck far below. Titans in varying states of readiness already lined the walls, magna-bound in place, standing sentinel until they were called for loading into the great red-iron planetary landers at the far end of the vast hangar. The landing craft were round, bulbous things, all armoured efficiency without artistry.

Lotara affected casual disinterest, not caring how unconvincing it sounded. 'I heard the primarch has commissioned a new blade from you.'

'Affirmative.'

The platform finally settled into the lower deck, locking in place. 'And that Khârn has secured your services for a similar project.'

'The resurrection of the blade Gorechild. This is also affirmative.'

Vel-Kheredar led them along the deck, his stalk-legs clicking three times for every thump of Lhorke's armoured feet.

'Did his servitor team find all the missing axe-teeth?'

Another binaric spurt of coded amusement. 'Not all. He seconded one of my preferred adepts to the task, but Lord Aurelian's orders to terminate the planet came before the excavation's completion. I am given to understand that Centurion Khârn improvised.'

She could easily imagine just how Khârn had improvised, no doubt taking a hammer to the skulls of the mica dragons in the Legion's Museum of Conquest, and stealing the teeth for use in the weapon's resurrection. She was willing to wager a year's pay that was what he'd done.

Of course, that triggered a darker thought – one she and her officers had lamented many times over shots of whatever spirit served as a nightcap in the officers' mess. Their pay, such as it had been, came from Terra. Rebellion had its downsides.

Vel-Kheredar walked ahead, turning to face them and walking backwards without effort or concern.

'You wished to speak with me over matters of vessel repair and weapon birth?' The tri-eyes clicked closed and back open, in imitation of a rare blink. 'This is uncharacteristically tedious of you, Captain Sarrin.'

She gave him her best smile, which was a weapon indeed. 'You've been with the primarch from the beginning.'

'Affirmative. In the interests of perfect clarity, I was disappointed at my appointment to the Twelfth Legion flagship. I was in contestation for assignment to the Seventh or Tenth Legions, but Kelbor-Hal – blessings upon his sacred wisdom – chose to the contrary.'

Lhorke grunted something as he followed. Some echo of Legion rivalry, perhaps. Lotara kept looking up at the backward-walking

Archmagos Veneratus. The mustering hangar was tomb-quiet, but for the sounds of the trio's passing.

'You were with the first surgical team that examined Angron's implants, all those decades ago.'

'Affirmative.'

'What did you find?'

Even without looking, Vel-Kheredar effortlessly paced around a stack of crates. 'My findings are easily accessible in the fleet's archives.'

'I've read them,' Lotara nodded. 'But there's no mention of any degenerative effects the implants might have.'

The tech-lord watched her in silence for several ticks of the augmetic metronomical machine that ran in place of his human heart. When he spoke, it was with reluctance.

'You are unsanctioned.'

She started, as if slapped. 'I'm what?'

Vel-Kheredar didn't answer. He diverted his attention to Lhorke. 'You were present at the time, Legion Master. You are aware of what I found.'

The Contemptor thudded along the deck, shoulders rolling side to side. 'The archives say nothing of degeneration. But what I'm aware of, Archmagos, is that each time I rise from slumber, the primarch is worse.'

The priest inclined his head, but it didn't seem to be in agreement. '*Worse* is a value measurement laden with relativistic emotional perspective.'

They passed beneath the staring eyes of the Warhound army, each head lowered as if to scent their trail as they passed, or wipe them from existence with a sweep of their weaponised arms.

Lotara wouldn't let Vel-Kheredar shake her loose. 'The World Eaters whisper it. Khârn has said it a dozen times or more, these last ten years. The records of compliances in the last century show a steady increase in our own casualties, as well as civilian losses. How many tactical briefings has Angron left before finishing, racked with head pains he never admits to? How many times has he failed to follow battle plans, only to lead the Legion in a frontal assault against the densest resistance, heedless of our own losses?'

She almost glared at the slender priest. 'Tell me, in the context of the last twenty years, that he's not getting worse. I've been with the fleet a fraction of the time you have, and I can see it clearly.'

Vel-Kheredar emitted an annoyed blurt of code. 'I can confess to observing a degree of undesirably erratic behaviour in Lord Angron's actions.'

'Oh, stop being so damn vague,' she scowled. 'Did you find anything in the Nails that suggested this… degeneration?'

'You are unsanctioned.'

Her scowl deepened. 'Will the Nails kill him?'

'You are unsanctioned.'

Lhorke emitted a vox-growl of his own. 'Is Angron dying?'

'You are unsanctioned.'

'I'm flag-captain of the World Eaters fleet, and Lhorke is the former lord of the Legion. How can we be unsanctioned? We have the highest clearance.'

'With respect, captain, you do not. Neither of you does.'

She breathed in through her teeth. 'How can we get sanctioned?'

He hesitated that time. 'You are unsanctioned.'

'Who ordered you to keep your silence?'

He answered immediately. 'The Omnissiah.'

Lotara hissed a triumphant *Yes*. Now they were getting somewhere. It wasn't about getting the right answers, it was about asking the right questions. Vel-Kheredar's orders were no doubt extremely, evasively specific. He wanted to talk, but a thin line of direct obedience needed to be… danced around.

'The Emperor–' she began.

'Correction,' stated Vel-Kheredar. 'The Omnissiah, avatar of the Machine-God.'

'Fine, fine. But the Emp– sorry, *Omnissiah*, demanded you sequester some of your findings?'

'You are unsanctioned.'

'We can guess,' Lhorke rumbled.

'What I can't guess,' Lotara mused, 'is why?'

'Easy enough. Morale within the Twelfth. We were a broken Legion back then, one of the last to find our lord. Bad enough that we were burdened with the only primarch to fail in conquering his homeworld. If we'd also discovered he was doomed to die before the Crusade's end, it would have annihilated what little morale remained.'

Lotara looked up at Vel-Kheredar. 'Is that why?'

'You are unsanctioned,' he said.

'Were you absolutely certain the Nails would cause degeneration?'

'You are unsanctioned.'

'Well... was it just a hypothesis that you didn't want leaked?'

Vel-Kheredar's tri-eyes whirred as they refocused. 'What I did or did not wish leaked is irrelevant. My personal preferences play no part in the equation, captain.'

'The Emperor, then. When you reported to him, did you know degeneration was a certainty, or was it just a possibility?'

'You are unsanctioned.'

'And the Emperor ordered you into silence.'

Another hesitation. 'He did. I defer to the wisdom of the Machine-God.'

Lotara glanced up at Lhorke by her side. 'Now we know.'

The Dreadnought looked down at her. 'Nothing we couldn't have guessed.'

She gave him a look. 'Not all of us were walking and talking a hundred years ago, Lhorke. The fact the mystery exists is all the proof I need. This is the reason Russ came for you, on the Night of the Wolf.'

'One of many reasons.'

She let that slide. 'Archmagos. Will the World Eaters implants kill them in the same way?' She licked her lips, feeling them suddenly dry. 'Will they kill Khârn?'

The robed priest seemed distracted, his eye lenses panning up one of the motionless Titans as it stood ready to walk again.

'Their implants are primitive copies of the malignant original,' he said. 'They erode stability and damage the subjects' capacity to reason. They impinge on higher brain function by rewriting emotional responses. However, they are not fatal – not degenerative in the terminal sense. The most important aspect of their implantation that they share with the original Nails is that they cannot be removed without killing the host, or – at best – inflicting severe and irreparable brain damage. But they are not, as you say, likely to kill Khârn. Or indeed any World Eater.'

Captain Lotara Sarrin punched a fist into her open palm. 'The things you learn,' she smiled, 'with a little curiosity.'

Vel-Kheredar *click-ticked* in amused disapproval. 'There is an ancient Terran proverb regarding curiosity, flag-captain. It involves felines and murder, thus I confess it makes little sense to me.'

'I have a better one: *"The only good is knowledge and the only evil is ignorance"*.'

'Intriguing.' The priest nodded. 'A sentiment close to my heart. Who spoke those words?'

'One of the Thousand Sons, apparently. Khârn quoted it to me once. I liked how it sounded.'

Vel-Kheredar returned to his personal chambers, craving the respite of solitude. Iron gargoyles leered down from the high walls, and his menials scattered before him, preparing the forge-fires in case he wished to work.

And he did, of course. He always wished to work. His chamber was more a foundry than anything else. His stalk-legs *clanked* on the deck as he moved to the workbench facing the panoramic window.

'Remove shields,' he commanded. Activated by his voice, the three-metre-thick armour plating blocking the windows started its laborious withdrawal. At first there was nothing but a slit of burning brightness, widening as the armour retracted. Soon enough, the warp's boiling, thrashing light played havoc with the chamber's shadows. Angels and devils danced across the walls, most cast by the leering gargoyles carved into the architecture. Most, not all.

Vel-Kheredar stared into the chaotic depths of the immaterium, occasionally letting his three eyes take picts for later reference. Though a baseline human would likely have been driven to madness by the sight, he did this often, and found the results hauntingly quaint. In many of the still images, he thought he could make out human faces in the murk. They were screaming, always screaming.

Vel-Kheredar set to work. He reached for the blade Gorechild with one hand, drawing his tools closer with the other.

But distraction reigned. The mortal captain's questions drifted through his mind, looping like a corrupted playback.

He'd never actually met the Master of Mankind, but the Palatine Aquila had marked the sealed scroll handed to him by Malcador the Sigillite. A message from the Emperor's own hand. He had it still – for who could ever disregard such a relic? – stored in his encrypted safe.

He kept faith with the secrets he was told to carry, though he never really saw what harm they might inflict. It was only a supposition, anyway. Back then, any hint of cerebral cortex degeneration was nothing more than an untested hypothesis.

He'd made an educated estimation, though. He'd made it while the primarch was still rendered somnolent by Malcador's touch, and after the XII Legion's Techmarines and Apothecaries had been ordered away. That made it Vel-Kheredar's turn, and he'd done his examinations over the course of seven hours, all under the Sigillite's watchful eyes.

'I cannot be certain,' he'd confessed finally to the man who was somehow both ancient and ageless at once. 'But I can make an estimation based on the little data available.'

Angron had grunted, shifting in his sleep upon the surgical slab. Vel-Kheredar had flinched back, in an unwelcome and accidental display of unease.

Yet time was proving him correct. The primarch was, to use Lotara Sarrin's crudely effective word, *worse*. Less human – if he could ever have been called such – in his responses, and increasingly slaved, emotionally and physically, to the Nails. A slow degeneration, slow enough that the erosion could be ignored for the first few decades. It had been easy to deny the Wolves, to refuse them and to fight them. Things weren't quite so noticeable then as they'd since become. Deterioration set in quicker in the following decades, but the spread of the Crusade fleets made management of resources and punishing the wayward something of a fool's dream. Reports didn't always make it back to Terra. With thousands of expeditionary fleets, it mattered little.

And now they were all at war. The slow erosion had become a catastrophic decay, as the primarch's rages burned hotter and lasted longer now he was truly free of the Emperor's leash.

Vel-Kheredar held no grudge against the one he called *Omnissiah*. Ultimately, whether he truly was the avatar of the Machine-God or merely an extraordinarily knowledgeable false prophet, it mattered little. Horus and Kelbor-Hal had declared him a false messiah, and as always in matters of empire-building, politics and military power came before the truth. They weren't mighty because they were right, they were right because they were mighty. History would be, as it always had been, written by the victors. In this case, it wasn't just history at stake, but the metaphysical truth: victory determined just who was divinely born and who was a false god.

The Archmagos deployed secondary arms from beneath his robes, letting them unlock and uncoil from where they'd formed his ribs. Each of these new hands had thin, prehensile filament-tendrils, much more adept at finer machine work than his too-human fingers.

Gorechild. Every weapon had a soul, and this one's was a shrieking, wrathful thing trapped in the toothless blade.

It didn't pain him to violate XII Legion tradition regarding the ill luck of abandoned weapons, for two simple reasons. Firstly, they broke their own laws all too often in the heat of a battle. Necessity was forever the bane of tradition.

Secondly, he didn't believe their foolish superstitions for a moment. He liked Khârn, though. The Eighth Captain was a difficult soul to dislike.

Bathed in the hellish light of the Sea of Souls, the Archmagos Veneratus – lord of a city-state on distant, sacred Mars – worked alone on an axe that had been cast aside by a genetic demigod. He cast occasional glances to where the sketched plans for a new weapon lay on the edge of his desk. A great black blade, to be forged for a primarch's hands.

They would reach Nuceria soon. May whatever gods were true have mercy on the souls that were there when the fleet arrived.

FIFTEEN

Warnings
Brotherhood

THE NINTH TIME the *Conqueror* translated from the warp without warning, Khârn received word from Argel Tal aboard the *Lex* – a short-range vox-pulse, ship-to-ship – requesting that he come aboard the Word Bearers flagship at once.

Intrigued, he'd done exactly that. Kargos had wanted to come, as had Skane, but Khârn refused permission to both of them. They had enough difficulty getting on with the Word Bearers at the best of times, and with tensions running hot after Armatura's cities finally fell, it was anything but the best of times.

What had really taken Khârn aback was that Esca, of all his warriors, had also asked to accompany him. The Codicier had seemed hesitant and worried, but that was nothing new where Esca was concerned.

'I sense something foul aboard the *Lex*,' he'd confessed.

'That is no way to speak of our brother Legion,' Khârn had said with a tired smile. The Nails gave a half-hearted pulse, as if punishing him for trying to enjoy a moment without an axe in his hand.

He knew, objectively, they didn't function like that, and it was almost certainly the Codicier's presence that was aggravating his implants. Even so, it was hard to deny the coincidence.

'I know we are far from close,' Esca said, 'but you are still my commanding officer. Be careful, captain.'

Khârn hadn't replied. He'd not known what to say.

So he went alone. He went alone and listened to Argel Tal make a case for madness.

KHÂRN REMAINED ABOARD the *Lex* as both flagships tore their way back into the warp, but with their destinations the same, it meant little.

The brothers spoke together in the foul serenity of the *Lex*'s winding corridors, which were forever home to chanting voices carrying through the ship's metal bones. Sometimes Khârn heard weeping around a corner ahead, only to find the passageway empty when they reached it. Sometimes it was screaming, or earnest hymns sung in a language he couldn't understand. Argel Tal seemed to notice none of it, and if he did, it never bothered him.

Khârn used the edge of his boot to nudge an abandoned lasgun, left to rust on the deck. Half the corridors they travelled through were thick with detritus and the mess of the foulest inhabitation. In several, they'd already stepped over corpses. Most showed the marks of the knife-wounds that had ended their lives, but Khârn had also seen signs of strangulation and gunshots.

'Why has the *Lex* become such a den of filth?' he asked.

'Most of our ships look like this now. Too many new, faithful souls coming aboard. Their filth and waste spreads, as does sickness in the lower decks, where the cultists live herded together like beasts.'

Khârn heard the sneer in his battle-brother's voice, despite the fact that Argel Tal's features remained hidden behind his helm. Khârn shook his head.

'It's a disgrace.'

Argel Tal nodded. 'Maybe so, but it's difficult to manage. Our fleet's holds are swollen with faithful mortals. Once we reach Nuceria, we'll transfer the remaining crew and slave-castes to the *Trisagion*. Lord Aurelian wishes it to serve as his new flagship.'

Khârn cursed in Nagrakali. *Nuceria*. That was a host of fresh trouble just waiting to dawn.

'What of the *Lex*?' he asked.

'I believe Lorgar means to make it a gift,' the Word Bearer replied.

'To whom?'

'To me.'

They walked in silence a little longer, listening to the sounds of the ship. 'It's either cursed or haunted,' said Khârn, trying to smile.

'Both,' confirmed Argel Tal with weary seriousness. 'Thank you for staying aboard. I need your blade by my side for this.'

The World Eater fought to keep the concern from his face. The one thing Argel Tal loathed above all was pity.

'You cannot mean to try it,' Khârn said. 'It can't be done, not that it matters. The intent itself borders upon depravity.'

The Word Bearer gave a grunt that could mean everything at once or nothing at all.

Khârn carefully kicked another dead body out of the way. Clad in rags, it flopped against the wall with a dull thud. The entire ship stank of the freshly dead and the sickened living – it wasn't quite the ripe scents of decay or disease, but carried elements of both.

Corruption. The word came to him unbidden. That's what Khârn could smell. Corruption.

'A few more decks,' said Argel Tal through tightly gritted teeth.

'You don't even have her bones,' Khârn said. 'You told me devotees stole them.'

Argel Tal grunted again, this time spicing the sound with speech. 'Where do you think we're going, brother? What do you think we're going to do?'

* * *

They'd descended through the ship's filthy innards for more than an hour. The stench only grew stronger, setting Khârn's teeth on edge.

'Argel Tal,' he said gently, as they traversed the chanting darkness. 'I'm concerned for you. For your Legion.'

'Spare me,' the Word Bearer replied. As if reading Khârn's thoughts – a possibility the World Eater didn't disregard – Argel Tal turned his helm towards his brother. 'I need no pity. I chose this path and I walk it willingly.'

Khârn breathed in the ship's rank air. 'Have I ever argued against the wisdom of you allowing a xenos parasite to share your body?'

'*Daemon*, Khârn. It is no mere alien.'

'Call it what you will. I've allowed it thus far, haven't I?'

Argel Tal's eye lenses were ice-blue in the gloom of the bowel-corridors. '*Allowed* it? What a curious choice of words.'

'I could have killed you by now. I could have killed you to free you of the thing you call Raum, but I haven't. For better or worse. I've trusted you. I've let you abide in your faith.'

A brief screech of wrenching ceramite split the air, and Argel Tal stumbled. Silver light burned for a heartbeat's span in his eye lenses.

'Do not threaten us.'

'Us?' Khârn asked.

'Me,' Argel Tal amended. 'Don't threaten me.'

'I'm not threatening you. Stop for a moment. *Stop.*' Khârn gripped his brother's shoulder guard. 'Take your helmet off.'

He heard Argel Tal grunt again. 'I can't. It's been this way since Armatura. The Change isn't... reverting all the way, as it once did.'

Khârn was implacable and unmoving. 'Does Lorgar know?'

'Does it matter?' Argel Tal countered. 'Come. We have to retrieve the Blessed Lady's bones.'

Khârn watched the other stride onwards for a moment before once again falling in step alongside him.

'How do you know where to find her remains? Haven't you been hunting for months?'

Argel Tal muttered something.

'What?' Khârn asked.

'I said, Erebus told me where to find her bones.'

The World Eater's mouth fell open. 'What's wrong with you? How is this anything more than the crudest manipulation?'

'*We know it's a trap.*' Argel Tal snarled, stopping suddenly. 'It changes nothing. We have to bring her back.' The Word Bearer breathed slowly, calming himself. 'I have to bring her back.'

He turned to walk ahead, but Khârn tightened his grip, halting him in place.

'All these accusations of the Nails killing Angron, and the implants ruining our Legion,' the World Eater said, 'and yet you're warping before my eyes. I'm *worried* about you – about the whole Seventeenth. Your ship reeks of some unnameable malaise. You're planning to raise the dead by giving your friend's corpse to a man you despise, purely so he may commit some impossible act of necromantic superstition and bind you into his debt. Tell me, brother, am I doing my duty to you if I just allow this? If I help you with it?'

Argel Tal shrugged free of the other warrior's grip. 'Times change, Khârn. We all walk the Eightfold Path now, whether we keep our eyes open or move in ignorance; whether we desire this journey or not.'

The Eightfold Path. More religious madness.

Khârn hesitated within himself. If it was just superstitious nonsense, why then did the words seem so familiar, the way one remembers a dream for a few precious moments after waking? For a tantalising instant, the hallway's repellent stench felt stronger. He heard a woman's scream in the distance. She sounded young.

'I hate this ship,' Khârn said, adding a curse in Nagrakali. 'I'll come with you for this, but I do not trust Erebus. I can't imagine why you suddenly do.'

Argel Tal was free, but didn't keep walking. His fevered need to move forwards seemed to have abated.

'I don't trust him,' the Word Bearer said in his dual voices, 'but you'll have to forgive me the desperation of a little hope. If he can bring her back…'

'But at what cost?' Khârn sighed. 'What price will you have to pay?'

Argel Tal started walking again, slower this time. After a long moment, Khârn followed.

'I am not going into this blind,' said the Word Bearer eventually. 'Erebus is not without his weaknesses. He can be out-thought, and outfought. It's worth the risk, brother.'

Khârn said nothing. He let silence disagree on his behalf.

'And there's something else I need to tell you,' Argel Tal continued. 'Erebus was his usual serpentine self about it, hinting and suggesting rather than speaking it outright, but he wants you dead.'

Khârn cocked his head, unsure he'd heard properly. 'Me? We've crossed paths once or twice in the last decade. Why would he consider me a threat?'

Argel Tal thought carefully before speaking again. 'I detest him, but I can't deny his genius. His mind works on a hundred levels at once and he sees the thousand different futures from every action he takes. Somehow, at some point in one of those many possible futures, your actions will lose us the war. If you die now, you won't be there to influence the Siege of Terra.'

Khârn felt the sudden need to check his weapons: the plasma pistol and the replacement chainsword he'd taken from his personal armoury.

'That's what he told you?'

'That's what he told me.' Argel Tal led them down a curving staircase, far too ornate and gothic to belong in the stinking underdecks of a Word Bearers capital ship. 'I believe he hoped I'd be the one to kill you, out of affection for him and respect for his vision. But Calth rather leeched the last of my admiration for my former master.' Argel Tal looked over at Khârn as their bootsteps echoed into the dark. 'Just be careful.'

'You're the second brother to warn me with those words tonight,' said Khârn. 'Esca was the other.'

Argel Tal nodded.

'You treat your Librarians shamefully, you know. Esca deserves better.'

Khârn laughed for the first time in days. 'Lessons in morality from–'

'From a man with a daemon in his heart,' Argel Tal finished, smiling behind his faceplate. 'I know, I know.'

The two warriors came to a sealed bulkhead set against the left wall. The Word Bearer stroked his hand across its surface.

'Wait here. Kill anyone who tries to escape.'

Khârn looked at him as if to check he was serious, then nodded. 'You owe me for this.'

'You owe me for saving your life at Therakan. This will make us even.'

'Therakan was three decades ago. And you still owe me for Jurade.'

Argel Tal grinned and turned the bulkhead's locking ring with one hand.

'This won't take long.'

He was right. It took less than seven minutes.

Khârn stood outside the chamber, listening as the people were – for want of a better word – culled. Meaty thumps and cloth-ripping tears heralded every blow Argel Tal landed on the worshippers within. Never once did he hear the Word Bearer demand an answer or explanation. Never once did he hear them resisting, either. In his mind's eye, he imagined ranks of ragged humans kneeling in concentric circles around a central pulpit or altar, shrieking and praying and gasping and weeping as they were slaughtered.

Perhaps they accepted their fate and welcomed passage to the afterlife. Perhaps terror kept them in place.

Candlelight bled faintly through the open slice of the bulkhead door that Argel Tal left ajar. Amongst the Colchisian cries and murmurs, he made out several repetitions of *Great Lord, Great Lord*. The twin tang-smells of blood and urine soured the air.

Just as six minutes passed, everything fell silent.

Before the seventh minute, Argel Tal emerged from the chamber, awash with blood and carrying a body. Whatever was left of the woman after a year of decay and many months in the reverent care of the cultists had been wrapped in a black silk shroud. The gravesmell was raw and sharp and thick enough to taste. Khârn leaned back as it washed over his senses, and reached for the helm locked to his belt. Once he was behind the familiar aura of targeting locks and inhaling the odourless air of his armour's filtration systems, he spoke again.

'How many were in there?'

'A hundred and three.' Argel Tal was already moving, cradling the shrouded corpse like a sleeping child. 'Come on.'

Vorias and Esca waited where they weren't welcome, but kept a respectful distance. Beneath them, the vehicle hangar was given over to several circles of World Eaters cheering on their kindred, who fought bare-chested or in bodygloves. An inactive procession of Fellblades and Land Raiders lined the walls, their turrets pointing open-mouthed at the warriors whose colours they shared.

The two Librarians remained apart, watching from the balcony deck above the hangar. Just distant enough so that none of the warriors below could sense their presence through accidental implant malfunction.

Vorias, eldest of the remaining Librarian coven, had worked with Kargos, Vel-Kheredar and the others in trying to determine just why the Nails reacted so poorly in the presence of psychic minds, but the line of research was abandoned when they had come to realise the context of their work: no one cared. No one but those cursed with a sixth sense. Besides, their efforts had always ended in vain, and killed too many 'loyal' World Eaters who were unfortunate enough to be near the unstable Librarians.

The primarch brought few traditions from his world into the Legion, but a mistrust of anything 'unnatural' was one of them. Soon enough, all of the Nail-bearing legionaries were spitting onto the deck before their own Librarians, to ward off the 'bad luck' of being near them.

How quickly superstitions were adopted into fact. *Primitive,* thought Vorias, *primitive and so very sad.*

Nothing had changed his perspective in the decades since. Quite the opposite, in fact. What followed was the gradual deterioration of any sense of brotherhood. With the death of kinship often came the death of loyalty, but Vorias was gene-born into the XII Legion and he'd be one until the day he died. He didn't hate them for the way they scorned him, nor did he resent them for the way they spurned his talents as something dangerously worthless. He understood it perfectly. His presence caused them pain, and the Legion had no need of his psychic gifts. Even before Nikaea, such powers had never been factored into Angron's battle plans, as blunt and uncomplicated as those plans were.

Vorias was sanguine, accepting the truth beneath it all: he wasn't one of them. They were World Eaters. He was a War Hound. The Legion had moved on and left him behind with his ever-diminishing coterie of gifted brothers.

He watched Esca watching the melees below and felt the stirrings of a melancholic smile. The Codicier flinched at the hardest blows and twitched at the best strikes, as if landing them himself.

'You wish to join them?' the older warrior asked.

Esca's answer was a question of his own. 'You don't?'

Vorias had a thin, aquiline face with eyes the same green as Terra's extinct forests. It was in all ways a scholar's face, the face of a man not easily riled to rage, which was true to his temperament. He was one of the few souls – human, legionary, or otherwise – with no desire to let his face reflect anything but the absolute truth of his feelings and thoughts. Those who kept his company admired that about him. His detractors considered it one of his many flaws.

'I used to,' he admitted, leaning on the railing as he watched the warriors below. 'I used to crave the fellowship, the hot-blooded rush of running with the pack. But you and the others are enough for me, Esca. We need to appreciate what we have and strive for what we can achieve, rather than reach for what's denied to us.'

Esca grinned, though his ravaged, sutured face made it more of a grimace. 'Sounds very passive, Lectio Primus.'

'Passivity implies apathy or cowardice,' the slender warrior corrected. 'I'm merely a realist.'

They watched the fighting below for another few minutes. One of the matches ended with first blood and riotous cheering. In the aftermath, Delvarus stepped into the circle, carrying his meteor hammer, already whirling the deactivated morning star in readiness.

Esca nodded down to indicate the Triarii captain. 'Evidently, Lotara freed him from his quarters.'

Vorias gave a thin-lipped smile. 'The flag-captain knows her trade. She shamed him in the finest way: she showed him as a warrior that couldn't be trusted by his brothers. Very artfully done. Now we get the dubious pleasure of watching him seek to prove himself again, the only way he knows how.'

Below them, Delvarus was roaring into the crowd, baying at them, building their cheers for the fight to come. Like many World Eaters, Delvarus was inducted from a planet conquered in the Legion's earliest decades rather than from a specific homeworld. No Legion except the Ultramarines was as diverse, coloured by so many shades of skin from so many different worlds. Where the Word Bearers were uniformly dusky-skinned from the desert world Colchis, and the Night Lords were pale from their years on sunless Nostramo, the World Eaters reflected a diversity of flesh overruled by the bonds of brotherhood.

Delvarus was unhelmed and unarmoured for the pit-fight. His dark skin marked his genesis in the jungles of whatever planet he'd once called home, and he bared iron teeth at his kindred, demanding one of them step forwards and face him.

'His popularity seems unaffected,' Esca pointed out.

'You'll see,' Vorias replied.

Skane was the first to step forwards. The Destroyer's pale skin showed an unhealthy lightning-storm of veins and blood-bruises staining his flesh, from proximity to his own toxically lethal weaponry. His neck was collared in dark metal, forming armour around his augmetic throat. An aggressive cancer had stolen his vocal chords, but Kargos had given him new ones.

'First blood?' Delvarus growled at his brother. For years, but for the rarest bouts, first blood was almost all they ever asked of him.

'Third blood,' Skane replied, and lifted an inactive chainsword.

The fight was painfully, though not shamefully, brief. Skane went down to third blood in two minutes, losing to Delvarus without the Triarii captain even breaking a sweat.

Before Skane had even picked himself up, another World Eater stepped forwards to take his place. Delvarus was still laughing.

'First blood?' he asked again.

'Third blood.'

The fight went the same way. As did the next, and the next, and the next. As did the one to follow that.

By the seventh fight, Delvarus was breathing heavily, his skin beaded by effort. 'Who's next?' he cried over the hamstrung brother at his feet. 'Who's next?'

'Third blood,' said yet another World Eater, lifting a stilled chainaxe.

This fight went to four minutes, ending with Delvarus smirking through the cheers. Tradition stated no warrior should fight more than eight bouts in a single night, else he attracted accusations of arrogance and vainglory, putting himself above his brothers. The Triarii cast his meteor hammer to the deck, raising his fists in triumph. The cheers, however, had stopped cold.

Delvarus turned to leave the circle and rejoin the crowd, but the World Eaters didn't part to make way for him. One of them, a warrior with a face almost as badly sutured as Esca's, thudded chest to chest with the Triarii.

'Third blood,' he said to Delvarus. There was a chainsword in his hand.

'I've done my eight,' the warrior grinned.

'Third blood,' the World Eater repeated, and shoved Delvarus back into the circle.

The Triarii reclaimed his flail, hesitating a moment before setting it whirling again. His eyes were utterly untouched by the amusement plastered across his dark features.

Above all of this, Esca started to smile.

Three more fights ended just as the first eight had. Delvarus was no longer amused, and no longer trying to leave the circle. He knew where this was going.

Another fight. And another. And another – on this, the fourteenth, Delvarus's opponent raked the motionless teeth of his chainaxe across the Triarii's bicep, drawing first blood. In a rage, Delvarus retaliated with first, second and third bloodings in as many swings.

'Next,' he breathed through clenched teeth, looking out at the ring of his brothers who stared at him in silence. He was panting now, no different from the breathlessness of the front lines. Legionaries were gene-engineered to fight for days on end against human and inhuman enemies alike, but on even ground...

When brother fought brother in a place as brutal as the XII Legion's fighting pits, the rules changed with the game.

He beat the next opponent, and the next, and the nine that followed those. With cramping muscles, he put his twenty-fifth opponent down on the deck and caught his heaving breath.

The twenty-sixth was tied at second blood for a dangerously long time. His opponent landed a lucky kick to his chest after almost half an hour of duelling, and Delvarus staggered back against the wall of World Eaters. Where duellists were usually pushed back into the fight with cheers and good-natured jeers, he was shoved unceremoniously forwards in vicious silence, almost stumbling over onto his hands and knees. He recovered in time to block the descending blow, his flail's chain wrapping the incoming sword and tearing it from his foe's fingers. Delvarus cannoned a fist into the warrior's face, breaking his nose and winning on third blood at last.

He dragged in another breath. 'Next.' The challenge was almost a wheeze.

Kargos stepped forwards. '*Sanguis extremis,*' he said. 'To the death.'

Delvarus narrowed his eyes, giving a snarl that wouldn't have been out of place rolling from the throat of an Ancient Terran tyger, or Fenrisian wolf.

'So eager,' he breathed, 'to die, Apothecary?'

Kargos gave a crooked, nasty smirk and held out his hand towards Skane. The sergeant handed him a power sword without a word.

Their weapons came alive in the same moment: Kargos's borrowed blade and the spiked flail-head crackling with opposing power fields. Neither warrior went to parry. Neither did anything beyond trying kill strike after kill strike, weaving aside when death came too close for comfort.

Desperation gave strength to Delvarus's sore muscles, but it couldn't give him the agility he possessed while fresh. Kargos's first blow came after the first minute, cutting a shallow line of sizzling flesh down the Triarii's cheek. Delvarus's face twitched as his Nails pulsed and he launched back at the Apothecary.

He scored the next hit, his flail's head catching Kargos on the jaw. The barest scratch, too weak to even flare the power field, but it painted blood over Kargos's pale skin and left his gums bleeding. That was enough to bring Delvarus's smile back.

He was wise to Kargos's games. He flinched aside when the Apothecary spat bloody saliva in reply, ready for the oldest of tricks that earned Kargos his pit-fighting name.

'A filthy habit,' Delvarus grinned. His return blow lashed through the air with a whine of energised metal, pulled back before it could crash into the deck and wedge in the iron.

Kargos's reply came with another smile, this one with blood-reddened teeth. 'You look tired,' he said.

Delvarus sprayed spit as he roared in reply.

Above them, Vorias narrowed his eyes in thought. 'Did you feel that?' he asked softly.

Esca nodded. He'd felt something change in the air, a *tightening* of the atmosphere around the circle as Delvarus's implants ramped up. The Triarii's blows were wilder, heavier, accompanied by grunts and snarls.

'Six seconds,' Vorias said in the same quiet voice. 'Maybe eight.'

It was six. Kargos parried for the first time, cleaving through the meteor hammer's chain in one chop. The deactivated flail head crashed into the closest World Eaters observer, raking across his bare chest.

At the mercy of his implants, Delvarus reached for Kargos with his bare hands, only to find the point of the Apothecary's blade at his throat. Even with the Nails stealing the edge from his reason, the threat of imminent death penetrated to his hind-brain instincts, forcing him to hesitate. The silence was louder than the cheering had ever been.

'Finish it, Bloodspitter.' Saliva trailed in a thick string down the Triarii's chin. 'You've proven your point. All of you have. So finish it.'

Kargos kept the blade against Delvarus's throat. 'The other Legions have primarchs that lead them to glory. They have homeworlds to honour and cultural legacies to live by. We have scraps of stolen tradition and the trust between brothers. That's all. *Brotherhood,* captain. A brotherhood you broke when you abandoned your duty and lied to your sworn kindred.'

Delvarus was clearly fighting the Nails, forcing his twitching fingers into fists to maintain a semblance of control. The sword's tip blackened his throat where it touched and scorched the flesh.

'I recognise my failing–' he growled the words '–and will be sure to correct it.'

Quoting the traditional apology of the VI Legion earned a guttural tide of chuckles. Even Kargos smiled, and this time without the shadow of malice that had backlit every one of his expressions thus far. The Apothecary stared hard into the Triarii's eyes.

'Are you my brother, Delvarus?'

The Triarii exhaled, tilting his head back to bare his throat for the final thrust. 'I am. And I'll die as your brother. Finish it.'

Kargos deactivated the blade. He lowered it, and tossed it back to Skane at the circle's edge.

Delvarus stared, wide-eyed, the Nails sparking in his brain. '*Sanguis extremis*,' he said. 'To the death. To the *death*.'

'We've all broken traditions in our time,' said Kargos. 'You're one of our best, Delvarus. Remember that. Remind us why we've spent so many years thinking it.'

The dark-skinned warrior met the eyes of his surrounding brothers. 'You all stand by his words? Any who would make a liar of Kargos step forwards now.' He spread his arms wide. 'Plunge a blade through my breast. I will stand here and let you.'

No one came forward. A few warriors smiled, others nodded in a respect that passed for forgiveness.

'I sense Khârn's hand in this,' Delvarus said to Kargos. 'It smells like his wisdom, carried out by other hands.' That earned more quiet laughter; no longer was it the sound of mockery.

'I couldn't possibly comment,' the Apothecary replied.

Above the dispersing confrontation, Esca finally turned to Vorias. 'They still have nobility in them. The Nails haven't bled them dry.'

The Lectio Primus nodded. 'Yet.'

As both Librarians turned away and left their brothers to the comfort of comradeship, Vorias spoke without looking into his protégé's eyes.

'Legion Master Lhorke came to me earlier today. He believes the primarch stands on the precipice, and a reckoning is long overdue.'

Esca didn't answer at once. 'That almost sounds like a threat,' he said at last.

'Yes,' Vorias agreed. His scholarly face was cadaverous away from the hangar deck lighting, now a mask of pale angles and worn lines. 'It does, doesn't it?'

SIXTEEN

Regenesis
Blessed Lady
Vakrah Jal

KHÂRN EXPECTED CHANTING, candles and all the cringeworthy trappings of superstition. In this, he was not disappointed.

Erebus maintained personal quarters aboard the *Fidelitas Lex*, despite commanding his own warship, *Destiny's Hand*. It was here that he brought Argel Tal and Khârn, and it was here that he prepared to commit blasphemy against the natural order.

Khârn knew little of Erebus beyond what Argel Tal had told him, and his Word Bearers brother was the kind of soul who disliked speaking ill of anyone without sincere and inviolate reasons to do so. Argel Tal would face down someone he despised and threaten to pull them apart, but he consistently refused to spread foul word about any other warrior once their backs were turned. 'Defamation,' he always claimed, 'is for cowards and insecure children.'

Still, Argel Tal's dislike for Erebus had come up more than once in conversation over the last year since Isstvan V, when Khârn and the Gal Vorbak warrior had renewed their acquaintance as respective subcommanders of their Legions' forces, in readiness for the Shadow Crusade.

To Khârn's thinking, the name Erebus chose for his battle-barge perfectly summed up the First Chaplain's attitudes towards fate and his place in shaping it. *Destiny's Hand*. Such arrogance. Such ardent, seething hubris.

Such an attitude led to... Well, it led to this.

Erebus had gathered a coven of slaves in his quarters, seventeen of them in all, each one chained by the throat to the central altar. The oldest was a crone who would never see eighty again. The youngest was a boy who couldn't be long into double figures. Quite how they managed to chant from their parchments while breathing in the stench of the Blessed Lady's bones was beyond Khârn. He'd seen unaugmented humans vomit at much less provocation, yet these murmuring worthies stared with dead eyes into the parchments clutched loosely in their dirt-stained hands. They chanted, but he wasn't sure they were even reading.

Candles lined the chamber's iron walls, each one marked with a meticulously etched Colchisian rune in its red wax. Shrieking angels and serene gargoyles formed of the same metal as the walls looked down from their perches sculpted into the ceiling. Several of the statues were reaching in motionless need, warped hands striving to touch the room's inhabitants – perhaps to bestow a blessing, perhaps to mutilate them on devilry's whim.

Most legionaries kept their arming chambers as places of meditation and training, filled with mementos of victories stored alongside their personal armouries. Erebus had made his haven into a heathen temple. The altar was a central table of filigreed black steel, complete with manacles for reasons Khârn didn't care to know but had no trouble imagining. Blood channels were cut into the table's surface: deep grooves that would funnel gore and whatever else into a shallow bronze bowl beneath the altar.

'What's the bowl for?' he'd asked upon entering.

'Scrying,' Erebus had answered. 'Now be silent and show some respect.'

Khârn had complied with the former. He wasn't certain he could convincingly feign the latter.

Argel Tal remained at Khârn's side, arms crossed over his breastplate. If his features were brightened by hope or darkened by distrust, his helm blocked all insight. Crystal blue eye lenses fixed on Erebus and the mouldering, disconnected bones resting on the burial shroud. The Word Bearer watched everything and revealed nothing.

'Brother.' Khârn spoke softly, so as not to interrupt the vileness taking place before him. He could hear drumming on the deck above, and weeping from another chamber nearby. A plague on this wretched vessel; this ship of the faithful damned.

Argel Tal turned with a low thrum of active armour joints. His twin voices were pitched low, leaving his human voice almost as soft as the daemon's whisper.

'What?'

Khârn inclined his crested helm to the chanting beggars. 'Will they survive this ritual?' he asked, his tone edged.

The Word Bearer looked back to the muttering choir. 'I don't know.'

'You don't know or you don't care?'

'I don't care,' Argel Tal admitted.

'You'd kill them to save her soul?' Even knowing it was too late, Khârn wouldn't back down. 'Is that who you are?'

Argel Tal breathed out a rueful sigh. 'It might be. I don't yet know. I'm willing to become it, to bring her back.'

The World Eater gestured to the chanting mortals. Chains rattled on his bracers as he swept his arm to encompass them all.

'This is how it begins,' Khârn said. 'This is how the coldness you so despise in Erebus first takes root in you.'

Argel Tal shook his head. 'Don't act as if this is new to either of us; as though neither of us has butchered hundreds of innocents, young and old, with our own hands. This isn't a game of selective morality, Khârn. We slaughter the innocent and guilty alike, whether they hold lasguns, bolters, or cower in their homes holding only each other.'

'I was Lost each time I killed civilians.' Khârn gritted his teeth. 'Lost to the Nails.'

'You can lie to yourself and your Legion – but not to me, brother. Even if you were "Lost", does that excuse what you have done? Does it make everything better? As you tore those men, women and children apart, did any of their screams even *once* turn to understanding smiles? Did they reach up during their own massacres to give your their blessings, forgiving you for the fact you can't control your own rage?'

Argel Tal looked back to the preparations as he continued. 'We are the Legiones Astartes. We choose who lives and who dies in this galaxy. It is the way of things.'

'This is murder,' said Khârn. 'Not war. *Murder.*'

'Just because we are soldiers in a warzone, it is no less murder if we slaughter unarmed civilians. The context is irrelevant. But I will not argue with you.' He nodded towards the remains on the altar. 'Her life is worth a thousand others. These are... humanity's dregs, but they are not here completely involuntarily. Look at them. You'd not think twice about breaking their skulls open if they were in your way. The only reason you're roused to disgust now is because this heathen ritual makes your skin crawl.'

Khârn had no reply. His brother knew him too well.

'It makes mine crawl, as well,' Argel Tal confessed. 'How many times have I told you I wished this Truth *wasn't* true? But it is, Khârn. It is true – *the* Truth – and we face it. We will not live a lie.'

Despite their surroundings, Khârn felt himself at risk of smiling. 'You sermonise well, brother. You should give more speeches to the Seventeenth.'

Argel Tal shuddered, his gaze never leaving the mouldering bones. 'I'm no preacher.'

Khârn fell silent. One minute he'd tell himself he would interrupt the rite by drawing his chainblade and threatening Erebus's life. The next he'd confess to a curiosity of his own, fierce even in the face of the distant drums and the chanting that pressed against his senses like an unwelcome smell.

As for the Blessed Lady herself, she was a year on the wrong side of the grave. With no real experience in how religious cultures preserved the remains of their 'saints' as relics, Khârn had expected her bones to be bleached and polished, or for her wounded body to be preserved in stasis at the moment of her death.

The reality was altogether more macabre. Full decay hadn't yet left her entirely fleshless – her initial interment in the mausoleum's hermetically-sealed casket had protected her at least a little – but it was clear that the worshippers who stole her body had been praying to a decomposing corpse for almost a year. All that remained of the XVII Legion's Confessor of the Word was a ragged skeleton, with a touch of ripped-parchment skin and rotted grey-green strings of tendon clinging to her joints. Her eyeless, jawless skull stared blindly at the gargoyles carved into the left wall. Skinless hands were nothing more than fragments of bone scattered on the black shroud. The last bits of organic matter she possessed gave off a cloying, musty reek as they broke down through the slow, slow process of inevitability. It was the befouled burial shroud that gave off the stench more than the pathetic remnants of her corpse.

Khârn knew Argel Tal as well as the Word Bearer knew him. Several long compliances and joint campaigns during the Great Crusade had seen to that, and respect had quickly grown between them. Khârn knew full well the nature of the repentant symbolism that his brother so often felt was necessary, and he could all too easily see Argel Tal wearing that burial shroud as a ceremonial cloak, whether this madness worked or not. Khârn resolved to put a stop to that, one way or the other. There was symbolism, and then there was morbid obsession. The Word Bearers – even the saner ones – often seemed to struggle telling the two apart.

'What of the Geller field?' he asked. With the *Lex* in the warp, its protective shielding guarded the hull against the touch of the Neverborn thrashing through the Sea of Souls.

'Geller fields ward metal and flesh,' Argel Tal replied. 'Nothing can fully ward the human soul.'

The breeze came from nowhere. Just gently at first, tugging at the parchments bound to Erebus's and Argel Tal's armour; curling the edges of the scrolls held in the slaves' hands. The temperature gauge on Khârn's retinal display flickered, telling him it was too cold in the chamber to sustain human life, then scrambling with static a second time and reporting that it was hotter than the surface of a weak sun.

'What are they chanting?' Khârn asked. He spoke Colchisian close to fluently, yet struggled to make out a single word leaving the slaves' lips.

Argel Tal's answer was several seconds in coming. 'Names,' he said in Raum's slithering voice. 'Thousands of names.'

Khârn's Nails gave an irritated *tick-tick* pulse, sending pain dancing down his spinal column. 'What names?'

'The names of Neverborn,' Raum replied, his tone in the velvet border between caution and unease. 'Daemon-names, rendered crudely by human tongues. Erebus is drawing their eyes to him, asking the denizens of the warp if they have seen Cyrene's soul.'

'*Seen* it?'

'Captured it. Immolated it. Flayed it. Flensed it. Devoured it.'

Khârn grunted, watching as the wind from nowhere clawed at the slaves' rags. The candles cast cavorting shadows of long-limbed things that weren't present in the chamber. The drums grew louder – the ship's own heartbeat pounding against the walls.

He was reaching for his weapon, whether the gesture was futile or not, when the first of the murmuring choir died.

The woman, clad in beggar's robes, tore the parchment in her hands, crying out as she ran towards Khârn. Revelation was a sick sunrise behind her eyes.

'*Betrayer!*' she screamed. '*Khârn the betrayer! Khârn the betrayer!*' The chain leash around her throat pulled tight when she reached the end of its slack – the sound of a splitting tree trunk cut right through the drumbeat – and the woman tumbled to the ground, her neck snapped.

Khârn's skin prickled beneath his armour. Argel Tal – or was it Raum? – turned to regard him. Liquid mercury coalesced and clashed in the Word Bearer's eye lenses. Neither warrior said a word. The drums intensified, furious now, mimicking a dozen hearts beating in opposition.

Across the chamber, Erebus watched the bones and only the bones. Khârn saw the Chaplain's mouth moving, but he read from no parchment or tome. Whatever he whispered, he did so from inspiration or memory.

A dishevelled man was next. He cried out in ugly, staccato shrieks as he smashed his face repeatedly into the altar, spattering the Blessed Lady's thigh bones with dark cranial blood and brain matter. It took him eleven impacts to kill himself; on the last, he slumped to the deck, twitching.

Khârn felt fingers scraping and scratching faintly at his armour. Uncertain target locks kept trying to track half-formed shapes of things that weren't really there.

He drew his blade and rested a hand on Argel Tal's shoulder guard. 'Brother, *nothing* is worth this foulness.'

Argel Tal never had a chance to reply. The moment Khârn finished speaking, Erebus voiced a single word: an unknowable command in that jagged, alien tongue. The skeleton on the altar rattled, shivered.

And then, with no lungs or vocal chords, it started screaming.

IN THE TORMENTED years to come, on the rare days Khârn possessed enough self-control to speak – let alone tell the tale of that night's events – one of the few things he remembered with clarity was the way the choir died.

Fifteen men and women, raking at their own flesh with dirty fingernails and ritual knives, came apart where they stood. They burst as if shattered by the invisible hands of gods. Some of their ruined flesh was contained by their clothes, the rest slopped across the chamber. The sound of their sanctified demise was somehow porcine – a squeal of piggish panic coupled with the fatty splash of wet meat falling to the floor. Their innards rained over the altar, bathing the writhing skeleton in the viscera it so utterly lacked.

As if in sympathy, the iron drums slowed to one gigantic heartbeat, rather than battering mercilessly to represent many.

Dappled in gore, both Khârn and Argel Tal stepped back from the grotesque performance – the World Eater wiping his gauntleted fingers over his faceplate to clear his eye lenses; the latter staring at the resurrecting corpse through blood-streaked vision.

Erebus ignored the howling aetheric wind and the lamenting of souls caught in its grip. He raised his voice, aiming his crozius maul at the revenant on the altar, commanding it to reclaim its place in the world of flesh and blood and bone and steel.

Khârn saw the still-screaming corpse lift a hand – a claw of bone now articulated by fresh, bloody meat – before the chamber plunged into absolute darkness. The blackness was an entity itself, too deep and true to be the mere absence of light. His thermal vision cycled live, showing nothing. His echolocation sight clicked active, showing the same. No matter what his retinal display did to compensate for the sudden blindness, he was left in the dark.

His blade came up *en garde*, revving and chewing air. Something smashed it from his fists; he hoped it was Argel Tal.

The screaming became more human, echoing around the chamber rather than through Khârn's mind. Blessedly, it ceased tearing at the Nails in his head.

He heard bare feet on the hard deck, and a young woman's hoarse shrieking finally falling into wet breathlessness. He heard, beneath all else, a rheumy dripping that conjured thoughts of carcasses hanging in an abattoir.

When his vision returned, it was almost with reluctance, more like emerging from an ink-cloud than merely opening his eyes. Shadows recoiled from each of them, dissolving away in the candlelight and leaving ripples through the pools of blood. Not a single candle had been extinguished by the wind, or in the blackness that followed it.

Erebus stood by the altar, his expression one of immortal patience. Indulgence, even.

Crouched in the corner, naked but for her burial shroud and the scraggly protection of her hazel hair now blood-darkened to black, Cyrene Valantion shivered and stared at Khârn and Argel Tal with wide eyes the colour of burnt auburn.

She looked at them. She *saw* them.

'You're not blind,' Argel Tal said in a stunned whisper. Not 'You're alive', or 'Are you all right'. Shock had hit him, and hit hard. 'You're not blind,' he said again.

Cyrene kept shivering, kept staring, and kept her silence.

WORD OF HER return spread like grassfire through the Word Bearers flagship. Mere minutes after they left Erebus's chambers, mortal crew were crowding the halls, calling her name, desperate to touch her skin for luck, or steal a scrap of her burial shroud as some funereal token of the Pantheon's favour.

Cyrene stared out at all of this with mounting horror. Before her murder in the skies above Isstvan V, she'd sailed aboard the Word Bearers warship *De Profundis* for over forty years. All the while, she'd been hailed as a living icon of the Legion's past, one of the last survivors of the Perfect City, annihilated on the Emperor's orders to punish the XVII Legion for their misplaced faith. The primarch himself had wept upon meeting her – the single, slow tear of a demigod's sorrow – and asked her forgiveness. That story, too, had spread with the tenacity of unchecked flame. All the more fervently for the fact it was true.

Her life was a lesson for the Legion to remember, and an acknowledgement of its guilt. She was also a treasure to be protected, finding a place within the XVII Legion the way men and women of faith and courage had been finding places among holy armies since time out of mind.

She'd listened for four decades, hearing the confessions of Word Bearers, Imperial Army soldiers, and the thousands of human crew of Argel Tal's warship. When the 301st Expeditionary Fleet linked up with other armadas prosecuting the Great Crusade, Word Bearers officers from other fleets always sought time in her presence, unburdening their hearts and consciences of the past's sins and the treacheries yet to come. She listened for almost half a century, hearing and forgiving the trespasses of the only Legion ever to fail the Master of Mankind, and the first Legion to learn of the truth behind reality.

She'd learned that truth with them. She was as faithful as any Word Bearer, and plainly more pious than most.

Rejuvenat surgery kept her young, strong, and a frequent figure for immortalisation in the statues and stained glass windows that decorated the cathedrals and monasteries of so many Word Bearers warships.

But she'd lived those years without ever once seeing a single warrior or worker that came for her blessing. The Ultramarines incendiary weapons took her sight when they erased the Perfect City from existence. Cyrene watched her city die to an orbital bombardment many times brighter than her world's sun, and the flash burns to her corneas and optic nerves had never healed. She'd refused augmetic replacements, for reasons of faith and the hope that her own eyes would heal.

Not once had she ever seen the interior of the vessels where she'd led sermons and taken countless confessions. She'd never seen Argel Tal, nor Khârn, nor even Lorgar. Her only experience of seeing any Space Marine in the flesh was watching the sons of Guilliman executing rioters and marching the population of the Perfect City from their homes, to minimise casualties before the skyfire began.

Now, in the corridors aboard the *Lex*, Khârn was glad he'd stayed for the ritual and its aftermath. He led the way back to Argel Tal's arming chamber, fighting back the zealous crowds lining the halls. Argel Tal kept her close, guarding her with a drawn blade held crosswise before her. He'd allowed the Change to come, and shielded her with his great wings – those red-black pinions he'd been forming over the course of the year since Isstvan. They horrified Cyrene, that much was obvious; she was overcome by the immensity of everything around her.

'Get back,' Khârn warned the tide of humanity crushing itself against him. Grimy hands sought to push him aside in their fervency. There were even Word Bearers in the throng, chanting the Blessed Lady's name, heralding her as the Saint Reborn.

'Get back.' He snarled the words, backing them up with a kick to one man's sternum. Bones broke in the human's chest, and the blow shoved him down to the deck, surely to die beneath the smothering tread of his fellows. Khârn felt a nasty little smirk take hold; Argel Tal was right. This wasn't a game of selective morality.

Between the calls of *Cyrene! Cyrene!* and *Blessed Lady!* he heard a softer voice from behind, a girl's tremulous whisper.

'Who are you?'

He risked a glance back, just as he threw an elbow into a Word Bearer's faceplate, sending the warrior staggering. Cyrene was pale, anaemically so, though whether from the potent stench of her entombment shroud or the insanity of her ordeal, Khârn couldn't be sure.

'It's me,' he told her. How many times had they met? How many times had he listened to her and Argel Tal debate faith, philosophy, or the nature of the soul? He'd never believed a word of it back then, but tonight's events forced an unpleasant re-evaluation upon his scepticism. He'd let her touch his face to feel his features; he'd even let her run her fingers over the scar at the back of his head, the only wound that wouldn't fade, where his Nails had been implanted so many years before. He'd told her of the Nails and what they did to his brain.

But here, now, she didn't know who he was. She was looking at him, *seeing* him and not recognising him, rather than feeling his face or knowing him by listening to his voice.

'Khârn,' he said to her. 'I'm Khârn.'

She stared at him, at the mask over his face. *'You're* Khârn?'

He had no chance to reply. The crowd pushed against him hard enough to almost press him back into her. Khârn lashed back with his chainsword, tearing the closest human in half. He felt sick, fighting cold like this. The Nails pulsed – not with pain but with a tantalising stroke of warmth that set his heart racing – offering pleasure drip-fed into the emotional core of his brain if he'd only let go and butcher with impunity.

'Back away,' he growled. *'Back away.'*

He swallowed the urge, battered another two humans aside, brained a third with the hilt of his chainsword, and crashed his fist full into another worshipper's face, snapping the man's head back and sending him to the deck.

It wasn't enough. The tidal push came on, humans squeezing past him, even slipping between his legs. Sheer numbers overwhelmed him, forcing the thought into his mind of peasant farmers with pitchforks dragging an armoured knight from the saddle. He'd seen that once, on a grainy hololith pict-feed, and it had left him laughing hard enough to bring tears to his eyes. It seemed somewhat less amusing now. Khârn banished the flicker of distraction and gave in to temptation. He gave in to the Nails, no different from the way an exhausted traveller surrenders to sleep. He simply stopped fighting it.

Pleasure came in an immediate trickle, revving as surely as the chainsword in his hands. Killing was exhilarating the way nothing else could be, and the Nails played their neurochemical game to make it so. He knew, in his moments of dull, grey peace, that when the Nails sang they stunted the serotonin in his brain to encourage instinctive aggression, just as he knew they deadened emotional response and electrical activity to anything but the flow of adrenaline. Amongst the archeotechnological whims of the Butcher's Nails, these were the effects his Legion had detailed most extensively in their long-abandoned studies.

All that cold and considered knowledge meant little. The pain engine in his skull forced him to enjoy killing above everything else, and all the calm-voiced hypothesising about the whys and wherefores changed exactly nothing. Even the comfort of brotherhood paled – one of life's few remaining pleasures outside of battle. So Khârn killed, just as his brothers always killed, because killing meant feeling something beyond slow, unfocused spite.

And as always, with the promise of pleasure came the burn of overworked muscles. Between the Nails and the combat stimulants swimming through his bloodstream, he fought harder, moved faster, struck with more fury. Pleasure was the reward for every swing of the blade.

Word Bearers were joining the worshippers now, decorum overcome by their zealous faith. One of them came at him with a chainsword of his own – Khârn cannoned his elbow into the warrior's throat, slashing his blade across the exposed power cables on his foe's thigh, and then reached to grasp at a human woman seeking to run past him. He balled his fist in her hair, breaking her neck with a single sharp pull.

Yet nothing he did could stem the tide. For each of them he knocked back or bludgeoned to death, more of them crawled or squeezed past in the press of bodies. The sheer amount of frantic humanity stole most of the room he needed to swing the blade or throw a fist.

The first sign of respite came from the rearmost ranks, with agonised wailing preceding the grisly smell of burning pork. Smoke, gritty enough to blacken the tongue, misted its way through the corridors, accompanied by the storm's-breath *fssshhh* of flame weapons unleashed in the closest quarters.

What little Khârn could make out of the firebursts set his lips peeling back in a snarl owing as much to laughter as to rage. The flames were green: licking tongues of vital, phosphorous jade. He knew the nature of that fire, as did any soul that had fought alongside or against Argel Tal's Chapter of Consecrated Iron in the year since their honoured founding.

Froth stung at the edges of Khârn's mouth. Saliva ran down his chin, acidic enough to hurt. He took one man's arm off at the shoulder, killing the poor human with a backhanded slap to the face before the man could even scream. Behind him, he heard Argel Tal's energised blade thrumming left and right, buzzing as it fried the blood trying to stick to its sacred steel. Argel Tal killed while holding Cyrene in one possessive, protective arm, his weapon needing no chain-teeth to chew. The Custodian-blade's force field rent organic matter apart, going through bone as easily as flesh.

The two warriors turned with unspoken understanding, herding the terrified woman between them, standing back to back against the horde. Both of them lashed out with blades, boots and fists. Argel Tal had the advantage of his wings, slamming them against mortals, throwing them from their feet.

'I see the jade fire,' Khârn called over his shoulder. *About time,* he silently added.

'Now stay alive until they reach us,' the Word Bearer grated in reply.

Khârn's chainsword lodged halfway through a man's torso, slipping from his grip where blood made his clutch treacherous. The blade's teeth clicked, caught against the bone. Khârn left it on the deck, sheathed in meat where it belonged, and resorted to killing them with his armoured hands.

It wasn't the first time, and it wouldn't be the last.

IT WAS FAIR to say that few Word Bearers had ever impressed Khârn. They waged war with zeal – passion's unhealthy cousin – and their chanting advances beneath morbid banners and divine sigils were difficult to admire. In some battles, a Word Bearers force could be relied upon to cleanse and purge every enemy soul, and salt the very earth on which the foe had lived. In others, they would crumble into praying, murmuring regiments and lose themselves in torture or some other ritual debasement to appease whatever gods they believed were watching. If there was a way to predict their inclinations before battle was joined, Khârn hadn't yet discovered it.

Even the Gal Vorbak, Argel Tal's daemon-blooded brethren, were as much animals as men. Few of the so-called 'Blessed Sons' restrained themselves to the degree shown by their former commander, and most were petty warlords over their own squads and hosts, ruling in their daemonic form more often than not, issuing commands not from the Legion, but from the Pantheon.

The exception to Khârn's hesitant disgust with the XVII Legion was the Vakrah Jal. The Chapter of Consecrated Iron rose from the ashes of companies devastated on the killing fields of Isstvan V. Argel Tal had gathered hundreds of leaderless warriors and given them unity from ruination. Forsaking his oaths to the annihilated Chapter of the Serrated Sun, he gained Lord Aurelian's permission to raise a new Chapter in its stead.

Many of them were berthed aboard the *Conqueror*, given the honour of duelling in the fighting pits. Only a few hundred remained aboard *Fidelitas Lex*, but they were making themselves known at last.

They were the bearers of the jade fire, and they went to war behind faceplates of burnished silver.

These were the warriors incinerating their way through the crowded corridors.

HIS BOOTS SLOPPED through the pools of sticky wreckage that remained. Where the floor was iron grille-work, molten flesh and metal dripped through the holes, trickling down into the nameless dark between decks. Khârn was fighting off the familiar disorientation of coming down from the Nails, but he was aware enough to note the caution in the Vakrah Jal's movements as they approached him. Several cut right past him to reach Argel Tal and Cyrene, but a few lingered, not entirely certain of his temperament.

One of them risked touching him, resting a hand on Khârn's back-mounted power pack.

'Captain?' the warrior asked. 'Do you require an Apothecary?'

Khârn moved away from the warrior's touch. 'No. My thanks, though.' His eyes were warm and weighty, threatening to close. He felt as if he could sleep for a week. Curse this damn ship – even the Nails pushed heavier on his mind here, leaving him weaker in the aftermath of their soaring song.

The warrior stepped back, his boots thudding in the organic slush as he deactivated and sheathed his curved Colchisian blade. A moment later, Khârn heard the telltale hiss of the Vakrah Jal's wrist-mounted flamer ports shutting down. The pilot lights snapped out of existence with twin sparks. The sight almost made the World Eater grin. Nothing but the Mechanicum's priceless best for the XVII elite.

'Eshramar,' he said to the Vakrah Jal sergeant.

'Sir?' The warrior turned his silver faceplate back to Khârn.

'You melted half of this hallway,' the centurion pointed out, and it was no exaggeration. The Vakrah Jal's alchemical cling-fire had dissolved long swathes of the deck and turned the walls to slack, cooling sludge. Although the ventilators battled the spoiled-pork stink and the clouds of smoke, there was only so much air filtration could hope to achieve without hours to work on this mess.

'We also saved your life,' Eshramar pointed out. His voice was a vox-drawl, but there was no hiding the amusement. 'Ungrateful Twelfth Legion bastard.'

The Nails' bite was just fresh enough for Khârn to find that funny. His implants allowed him a smile, still stinging pleasantly from the adrenaline in his bloodstream.

'Brother.' He turned to Argel Tal. 'We have to move. More will come.'

SEVENTEEN

Voices in the Night
Russ's Lesson
Warp

Lorgar was listening to worlds die. Above and around him, kept at bay by the warded glass dome, the warp thrashed and surged in a dance of colours that couldn't exist. He saw things in the boiling tides, as everyone did, but the tormented faces and helpless hands were easy to ignore. All that mattered was the melody.

The rest of the song continued in its arcane flow, coming closer and closer to the crescendo he required. Not long now. Soon, the tune would reach such aetheric artistry that he would be free to channel it for the material realm to hear. Each world enslaved to their suns had a part to play, which is why they had to die in perfect harmony with one another. All Lorgar lacked was a conduit to release the accrued power, and that would come in time.

Serving as conductor for an astrological orchestra was more taxing than he'd dreamed, though his blunter, more militant brothers would struggle to grasp the finer points of his efforts. Exhaustion left him wondering, even if only briefly, whether absolute peace would create a stellar song as divinely inspired as absolute war.

Fate had played its hand and Chaos was destined to swallow all creation whether or not Horus and Lorgar raged against the Imperial war machine, but if what if they'd stayed loyal to the Emperor? What then? Would the Great Crusade have shaped a serene funeral dirge, to play behind the veil as humanity died in a defenceless harrowing?

Therein lay the fatal flaw. The Emperor's way was *compliance*, not peace. The two were as repellent to one another as opposing lodestones. It didn't matter what enlightenment the Imperium stamped out in its conquering crusade when obedience was all its lords desired. It didn't matter what wars were fought from now into eternity. The Legiones Astartes would always march, for they were born to do so. There would always be war; even if the Great Crusade had been allowed to reach the galaxy's every edge, there would never be peace. Discontent would seethe. Populations would rebel. Worlds would rise up. Human nature eventually sent men and women questing for the truth, and tyrants always fell to the truth.

No peace. Only war.

Lorgar felt his blood run cold. *Only war.* Those were words to echo into eternity.

He didn't trust the Ten Thousand Futures the way Erebus claimed to. Too many possibilities forked from every decision made by every living thing. What use was prophecy when all it offered was what might happen? Lorgar was not so devoid of imagination that he needed the warp's twisting guesswork to show him that. Anyone with an iota of vision could imagine what might happen. Genius lay in engineering events according to one's own goals, not in blindly heeding the laughter of mad gods.

More than that, Lorgar sought to keep one thing in mind above all else. The gods were powerful, without doubt, but they were fickle beings. Each worked against its own kin more often than not, spilling conflicting prophecies into their prophets' minds. Perhaps they weren't even sentient in the way a mortal mind could encompass. They seemed as much the manifestations of primal emotion as they did individual essences.

But no, there was a wide gulf between hearing them and heeding them. Gods lied, just like men. Gods deceived and clashed and sought to advance their own dominions over their rivals'. Lorgar trusted none of their prophecies.

He'd even seen glimpses of potential futures where the Imperium came to worship the Emperor as a god. What would have to transpire in countless trillions of human hearts for that faith to ever take hold? The very faith Lorgar was chastised for spreading, the very beliefs he was punished for believing – how could mankind's empire ever embrace their lord as a deity, after the XVII Legion had been humiliated for daring to claim such a truth?

He shook his head at the thought and sighed softly.

'Lord?' one of the choir asked, interpreting the sigh as one of displeasure.

Lorgar softened the interruption with a golden smile. 'Forgive me a moment's distraction,' he said. 'Please, continue.'

The choir numbered fifty-one souls, and they all spoke over one another. Each of them wore the white robes of their calling, almost priestly in their sombre regalia. They stood in loose disorder, with no discipline to their formation beyond the accidental artistry that each of them faced Lorgar, sharing their words as if they truly spoke to him.

Several mumbled. Others cried out. Most spoke in a placid monotone, bleaching their words of all emotion.

'*My legs,*' one of the choir said without any expression at all, standing perfectly straight. '*Mikayas, help me, I can't feel my legs.*'

'*The Western Adelfia District is already lost,*' droned another, staring with eyes both wide and dead. '*Aren't you listening to me? The World Eaters took it an hour ago. I need more men, governor. I need more men.*'

A third swayed on her feet, her unremarkable face striped by an unattended nosebleed.

'My son,' she whispered. *'My son is trapped under there. Don't shoot. Please. Don't sh–'*

Her sudden, abrupt silence made Lorgar wince.

At the choir's edges, several of his thrall-scribes noted every word, doubtless to be pored over later for any lost significance. They paced across the cathedral floor, weaving between the astropaths, careful not to brush against any of them.

Angron entered the basilica, armoured in his usual stylised bronze and ceramite and with two oversized chainswords strapped to his back. He even wasted time with a greeting, raising his hand in the first time Lorgar could ever remember such a gesture from his broken brother. The Word Bearer tried not to let his amazement show at his brother's new consideration.

'Lotara says you stole her astropathic choir.' Angron's lipless smile was a ghastly thing indeed. 'I see that she may have been correct.'

'Stole is a strong word. "Appropriated" seems much less ignoble.' Lorgar spared a glance for the skies above the cathedral, as the *Lex* ripped onwards towards Nuceria.

'What do you need them for?' Angron asked. His wounds from being buried alive had already faded to scrunched scar tissue pebbling his flesh, just another host of scarring to overlay the last.

The Devourers lurked behind him, stomping into the cathedral without the primarch sparing them a glance. To be one of Angron's bodyguards was no honour, despite how fiercely the World Eaters champions had fought for it in the first, optimistic years. Angron ignored them no matter where they went, never once fighting alongside them in battle. In their Terminator plate, they'd never managed to keep up with their liege lord, and they were as prone to losing control as any other World Eater, meaning any hope of them fighting as an organised pack was a forlorn one at best.

Lorgar watched the Devourers – those warriors who'd spent a century learning to swallow their pride and pretend they weren't ignored – speaking amongst themselves at the basilica's entrance.

'Hail,' he greeted them. They seemed uneasy at being addressed, offering hesitant and wordless bows.

Angron snorted at his brother acknowledging them. 'Bodyguards,' he said. 'Even their name annoys me. *"Devourers"*, as if I'd named them myself – as if they were the Legion's finest.'

'Their intentions are pure,' Lorgar pointed out. 'They seek to honour you. It's not their fault you leave them behind in every battle.'

'They're not even the Legion's fiercest fighters, any more. That rogue Delvarus refuses to challenge for a place in their ranks. Khârn laughed when I asked him if he'd ever considered it. And do you know Bloodspitter?'

'I know Bloodspitter,' Lorgar replied. Everyone knew Bloodspitter.

'He beat one of them in the pits, and carved his name into the poor bastard's armour with a combat knife.'

Lorgar forced a smile. 'Yes. Delightful.'

Angron's face wrenched again, at the mercy of misfiring muscles. 'What primarch ever needed guarding by lesser men?'

'Ferrus,' Lorgar said softly. 'Vulkan.'

Angron laughed, the sound rich and true, yet harsh as a bitter wind. 'It's good to hear you joke about those weaklings. I was getting bored of you mourning them.'

It was no joke, but Lorgar had no desire to shatter his brother's fragile good humour. 'I only mourn the dead,' Lorgar conceded. 'I don't mourn Vulkan.'

'He's as good as dead.' The World Eater smiled again. 'I'm sure he wishes he were. Now, what are you doing with Lotara's choir?'

'Listening to them sing of other worlds and other wars.'

Angron stared, unimpressed. 'Specifics,' he said, 'while I have the patience to hear such details.'

'Just listen,' Lorgar replied.

Angron did as he was bid. After a minute or more had passed, he nodded once. 'You're listening to the Five Hundred Worlds burning.'

'Something like that. These are the voices of the freshly dead, and those soon to join them. The mortis-moments of random souls, elsewhere in Ultramar, as our fleets ravage their worlds.'

'Morbid, priest. Even for you.'

'We're inflicting this destruction on them. We mustn't consider ourselves distant from it. It may not be our hands holding the bolters and blades, but we are still the architects of this annihilation. It's our place to listen to it, to remember the martyred dead, and to meditate on all we've wrought.'

'I wish you well with it,' said Angron. 'But why steal Lotara's choir? What happened to yours?'

'They died.'

It was Angron's turn to be surprised. 'How did they die?'

'Screaming.' Lorgar showed no emotion at all. 'What brings you here, brother?'

'Curiosity. I've followed you so far. We've killed the worlds you wished to kill, and now you owe me an answer or two.'

Lorgar laughed. 'You've killed several worlds in the last year that I wished to sail right past. Do not pretend you've been an obedient war hound, brother. Armatura was the first engagement I actually wished you to prosecute for me.'

The reply didn't entirely banish Angron's stable mood. 'I have a question that you will answer, Lorgar.' The World Eater finally turned to acknowledge his Terminator elite. 'Be somewhere else,' he told them.

They saluted, and did exactly that. Several of the Vakrah Jal stood at the basilica's immense doors, watching the Devourers thud past. They turned to Lorgar, awaiting his order before following their cousins of the XII Legion. The primarch nodded, granting them leave to go. He looked next to the astropathic choir, who were slowly coming to their senses.

'You may return to the *Conqueror* when the ships next fall from the warp. Leave us, please.'

They bowed and shuffled from the chamber in a slow, dazed procession.

Once the two brothers were alone, Lorgar raised a hand as if to stall Angron's words. Ephemeral light ghosted into the space between them, swirling into spheres, mirroring the universe's formation so many millions of years ago. Suns coalesced first, then the planets that depended on them. All of it drifted in a slow, stellar dance: the gravitic ballet of creation. A hundred stars rotated in the air, each with worlds revolving around them.

Angron bared his teeth at his brother's shadowplay. 'Ultramar?'

'Ultramar,' Lorgar confirmed. 'A mere one-fifth of mighty Ultramar.' He walked to one star, cradling it between his curled fingers. The sun paled to a murky grey, spreading white mist from its pulsing core. 'Calth's sun,' he said. 'The star Veridian.'

Angron's mouth pulled into another sneer. 'I am not an idiot, Lorgar.'

The Word Bearer's smile was sincere enough. 'Indulge me a moment more. Watch.'

Several stars paled the same way, while others played host to worlds that darkened and died in whirling clouds of subtle fire. Sure enough, tendrils of the white mist lengthened from their genesis at Calth, reaching across the heavens in slithering jealousy. They started to spread, but behaved as stunted, directionless things, never reaching any of the other orbs.

'I once sailed to the edge of reality,' Lorgar said softly, 'and instead of godless, hopeless infinity, I found the remains of an empire destroyed when a god was born. The eldar gave birth to a deity that killed them because of their ignorance, Angron. The Great Eye is Slaa Neth's afterbirth, joining reality and unreality as one holy realm. The Imperium has archived such events as warp storms, but – to my regret – I know better.'

At last, he came to an unremarkable star on the edge of his illusory display. A lone world turned around this sun: no more notable than any other globe, and less remarkable than many. Blue marked its oceans and great lakes. Green, grey and yellow marked its various landmasses, with the white of ice at both poles.

'Here,' said Lorgar. 'The answer to your unspoken question.'

Angron wasn't a creature given to hesitation, nor to patience. Even so, in that moment he seemed reluctant to speak, for once showing no annoyance at his brother's lengthy, poetic scheming. Even the Nails were still, not forcing his face to twitch.

'Nuceria,' he said at last, and his voice cracked on the word. Iron teeth pushed together hard enough to give a metallic whine. 'I have no wish to return there, Lorgar. No wish, and no need.'

Lorgar nodded, the sympathy of kinship in his eyes. 'I know. None of us are the souls we once were, when the Emperor first brought us up into the stars. Each of his sons has grown, either learning from the past or throwing its shackles aside. But look.'

As the world drifted past, Lorgar reached out to touch it, the barest brush of his fingertips. The globe was swallowed in worms of fire, blanketing all detail beneath the burning cloud cover.

'The conduit,' Lorgar said. 'It seals the pattern, and makes it whole. Watch.'

The tendrils of light straining at Calth suddenly leapt from world to world, grasping and curling across the reaches of space. As they spread across Ultramar's borders, they looked undeniably eager – they looked *hungry* – clawing towards the burning orb of Nuceria. By the time they reached it, they'd formed a misty boundary between the Five Hundred Worlds and the rest of the Imperium.

Angron heard Lorgar's gentle exhalation, even from almost twenty metres away.

'Nothing from Terra will get in,' the Word Bearer said, walking the misty line, 'and nothing will get out. Not even an astropathic whisper will pierce this storm. We'll set fire to Guilliman's corner of the galaxy, and only you and I will know the way back through the flames.'

Angron's voice was rusty metal, chewed up and spat out in a snarl. 'Why *Nuceria*? You could choose any world near Ultramar's borders to form the other end of this… barricade. But you chose Nuceria.' The World Eater's blink was lazily predatory, almost crocodilian.

'You will answer me now, priest. Why Nuceria? What waits for us on that world that makes it such a tempting target?'

The Word Bearer lowered his hand and the illusory stellar cartography ceased to be. 'It must be Nuceria,' he said.

'Not good enough.'

'Why are you so reluctant to return?' Lorgar asked quietly. *Reluctance*. This was something he'd simply not expected from his warlike brother, even on this most difficult of decisions.

'How many times have I said this to you?' The World Eater grunted, his throat forming a lingering *'Hnnngh'* sound. 'I died there. Everything after it is meaningless. Do not reduce me in your mind to a snarling, inhuman thing forever blinded by its own anger. I am still a man, no matter what they did to me. I chose to let the world live. There's nothing there for me now.'

Lorgar nodded, sensing he had to make some small allowances to chain his brother's temper.

'Vengeance is there, Angron. Is that so meaningless?'

'*Hnh*. Vengeance for what? Will it bring my brothers and sisters back from unfair graves? The bones of my past have long grown cold, Lorgar.'

The Word Bearer pressed harder, his eyes narrowing. 'There was talk that the Emperor concealed the world from you. I'd always thought–'

'You thought wrong.' Angron spat on the mosaic deck. The saliva was red. Something in his skull was bleeding.

'You played the Emperor's games,' Lorgar allowed. 'You wore his collar before the rebellion. You tried to be the son he needed you to be. You were exactly that, beyond the moments you lost control. But now, whether you wish it or not, I need Nuceria dead. And you are the perfect architect of its demise, brother.'

Angron hesitated. Despite his words, there was no concealing the slow rise of fire in his eyes.

'Why Nuceria?'

Lorgar looked rueful. The Word Bearer usually wore his feelings on his face, but he could be difficult to read when he chose to be, and Angron was no master at the subtleties of human expression.

'The metaphysics are complicated,' said Lorgar.

That had Angron growling. 'I may not have wasted days in debate with you and Magnus inside our father's Palace, but the Nails haven't left me an absolute fool. I asked the question, Lorgar. You answer it. And do so without lying, if you can manage such a feat.'

The Word Bearer met his brother's eyes, and the rarely-seen palette of emotions within their depths. Pain was there in abundance, but so was the frustration of living with a misfiring mind, and the savagery that transcended anger itself. Angron was a creature that had come to make his hatred a blade to be used in battle. He'd weaponised his own emotions, where most living beings were slaves to theirs. Lorgar couldn't help but admire the strength in that.

'We're going to Nuceria,' he said, 'because of you. Because of the Nails.'

Angron stared, and his silence beckoned for his brother to continue.

'They're killing you,' Lorgar admitted. 'Faster than I thought. Faster than anyone realised. The rate of degeneration has accelerated even in the last few months. Your implants were never designed for a primarch's brain matter. Your physiology is trying to heal the damage as the Nails bite deeper, but it's a game of pushing and pulling, with both sides evenly matched.'

Angron took this with an impassive shrug. 'Guesswork.'

'I can see souls and hear the music of creation,' Lorgar smiled. 'In comparison, this is nothing. The Twelfth Legion's archives are comprehensive enough, you know. Your behaviour tells the rest of the tale, along with the pain I sense radiating from you each and every time we meet. Your entire brain is remapped and rewired, slaved to the implants' impulses. Tell me, when was the last time you dreamed?'

'I don't dream.' The answer was immediate, almost fiercely fast. 'I've never dreamed.'

Lorgar's gentle eyes caught the warp's kaleidoscopic light as he tilted his head. 'Now you're lying, brother.'

'It's no lie.' Angron's thick fingers twitched and curled, closing around the ghosts of weapons. 'The Nails scarcely let me sleep. How would I dream?'

Lorgar didn't miss the rising tension in his brother's body language – the veins in his temples rising from scarred skin, the feral hunch of the shoulders, no different from a hunting cat drawing into a crouch before it struck.

'You once told me the Nails stole your slumber,' Lorgar conceded, 'but you also said they let you dream.'

Angron took a step closer. He started to say 'I meant...' but Lorgar's earthy glare stopped him cold.

'They give you a serenity and peace you can find nowhere else. Humans, legionaries, primarchs... everything alive must sleep, must rest, must allow its brain a period of respite. The remapping of your mind denies you this. You don't dream with your eyes closed. You dream with your eyes open, chasing the rush of whatever peace the Nails can give you.' Lorgar met Angron's eyes again. 'Don't insult us both by denying it. You slaver and murmur when you kill, mumbling about chasing serenity and how close it feels. I've heard you. I've looked into your heart and soul when you're lost to the Nails. Your sons, with their crude copies of your implants, have their minds rewritten to feel joy only in adrenaline's kiss. Those lesser implants cause pain because they scrape the nerves raw, thus your World Eaters kill because it gladdens their reforged hearts, and ceases the pain knifing into their muscles. Your Butcher's Nails are a more sinister and predatory design, ruining all cognition, stealing any peace. They *are* killing you, gladiator. And you ask why I'm taking you back to Nuceria? Is it not obvious?'

Angron backed away, his eyes hot where his brother's were cold. 'They cannot be removed. And I would fight anyone who tried. If they are killing me, it's a slow enough death that I feel neither fear nor regret.'

Lorgar's stare was blazing now. 'I will save you, Angron. Fight me, hate me, or trust me – it matters not. I will drag you into the immortality you deserve.'

'They cannot be removed!' Angron reached for his chainswords, stopping just short of pulling them. He ached to master his emotions, as if here and now, succumbing to rage would somehow prove Lorgar right.

'I will not remove them,' Lorgar stepped closer to his brother, his hands outstretched in placation. 'But the overlords that hammered them into your skull will know more of their function. I will learn all they know of their insidious designs, and then I will burn their loathsome world until its surface is naught but glass. And you will stand with me, taking the vengeance you pretend you no longer desire. If there is a way to save you, somehow, some way, I will do it. This I swear.'

Angron swallowed. Not nervous, for he knew nothing of that particular stripe of unease, but something in Lorgar's intense, spit-wet whispers had the World Eater grinding his teeth yet again.

'If what you say is true, why save me?'

Disappointment was clearly etched across Lorgar's calm features. 'Why is that a question every one of our bloodline must ask in a disbelieving snarl?' He sighed. 'You are my brother. I would spare you any pain I can, and protect you from harm if I'm able.'

Angron said nothing for several heavy, heavy beats of his ursine heart. 'Blood is not always thicker than water, Lorgar. There are many souls I honour above my own brothers.' He started pacing, a caged animal, frustrated by the very fact his brother sought to show regard. The unfamiliarity of the moment was venomous. 'You are weak,' Angron said at last.

The golden primarch's eyes unfocused, but he showed no offence beyond his faint distraction.

'*I* am weak?' he asked softly. 'Did I hear you correctly?'

'You heard me,' replied Angron. 'Let history mark my words well, for I care nothing about who sits proud on the Throne of Terra when the last day dawns. Horus is a fine commander, but that's the limit of my admiration for that arrogant, preening bastard. I joined his rebellion because I can tolerate him easier than I can endure the abomination that names himself Master of Mankind. You want the truth of my life and death? I am Angron, the Eater of Worlds, and I am already dead. I died over a hundred years ago, in the mountains north of the city that enslaved me. I died after Desh'ea.'

Lorgar clasped his hands together, and the smile that curved his lips held nothing but amused understanding.

'*I* am weak,' Lorgar said again. '*Me*. Is that really true, brother? Am *I* the only primarch never to conquer his homeworld? Or is that the great and powerful Angron? Am *I* the first primarch to feel the breath of the Wolves on his throat, or was it Angron and his mighty sons who suffered on the Night of the Wolf, beaten bloody by Russ in the rain?'

Angron roared as he came forwards, though he drew no blade and aimed no blow. 'I had him! *I had Russ at my mercy!* You dare say otherwise, when *he* was the one sent fleeing back to his gunship?'

Lorgar wasn't cowed. 'Was that how it happened, brother? Truly?'

'I... Yes.' Angron checked his advance, suddenly on edge. 'We fought. Our Legions fought. The Wolves fell back. We... we chased them.'

'If you speak the truth,' Lorgar watched him carefully, 'then... tell me.' He almost asked to see, to touch minds and perceive the memory through Angron's sensory recollections, but hesitated at the last moment. Despite their inanimate lifelessness, the Nails felt any sixth-sense intrusions and tended to bite back. Lorgar had probed and scryed enough to know the truth of that. Better to hear the tale in his brother's words than to agitate Angron further.

'You're wrong.' Angron spoke in a hoarse snarl, husky not from anger but from the weight of emotion. 'You're wrong, it wasn't in the rain; it was at sunset on a day already darkened by the burning city behind us. My blade broke, but it didn't matter. I pulled his chainsword from his fists, and broke it in my hands. We fell into the mud, brawling. We'd both known that fight would end up on the ground. I had him, Lorgar. My boot on his throat, at the very end. I stood above him at last, and Russ...'

...and Russ had to crawl away, fanged teeth clenched, breathing spit as much as breath. Strings of it tumbled from his cracked lips with each rasping exhalation. Angron chased as the Wolf King staggered to his feet, but Russ opened his arms wide, offering no fight.

'Do you see?' he said. No, he barked it. He barked it not like a simple beast, but with human passion backed by canine ferocity. Conviction burned in his eyes – the same instinctive viciousness of a dog defending its family. 'Look, damn you. Look around you. Do you see what you've done to your sons?'

At the battle's core, sense pierced Angron's aching sight long enough to leave him speechless. The axe in his hand lowered, and he looked out at the ranks of Wolves facing him with their bolters raised. They came in ragged packs, abandoning the warfare to form a ring around the primarchs. Wolf after Wolf – close enough for Angron to make out the individual totems and talismans rattling against their storm-grey armour – moving to stand in ragged ranks with their brothers.

One of them, a tribal leader of some kind, stood out by the elaborate blue pack markings over his faceplate.

'It's over, Lord Angron,' he said.

'Russ.' Angron turned to his brother, and pointed with one bloody hand over the encircling wolf packs, to where the Legions still fought across the rest of the battlefield. 'Your Legion is bleeding.'

Russ didn't deny it, for it was true. Beyond the encircled primarchs, the World Eaters were tearing through their cousins' grey regiments, fighting without sign of formation, just as they fought without any regard for their primarch. Even in those early days, they were used to Angron fighting alone, and their fresh implants stole any hope of cohesive battle planning. Their stunted brains wouldn't let them bring order to the chaos.

The few World Eaters in possession of their senses – Lhorke's towering ironform was one, Angron noted through narrowed eyes – were throwing themselves at the Wolves entrenched around the duelling primarchs, but they lacked the numbers to break through Russ's defensive packs.

'My men are dying,' Russ admitted. 'Yet here we stand at the battle's heart, and only one Legion is about to lose its primarch. Do you see why I came? Do you see how you've broken your sons?' He threw an arm to take in a wide pass of the battlefield. 'The Wolves are soldiers taking an objective. They fight to win, while your World Eaters fight only to kill.'

'Victory comes,' Angron smiled, showing a crescent of bloody teeth, 'to the last man standing.'

Russ spared a glance to the wider battle, wincing at the devastation being inflicted upon both Legions.

'That is true in the gladiator pits, Angron. But our father desires soldiers and generals. Not gladiators. Death is a necessity – it comes for our foes, and it comes to our own soldiers when we cannot spare them. You spend your Legion's lives like a lord spends coin. It cannot continue.'

Angron had followed Russ's glance, but where the Wolf King gave the battle a mere glimmer of attention, Angron was paying full and amused attention.

'War is only won when every enemy is dead. A pacified enemy is still an enemy.'

'More gladiator wisdom, Angron. Look at my men surrounding you. Have you honestly learned nothing from this?'

'Your men are losing, Leman.' He grinned at his brother. 'Let's take this to the last breath, eh? Let the bloodshed play out with the dance of cutting blades. We'll see which Legion still stands.'

'Neither will stand. But you die the moment my men open fire.'

'Death holds no sacred mystery to me, Russ. It holds no terror.' He laughed then, through the Nails' pain, laughing hard enough that his eyes watered. 'I may even welcome it! Are you empowered by our "beloved" father, dog? Can you really give me death, or has your posturing already gone too far? Will you run back to Terra and report that you lost control of your mongrel-blooded curs in the same way you slander me?'

Angron's pain-slitted eyes locked to his brother's, and he laughed even harder. 'This was never meant to come to battle! I see it in your eyes – you took a step too far, little executioner, now you fear how this will all end.' He stepped closer, his amusement turning sick and savage. 'Executions are the murder of helpless prey, Russ. What you've committed to here, "brother", is a fair fight.'

He nodded over the battlefield again. 'And I say once more – your men are losing. You know why? Because yours have something to live for. They care. Mine fight for pleasure, knowing any life outside of war is denied to them. Their own lives are as meaningless to themselves as they are to me, and that *is* the gift given by the Butcher's Nails. Warriors, not soldiers. Warriors with no fear of death, and no caution to guard against it. They don't protect, they kill. They cast aside all thoughts of their own lives in the hunger to end others'. Remember that, Russ. Remember it well.'

'This isn't over,' Russ promised.

'Whatever soothes your bruised pride, dog.'

Leman Russ, Primarch of the Vlka Fenryka, took in one long, deep breath, and cast his howl to the sky.

'He howled?' asked Lorgar. His eyes were wide, pearly with soft wonder.

'The call to retreat,' Angron replied. 'A fighting retreat – it took longer than you can imagine for the World Eaters to realise the battle was over. I had whole companies still trying to fight the Wolves as Russ's Legion ran for their gunships.' He chuckled. 'They took a lot of trophies for their tallies. Many wear them still.'

For several moments, Lorgar had to watch his brother's flawed face to make sure this wasn't some elaborate jest.

'You didn't answer Russ's question,' he said. 'Did you truly learn nothing from that fight?'

Angron blinked, the dull edge of surprise coming into his eyes. 'What revelation should I have come to? I learned he wasn't allowed to kill me. I learned he postured in the hope of bringing me back to Terra, collared and submissive to his whims.'

'No.' Lorgar was almost breathless in disbelief. 'No, no, no. Angron, you stubborn fool. None of that matters.'

'There were more dead Wolves on that field than dead World Eaters. That matters.'

That, thought Lorgar, was also arguable, but he let it pass. 'Russ had you cold. You said you had him at your mercy, but he crawled free.'

'He *crawled*.' Angron chuckled again, making a meal of the word.

'And when he rose, he had you surrounded. He could have killed you.'

'He tried and failed.'

'His *men*, Angron. His Legion could have killed you. Whether the Emperor ordered it or not, Russ spared your life. He didn't retreat in shame, you arrogant...' Lorgar sighed. 'He was probably lamenting your thick skull all the way back to Terra, hoping you'd heed a rather consummate lesson in brotherhood and loyalty. Look what happened. Yes, you beat him in a duel. Yes, your men took down more of his than his of yours. And yet, who won the battle?'

'The World Eaters,' Angron said without hesitation.

Lorgar just stared at him for several seconds. 'I appreciate that every living being must, by the nature of perception, understand and process life in a different way. But even for you, brother, this is achingly obtuse.'

'You're saying the Wolves won.' Angron looked more amused than confused.

'How can you not see it?' Lorgar steepled his fingers, trying to rein in his own temper. 'They won a victory worthy of engraving on their armour for all time. While you were glorying in your strength, Russ's sons were loyal enough to come to him, to surround you both, to threaten your life while you stood at the vanguard of your own Legion. That may be the most comprehensive moment of outmanoeuvring in the history of the Legiones Astartes. It's almost poetic in its elegance and emotional resonance. He proves his sons' loyalty, while yours leave you to die. He proves the damage the Nails are doing to your Legion. He proves the tactical strength of taking an objective rather than fighting purely to kill. He *spares your life* in the hope you'll see all of this, in a lesson it cost him heavily to teach you, and your reaction is to grin and claim yourself the victor.'

Angron didn't chuckle that time. Lorgar could see it in his brother's tensed muscles – some cognitive switch had clicked somewhere in his consciousness, and Angron's rage was rising again.

'Only one of us ran away that night. He's weak.'

'Gods' blood.' Lorgar was still managing, barely, to speak calmly. 'The primarchs are the bridge between the Emperor and the species he leads. We are all weak, for we are all equal. *All of us.* We are humanity magnified: its virtues and its flaws.'

'I am not weak. I have never been weak.'

'You are not only weak if you fail to understand Russ's lesson, you are also a fool.'

Lorgar could see in Angron's eyes just how much it strained the World Eater to resist closing his hands around his brother's throat. He was drawing breath to comment on Angron's self-control when the ship shook beneath them, and they fell from the warp once more. Metal groaned beneath their boots as the ship itself writhed in torment to be plunged back into the cold un-tides of realspace. The *Lex*'s noble machine-spirit was coming to love its journeys through the Sea of Souls.

Angron breathed out in a slow, bearish huff. His bloodshot eyes lost their unhealthy glint, and the shaking eased in his hands.

'Forget the Night of the Wolf. I came because of Nuceria.'

'And I have answered you,' Lorgar countered, still watching the way his brother's wrath faded as the ship dropped from the warp.

The scarred primarch returned the golden one's gaze. For the first time, Angron realised that the only injuries Lorgar had failed – or perhaps refused – to heal were the talon-gashes across his cheek, inflicted by Corax on the Killing Fields.

He was already weary of falling into Lorgar's gentle conversational gambits, and just this once, he wouldn't rise to his brother's baiting words.

'I respect you,' he admitted. 'But I will never like you.' With rare concern and consideration, Angron met his brother's eyes. 'You *do* owe me, though. I saved your life. So I'll let you save mine.'

Lorgar bowed, priest-like, as he smiled. 'Make ready, then,' he said. 'We'll reach Nuceria in a month. You are going home, Angron.'

Angron gave the low, throaty *'Hnngh'* growl again. A slow, iron-fanged smile dawned over his devastated features. 'I wonder if they still remember me.'

TIME PASSED IN the warp like nowhere else. Even on warded vessels, unreality's caress would drip through to twist the hours in the muscles and minds of the mortals aboard. Tasks that took minutes might leave someone exhausted as if they'd done hours of work; sleep came uneasily to all, and dark dreams plagued many. When a crew member's cycle of rest came, it wasn't uncommon for them to leave their quarters at the beginning of their next shift irritable and scarcely rested at all.

Lotara Sarrin dreamed of her brother – of his death in her youth, when he'd sickened and died beyond even her father's infinite financial resources. It was the first time in her young life she'd realised that you couldn't heal all problems by simply hurling money at them. Towards the very end, she'd hated seeing her brother at all, and the years did nothing to soften the bite of that shame. He'd raved and cried, looking dead already, staring at them with sunken yellow eyes and shivering from a host of malfunctioning organs.

Many nights that month, she dreamed of that writhing boy, and when her insomnia was at its least merciful, keeping her awake for days on end, she heard him crying in the air ducts.

Angron cared nothing for the *Conqueror*'s command, trusting it to the officers trained for the task; he cared similarly little for his warriors' training, trusting the centurions to handle the mundane aspects of Legion life. Several times, he was seen in the company of Vel-Kheredar, entering or exiting the Archmagos's forge-chambers. Other times, he walked the wide halls of the *Conqueror*'s war museum, pausing for long conversations with the archivists when his skull's aches allowed him the patience to do so. When he spent any time among his men, it was never with any preferred Chapter or company; always with his attention divided between them. The *Conqueror* housed precious few of his Legion, while the rest were engaged in the pacification of Ultramar, and those present saw more of their primarch in that one month than they had in the several years before. He drank with them, watched their gladiatorial duels, laughing as they laughed and sharing the warmth of brotherhood in a way few primarchs enjoyed with their men.

LORGAR'S SECLUSION WAS one of effort and focus, rather than disgust at the nearness of others. He'd taken to transcribing the melody behind the veil, writing with ink and quill upon the walls and floor of the basilica in a language that was and wasn't the jagged rune-lore of Colchis. Magnus came to him once more, to speak of the stars and the nature of reality in the realm where gods and mortals meet. Lorgar never looked up from his transcriptions; never even noticed his brother's manifestation. All that mattered was the song. He felt it as much as heard it now – it was a wind against his skin and a drumming in his bones. You could take a thousand orchestras on a thousand separate worlds, using instruments and melodies known only to those cultures, and you would still never come close to the scale of the orchestral undertaking playing through Lorgar's mind. It wasn't one song, it was a billion songs playing over each other, and it was his place to listen and ensure every note hit its beat. He heard trillions of men, women and children dying in every way it was possible to die. He heard the death-scream of whole worlds, as their surfaces burned and their cores cried out under the strain. He heard it, felt it, and wrote and wrote and wrote.

By the time the *Lex* finally fell from the warp in Nuceria's system, he was left wondering if this was what madness felt like. Was this madness? Would he know? Did the insane ever know they'd fallen so far?

He didn't stop writing, though. The cathedral was a canvas of runic text, senseless in how often it was overwritten, and although he slowed in his scrawls he didn't quite stop.

Not yet.

SKANE DREAMED OF home, and spent many hours watching medical diagnostic hololiths picturing the exact radiation degeneration of his body over the years. He was offered the chance to leave the Destroyers. He refused.

DELVARUS DREAMED OF a redemption denied, and fought twice as hard in training to defy the possibility.

KARGOS INSPECTED THE gene-seed vaults, indulging in a momentary melancholy at the names etched across the cryo-storage units. When he dreamed, he dreamed of past victories. The warp's touch never seemed to play on him as it did on others.

CYRENE VALANTION, SHE Who Lived Twice, dreamed of swimming through fire, chased by howling daemons clawing at her ankles. Her own screams woke her each night, sitting bolt upright in her new quarters, sheened with cold sweat. Some nights, she could hear the Vakrah Jal guardians outside her door ordering worshippers to clear the area. Other nights, she woke to see Argel Tal sat hunched with his back to the door, the sword that killed her in his hands. His cold blue eye lenses burned through the gloom as he watched her. The two of them would while away the following hours in quiet talk, with him telling her of the last year's warp journeys after Isstvan, and her swearing she remembered nothing of the year she spent dead.

For her sake, he said he believed her.

ARGEL TAL HIMSELF spent much of his time training with the Vakrah Jal, or being ignored on his daily attempts to speak with his primarch. With the *Conqueror* repaired, there were fewer chances to cross over to meet with Khârn.

As for Khârn, he never told anyone of his dreams, if indeed he had any at all. He pushed his men harder than ever before, amalgamating several broken companies to reform his own. His focus was on Nuceria. Specifically, on *surviving* Nuceria. Despite the world's undeniably soft defences, he couldn't shake the threat of discomfort severe enough that it felt like a premonition.

Argel Tal's warning stayed with him, to the point where he considered killing Erebus and simply being done with all thought of it. Kargos considered it nonsense – *'I cannot believe you are even giving this consideration, captain'* – and Skane considered it hilarious. His augmetic throat laughed like a Rhino tank changing gears.

Twenty-seven days after the *Conqueror* and the *Fidelitas Lex* left Armatura in ashes, they broke from the warp at the edge of Nuceria's system. The *Trisagion* was waiting for them.

Lorgar looked up from his scrawling, saw the distant world turning in the night, and shuddered. Here was his conduit to release the energies of a hundred massacred worlds and bathe Ultramar in holy fire. Here, on the planet where Angron was raised, Lorgar's brother would face the most vital choice of his life.

And as always, it would come down to blood.

EIGHTEEN

**Field of Bones
Betrayer
A Simple Order**

Oshamay Evrel'Korshay of the Thal'kr Kin-Guard was making her rounds when the sky caught fire. She walked the city walls at sundown, speaking with her artillery crews and line captains, never kind but never unfair, always preferring professional distance to any shared warmth. Better to be admired than loved. Her artificial arm whirred and purred smoothly, obeying at will. She'd lost her flesh and blood limb nine years ago, during the trench fighting of the Last War. Since then, that name had become something of a sour-tasting joke. The War to End All Wars hadn't been the last after all. With the city-states changing sides so often, she honestly wasn't sure if they were all fighting a different conflict, or if the Last War merely spread down the years, its boundaries and bitterness changing with the seasons.

When the fire-rain first showed in the sky, trailing down between the evening's first stars, her first thought was that their enemies were doing the impossible. Somehow the Great Coastal Union was attacking Desh'ea from the air, despite lacking all resources and munitions to do so. What political shifting had taken place to allow it? Had they unearthed one of the First Kingdom's arsenal-crypts deep under the coastal waves, or buried beneath the mountains? Impossible. There could be none left, every site had been dug up or dredged centuries ago.

Even so, the very first thing she did was activate the telemetry unit built into her uniform's metal epaulette. Its single light started blinking urgently, trading electronic panic with its main cogitator elsewhere in the city.

'General,' said one of the wall-gunners at her side. 'Is it the Imperials?'

The Imperials, he said. Like a curse.

'We *are* Imperials,' she pointed out, still watching the comets fire-trailing down.

He shrugged. Compliance had held on Nuceria since their grand-parents' days, but the Imperium was a distant master at best. There'd been no visiting vessels since the Emperor – praises upon him, Lord of Old Earth! – ended the Gladiator-King's Rebellion over a hundred years ago. Like so many worlds in the nascent Imperium, Nuceria was left alone as long as it paid its tithes in loyalty, coin, iron and flesh.

'Maybe they've come back,' he said, and she pitied him for the hope in his eyes. 'They've come back to end the Last War.'

'We don't need their help to end the Last War.' She trotted out the old trope without a thought, speaking on instinct. How many times had the Praxury, and his father before him, told his war council that they would never send to the Imperium for aid? Not even the forces of Ultramar, rumoured to be so achingly close by, would be summoned for assistance.

'It must be the Imperials. The Alliance has no weapons capable of... whatever this is.'

Sirens started wailing across the city, warning of an incoming air raid. The sound was so alien it almost made her laugh, though her smile was a peeled-back thing, unpleasantly grim.

'Give me your magnoculars,' she ordered. He did so, and she aimed them high, staring up at the teardrop pods streaming contrails of flame through the heavens.

'Is it them?' the man asked. 'The Imperials?'

'Wish in one hand,' she told the soldier, handing back his viewfinder, 'and crap in the other. See which hand fills up first.'

THE GENERAL MADE her way to the war room, generously deploying her scowl to move any junior officers out of the way. The Palace Praxica was a monument to excess, with reskium metal and black marble displayed in such quantities that they crossed the border into garishness from the moment one entered the first receiving chamber. Oshamay had no patience for yet more statues of lithe dancing girls or another mural of past Praxuries standing triumphant over battlefields where they'd never even drawn a pistol or blade.

When she entered the war room after making her way through the palace's crowded corridors, a sea of salutes and wide eyes awaited her. She returned the only salute that mattered with her own robotic arm.

'Our one lord,' she greeted Praxury Tybaral Thal'kr of the First House, Protector of Desh'ea, Imperial Magnate of Nuceria.

He waved her closer, his eyes as wide as those of his servants and soldiers. Blue eyes, like his father. Dark hair, like his mother. Somewhat drowned in his purple robes of office, and clutching the aquila-topped reskium sceptre as though it were a weapon to save his life. Perhaps it would, if this really was the return of the Imperials.

He would be thirteen years old next month. *Assuming*, Oshamay thought, *that we all survive until next month. Or the next hour.*

'General Evrel'Korshay,' the Praxury greeted her. 'The sky is crying fire. It's a sign.'

'Yes, our one lord. A sign, as you say.' Her heart sank upon seeing him. What they really didn't need, on the edge of this crisis, was their mad little cockroach of a king slowing them down with his idiocy. 'With your permission, I've mobilised the Kin-Guard, and–'

'No.' The frightened boy controlled his voice to perfection, no surprise given his endless elocution training. If she couldn't see the fear in his eyes, she'd never know from his firm voice that he was on the edge of terror.

'Our one lord,' she said, careful not to glance to any of his courtiers and other officers for support. 'The city is about to come under attack.'

'You do not know that,' he pointed out. He limped over to the map table, messy as it was with scrolls, wincing at the gout he'd developed years before and never managed to fight off. 'I believe the Imperials are returning to end the Last War.'

Oshamay didn't know what the pods of fire that rained down from orbit actually were – such a technological marvel was far beyond her frame of reference, and had no mention in the city-state's archives. Even so, when they began to light up the sky, she needed no help guessing what was going on.

'Using transport pods for either men or materiel suggests assault, our one lord. If they came in peace, surely they'd land with a little less vim.'

She saw the doubt in his eyes. It lasted a moment, replaced almost immediately by a calcification of confidence. Heaven forbid the mad little lord ever doubted himself.

'No,' he said. 'No, they are merely arriving with as much grandeur as would be expected.'

'Then I shall mobilise the Kin-Guard as a ceremonial effort to greet them, our one lord.'

He nodded to that, unaware that Desh'ea's soldiery had already been mobilising for ten minutes.

'Very well.'

'We have reports of several craft coming down in the Desh'elika Mountains, far from the main army. With your permission, I'll send outrider skimmers to investigate.'

The boy waved acquiescence. 'As you say. I shall receive the Imperial emissaries in the throne room. Come with me, general.'

Oshamay bowed and obeyed.

KHÂRN WALKED ACROSS the field of bones, listening to the ghosts in the wind. This high in the mountains, the wind had a howling edge. All too easy to hear the voices of the long-lost and ancient dead in its breath. They weren't high enough for year-long snowfall, but Khârn looked up, and for a moment he was a boy again, climbing the jagged peaks where he was born, feeling close enough to touch the stars. The world that had been his cradle was halfway across the warring galaxy, but not even the Nails could steal his short-lived smile at the clear, clean memory.

The primarchs walked ahead of their shared pack, paying no attention to the mixed grouping of Khârn's Eighth Company and Argel Tal's immolators. Behind the squad, two Thunderhawks still glowed hot from daggerish atmospheric dives, steaming in the cold mountain air.

Bones decorated the alpine tundra. Bones with no cohesion and little suggestion of form or function. A century of weathering had eroded them to nubs and slivers, but here and there among the open graveland, the eye was drawn to something recognisably skeletal.

Khârn reached down to pick up what remained of a skull. His armoured fingertips scratched across its timeworn surface with a gentle whisper. From what was left of its structure – the side not planed smooth by the wind and rain – it had belonged to a male.

'Don't,' warned Argel Tal, coming to stand with him.

'Don't what?'

'Don't touch anything. The skull. These bones.' His brother's helm nodded towards Angron, then looked back at the skull in Khârn's hand. 'This tomb site is your primarch's heart, pulled open and laid bare. Look at him.'

Khârn did so. Angron's back was to the others. He was swaying on his feet, thick fingers twitching. A keening, mournful whine left his clenched teeth – a sound of vulnerability without weakness; the sound of indescribable pain vocalised in bestial simplicity.

'Tread lightly,' Argel Tal added, 'and touch nothing.'

Khârn crouched, replacing the skull where he found it. It stared up, accusing him with its one eye socket. With the edge of his boot, Khârn rolled it over, leaving it exactly as it had been before his interference. When he spoke again, his voice was pitched low, despite speaking over a personal vox-channel.

'Angron should have died here. This is like walking through a memory that never happened.'

Argel Tal walked around a boulder with a pile of bones at its base. 'I can still smell the blood that watered this worthless soil.'

'That's your imagination,' Khârn told him.

Argel Tal didn't answer.

ANGRON HAD WEPT once, and only once, in all the years of his life. He remembered it well, for it was his first memory outside the stifling confines of his gestation tube. He'd pulled himself from the sundered warmth of his birth-pod and into the freezing mountain air. All he could see was red, and all he could taste was his own blood. The wounds across his body froze as soon as he crawled free, ice-burned and cauterised, after a fashion. He was a boy, just a boy, and he was bleeding all over.

They'd come for him then. Spindly shadows, quick as the wind, howling and laughing and cursing in a language he couldn't follow.

He'd killed them. Of course he'd killed them. The moment he sensed them drawing near, he smelled the metal of their weapons and struck at them, without knowing any more than that the metal-scent meant danger and death.

He'd beaten several of them to death with a rock the size of his fist. Others had tried to run, but the bleeding boy had chased them over the tundra, bringing them down and tearing at their throats with his fingers and teeth.

But he'd wept that day. Not because of his attackers, whoever they were. Not because of the pain of his wounds, though he was but a boy, and none would judge him harshly for crying a boy's tears at the wounds he'd suffered.

No. He'd wept upon his first emergence from the pod because of the wind against his skin. Even as the gale bit his injuries with cold teeth, the feeling of freedom brought tears to his eyes. In all the decades since, he'd never shed a tear, until now. Two saltwater droplets, freezing to his mangled face the moment they trailed down.

'All dead,' he said softly. 'My brothers. My sisters.'

Lorgar approached, careful where he walked, doing all he could not to disturb the sacred ground.

'What did you name your enemies?' he asked.

'High-riders,' Angron replied. 'We called them high-riders, for how they stood above us, watching us die in the arena's dirt.'

'The high-riders took their dead with them,' said the Word Bearer. 'There aren't enough bones to be the remains of both armies.'

'My brothers and sisters,' Angron said again. 'I swore I'd stand with them. We would die together. Life had never seen such fighters, Lorgar. Klester, riding her shriekspear. Jochura with his strangling chains. Asti, Little Asti, stealing knives to throw and cut and stab. His grin warmed the cold nights. Larbedon, who lost his arm to gangrene, shouting for the high-riders to follow if they dared. He had my back, as I had his. We'd slip on the gore together, grinding the fallen beneath our boots.'

Angron shook his head as he continued. 'Words don't do them justice. We came from the red sands, growing in the filth, eating the shit the high-riders fed us. But we broke free. Thousands, Lorgar. *Thousands of us.* We were free, and we lived and laughed and we made the bastards pay. The Nails hurt – ah, how they hurt, even then. But we made the high-riders and their paperskin Kin-Guard pay.'

Lorgar listened in silence as Angron lowered his head. 'I should have died here. I *did* die here. The primarch of the World Eaters is nothing but a shade. An echo. This is where I belong. The greatest battle of my life, and it was stolen from me.'

Now Lorgar spoke, not without a slight smile. 'There will be a greater battle, brother. Terra. And I promise you, no one will deny it to you.'

'Terra. Terra!' Angron laughed, the sound rotten with bitterness. 'I piss on Terra. I care nothing for Terra, or Horus, or… or Him. *Him*. The Emperor.'

'Then why do I hear such hatred in your voice?' Lorgar asked quietly.

Angron pulled the chainblades from their scabbards on his back, clenching the handle-triggers and setting them roaring.

'*Hnngh. Hnh.* He took me! He dragged me into the sky! The Emperor. The gods-damned Emperor.'

'You'll have your vengeance, Angron. We will stand upon Terra's soil again before long, you have my word.'

'My brothers,' Angron continued, murmuring low, not hearing his brother's oath. 'My sisters. Slaves, all. Pit-fighting slaves. Our lives were mud to the high-riders that held chains around our throats. But our masters paid, oh how they paid. This world burned when we broke free. It *burned*. I promise you that.'

The other primarch nodded in slow understanding. 'I believe you.'

Angron still wasn't hearing anything but the ghosts in his mind. 'The war dragged on. Season after season. City after city. The rivers ran red with high-rider blood! We fought. We fought everywhere, I swear it. The high-riders charged our shield-wall at Falkha. They charged us! Their lordlings demanded it of them, and they rose to the bait. I still hear the thunder of both lines meeting. Do you hear it?' He turned wild eyes on Lorgar. 'Do you hear the thunder?'

Lorgar smiled, his rune-painted face ruthlessly kind. 'I hear it, brother.'

'But we fled when the seasons turned. We had to run into the mountains, to the ridges, to survive the winter. Too many high-rider armies were coming for us, with their lasers and grenades and machine guns rattling all day and every night. I swore I'd die with my brothers and sisters in the mountains. We were free. It was our death. The death we earned, the death we wanted. We laughed and called them closer! High-rider bastards!'

Angron turned, living the moment a second time, vaulting onto a boulder and throwing his arms wide. He shouted – nay, screamed – his laughing challenge to the sky.

'Come and die, dogs of Desh'ea! I am Angron of the pits, born in blood, raised in the dark, and I will die free! Come, watch me fight one last time! Is that not what you want? Is that not what you always wanted? Come closer, you dog-blooded cowards!'

Khârn watched his primarch standing against the rising wind, seeing history repeating itself to the tune of maddened memory. Angron raised his chainswords, miming the first cuts and carves of that last fight. The teeth roared with every sweep. The gathered legionaries were transfixed, staring in silence.

'And then. And then. *Hnh.* The Emperor. *Hnnngh.* The Emperor. He stole me, trapped me, banished me to the *Conqueror*'s dark belly. Teleported me up into orbit, though at the time, I knew nothing of such technology. I was alone, alone in the dark. And my brothers and sisters died here. They died without me. I swore. We all swore. *We swore to stand and fight and die.* Together. *Together.*'

Angron rocked back and forth, the blades lowering, his eyes unfocusing. 'The Emperor. High-rider dog-filth. When Horus called, I gave my word. I gave my word, because I lived when I should have died. That's no gift. He made me a traitor! He made me betray the only oath that mattered! I lived and my brothers and sisters died here, their bones left for the vermin, the wind, the snow.'

The two brothers could have been alone for all the attention they paid to their nearby warriors. Lorgar walked to Angron again, careful not to touch him, but pitching his voice in what felt to Khârn like an insidious caress.

'No purer emotion than rage,' said Lorgar. 'No more righteous ambition than vengeance.'

The light of recognition dawned in Angron's eyes. 'Vengeance, aye. Revenge. Food for the soul, brother.'

'Why were you different?' Lorgar asked. 'Why did our father treat you as he did?'

Angron shrugged away from the insipid kindness in his brother's tone. 'You kept that mule Kor Phaeron. Russ kept his kin-friends. The Lion kept Luther. Humans – brothers and foster fathers – saved and raised into Legion ranks. But not me. Not Angron, no. Did the Emperor teleport his gold-wrapped Custodians down to help me and my army? No. Did he free the War Hounds and order them to battle, to fight alongside me? No. Did he save my brothers and sisters the way he spared and honoured the Lion's closest kin? The way he honoured Kor Phaeron? No, no, and no. No mercy for Angron. Angron the Oathbreaker. Angron the Betrayer.'

The World Eater jumped from the boulder, looking down at the bones but still speaking to Lorgar. 'Did he stay on my homeworld for weeks, as he did with you on Colchis, Vulkan on Nocturne, and Russ on Fenris? No. No contest of strength and will with the Emperor for Angron the Slave. No weeks of laughter and joy and healing the world's wounds. Instead, he stole me from the life I'd lived and the death I'd earned. He made me break my oath to those who needed me.'

Lorgar's eyes were fierce now. 'But *why*? Why did he let your army die? Why did he steal you in a teleportation flare, when he could have remained here for a time, as he did on so many other worlds? He had a Legion – *your Legion* – in orbit, Angron. A single order, and they would have bloodied their blades at your side, saving your rebel army and hailing you as their gene-sire. Instead, he collared them, as he collared you.'

Angron drooled, thick and wet, down his chin. 'I'll never know why. He never answered me. But he'll pay, as the high-riders paid.

And when I stand before him on Terra, I will ask again. And then, Lorgar, our father will answer.'

The Word Bearer sighed, in the grip of something sublime and unshared. 'You deserve an answer.'

'Desh'ea,' said Angron. 'I have to go there. I have to see who rules the city that claimed to own me. The city that murdered my brothers and sisters.'

'As you wish,' Lorgar agreed. 'As you wish.'

IT GALLED HER that the Praxury was right. Despite their hurried arrival, they did seem peaceful. Reports listed thousands upon thousands of them making planetfall on the plains outside the city, unquestionably landing an army, but making no assault upon Desh'ea itself. Stuck as she was by the royal throne, she presided over a procession of officers bringing her updates and observer reports, whispering in her ear and swapping data printouts.

The Praxury sat straight in his throne, half the height of his father and twice as ridiculous as that pompous fool had ever been. His periapt of office was an amulet of polished silver shaped into a clenched fist – young Tybaral wore it around his neck, though it hung almost to his stomach. Every now and again, he'd sigh, as if the weight of the world rested upon his shoulders.

'How many houses have mobilised?' Oshamay asked one of her subcommanders. He was nervous, she saw it in his eyes, but he dealt with it cleanly, purely, masking it in the efficiency of a busy soldier.

'Perhaps half are already at the walls, general. Most of the rest are choosing to defend their own estates rather than join the communal defence force.'

She dismissed him, not surprised in the slightest that so many houses were choosing to reinforce their own estates; in fact, she was shocked so many were choosing to send their soldiers to man the walls. It wasn't like the noble bloodlines to actually act with any unselfish vision; she knew that well from almost thirty years as an officer in the Praxury's court.

To the next of her officers that approached, she leaned in close to speak into his ear. 'If they do attack the city, be ready to free the slaves.'

To his credit, he didn't ask if she was sure, or argue at the idea's inherent madness. If the city was attacked, the several thousand slave-caste warriors in the arena's fighting pits might at least help shore up the defenders' numbers. And if they revolted and rioted? It hardly mattered, the city was doomed anyway.

'I'll see to it,' the officer promised.

'Good luck,' she said. That made him hesitate – no one was used to hearing affection from the general's thin lips. Oshamay was glad he decided not to acknowledge her momentary slip. Her nerves were as frayed as anyone's, given what was taking shape out there on the plains.

They didn't have to wait for long. Heralds ran through the great stone doors at the throne room's southern entrance, escorted by soldiers running and looking back over their shoulders.

Oshamay swallowed. This didn't look good.

'Our one lord!' the heralds cried, babbling and speaking over each other. The boy-king endured this display with regal, practiced patience. He never got the chance to speak, however.

The first figure to stalk through the black marble archway was so tall he had to lower his head. Oshamay literally felt the hundreds of courtiers' unified intake of breath; they gasped as one, many backing away to the walls as the towering figure made its entrance. He was taller than any human, clad in armour of cold red and lustrous, clean bronze. Dreadlock-cables ran from the back half of his shaven and tattooed head, down into the active powered suit of armour. Everyone staring up in awe at the warlord knew those implants – Butcher's Nails, the cyber-crest of a slave.

Two toothed, motorised swords were lashed to his back, though the idea of this creature, this avatar of brutality, requiring weapons to strike his foes down was laughable. He stalked down the red carpet leading to the Reskium Throne, his boots sending tremors through the stone floor. The throne's polished surface reflected the artificial lighting strips above, and the cringing figures of almost two hundred courtiers. Several Kin-Guard soldiers went for their guns with trembling hands. Others recognised the sheer futility of the gesture. Oshamay was one of the latter.

The figure stopped, turned, regarded his surroundings. The lipless face was the visage of a broken angel, scarred and ruined, denied any echo of what might have once made it handsome.

'So,' he said, and his voice was the grinding of bitter stonework. 'Who sits in ascendancy in this age?'

On the throne, the boy-king started crying. His Kin-Guard, life-sworn to defend him to their final breaths, started retreating away from the throne. The god-warrior saw their slow retreat, and it made him smile.

'Is it you, boy? You're Praxury of Desh'ea?'

The boy curled into his throne, crying louder. The god came closer, taking the stairs slowly, four at a time.

'Boy,' he said, his gravelly voice now a dusty whisper. 'What family are you from? What blood beats in your filthy high-rider veins?'

It was Oshamay who answered in place of the crying child. She alone hadn't cowered back from the Reskium Throne.

'You stand before Tybaral of House Thal'kr.' She almost managed to keep her voice level.

The god's face tightened at the name, tautening into a grimace that failed to be either a scowl or a smile.

'Thal'kr,' he said. 'That family still rules? After all this time...'

'They still rule.' Oshamay stood straighter, fear-tears in her eyes. Her heart beat fit to burst.

'The Thal'kr held my leash,' the warrior said. 'They owned me.'

Other invaders were entering now. The first of them was as tall as the dreadlocked god, his skin pale gold where the blade-bearer's was scarred and tanned. He carried a spiked and ridged maul over one shoulder, and a cloak the colour of bloody sunsets cast back to reveal armour of the same vascular hue. His features were sculpted in statuesque masculinity, somehow protective and serene and confident all at once. Up close, through the tears in her eyes, Oshamay saw the gold on his skin was runic script tattooed onto his flesh. The only flaw was the claw-scars along one cheek, from temple to his jawline, though they added to his presence rather than stole from it. At first sight of him, dozens of courtiers fell to their knees. Others wept – not the shameful tears of fear but the silent weeping of purest awe.

Trailing behind the golden god were armoured knights in clean white and sanguine red. Thirteen of them in total – the warriors in white held axes in loose fists; the knights in red bore parchment strips bound to their battle-plate, and carried curved blades in their hands, while armoured fuel tanks sloshed on their backpacks. Each of them stared from a snarling helm with a silver faceplate. They seemed to be guarding a lone female – a precious, fragile girl of two and a half decades' life, clad in red silk. She was willowy in shape but utterly fearless, surrounded by her protectors. Dark hair framed dusky features and dark eyes that danced from face to face, weapon to weapon, painting to painting.

'Lorgar,' said the dreadlocked god by the throne. He said that one word, with his shoulders shaking. Then he threw his head back, and started laughing as loud as the ghost-wind back in the mountains.

KHÂRN AND ARGEL Tal hesitated – as did every World Eater and Word Bearer – when Angron's laughter cut the sterile silence. It was more than mere laughter, it was a slice of life brought to the chamber's mournful, stunted emptiness. Those who'd been cowering withdrew further. Those who'd been standing their ground found their skin crawling.

'Lorgar.' Angron was still laughing, his bloodshot eyes wet with amusement. 'Behold, brother! Behold the last scion of the family that once owned me. How the mighty have fallen!'

Khârn watched Lorgar ascend the steps to the throne, standing next to Angron, casting the poor, crying child into the shadow of two primarchs. For the first time Khârn could ever recall, the primarch of the XVII Legion looked unsure. Doubt warred with bemusement across his features.

Understanding passed between the two warlords and Angron slapped his brother on the shoulder. The laughter faded from his throat, but never left his eyes.

'I will handle this,' he said to Lorgar. And then, 'You. Woman. Come here.'

Oshamay, who'd never been spoken to like that in her life, put all her effort into swallowing the lump in her throat.

'You're not him,' she stammered. 'You can't be him.'

Angron clacked his teeth together, a feral snapping bite aimed at the air. 'Can't I?'

'Angron-Thal'kr died a hundred years ago,' Oshamay whispered. 'He fled at the Battle of Desh'elika Ridge.'

'He… He…' There was no laughter now. The life in his eyes faded, leaving them pearlescent with numbing pain. Angron brought his whole body around to face her, to look down at her. 'He *fled*. You said those words to me. You said Angron-Thal'kr fled.'

General Oshamay Evrel'Korshay tried to speak but it left her clattering teeth as a weak moan while her bladder emptied itself down her thighs.

'Speak,' Angron almost purred, hatred souring his breath.

'He led a rebellion of slaves. He left them to die in the mountains. He…'

'You.' Angron wrapped her whole head in a scar-thickened fist. 'You lie, woman. You will– *hnnngh*, you will tell the truth now.'

She sobbed instead, and her crying killed her. Angron closed his fist, ending her distinguished career in a crumbling of gory skull fragments that he didn't bother shaking from his hand. The body toppled; Angron looked at it on the floor, seeming annoyed that it had died, as though he had nothing to do with it.

'You.' He pointed a blood-wet hand at the closest officer. The man wore a breastplate over his black toga, marking him out as a captain. Angron recognised that much; so little had changed in the century he'd been gone.

'Please,' the man said. 'Please. Please.'

The primarch's breathing was carnosaur-low, carnosaur-heavy. 'You,' he said again, and now his own great hands were shaking. Khârn recognised all the signs of Nails-pain. 'You will speak,' Angron said. 'Tell me of this battle. The Battle of Desh'elika Ridge.'

'You're him,' the officer whispered. 'You're him.'

'*Speak.*' The roar rocked the man onto his heels, driving him back against a pillar.

Khârn risked a glance at Argel Tal. The Word Bearer stood by Cyrene – who'd insisted she was making planetfall with them – with his silver faceplate tilted to regard the primarchs. Behind them both, Vorias and Kargos were equally emotionless behind their Sarum-pattern visages.

'Captain,' came Esca's voice over the vox. The Codicier stood far back, close to the doors with several of the Vakrah Jal. 'The fear in the chamber is threatening to reach breaking point. The human herd instinct will force them to flee.'

Khârn didn't need to be psychic to know the Librarian was correct. He could see it in their tremulous movements, and smell the copper on their breath.

'Kill any who bolt for the doors.'

'Aye, captain.'

On the platform with the throne, Lorgar was a statue carved in honour of patience. Angron loomed over the whimpering Nucerian officer, closing a fist around the man's armoured torso and dragging him from his feet.

'You will speak,' the primarch breathed, 'or you will die.'

'A hundred years ago,' the man whined. 'A legend. An old story. Angron-Thal'kr and the rebel army, massacred in the mountains. He... You...'

'*Say it.*' Angron shook the man, dropping him to the floor with the clang of breastplate on stone, and the snap of one leg bone. The officer cried out until Angron leered down at him, iron teeth wet with strings of saliva. *'Speak.'*

'The army died to a man. Angron-Thal'kr left them to die–'

'No. *No! That was never my name. Never! I refuse that slave name!'* Angron crushed the man's skull beneath a boot, smearing the wreckage across the stone. 'Can no one speak the truth? Can no one remember anything but lies?'

He turned on the crowd, still raving, crashing his chainswords together. 'I never ran! You filthy high-rider dogs. Is nothing sacred? Is nothing spared from your vileness? You are murderers, and the sons and daughters of murderers. Slavers, and the sons and daughters of slavers. We burned your cities! I stood and breathed in the death-smoke of Ull-Chaim on the finest day of my life. I pulled out the princeling's eyes. *Pop* and *crunch* and scream, scream, scream.'

His voice rose, manic in imitation of a man dying in woeful pain. 'No, Angron, no! Please! Mercy!'

Lorgar watched all of this in silence. Khârn could scarcely believe the other primarch stood so impassively.

'Sire–' Khârn began, but Angron slapped him aside with the flat of one chainblade. It hit with the force of a forge hammer, hurling him back against Argel Tal and Eshramar, who awkwardly caught and righted him.

'I never ran. Never. The Emperor… *Hnnngh.'* The effort was monumental, but Angron let the chainswords fall idle, no longer gunning their motors. He was silent for a long while.

'Khârn,' he said at last, his voice a grating hiss. 'Argel Tal.'

The Eighth Captain stepped forwards, as did the commander of the Vakrah Jal. 'Sire?' they asked in unison.

Angron looked up, his gaze one of old hurt and dull, emberish fury. He didn't glance at the warriors – instead, he raked his eyes over the gathered courtiers, no longer recognising them as people at all.

'I want every World Eater and Word Bearer to heed a simple order.'

'Anything, sire,' Khârn said.

'Speak, and it will be done,' said Argel Tal.

Angron looked back to the cowering child on the throne – the last living remnant of the bloodline that had owned and mutilated and ruined him.

'Kill everyone in this city.' Angron closed his eyes. 'Then kill everyone on this world.'

NINETEEN

Dead Eyes
Perpetual
A Thinker's War

THERE WOULD BE no great war for Nuceria. Nor, much to Lotara's guilty disappointment, would there be any bombardment. She spent the days on the *Conqueror*'s bridge, watching the orbital cartography, seeing the cities burn beneath the tide of the two Legions and their Audax forces. They only had twenty thousand legionaries down there, but when you were dealing with warriors of that calibre, 'only' was a relative statement. Several hundred could take a world in months. Several thousand barely needed a week.

Lhorke had made planetfall with them, leaving Lotara with a curious feeling of isolation. She'd grown used to the former Legion Master remaining by the side of her throne this last month, offering his grinding, veteran observations on everything that took place. She wondered if he'd paid this much heed in the years he'd been lord of the War Hounds, standing by the thrones of her predecessors and rumbling with advice and criticism whether or not it was sought.

She'd tried playing cards with him at one point to pass the time during their month in transit. Lhorke was, she learned, a very sore loser, and his massive gauntlets precluded a card player's finesse. In the end, they'd had to use a servitor to hold his cards. He only played once, and not for more than two minutes.

'This is ludicrous,' he'd stated, and that was that.

When he'd announced he was making planetfall, she'd let her raised eyebrow ask the question for her.

'War calls,' he'd answered.

'And this has nothing to do with you not trusting Angron?'

'War calls,' he'd said again. And that, also, was that.

Desh'ea had fallen first. She'd watched it die, in the familiar way that civilisation burning always looked shamefully beautiful from orbit. The two Legions marched through the streets, massacring the population, bringing death to every slaver, and every man, woman and child that had ever tolerated slavery in their society. Her one and only transmission from Angron had come when Desh'ea was blanketed in the smoke of its last breath. He'd looked more alive than she could recall, and yet his eyes were deader than ever.

'Justice,' his hololithic image had said, fiercely intense. 'Vengeance. Every slaver dead. Every wretched soul that ever cheered at the gladiator games. Every one. All of them, Lotara.'

She saw Lhorke behind the primarch, stomping past, crossing her field of vision. A Fellblade trundled by afterwards, making the image shake.

'Will every city face the Legions?' she'd asked.

'Every city.'

Lotara had feigned a casual air, pretending to toy with a data-slate. She didn't like looking into his unfocused eyes. Despite his vitality and the fire in his voice, Angron stared like a corpse, tensing with Nails-pain. She feared whatever had happened in the Praxury's throne room had damaged what remained of his mind still further.

'What of Lord Aurelian's plan?'

'Soon. *Hnnh*. When the cities are dead. They will burn. They will be funeral pyres for my brothers and sisters, one hundred years gone. Then we can deal with Lorgar's madness.'

She shivered at his voice, glad she was two hundred kilometres above him. 'Good luck, Angron.'

He'd grinned then, pleased at not being called 'my lord' by her for once, even as a joke. The image blanked a second later. That was the first night.

Now, six days after arrival, she paced the bridge, hoping for something – anything – to do. On the surface, with the city of Meahor being assaulted at sunrise, part of her wanted to be there to see it with her own eyes. Part of her – the much shrewder, wiser part – wanted to be nowhere near.

She stood by Lehralla's console table. The crippled girl smiled down at her, with those watery, fey eyes of hers.

'My captain,' she greeted Lotara in a soft voice.

'Scrymistress,' Lotara replied. 'Do you ever get bored?'

'No, captain.' And for a wonder, the halved girl seemed to be sincere. 'Never.'

Lotara gave a soft laugh and moved on. She was by Vox-master Kejic's array of frequency controls and transmission stations when the bridge's southern doors rolled open on their sonorous tracks. Several heads turned; the main crew thoroughfare was from east to west, and few used the southern doors.

Tarn, her Master of Astropaths, stood in the entranceway. Blind as all astropaths were, their sight stolen to magnify their powers, his milky eyes were wide beneath his white hood.

'Captain,' he said. 'I hear something.'

Lotara hid her sigh behind a false smile, hoping it would steal the edge from her tone.

'Tarn, if you've come to give me another lecture on Lord Aurelian's great song, you have my permission to turn around and leave me in peace.'

He clutched at his medallion of office with skinny hands, his fingers gnarled by gout.

'No, captain. I hear something approaching.'

Across the bridge, Lehralla turned on her plinth, the cables leashing her to the ceiling lashing like snakes.

'Warp nexus,' the girl called. 'Warp nexus in the fifth meridian. Hololithics activating.'

Lotara sprinted to the central hololithic table as it flickered into life.

'What's coming through? All eyes on the nexus. Track it and codify it at once.' The wait was agony as she stared at the hololithic rune flickering in the air, waiting for it to resolve. A warp-wound, that much she knew. A ship breaking back into reality.

'Scry-locked,' Lehralla said in a distant voice. 'I see it.'

Lotara saw it a moment later. The rune resolved, showing a transponder code; then several transponder codes; then several more.

'Prime weapons and shields,' she said calmly. 'All crew to battle stations.'

HER FACE APPEARED in ghostly resolution at the edge of Khârn's retinal display. In profile, as always, from the pictfinder mounted on the side of her throne.

'This is Captain Sarrin to all ground forces. The Thirteenth Legion warship *Courage Above All* has broken warp at the system's edge, at the head of a void armada. Their outrunners will be in range to engage in nine minutes. All Legion forces, get back to your drop-ships and landers for immediate withdrawal.'

The city Meahor stood defiant on the horizon. The two Legions had lined up in siege formation, ready for the grim march towards the walls. Audax's Titans were with them, row upon row of Warhounds standing above the massed infantry and their armour divisions. Vindicators, Land Raiders, Fellblades, Mastodons – entire tank divisions, awaiting the order to roll forwards at dawn. No swift, clean attack for the cities of Nuceria. Each of them so far had watched their demise come rolling closer in a tide, and died when the World Eaters and Word Bearers pulled their walls down.

Meahor would be the last. Now it seemed to be spared, minutes from the order to march.

'Lotara,' Khârn voxed back, knowing every legionary, Titan crew member, and skitarii in the ranks could hear him.

'Centurion,' she replied. She looked eager, eyes narrowed, a huntress ready for any tricks her prey might play.

'Extraction is impossible. Can you keep them at bay?'

'Khârn,' she said with a sigh, then seemed to recall the fact every single soul on the surface could hear what she was saying. 'Captain, you have no conception of the host sailing its way into lance range. We outweigh them and outgun them, but we'll still die deaths from a thousand cuts. If you can't withdraw, then *take the city now*. Find cover, because they will break past us, no matter what I do up here.'

'Understood.' Khârn looked down the line of several thousand Space Marines in scruffy formation. He raised his axe, ready to give the signal to advance.

'Wait,' said a voice of gargling gravel.

'Sire?' Lotara replied. She looked away across the bridge, her voice distorting for several seconds. 'Feyd, are those fighters in the sky?' She turned back. 'Angron, with all due respect, hurry up.'

'They want us,' the primarch replied. Khârn could see his gene-father back in the ranks, standing atop a Bloodhammer super-heavy assault carrier, both chainswords in his hands. 'They want us dead. That means proof. It means planetfall. We'll take the city and force them down to dig us out. Repel bombardment, at all costs. Do you understand me? Repel bombardment, even at the cost of the ship.'

'Understood,' Lotara said, and her image died in the retinal displays of every legionary on the surface.

Lorgar's voice was a gentle interruption over the shared vox. 'Guilliman is up there.'

'*Hnngh*. I know. The vengeance of Calth is coming at last. Warriors of the Twelfth and Seventeenth Legions! Take the city! *Charge!*'

As the sun rose over the Jehzr Plains, the Legions tore their way overland, to bring down the walls of Nuceria's last city and use its ruins as a fortress.

Aboard the *Fidelitas Lex*, a slender young woman walked through the mausoleum, approaching her own tomb. Her skin was dusky – a desert tribeswoman's tan – and her long hair fell in soft brown curls, neither dark nor light but a healthy, earthy compromise between the two. She wore a robe of Word Bearers red – that unmistakable blood-claret darkness – cut in a flowing shape that clung to her waist and flared outwards from there on down. She looked a little like a bride, and a little like a priestess.

The ship shook beneath her. Another battle. How many battles had she lived through on the *De Profundis*, seated in the quiet of her chamber while the walls shook and the decks vibrated from cannonfire? You could get used to anything. That was the sad truth.

Her Vakrah Jal guardians waited outside the chamber, four of them in all, ready to incinerate any mortal or Word Bearer that sought to lay a hand on her or bar her way. With Argel Tal on the surface, she'd decided it was time to come see herself as she'd been… before.

When she passed the statue of Xaphen, she dared to reach out and touch its breastplate, unconsciously echoing the gesture Argel Tal always made here. He'd told her how Xaphen died. He'd even shown her the weapon that did it, and admitted the secret of how he'd managed to break the gene-coding to activate his stolen relics.

Blood. Didn't it always come down to blood?

Her skin crawled as she caught sight of her own statue from the corner of her eye. Even without looking at its details, the thing's presence spread the taste of bile over her tongue.

Bracing herself, she walked towards it. A robed servant stood by the pedestal, tending to the three braziers at the stone lady's bare feet. Unless a senior Word Bearer decreed otherwise, the Hall of Anamnesis was often populated by menials and thralls tending to the monuments.

The sight of herself graven in stone felt much worse than she'd imagined. She didn't want to look at it, let alone touch it. The sculptor's artistry was undeniable, but therein lay the problem. It looked too real. It wasn't a stylised statue raised in honour of her deeds. It was a tomb marker, a monument to her death. And it was blind – the stone girl's eyes wreathed in a sculpted blindfold. That was doubly unnerving, though she wasn't sure why. She'd spent most of her life blind, and in the month since her rebirth – what Cyrene hesitantly called her 'reawakening' – she had spent many hours in her chamber alone, lights dimmed and her eyes closed, listening to the ship around her. It felt more natural than seeing the million things she'd lived amongst and never witnessed before.

Despite herself, she touched the statue's outstretched hands, fingers to fingers, flesh mirrored perfectly in stone. For a churning moment, she wasn't sure which one of them was really her: the reborn girl or the statue of the dead one. Both, perhaps. Or neither.

'It's a very fine likeness,' said the robed servant. She started at the sudden voice – Argel Tal had told her the mausoleum thralls took a vow of silence upon pain of death. He kept his face hooded, but she saw the edge of a smile in the shadow. 'I'm sure you don't miss the blindfold, though.'

Her blood ran colder; he'd not spoken in Gothic or Colchisian. The words were Uhturlan, the dialect of the Monarchian city-state where she'd been born on distant Khur.

'Show yourself.'

He did. He wasn't particularly handsome, nor was he especially youthful. He looked to be in his mid-thirties, edging towards middle-age, and like anyone spending their lives aboard the vessels of a war-fleet, he looked like he'd lived hard for those decades.

He was also, without a shade of doubt, not what he was pretending to be. His eyes were bright and alive and full of laughing lies.

'Don't,' he warned her. 'Don't shout for your guardians.' A moment later he added, 'I could see you were about to.'

She'd been about to turn to see if there were any other thralls nearby, but she didn't scare so easily as to shriek for her Vakrah Jal purely because of a deceitful rogue trying his luck. And she had a ritual *qattari* knife strapped to her thigh, beneath the flowing robe.

'How do you speak the tongue of a dead city?' she asked, folding her arms beneath her breasts, hugging herself as if cold. Hearing her language, seeing this statue… It was surreal enough to drive her to distraction.

'I speak any tongue I put my mind to.' His eyes locked to hers with sincerity, but without threat. 'Pardon me for saying so, but you're breathtaking in the flesh. I have an avowed weakness for dusky women.'

He wasn't putting her at ease, but something in his voice was more palatable than the solemn reverence in almost every Word Bearer's tones. Even Lorgar, upon seeing her again, had been awestruck and priestly – praying for her soul and naming her resurrection a miracle. He'd not commented on Erebus's role in her rebirth, and never once tried to ask any of the questions so many others came to her with. Lorgar didn't ask her if she recalled being dead, or what it was like beyond the veil. She suspected it was because he already knew.

All Lorgar had done was kneel before her, bringing himself close to her height, and kissed her closed eyes.

'I once apologised for my sins bringing the fire that blinded you,' he had whispered. *'Now I apologise for them bringing the blade that harmed you. My heart sings to know you breathe again.'*

She'd wanted to reply, but in a primarch's company, she did what so many humans had done and would continue to do. She stared, shivered, and tried not to weep at his majestic, impossible presence.

Understanding her breathless indecision – as he always seemed to understand those beneath him – Lorgar had released her with an apologetic smile.

'Go in peace, Blessed Lady. You were always a gift to my Legion, and my sons have missed you. Anything you ask of me will be yours.'

Here, in the mausoleum, Cyrene blinked to banish the memory.

'Whatever you're trying,' she said to the false thrall, 'you'll have to try harder.'

'This is just the opening volley, I assure you. We have to talk, Cyrene.'

She scrunched her nose at his pronunciation. *Sy-Reen*. Despite speaking her native language, his pronunciation held traces of Gothic clumsiness, and Gothic wasn't kind to her name.

'It's *Sih-renny*,' she replied.

'Forgive me, John was always better at languages.'

'Who's John?'

'A friend. An idiot, but a friend. It doesn't matter – he's busy. I was sent here, for you. We have to talk.'

She'd not spoken her homeland's dialect in half a century, yet it was like honey on her tongue. 'We're already talking. Tell me your name, if you please.'

'I wonder, why is it that the simplest questions have the hardest answers? Most recently, I've been going by Damon.' He offered his hand for her to shake. Unfamiliar with the Terran custom, she simply glanced at it, then stared back into his eyes.

'Just *Damon*.' Disapproval made it a question.

'Damon Prytanis,' he said.

'That isn't your real name.'

'It isn't the name I was born with,' he admitted with a smile, 'but that doesn't make it any less real, or any less mine.'

'I am leaving,' she lied. The *qattari* knife was starting to feel tempting.

'No you're not. And don't reach for that blade. I'm not here to hurt you. I'm here to save you.'

'You think I need saving?'

'I *know* you need saving. Everyone does, from time to time. Do you have any idea how difficult it was for me to infiltrate the Word Bearers flagship just to have this conversation?'

Infiltrate. He said *infiltrate*.

He wasn't on their side.

'I'm not on anyone's side,' he said, though she hadn't spoken a word. 'I know,' he added. 'I can read your mind.'

She turned to run, but Damon reached for her wrist, holding it tight. 'You died and came back again,' he said to her gently. 'We have that in common. The Cabal have taken an interest in you, and for humans that's almost always a bad thing. But you're like us now. The Seventeenth Legion made you into one of us. I can't say whether they meant to. I wouldn't even want to guess.'

'One of what? What are you talking about?'

'The undying. The Perpetuals.' Damon Prytanis didn't smile that time – he outright grinned. 'Come with me, Cyrene.'

'Eshramar!' she shouted. *'Eshramar!'*

The Vakrah Jal warrior entered at the other end of the chamber, taking less than a heartbeat to see her and the danger she was in. The turbines on his back screamed into life as he started running, and after three steps he kicked off the deck, jump pack howling.

Damon refused to release Cyrene's wrist, even as he faced the Word Bearer diving through the maze of statues, streaming smoky fire. He swore in several languages, one of which sounded like a particularly elegant eldar dialect, and none of which Cyrene understood.

The Vakrah Jal sergeant landed with a crunch of ceramite on the deck, both wrist-mounted flamers aimed at the false thrall. Alchemical fire bubbled in the connective cables along his arms, boiling, waiting to roar into the air and turn from liquid to true flame.

'Move away from her,' Eshramar demanded. His silver Mark III faceplate stared with surprising vehemence. Smoke wisped around the three of them, trailing from the exhaust vents in the Word Bearer's turbine backpack.

'Listen–' Damon began.

'Move away from her.'

'Listen to me.'

'Move away from her.'

'Cyrene, I can explain everything,' he said.

'Move away from her.'

Damon raised his hands and took a single step forwards. In the same moment, Cyrene rammed her ritual knife into his shoulder. She'd been aiming for his neck, but he wove aside even with his back to her – the man's reactions were far too fluid to be entirely human.

He didn't scream, didn't even curse, but he did lose his grip. She threw herself to the side.

'Wait,' he said. 'Cyrene, wait!'

Eshramar closed both hands into fists, triggering the pressure pads in his gauntlets' palms. Fire the colour of diseased jade burst from his wrist-flamers, bathing the human in a sustained, semi-liquid torrent. It dissolved the meat from his bones in the time it took Cyrene to pick herself up and turn to look back.

Damon Prytanis died before their eyes, in what might be the most painful way to meet one's end.

It was the first time he'd died in flame, but not the first time he'd died laughing.

LOTARA LOVED THE calm that took hold in moments like this. This was what she was best at, and all she ever needed was free rein to play the game her way. Outwardly, she was relaxed in her throne, but her eyes were everywhere at once – locator and vector hololithics; targeting array displays; the multisected oculus screen; and even her own officers, to make sure they were bearing up as expected.

They had two Gloriana-class flagships and whatever in the hells the *Trisagion* was supposed to be. There was no way Lotara Sarrin was going down without a fight, no matter how devastatingly, hopelessly outnumbered they were. In fact, she kept finding herself wanting to laugh.

The enemy armada came running close, each squadron falling into attack formation and holding with admirable unity. Every battleship and carrier was defended by destroyers and frigates, and each squadron was led by cruisers with their own lesser escorts.

'Forty-one,' Lehralla said, her voice distant the way it always was when she was seeing through the ship's scanners rather than her own eyes. 'Forty-one enemy vessels.'

Lotara heard Ivar Tobin's quiet curse to the side of her throne. It was, she agreed, an insane force to face practically alone. What few escorts they'd kept with them would be nothing more than sacrificial lambs in the maw of the enemy fleet, but Angron and Lorgar had needed to spread their Legions behind enemy lines, and Captain Sarrin would work with what she had left. She hadn't earned the Blood Hand for whining about the odds.

Even so, she estimated those odds were about even. The *Trisagion* could take twenty lesser vessels alone, and there were many, many reasons Gloriana-class battlecruisers were used as Legion flagships. Plenty of the Ultramarines armada already looked wounded, or cobbled together from separate fleets. It wasn't a dedicated interdiction war-fleet, it was clearly a ragtag strike force: a lance thrust to the enemy's heart. Someone – perhaps even Lord Guilliman himself – had done the best he could with limited resources.

If she had been leading that enemy fleet, she knew how she'd roll the dice in this fight. The Ultramarines victory counted on two factors. First, that the *Conqueror*, the *Lex* and the *Trisagion* would be torn apart by the massed firepower of smaller ships. The XIII Legion's cruisers and battleships would run abeam for repeated exchanges of broadsides, offering targets too big and powerful to ignore, while the rest of the fleet used calculated lance strikes from safer range. She suspected the armada would divide its assault potential, doing its damndest to kill either the *Lex* or the *Conqueror*, and taking the other by boarding parties. The *Trisagion* was too vast and deadly to take with boarders or with a divided fleet, but nor would any sane void commander devote their entire focus to attacking it first. The two Legion flagships would be free to inflict unrivalled damage in the time it took to cripple the king-ship.

The second factor was planetfall. The Legiones Astartes excelled at fighting void wars and surface battles at once, and this attack run reeked of something personal. The Ultramarines were coming for revenge here, just as they were apparently pursuing Kor Phaeron all the way to the Maelstrom on the other side of Ultramar.

Several ships would make a run for Nuceria, haemorrhaging drop pods, landers and gunships, forcing planetfall by any means necessary. They'd have to come in close – close enough to brawl, just as Lotara liked it – but they'd get the job done, and Meahor would be crawling with the enemy in no time at all.

This was what she loved about void battles. Up here, in the coldness of space, you were trading death at unthinkable distances one minute, and manoeuvring city-sized warships close enough to scratch each other's paintwork a minute later. It didn't lack the adrenaline and frantic focus of a ground battle, it simply refined it into something much more civilised.

Void war was a thinker's war.

Lehralla's cabled head turned again. 'Captain, fourteen of the enemy vessels, those in the axial formation marked now on the hololith, bear transponders correlating to the Martian Mechanicum. Several appear to be Titan-carriers.'

Lotara resisted the urge to swear at length and in great detail. Whatever broke through their blockade – and plenty was going to make it through, no question there – would make life murder for those on the surface. Ultramarines were bad enough. Ultramarines and Titans was about the worst news she could receive.

'Inform the primarchs and Legion captains they are likely to be dealing with Titans as well,' she ordered Kejic. 'Weaponmaster, time to maximum range?'

'Enemy vanguard will reach maximum lance range in one minute, fifty seconds.'

'Good, good. Feyd, status of our fighter squadrons?'

'All flying free, ma'am.' The young lieutenant didn't look up from his scanner console. 'Captain, I have an idea regarding phase two of the engagement.'

'As long as it's not about capital ship movement, I wait with bated breath. Let's hear it.'

Rather then tell her, he showed her. The tactical suggestion played out on the hololithic display as Feyd ran a simulation over the course of ten seconds. By the end, the flag-captain was smiling.

'Do it,' she said. Her confidence in him wasn't idle assumption; no one oversaw a spread of fighter squadrons quite like Feyd, which was why Lotara had poached him from the battleship *Interregnum* for her own command crew.

She waited, drumming her fingertips on the armrest of her throne. 'Keep an open vox-link to the *Lex* and *Trisagion*.'

'Aye, ma'am,' Kejic replied.

'Are they in position?'

'Yes, captain,' replied Lehralla.

Lotara looked up at Tobin, ever-loyal, ever by her throne. 'Did you imagine you'd die in Ultramar, Ivar?'

'I try not to imagine dying at all, ma'am. Weapons primed and awaiting your mark.'

'Thank you, Ivar. I suspect they'll choose to board the *Conqueror* and destroy the *Lex*, given the grudge they surely carry against Lord Aurelian's Legion, but if it happens the other way around, I'll just say now that it's been a pleasure serving with you.'

'I'm honoured you'd say so, ma'am.'

The command crew exchanged glances and smiles as they listened to their ranking officers.

'Now then.' Lotara cleared her throat. 'Let's start killing.'

TWENTY

**Blood in the Void
Going to the Triarii
He Dies Here**

It didn't take long for her to lose all track of the surface war. The Ultramarines fleet swept over and against them like an insect horde, robbing any attention she'd have liked to let linger on how the Legion was doing. Her world erupted in a kaleidoscopic mess of weapon flashes, shield flares, and the insistent flicker of sirens. Every officer was reporting at once, while still shouting at their own underlings. The ship shook in a tempest's grip, and the bridge smelled of unwashed skin, rancid breath, and the faint smoky spice of internal systems burning.

Lotara was a dervish, delivering a ceaseless stream of orders between tracking the constantly-updating hololithic projections. Her most pressing concern wasn't that her ships were taking a beating, but that trying to stop the enemy getting past them was a game of fighting back an ocean tide with cupped hands and harsh language.

'The *Ceres*,' Lehralla called, twisting in her socket cradle. The legless girl had to shout over the shaking chamber. 'The *Ceres* is running past us.'

Lotara gave three precious seconds to her personal hololithic display, beamed up from the microprojectors in her armrests. The *Ceres*, the *Ceres*... There. Bulk cruiser. A Dominus-class battle-barge. That meant troops, thousands of troops. Damn it, damn it, *damn it*.

The *Ceres*'s rune flickered past the sigil marking the *Conqueror*. There were still two Ultramarines warships between the World Eaters flagship and the ship it needed to stop, and seven others rolling above and below, in the middle of their own laborious strafing runs.

If Lotara came about, she'd abort her kill-run against the *Unbroken Vigil* and risk another full minute of broadsides from the... No, it didn't matter. The *Ceres* had to die.

'Come about,' she called, ready to shoot the first officer to dare argue.

'Come about!' Tobin relayed the order in a roar.

The ship groaned beneath them, at the mercy of momentum, retros and protesting roll/pitch/yaw thrusters.

'Everything on the *Ceres*,' Lotara ordered. 'Broadsides as we turn, then lances from the forward array at one-eighty degrees. Send that bitch to the ground in flames.'

'The *Legendary Son* and the *Glory of Fire* are–'

'I see them,' she interrupted Feyd. 'I'm not letting them get in our way. Engines to full burn.'

'That will alter our turning arc to–'

'I *know* where our arc will take us. I want the engines screaming. Cease starboard broadsides for immediate reload, I want them ready as we come about. We'll only have one try at the *Ceres*.'

The *Conqueror* lumbered around, dragging itself away from the encircling Ultramarines ships, sacrificing a kill-run Lotara had spent the best part of five furious minutes setting up while under intense enemy fire. She watched the *Unbroken Vigil* roll aside, safe and unharmed, when she should be tumbling away in flaming pieces.

'*Ceres* is manoeuvring for orbital release,' called Lehralla, her watery doe-eyes wide at the hololithic, and her brittle teeth bared in the face of the fight.

The stars rolled across the oculus as the *Conqueror* turned, turned, turned, slow, slow, slow. The deck, *her deck*, was shaking beneath Lotara's boots. They were taking one nightmare of a beating.

The *Ceres* hove into view, already kissing the atmosphere.

'Laser batteries rea–'

'Broadsides!' Lotara yelled.

The *Conqueror* answered its captain, its cannons booming into the night's silence. The deck heaved again, but it was a much more pleasant shudder this time. Space around the *Ceres* flared with luminescence as its shields resisted the torrent bursting against the ship's hull. After three beautiful seconds of defensive pyrotechnics, the cruiser's void shields shattered with enough force to send ripples of lightning across the ship's armoured skin. The *Conqueror* hadn't just broken through its prey's defences – it had overloaded them through power strain. A cheer went up across the strategium at the sight.

'Her shields are fouled.' Lotara was almost laughing in a heady, nasty mix of relief and predatory pleasure. 'Kill her.'

The *Conqueror* fired again, another broadside volley, then brought its forward weapons to bear as it finished coming about. The *Ceres* broke apart in high orbit, the barest touch of Nuceria's atmosphere giving enough air for its wreckage to burn. Lotara gave it another few seconds, just to drink in the image: tens of thousands of lives ending in fire.

'Status of the *Trisagion*?' she called, turning back to the bridge.

'Fighting like nothing I've ever seen before,' Tobin replied, more than a little awed at the figures spilling down his data-feed monitor. 'We'd have lasted less than three minutes without her. She might even win this once we're gone.'

'What are the odds of that?'

'Terrible, ma'am. But there's still a chance.'

'And the *Lex*?'

At that, Tobin shook his head. 'The *Lex* is dying.'

The *Fidelitas Lex* punched through the wreck of a smaller cruiser, ramming it aside. The Word Bearers flagship was already a ruin, its armour pitted and cracked, its shields a memory. The cathedrals and spinal fortresses barnacling along its back were gone, laid waste by the Ultramarines' incendiary rage.

The XIII Legion armada attacked in strafing runs and protracted exchanges of broadsides, trading fire with the superior ship and accepting their own casualties as the cost of bleeding the bigger vessel dry. Each assault left the *Lex* weaker, firing fewer turrets and cannons, taking punishment on increasingly fragile armour. Air and water was vented in silent gushes from holes in the hull, while fuel and coolant flooded from similar wounds. Crew – many of whom were praying as they died – were sucked from the hundreds of other hull ruptures. Lotara took this all in with a glance; it looked like the *Lex* was being turned inside-out, its innards aflame and pulled out into the void.

But she still fought. Crawling with smaller ships, the *Lex* lashed back with its remaining cannons, rolling in the light of its own burning hull.

The Ultramarines commander, whoever guided the battle from the command deck of *Courage Above All*, had made their choice. The *Conqueror* would be boarded, killed from within. The *Lex* would die first, killed in the death of a thousand cuts and swept from the game board.

The *Conqueror* couldn't rise in its sister-ship's defence. Both flagships fought alone, starved of support and suffering the endless attacks of the XIII Legion's ragged armada.

'A bad end for a fine lady,' Lotara commented, 'even if she is full of fanatics.'

Salvation pods were streaming from the *Lex*'s sides and underbelly, along with heavier Mechanicum craft and bulk landers. With the legionaries already on the surface, the ship's human population was fleeing in the vessel's final minutes. And *still* she fought – rolling, turning, raging. The Ultramarines cruisers drifting past burned as badly as the warship they were killing. Dirty fighting, too close for calculations, up close and personal. Lotara felt guilty for loving every second.

'She's still with us,' Tobin noted.

'Not for long. Can we break free to support her?'

Tobin's dry laugh was answer enough.

Lotara was staring hard at her personal hololith. 'You're no fun, Ivar.'

Eshramar had one duty, and it was proving the hardest one of his life. And unless it got easier, it would also be the last duty of his life. One he'd fail, as it happened.

It seemed so simple on the surface – all he had to do was get from *here* to *there*, with Cyrene in tow. The reality of the matter was that the damn ship was coming apart at the seams, and he was already exhausted from murdering his way down the crew-choked corridors. The killing had become farming, no different from the heft of a scythe and the reaping of wheat, day in and day out, from dawn until dusk. Except Eshramar's power scimitar, those newly-forged blades given to each Vakrah Jal warrior, was harvesting life.

He incinerated his way through the densest corridors, but after the corpse-smoke had almost asphyxiated the Blessed Lady, he'd learned to temper that response.

Half the raving packs of humans they came across were trampling each other in feral panic to reach the escape hangars. The other half rounded on Cyrene and shrieked for her favour, believing touching her would grant the fortune to spare them death in the void. Eshramar killed both creeds of crowd, caring little whether they shouted for mercy or cried the Blessed Lady's name as they died. Getting them out of the way was all that mattered.

'This way,' he said to her, pulling his sword from the last body in the hallway. She was struggling to walk, half-climbing over the piled, split-open cadavers. Horror widened her eyes, but that wasn't Eshramar's concern. He was bathed in gore, covered from helm to boots in the blood of his own flagship's crew, but that wasn't at the fore of his thoughts, either.

Ships died slowly – first in fire, then in silence. Eshramar knew they didn't have long left before the *Lex* crumbled around them, becoming powerless and fully open to the airless void.

'This way,' he said again. 'My lady, hurry.'

Cyrene scrambled over the slain, her robes slathered with their blood, her hands red to the wrists from where she kept falling. She'd been on warships for most of her life, but never on one being torn apart.

Eshramar led the way through the corridors, his wet boots thudding on the deck grilles. He was half-dragging her by the wrist, careful not to break her arm or pull it from its socket, but she still grunted with the stabs of pain as he manhandled her.

She knew where he was taking her. The Vakrah Jal had several of their Chapter's own gunships aboard, but she sincerely doubted they'd still be there by now. It had taken them almost half an hour to cross the ship so far. Elevators were inactive, leaving hollow tube-tunnels between decks. Ventilation access crawlspaces glowed orange with distant fire in the ship's veins. Entire swathes of decks were thick with bodies and debris.

Why even abandon ship? What was down there on Nuceria but a death delayed by a handful of hours?

That only made her run harder. She was a daughter of the Perfect City, and the Confessor of the Word. She wouldn't die here if there were even a shred of hope.

Eshramar dragged her to a halt before a sealed bulkhead. She could see from the cant of his head that it shouldn't have been sealed, even in an emergency lockdown. There was no handle, no transition bar, nothing.

'I don't...' he said, but never finished the thought.

'Can you burn through?' she asked, catching her breath. Her throat tasted of blood.

His wrist-flamers were more than capable of liquefying metal, but time wasn't on their side.

'It will take too long.' Eshramar turned away from the dead-end, meaning to double back and take another route. 'Come.'

He said nothing more. His helmeted head cracked back with a dull, ringing clang, sending him staggering against the wall behind. The silver faceplate was a mangled crater around his left eye lens, and Cyrene heard the dim sound of a flatline playing from inside his armour as he slumped to the deck.

At the end of the hallway, where she and Eshramar had run in, she could make out three robed Legion thralls through the smoke. One of them lowered a heavy, long-necked rifle. The other two started running towards her.

She'd have taken Eshramar's bolter if she'd had any hope of lifting it. Instead, Cyrene drew the *qattari* knife for the second time since her rebirth and ran at the men that had murdered her last guardian.

She didn't scream or shriek or laugh. She met her attackers in fierce silence, knuckles white around the ritual knife. The same way she died a year ago.

The first of them deflected her strike with his forearm, batting the dagger from her hands.

'Cyrene,' he said. 'Cyrene, wait, please.' Damon Prytanis pulled back his hood, looking into her eyes as he had an hour before. He was absolutely untouched by the fire that had destroyed him. 'Will you listen to me this time? Come with us.'

THE CONQUEROR HEAVED again, its overburning engines bringing it deep into a slowly-scattering enemy formation. Its shields were dead. Its battlements burned with the dissipating flash-flame of void wounds. Half of its guns had fallen silent. They would never fire again.

Lotara pushed her loose hair back from her face, sucking in air through her rebreather. The ventilators were struggling to cope with the smoke hazing the bridge.

'Come about to three-sixteen,' she called.

'They're running past us,' Tobin yelled back. 'Captain, the *Nova Warrior* and the *Triumph of Espandor* are cutting past. Weapon batteries firing.'

'Will it kill them?' Lotara asked.

'They're damaged, but not dying. This will push them closer to the edge. Don't hold out hopes for anything more, ma'am.'

Lotara touched a grisly, gushing slash on her temple, not remembering when she'd earned it. Her fingers came away red. Almost in a daze, she limp-ran to Lehralla's console. The Scrymistress hung slack and dead, slouched over, held up only by the cables and wires snaking between her head and the ceiling.

Lotara reactivated the central hololith, staring through its flickering indecision and tracking the runes of enemy ships. Blood of the Emperor, how could so many of them still be alive? Surely they'd killed the whole armada and more besides.

The *Conqueror* turned at the heart of a spreading sphere of enemy warships. Its remaining weapons spat wrath into the void, bruising, breaking, burning the Ultramarines vessels clinging to it.

The *Nova Warrior* and *Triumph of Espandor* blinked on the ethereal display, pulsing their way past the embattled *Conqueror*. But Tobin was wrong. They weren't cutting past quickly, they were making attack runs as they flew by. Given the enemy fleet's resources, that was exactly what she'd have done, too – they couldn't afford to keep their heaviest cruisers entirely out of the firefight, no matter the risk.

'Move us closer,' she called out across the bridge. 'Get me within range for the ursus claws. It doesn't matter who we hit in the turn, but those two barges aren't firing their drop pods onto Nuceria while I still draw breath.' Her smile was all white teeth in her sooty face. 'No one runs from the *Conqueror*.'

'If the *Chronicle* changes course...' Tobin warned.

'It will or it won't, but *no one runs*. I want the engines howling loud.'

The World Eaters flagship leapt forwards, engines roaring hotter and harder. Beyond manoeuvring speed. Beyond attack speed. Beyond pursuit speed.

Lotara, and all the surviving bridge crew, stared at the image blooming on the oculus. She heard Feyd curse in the same moment Tobin shouted, 'Brace, brace!'

The rising *Conqueror* met the descending *Chronicle*, both ships changing their heading along unpredicted arcs, and crashing together without void shields to cushion the impact. The strategium shook hard enough to throw everyone from their feet. Lotara's teeth clacked together – she felt several of them break.

The shriek of tormented, agonised metal lasted almost a full minute. The two warships slid against each other, and there was almost something shark-like to how they coupled in the dark. The *Chronicle* came off worse, far outclassed in size, armour, momentum and weight. Its entire port side disintegrated in a tidal tear of scrap metal, exposing thousands of crew to Nuceria's upper atmosphere. When the two ships slipped free of their grinding slide, the *Chronicle* rolled into a powerless fall, snatched by gravity, spearing groundwards and catching fire as it knifed through the world's atmosphere.

The *Conqueror* fared better, but earned black scarring across its entire port side. Entire fortresses of cannons and crew were raked clean off the hull. At her instinctive guess, Lotara estimated they'd lost several thousand crew, and were lucky it was so few.

But they were free, and bearing down on the running cruisers. Despite being forty kilometres away from her prey, in terms of void war Lotara was practically on their backs.

She gave the nod to Tobin.

VEL-KHEREDAR'S FINEST WORK was arguably the weapons array he'd spent over two years installing in the refitted *Conqueror*, soon after she first changed her name from *Adamant Resolve*. The flagship of the XII Legion outgunned practically any other vessel of comparable size, even with its standard armament. What really made the difference were the pursuit talons. The harpoons carried by the Warhounds of Legio Audax served their purpose well, but the *Conqueror*'s ursus claws were an extension of Legiones Astartes savagery on a scale unseen anywhere else.

As the *Conqueror* bore down on the running cruisers, it launched its talons right at their spines. Dozens of spears, each one the size of a frigate in its own right, burst from the warship's forward fire arc. Many missed, as they always did at such range. And many hit, as they always did when Lotara fired them in anger.

She watched the massive spears drive through the cruisers' spines, impaling them and digging deep. Great industrial drills at the head of every harpoon came alive, grinding and eating deeper into the struck ships. Electromagnetic seals charged. The spears, skyscraper-tall and skyscraper-thick, locked home in the puncture wounds they'd caused. The chains connecting the harpoons to their mothership were an alloy of Nostraman adamantium and Ferrekesian titanium, and each of them carried the same value as the annual tithe allowances of an average frontier world. The Imperium, in its sickening scale and ambition, spared no expense for its visionaries and warriors.

The harpoon chains straightened and grew taut. That was when the *Conqueror* killed its thrust. Massive Mechanicum-engineered pulleys – each one dwarfing a Titan in size and strength – began ratcheting the harpoons back.

Clawing a vessel was always a matter of complex calculation. The pursuit talons were designed for the most vicious, close-range breed of warfare, and if too many spears missed – or the enemy ship had too much power – it would be the *Conqueror* that suffered, losing its hold – or worse, being pulled along by the running prey. Neither failure had ever happened. Lotara knew the weapons array inside and out, from the names of the work shift leaders overseeing the slave population that manned the manual loading systems to the exact classes of ship she could bring down at different levels of thrust.

Both the *Nova Warrior* and the *Triumph of Espandor* were wounded, because every ship in the sky was wounded. Thanks to the *Trisagion*, they'd taken heavy fire along with the rest of the Ultramarines fleet, and suffered a massed broadside beating in their attack run past the *Conqueror*.

Weakened as they were, they were the perfect targets.

The claws had fired, sunk in, drilled deeper and bit hard. The chains had pulled tight, and the *Conqueror* fired everything it had into pulling back. Slowly, inexorably, the two Ultramarines vessels were dragged back in defiance of their thrusters, losing all forward momentum and leashed off-course.

Another cheer, this one much sparser, went up across the bridge.

'Pull them closer and finish them with lances.' Lotara limped back to her throne. 'Ram our way through the wreckage when you're done and come about to break the *Glory of Fire*'s escort squadron. Someone give me a status report on the *Lex*.'

'Dead within minutes,' Kejic called back. 'They're abandoning ship, marking twelve kills.'

Twelve. Lotara gave a small smile. *A good showing from the fanatics*.

'Order them to rise to minimum safe distance,' she said. 'I don't want them hitting earth while our forces are still fighting on the surface.'

Kejic relayed the order, but called back almost at once, 'They're going down, captain. Projected markers will have them strike the eastern ocean.'

Lotara swallowed, staring right at her vox-master. 'How far from the coast?'

Kejic looked pained. 'Seventeen kilometres. Twenty if we're lucky.'

'Everything depends on how they crash. It might be nothing, it might be everything.'

Lehralla's corpse shuddered like a string puppet as the bridge gave its heaviest shake yet.

'Captain!'

She turned to Feyd, overseeing the weapons teams and their army of consoles. 'Officer Hallerthan?'

'Three strike cruisers are running past the *Lex*.'

It had to happen. There was always going to be planetfall. Lotara knew that. And at least they'd stopped... who knew how many other ships?

She was still annoyed.

'Warn the Legions,' she said. They weren't easy words to speak. Pulling teeth might' have been less effort. 'And start your intentions for phase two – I want your fighters shooting everything out of the sky. Drop pods, gunships – whatever they see, I want it dead. Any Mechanicum craft making it past the *Lex*?'

Tobin hissed a curse. 'Aye, ma'am.'

'Very well. Ensure the Legions are aware the enemy is landing Titans. Order the *Trisagion* to ensure no enemy vessels are allowed enough time for pinpoint orbital bombardment. And Kejic, make sure our warriors know to brace for the *Lex* going down offshore.'

As the vox-master relayed her warnings, Ivar Tobin looked at his captain across the central table.

'What do you expect them to do, captain? We'll be fortunate if they don't all drown.'

'A fact I'm well aware of, commander. Status on the ursus claws?'

Outside the ship, the impaled Ultramarines cruisers were dragged closer to the *Conqueror*'s eclipsing shadow. The much smaller cruisers rolled and strained against their chain leashes, engines firing into futility.

The *Conqueror* gave a judder as its lances streamed again, knifing through the captured cruisers, bisecting them first, then taking them to pieces with the second beam.

'Retract the claws. Have the slave teams begin rearming lost spear chutes, on the miraculous chance we get to fire again.'

Kejic was about to confirm her order when Tobin interrupted.

'The *Armsman* on an intercept run.' He pointed at the rune on the display, looking for the closest weapons officer through the smoke. 'Another battle-barge! Kill it before it comes abeam!'

Lotara knew, even as her first officer gave the order, that he was asking the impossible.

'No time,' she replied, feeling a surreal, sudden calm. She lifted the vox-thief built into her dark iron throne, sending her voice crackling all the way through the wounded ship. 'All hands, stand by to repel boarders. Captain Delvarus, respond at once.'

Her heart kept pace with the passing seconds, as no answer came.

'Delvarus,' she said again. 'Respond, damn you.' *If you made planetfall, I swear I will crash the* Conqueror's *wreckage down onto your miserable...*

'This is Delvarus of the Triarii.' The voice crackled back clear and strong, despite the interference with the shipwide vox. 'I hear you, captain.'

THE FIRST DROP POD hammered into the empty marketplace, scattering handcarts and wooden tables with the force of its arrival. Sealed doors unlocked with pressurised hisses, blasting open to unfold as ramps. The first Ultramarines to set foot on Nuceria poured forth, bolters raised, a sergeant leading the way with his gladius high. They moved in the perfection of well-trained unity, drilled to exact movements through thousands of hours' training and hundreds of battles.

The World Eaters were waiting for them. Squads broke cover, sprinting from alleyways and nearby brick buildings, chainblades revving. Those not lost to the Nails at once had the presence of mind to note that these Ultramarines weren't the pristine cobalt-blue warriors they'd faced on Armatura. The legionaries of the XIII wore cracked armour, still scarred and burnwashed from some horrendous battle weeks or months before.

Argel Tal saw it. Khârn did not. The World Eater broke cover with his men, laughing and howling, lifted by the adrenaline rush igniting his pleasure receptors.

Erebus, armoured for war and crouched in the alley with Argel Tal, offered his former protege a rueful smile.

'You fear for him. I don't judge you for that, Argel Tal. Your loyalty is a gift.'

Argel Tal hesitated, half-risen and ready to run. 'What?'

Erebus rose as well, gesturing with his crozius. 'I told you, did I not? Khârn dies on a world of grey skies, in the murky light of dawn. Where do we stand now?'

Argel Tal refused the temptation to look up. 'Lies. Guesses.'

'*Prophecy*,' Erebus said softly. 'He dies on this world, my son. He dies today, with a blade in his back.'

Argel Tal turned back to the fight, where Ultramarines drop pods were raining fiery steel from the sky, breeding groundquakes each time one hammered home. The daemon Raum stirred within his blood, awakening to the taste of anger.

Prey comes. Let us hunt and skin and kill and feed.

These are the survivors of Calth. The warriors Erebus failed to kill.

So let us finish the Deceiver's failed work.

I have to save my brother.

The Slayer?

Khârn, yes.

Hunt and skin and kill and feed and save the Slayer. It is all the same game on this battlefield.

The beast was right. Argel Tal started running, his eyes on Khârn in the midst of the melee. With each step his wings stretched and grew, mangling free of the ceramite; horns rose from his helmet to form a crown of curling ivory; and his faceplate smoothed into the daemonic deathmask. Like something from the pagan nightmyths of the First Kingdoms, Argel Tal charged into battle to fight at his brother's side.

Above them, the dawning sky grew suddenly dark. Something – something *vast* – made its slow way through the clouds. It set fire to the sky on its way down, pushing the rippling tide of clouds apart.

'No...' the Word Bearer said. 'Please, no.'

LORGAR STOOD ALONE atop a Land Raider, the wind picking at the parchments bound to his armour. From his vista, he watched the surrounding city dying purely because three Legions happened to use it as the place they met. Was that fate? The city had been destined to die this very day anyway, but to see an entire population slaughtered purely because they were in the way was...

A waste? He'd almost considered it a waste. But that wasn't true, for their screams all melded with the great song. It didn't matter from whence the blood flowed. Simply by attacking, Guilliman's sons were bringing the song to its crescendo. It was coming to its apex, carried by the arrhythmic crashing of bolters and the grunts of dying men too proud to scream in pain.

Lorgar had to find Angron. It would be time soon.

His brother's bitterness at Desh'elika Ridge had almost been enough. In the Praxury's throne room, it had come even closer. Lorgar didn't know how the final note would sound, but he sensed it coming, the way ozone in the crisp air heralds the coming storm.

The Ultramarines drop pods were just the first wave. The XIII Legion came down across the city, deploying in force – even mauled by the loss of Calth, they were still numerous enough to fill Nuceria's heavens.

Behind them came gunships, drop-ships, heavy landers and the great black tower-ships of the Martian Mechanicum. Contact was sporadic with the void war above, but it was clear the enemy armada had enough strength to rain their troops onto the surface. The Ultramarines knew Angron and Lorgar were here, and they'd come to end both primarchs' brutal reigns.

As was their way, the Ultramarines established footholds at defensible positions in the dying city, clearing room for their reinforcements to land. For every one they held, another was overrun by the World Eaters in a storm of roaring axes, or lost to the Word Bearers chanting, implacable advance. The XII Legion crashed against the XIII in rabid packs, showing why Imperial forces had feared to fight alongside them for decades. Uncontrolled, unbound, unrestrained, they butchered their way through Ultramarines strongpoints, enslaved to the joy of battle because of the pain engines in the meat of their minds.

The XVII Legion also met their enemy cousins, replacing ferocity with spite and hate. The Ultramarines returned it in kind, hungry for vengeance on those who'd defiled Calth and killed its star. Word Bearers units marched, droning black hymns and chanting sermons from the *Book of Lorgar*, bearing corpse-strewn icons of befouled metal and bleached bones above their regiments.

The Legio Audax walked through Meahor, jackal-keen on the prowl, ursus claws harpooning tanks and vulcan mega-bolters eviscerating infantry. The inefficiency of the way they made war had never appealed to Lorgar, but he respected his brother's admiration for the Legio's savagery. One of their Titans, hunchbacked and hunting, clanked along an adjacent street – from the sounds of human panic, it was wading through the native population. The taller forms of other Titans – Reavers and Warlords – strode at the city's edge; the Ultramarines were landing their own god-machines, but too few, far too few. Audax was adept in its hunts against larger prey. The Legio loved to play as wolf packs bringing down lone bears.

Lorgar raised his gaze as the rising sun went black in the sky. Across the city, Word Bearers were looking up in the very same way, with the very same feeling uncurling in their guts. He could sense their despair – a feeling too melancholic and pained to be either fear or anger, but somehow more desperate than both. His sons' emotions reached him in a bitter wash, making it even harder to look away.

Such a blow to morale, to see one's flagship die.

The vast silhouette of the *Fidelitas Lex* cut through the clouds, big enough to stain half the sky with its immense gothic darkness, fire-ghosts dancing in its miniscule window ports. For several terrible pregnant seconds, another city hung above Meahor, shuddering on its way east, loud enough to shroud the sounds of thousands and thousands dying in terror. Almost loud enough – Lorgar actually smiled at this – to drown out the warp's melody.

Almost.

The behemoth passed overhead, dead engines like open mouths, debris and crew raining from the falling ship as it rolled in a slow drift towards the open ocean.

Lorgar watched it trail across the grey skies, and whispered a final farewell. The *Lex* had served him well, but all things must come to an end. He hoped the Blessed Lady had made it to the escape pods. How bitter it would be to be reborn, only to die in the agony of fire mere weeks later.

Down it rolled, achingly slow for something of such weight and scale, shrinking towards the horizon but never disappearing. Lorgar knew that a death in gravity's grip would deny the vessel any last claim to grace, as the weight of its immense engines inevitably dragged the stern down first, colliding with the ocean's surface far from shore.

But far enough?

'This is the primarch,' he said quietly into the Legion's vox-net, cutting through his warriors' lamentations. 'Even in death, the *Lex* shows her rage. Brace for the coming tidal wave, and remember the Canticles of Mourning. No dirges for those lost in righteous battle. Everyone to higher ground, avoid all battle in the east where the wave will crash. Take the battle to the west.'

Lorgar dropped from the battle tank's roof, sheathing his bloodied crozius and ignoring the Ultramarines bodies he crushed underfoot.

Another drop pod slammed earthwards at the far end of the street. Without even looking, he directed a mixed group of Word Bearers and World Eaters to deal with it, and reached out with his senses, seeking Angron's presence.

But the song distracted him. It jarred, leeching at his concentration, pressing at his skin with the same static itch as standing too close to his brother Magnus.

Lorgar reached out again, seeking the source of the discordant disruption. The answer came at once, because the answer was behind him.

The answer stood at the far end of the street, clad in bloodstained blue, dropping the corpse of the last Word Bearer from the grip of its oversized power fists. It started running towards him, shouting his name, and Lorgar knew with cold certainty that the reason the song had fallen so catastrophically out of tune was because Fate itself was laughing at him.

Princeps Ultima Audun Lyrac still felt buffeted in the seat. It wasn't exactly enough to shake his bones from their sockets – nothing more than a slight tilt side to side with each step *Syrgalah* took – but it marked him from Keeda and Toth, who both suffered no such discomfort. He kept casting glances to the veteran cockpit crew, soon realising they instinctively leaned left and right in time to the Titan's tread. A miniscule motion, barely noticeable. That was how in tune they were with *Syrgalah*, and he felt a stab of admittedly childish jealousy. He doubted they even knew they were doing it.

He didn't remark on it, of course. They'd been merciless in their attitudes to his practical inexperience, and though they'd been suitably polite the last month in transit, this was his first walk. He was perspiring freely, the dampness shining on his temples. His back was similarly filmed by greasy perspiration as he tried to recline for the hundredth time in the shivering throne. Interface needles in his skull and spine gave irritated twinges as he shuffled.

All in all, he was glad he was behind his moderati in their control thrones. The last thing he needed was them seeing how awkward he felt. *Syrgalah* herself was a presence, a voice and a snarling smile in the back of his head. Her intelligence felt like the embers of a fire, burning slow but too hot to touch. He could sense she wanted to hunt, but was she never satisfied? He'd lost count of how many tanks they'd already destroyed.

The Titan kept pulling west, as well. It wanted to walk west, kept pulsing the word *west, west, west* through his mind, but that was just one of several Ultramarines landing sites. He detected nothing anomalous there. Did *Syrgalah* sense the coming tidal wave? Even if it struck, she could ride it out. It might reach her waist, at best. Mechanicum calculations had been vox-spurted in a torrent, and the tsunami to come was eminently survivable. The *Lex* had died well, and they'd all live because of it.

West, west, west.

'What is it with this city?' Keeda asked. She asked Toth, Audun noted, not bothering to turn and include him. 'I thought this world was supposed to be advanced. This looks like they've barely pulled themselves out of an iron age. Most of these buildings are stone. Brick and mortar.'

'Weapons.' Toth sounded distracted. 'Their weapons are advanced. Not by our standards, of course. Their nautical technology is supposed to be impressive, as well. A coastal people.'

'They didn't even have satellites.'

'They did.' Toth held a hand to his earpiece. 'Just not many.'

'Someone's been reading the mission briefings.'

'Shut up, Kee.' Toth spoke without turning around. 'Sire, *Syrgalah* is scry-locking onto a heat signature at the city's edge. She keeps pulling towards it.'

Audun had to swallow before speaking, and he still worried his voice sounded tremulous.

'I'm sensing it, too. The machine-spirit hungers for whatever prey she scents out there.'

There was a moment's silence in the cockpit. Toth said nothing. Keeda busied herself with butchering three Ultramarines Rhinos in a torrent of white-hot bolter shells.

Audun sucked his lower lip. Was he trying too hard to speak as they did, in the same familiar terms of Titan interface? Were they laughing at him?

'That's it,' Toth agreed. 'That's the signal I mean. *Syrgalah* keeps turning to face it.'

'Do we have any 'hounds at the western edge?'

'They've reported a coffin-ship. Big enough for three Warlords.' He lifted a shoulder in a lazy shrug. 'Nothing we can't handle, especially if they're down here without support. I'm getting reports that the *Conqueror*'s fighters are shooting down every infantry lander they can.'

Toth sounded at ease, but there it was again: the insistent pull of the Titan leaning to the west. Audun had to make a decision.

'What Legio walks against us? The markings resemble several–'

'Oberon,' Keeda replied. 'Orange and black striping, and the sigil of the cleaved crown. It's the Legio Oberon – whatever dregs survived the Calth muster.'

Oberon. *Oberon*. As he silently said the name, *Syrgalah* gave another tug, wanting to walk west.

Oberon. An Oberon coffin-ship, ready to unload at the city's edge. Prey so tempting that the Titan herself wanted to hunt it. *Syrgalah* sensed an enemy warrior-spirit even from this distance.

'We go west.' Audun rested his slippery hands on his own control console. 'Bring four packs with us.'

'Aye, sire,' replied Toth.

Audun hesitated, working a quick calculation. 'Amend my last order, Toth. Bring five packs with us.'

'That's more than a quarter of Audax.' Keeda finally turned around, looking both surprised and alarmed.

'You're right. Make it six. And tell them to converge with all possible speed. We're going in together.'

Thirty Warhounds. Would it be enough? Audun Lyrac was certain it would – he was equally certain many of them wouldn't survive, and prayed to the Omnissiah that he wasn't about to end his career on his very first walk.

'Toth, I want you to ensure we advance with Legion forces in support, ready to finish the fight once we start it. World Eaters, Word Bearers, I couldn't care less. But I want legionaries at our feet, ready to strike. Get them to run with us aboard speeders and Rhinos. We'll only have one shot at this, and it will have to be quick.'

Toth didn't turn back, but the smile in his voice was evident.

'You sound like you know what Oberon is bringing to join the fight, princeps.'

'I do. Unless I'm very much mistaken, we are about to meet the *Corinthian*.'

Toth and Keeda shared a grin at his proclamation. Audun knew Audax's history and pedigree better than any soul living, except for perhaps Vel-Kheredar – 'honours upon his name'. He knew the Legio was founded on the principles of the hunt, of cutting in quick, gutting your enemies, and pulling back before retaliation could fall. He knew Audax crews were raised and trained to work in five-Titan packs to bring down larger prey. It was more than the Legio's specialty – it was the reason they were halfway to being legendary.

But he had never, ever seen two people eager at the prospect of facing an Imperator.

THE DEMIGOD IN gold and blue had the advantage of two weapons, but Lorgar's crozius gave him a reach that his brother lacked. When they first met, there was no furious trading of frantic blows, nor were there any melodramatic speeches of vengeance avowed. The two primarchs came together once, power fist against war maul, and backed away from the resulting flare of repelling energy fields. Their warriors killed each other around them both, and neither primarch spared their sons a glance.

Lorgar flicked the clinging lightning from the head of his crozius, shaking his head in slow denial.

'You're ruining the song. You shouldn't be here.'

Roboute Guilliman, Lord of the XIII Legion, stared with eyes ripened by hatred.

'And yet, here I am.'

TWENTY-ONE

The Mark of Calth
A Redemption Unseen
Crescendo

THE BROTHERS DUELLED in the stone street, their boots kicking up clouds of alkaline dust. Gone was any notion of humanity or mercy from either warrior – here, at last, were two men that despised one another, fighting to end each other's lives.

In Guilliman's eyes, Lorgar saw a wealth of purest, depthless hatred. A hatred not formed from one action and one event, but a chemical cauldron of emotion strong enough to twist even the calmest, most composed demigod in the Imperium. Anger flared in those eyes, of course. More than anger, it was rage. Frustration tainted it further; the desperation of not understanding why this was happening, and the ferocity of one who still believes he might find a way to stop it. Hurt – somehow, seeing the hurt in Guilliman's eyes was worst of all – also poisoned the mix and made it rancid. This wasn't the pure rage of Corax on the killing fields – the fury of a brother betrayed. This fury was saturated into something much harsher and much more complex. It was the pain of a builder, an architect, a loyal son who had done all that was ever asked of him, and had seen his life's work die in foolish, spurious futility.

Lorgar knew that feeling, had known it since he knelt in the ashes of the Perfect City, the entire settlement destroyed by Guilliman's fleet on the Emperor's orders. For the first time in all the years of their wildly disparate lives, Lorgar Aurelian and Roboute Guilliman connected as equals.

To his amazement – the shock leaving him cold-blooded – Lorgar felt ashamed. In his brother's face he finally saw real hate, and in that moment he learned a lesson that had evaded him all these decades. Guilliman had never hated him before. The Ultramarine had never undermined his efforts; never hidden his sneers while presenting false indifference; never held a secret joy over humbling Lorgar's religious efforts in Monarchia and the great Crusade beyond.

Guilliman hadn't hated him. Not until now. *This* was hate. *This* was hatred in totality, fuelled by a fortune of pathos. This was a hatred deserved, and it was a hatred that would see Lorgar dead, with the song unfinished and the False Emperor still enthroned at the head of an empire he didn't – in his ignorance – deserve to lead.

The Bearer of the Word felt a sudden, burning need to explain everything, to justify himself, to tell how this was all necessary, all of it, to enlighten humanity. The rebellion. The war. The Heresy. The truth of reality was foul but it had to be told. Gods were real, and they needed man. The human race could rise in union and immortality as the favoured race of the Pantheon, or die as the eldar died centuries before for the sin of ignorance.

Between blocking the hammer-blows of his brother's swinging fists, Lorgar started cursing the warp's song for distracting him. It played through his skull and before his eyes, insistent and ceaseless. Everything felt significant. Nothing sounded right. Every bell-toll of his crozius crashing against Guilliman's fists thrummed wrong, confusing the crescendo as it was supposed to be rising.

Both primarchs fought without heeding their warriors, their godlike movements an inconceivable blur to the Space Marines fighting around them. Here was a record of the very mythical action that the Terran remembrancer order had been founded to document, as two of the Emperor's sons raised weapons in the embodiment of those most ancient legends: Akillus, Destroyer of the fortress-city Troi; or Gulyat, Giant of the Fillestyne Tribe. None had ever imagined the heroes of this new age would take the field against each other, nor could they have predicted the wellsprings of spite between them.

'Calth.' The word was a weapon. Guilliman breathed it, infesting it with the same hatred colouring his eyes. 'Calth. Jursa. Kallas. Corum's Landing. Ereth Five. Quilkhama. Tycor. Armatura. How many of my worlds, Lorgar? How many?'

Lorgar parried another swing, spinning his crozius in a heavy retort. Guilliman blocked it as easily as Lorgar had blocked the punch. Their blows rang out across the battle the way temple bells called the faithful to worship.

'*Calth,*' Guilliman said again. 'No words now, "brother"? No reply for what your Legion has done across the Five Hundred Worlds?'

Lorgar held his tongue. Everything had changed after Isstvan. In the hours after the massacre, as he'd sat alone and let his face bleed from Corax's murder-talons, he sensed the shifting of fate behind the veil. The futures rewiring themselves, new pathways of possibility opening up. In this last year, he finally felt himself taking the mantle of the man he'd always meant to be. He even, in his less humble moments, hungered to face Corax again. Things wouldn't play out so perfectly in the Raven Lord's favour next time – of that, Lorgar was sure.

'The Mark of Calth.' Guilliman made the title into an accusation. Reserved dignity even flavoured his wrath: he refused to fall into the emotional madness of a berserk killer, instead fighting with a fury that burned cold.

Guilliman slammed his hands together, catching the falling maul with a harsh whine of protesting energy fields. Holding it there, he looked past their joined weapons and into his brother's eyes.

'Look at me. Look at my face. Do you see the Mark of Calth?'

His patrician's features were handsome in a stately, stern way, even when twisted by anger, but he could never be considered as made in the Emperor's image to the degree that played over Lorgar's tattooed visage. The only difference between Guilliman now and the Guilliman that had stood in the dust of Monarchia was a fine threading of dark veins along the primarch's throat and cheeks – scarcely noticeable to any but those who knew him best.

'Void exposure.' The Ultramarine refused to release the weapon, despite lightning dancing down his heavy gauntlets. Lorgar gripped Illuminarum's haft as the energy rippled down its length, biting at his gloved hands and setting fire to the parchments bound to his shoulder guards. 'Void exposure when you killed one of my worlds, and the fleet above it.'

Lorgar didn't spit back with harsh words. He shook his head, pitting his strength against his brother's.

Guilliman's statesman smile played across his features. 'You've changed.'

Lorgar grunted at his brother's accusation.

'So everyone tells me.'

This time, it was Lorgar who disengaged. He pulled Illuminarum free, and suffered a fist to the sternum for taking the risk. The blow sucked all the breath from his body, cracked his breastplate, and left him with a bloody smile at the poetic justice. He'd cracked his brother's breastplate in the Perfect City and now the favour was returned. Fate really was laughing at him.

'First blood to me,' Guilliman said.

The pity in that voice was acid in Lorgar's ears. He tried to speak, tried to breathe, and could do neither. The song had never sounded more wrong.

Guilliman's hands scrabbled and skidded across his armour, seeking a stranglehold to end the fight quickly. Lorgar repulsed him with a projected burst of telekinesis, weak and wavering with the song still so de-tuned, but enough to send his brother staggering. The maul followed, its power field trailing lightning as Lorgar hammered it into the side of Guilliman's head with the force of a cannonball. There was a crack that wouldn't have shamed a peal of thunder.

'*There's* your Mark of Calth,' Lorgar replied, backing away to catch his breath. Air sawed in and out of his lungs. He could already taste blood – Guilliman's blow had broken something inside him. Several ribs at the very least, and likely something more vital. He dragged in a breath, and exhaled it as blood down the front of his armour.

Both primarchs faced each other beneath the grey sky, one bleeding internally, the other with half of his face lost to blood sheeting from a fractured skull.

'Enjoy that scar.' Lorgar fought for his smile. 'It will be with you until your dying day.' He threw his arms wide, taking in the dying city. 'Why chase me, Roboute? Why? Your fleet will fall against the *Trisagion* and you'll die down here.'

'There is a difference between confidence and arrogance, cur. Surely someone has told you that.'

The Word Bearer spat blood again. 'But why come? Why come at all?'

'Courage.' Guilliman stalked forwards, ignoring his wound, and he didn't need to struggle for a smile – it came as easily as breathing. 'Courage and honour, Lorgar. Two virtues you have never known.'

THEY MOVED WEST, fighting every inch of the way, engaged in running battles with the Ultramarines who also withdrew before the coming tidal wave.

A concept often stated in the war chronicles Argel Tal studied was the notion of a warrior 'fighting as though possessed'. Possessed, in most cases, by some unquantifiable warrior spirit, the desire to defend one's homeland, or just to echo the essence of legendary ancestors.

Argel Tal *was* possessed, in the truest sense of the word, and without the parasitic symbiosis he shared with Raum, he doubted he could have kept up with Khârn. From the moment Argel Tal left Erebus's side, he'd spent the battle in his daemonic form, too hard-pressed to exult in his strength and hating the credence he was giving to his former master's prophetic warning. He kept telling himself it was a lie even as he acted to prevent it becoming truth.

The Eighth Captain of the XII Legion leapt fully into the visceral, laughing joy of battle, chainswords howling and tearing, wearing the blood-spray of defeated foes as medals across his white armour. He was scarcely even Khârn any more. Argel Tal's daemon-granted sixth sense was a stunted and mulish thing, but he could rake a mind for its surface thoughts easily enough. With Khârn, he sensed nothing but a rage hot enough to scald the thoughts of any who pried into it. Familiarity taught him to recognise the Nails' bite, and to leave well alone.

Keeping Khârn alive so far had been a crusade to match the fevered hours of Isstvan V. When Argel Tal came too close, he risked being carved open by his brother's blades. Seven times already Khârn had attacked him in blind rage, and each time it took longer for the World Eater to realise what he was doing and turn back to the closest enemy.

When Argel Tal strayed too far, he'd lose sight of Khârn in the swarming chaos of the running street battles. Easy enough to claw his way up the side of a building to get a better view of the fighting, or take to the air on his fleshmetal wings, but each time marked him out as a target to the Ultramarines below.

He didn't know how many he'd killed. Not enough, evidently. They kept coming.

Enough, Raum had seethed in the thick of it. **The Slayer does not need us. Fight with the Vakrah Jal.**

I will not risk you being wrong. I've failed every brother I had. Khârn is the last.

You have me.

You are madness made manifest. Argel Tal ripped his spear from the chest of a dying Ultramarine, ramming it back down through the warrior's throat. *You are Hell in my bloodstream.*

Khârn was somewhere to the left, chopping his way forwards. He'd been laughing, of all things, even as he moved ahead of his swordbrothers, carving deep into a crowd of Calth-scarred Ultramarines.

Argel Tal had seen the danger that Khârn hadn't. The Word Bearer spread his wings and kicked off from the ground, landing on the warriors seeking to outflank his brother. The first Ultramarine died with Argel Tal's spear through his helmet, rammed clean out the back of his skull. The second and third fell to the Custodian blade – cleaving one in two, severing the other's arm and half his head in a badly-angled blow.

The searing burst of bolter shells savaged his wings and back. Argel Tal turned with a bellow far too low to be human, and reached for the legionary with his twisted, gnarled claw around the warrior's throat. The Ultramarine's valiant attempt to fire again ended when the commander of the Vakrah Jal's faceplate warped into something wolfishly metallic, and broke the Macraggian's head in its fanged maw.

Another blade had raked across his back. Another bolter shell cracked into his shin with the force of a thunderclap. Argel Tal ignored every wound he took, clawing his way closer to Khârn. Were the Ultramarines seeking Khârn's blood because they were slaves to some prophesied fate? Was it as prosaic a truth as that they simply recognised his officer's crest, or his heraldry, and wanted him dead? Or was Argel Tal imagining it all, fuelled by Erebus's whispered prediction? What hope was there of knowing in this chaos?

He couldn't remember how long ago that had been. Five minutes.

Fifteen. Fifty. The sun was up, a sliver over the horizon. Blood of the gods, this world turned slowly.

Steadily and undeniably, they were growing outnumbered. For all he knew, the *Trisagion* and *Conqueror* were as dead as the *Lex*, and the Ultramarines had an open run to the planet.

He saw the helms of World Eaters he'd known this last year, training and fighting at Khârn's side. He saw Lhorke, forever where the fighting was thickest, devastating all that stood in his path. When his spear slipped from his grip, lost in the tempest, he relied solely on his Custodian blade. When that was shattered against a Terminator's thunder hammer, he let his bestial claws lead the way. They sang like honed steel, dripping with alchemical fire from his leaking wrist-flamers. There was no pain. For that, he thanked Raum.

Across the vox, Audax was calling for aid. Several World Eaters officers resisted the Nails long enough to guide the flow towards breaking out to the west, but it could hardly be considered a unified front line.

He prayed for Cyrene, beseeching the laughing, murderous gods not to toy with her soul. Another failure – bringing her back only to lose her again.

Khârn truly was the last of his closest kindred he hadn't yet failed, and the World Eater mattered more than any other. Khârn was as Argel Tal once was: still untouched by the warp, not yet hollowed out by the cancerous kiss of a daemon stealing his consciousness and igniting his blood at will. Raum was a blessing and a curse, for despite the strength the daemon offered, the Word Bearer wouldn't wish this gift on anyone else.

He thought he saw Skane die. There was the briefest moment when his eyes flickered down the embattled line and his muscles bunched to run to the Destroyer sergeant's aid. Skane, marked out by his black armour, was on his knees in the dirt, raising an arm that ended at the elbow.

Argel Tal resisted the urge, deflecting another chainsword

coming for Khârn's shoulder guard. The centurion looked over his shoulder, and for a moment Argel Tal thought the Nails had relented enough to allow Khârn time to catch his bearings. The truth came a half-second later, when Khârn lashed out at him with a twinned blade. The Word Bearer parried, snarling as the block cost him another cut to his arm from an Ultramarine in the press of armoured bodies.

'It's me,' his wolfish faceplate snapped back at his maddened brother. *'Fight the enemy, you maniac.'*

Whether he understood or not, Khârn turned to the closest Ultra-marine and disembowelled the warrior with both blades.

Argel Tal fought on, defending the frenzied brother who scarcely even knew he was there. But then, it was never written that redemption came easy, nor that it would always be recognised.

He had time to wrap his claws around the throat of his next foe before the vox flared into shouting activity. Argel Tal looked to the east, where the *Lex*'s legacy was making itself known at the coast. He saw the tidal wave bearing down on the far side of the city, and thanked the gods that the battleship had come down in a drift. If it had struck like a spear and lanced into the crust, half the planet might have shaken itself apart. At least this way, an already dying city would just add another layer of ruin to its memory.

From the vox-reports, the grey seawater hit the coast with unimaginable force. It was high enough to pound against three- and four-storey buildings, breaking them apart in the deluge, adding huge stone blocks to the vehicle-cluttered flood lashing through the streets. Towers toppled into the drink, broken at their foundations. The entire coastal district was swept clean from the city in a single blow, the bodies of Nucerian natives and shattered habitation blocks carried westwards by the tide.

The land drank it up, fought it back, but still the water kept coming. By the time it reached the embattled Legions at their fallback positions, it was a waist-high encumbrance that fouled light tanks and devastated the effectiveness of their allied skitarii.

Argel Tal fought on, sloshing through the saltwater, always following Khârn.

Khârn didn't seem to notice it at all. He pushed ahead, wading through the deep water as if it wasn't there.

THE COFFIN-SHIP OF Legio Oberon was by far the largest lander that Guilliman's fleet had managed to get past the sundered blockade. Its retros threw up a great cloud of alkaline dust, mixing in with the gritty smoke cloud already sent up by the city battle.

The term 'coffin-ship' was that rarest of titles: Mechanicum slang that wasn't coded or binaric in nature. An ugly name for an ugly vessel – what touched down at Meahor's western edge was a fat-bellied whale of a ship, its bulbous hull streaked with scorch marks from atmospheric entry. Its deployment ramps had taken a full five minutes to lower to the ground, on hydraulics loud enough to carry over half of the city. Preparing any Titan to walk was a solemn and involved ritual requiring hundreds of souls, but an Emperor Titan was an enterprise far beyond what was required with the lesser-pattern god-machines.

Within the shell, the *Corinthian* stood bound and leashed in place by thousands of fibre-cables, magnetically sealed into position between three gantried pylon towers. The structures required to board the Mechanicum walker and hold it in place were little different from the support towers once used to launch rockets to Luna in the dull ages of Man, when such things were laughably considered an achievement.

Depowered as one, the binding cables came loose in a whipcracking cascade, freeing the Titan to walk at last. Each of the giant machine's legs was a bastion in its own right, crewed by skitarii detachments of weaponised cyborgs. Its splayed, clawed toes were wide stairs leading out from the defence-towers of its legs.

Corinthian's first step shook the ground. Its second annihilated the city wall and three tall buildings, grinding them into dust. A war-horn sounded, almost a sonic weapon in its own right, announcing its presence. The Imperator's right arm would level an entire city district if it was allowed to fire once. Its left arm would chew through half of any army it faced. Above all of this, above even its skull-headed cockpit – which in turn was large enough to be more of a command deck – the *Corinthian* carried a fortress on its shoulders, with anti-air cannons and laser batteries lining the battlements.

The last sound of its cacophonic preparation ritual was the dragon's roar of its heart-core powering up to battle readiness. Searing liquid fuel washed through its veins, pushed out from the heart, and the magnetic coils of its plasma arm started the lengthy process of charging. If it fired, they were dead. They were all dead.

'Beautiful,' Audun breathed, watching the majestic avatar of the Machine-God take its first steps of freedom. They were closing on the city's edge, and *Corinthian* was already visible, towering over the hab-blocks. The floodwater lapped at the giant's foot-claws, not troubling it at all.

Syrgalah ran in a lurching hunch, leading her packs through the deluged streets; ignoring the Ultramarines firing up at them from below, accidentally crushing dozens underfoot. World Eaters land speeders slashed alongside them, bulked out for troop transport. Several of the Warhounds were serving as steeds themselves, their armour plating crawling with whole squads of Destroyers and assault troops clinging on as the Titans ran. Each Titan's footsteps sent up great splashes of saltwater – the tidal wave had settled, but refused to recede. It was here to stay; the city Meahor would end its life a flooded wreck as well as a destroyed one.

'So very beautiful,' Audun sighed, unable to take his eyes from the steel giant. 'We have to take it alive.'

'You think the Twelfth will bear that in mind?'

'We can only pray they do, Moderati Bly.' A moment's concentration activated Audun's personal vox-link to every one of his Legio's Titans. 'This is the Princeps Ultima. In the Omnissiah's name, the *Corinthian* cannot be allowed to fire. You all know what to do. This is the breed of battle that Audax was born for. Ursus claws ready, brothers and sisters. Let the hunt begin.'

There was another moment of relative silence in the cockpit. He found himself swallowing.

'Nicely said, sire,' Toth ventured.

Keeda nodded. 'Just like the old man.'

Audun Lyrac, master of a hundred war machines and several thousand augmetic warriors, felt his cheeks heat up. He mumbled thanks his moderati pretended not to hear, to spare him further embarrassment.

OF ALL HIS TITLES, given in glory or earned in infamy, Angron most despised being named the Red Angel. The Imperium already had an Angel in Sanguinius, and Angron had no desire to ape the fey mutant that commanded the IX Legion. For all his flaws, he was his own man, and took pride in that above all else.

Lorgar knew Angron loathed it, yet it was among his brother's most fitting titles. When the World Eater burst forth from the Ultramarines ranks, his armour was a shattered wreck, and both of his chainswords spat gobbets of ceramite armour plating and scarlet gore. After hours in the crush of the front lines, Angron was plastered with the blood of the slain – more than bloodstained, he was bloodbathed.

On his chest hung a bandolier of skulls taken from the mass grave at Desh'elika. Blood painted them as surely as it marked Angron. Even through the Nails' pain, that pleased him. He wanted his brothers and sisters to taste blood once more. He'd carried them with him across Nuceria, letting their empty eyes witness the razing of high-rider cities.

The World Eater launched himself at Guilliman, with his ruined face contorted to be perfectly reminiscent of an angel lost in murderous hatred. Lorgar and Roboute both turned in the same moment – one of them to meet this new threat, the other to welcome it.

Lorgar's breath caught in his throat. Not because he was exhausted – though he was – and not because he was relieved to see Angron breaking the deadlock – though, again, he was. His breath caught as his heart started pounding in fierce thunder, falling in perfect pitch with the warp's song once more.

The two primarchs fell into a seamless, roaring duel exactly where Lorgar and Guilliman had abandoned theirs. This high on the overlooking hill, the water was a dim and distant concern. Lorgar heard its serpent-hissing flow, but spared it no mind. It didn't matter. All that mattered was the song.

Lorgar could barely breathe as the song realigned in his mind. *Here,* he thought. *Now. Angron. Guilliman.* Roboute wouldn't destroy the song. He was part of the crescendo.

Two primarchs faced one, and Guilliman was cunning enough to back away and take whatever ground he could.

'You two.' He looked at them with eyes heavy with judgement. 'My brothers, my brothers, what a sorry sight you've become. Traitors. Heretics. No better than the treasonous cultures we've quashed for the last two hundred years. Did you learn nothing? Either of you?'

'Always the teacher,' said Lorgar, and there was admiration in his smile. 'It grieves me this was necessary, Roboute.'

Guilliman ignored him, aiming a gauntlet at Angron. 'I've heard Lorgar's puling heresies already. What brought *you* so low, brother? Did the machine in your skull finally refashion your loyalty into madness?'

'*Hnnngh.* They let me dream. They give me peace. What would you know of struggle, Perfect Son? *Hnh?* When have you fought against the mutilation of your mind? When have you had to do anything more than tally compliances and polish your armour?'

'Childish,' Guilliman sighed, gesturing to the burning, dying city. 'Does it really come down to this? So pitiably childish.'

'Childish? The people of your world named you Great One. The people of mine called me Slave.' Angron stepped closer, chainswords revving harder. 'Which one of us landed on a paradise of civilisation to be raised by a foster father, Roboute? Which one was given armies to lead after training in the halls of the Macraggian high-riders? Which one of us inherited a strong, cultured kingdom?'

Angron sprayed bloody spit as he frothed the words. 'And which one of us had to rise up against a kingdom with nothing but a horde of starving slaves? *Which one of us was a child enslaved on a world of monsters, with his brain cut up by carving knives?*'

The two primarchs met again. Guilliman's powered gauntlets should have easily deflected Angron's chainswords, but the World Eater's strength drove his brother back step by step. Chain-teeth sprayed from the weapons as eagerly as the saliva from Angron's lipless slit of a mouth.

'Listen to your blue-clad wretches yelling of courage and honour, courage and honour, courage and honour. Do you even know the meaning of those words? Courage is fighting the kingdom that enslaves you, no matter that their armies overshadow yours by ten thousand to one. *You know nothing of courage.* Honour is resisting a tyrant when all others suckle and grow fat on the hypocrisy he feeds them. *You know nothing of honour.*'

Guilliman parried, forced back further by the storm of Angron's blows.

'You're still a slave, Angron. Enslaved by your past, blind to the future. Too hateful to learn. Too spiteful to prosper.'

The Ultramarine finally landed a glancing blow, his fist pounding across Angron's breastplate. The chain of Desh'elika skulls shattered, bone shards scattering across the dirt.

Guilliman stepped back again, his boot crushing a skull's remnants into powder.

Angron saw it, and threw himself at his brother, his howl of wrath defying mortal origins, impossibly ripe in its anguish. Though he couldn't know it, the sound of his cry blended perfectly with the great song.

Lorgar saw it, too. The moment Guilliman's boot broke the skull, he felt the warp boil behind the veil. The Bearer of the

Word started chanting in a language never before spoken by any living being, his words in faultless harmony with Angron's cry of torment.

TWENTY-TWO

He Dies on this World
Claws of the Ember Wolves
Blood Rain

The hours hadn't been kind to Argel Tal. He tasted blood, and for once it was his own. Lacerations striped his armour, gouged into the flesh beneath. One of his horns was broken halfway down, cleaved off by a power axe. Scorch marks dappled his armour from flamer wash, and the bone ridges pushing through his armour were bleeding, by means he didn't understand and was too weak to investigate with any real intent. He kept his wings folded close to his back, doing his best to ignore the rents and blade-cuts painting them in fresh scars.

He'd kept pace with Khârn, side by side with his sword-brother to the last. He alone among the white-armoured squads didn't laugh and howl in triumph with each life they took and each street they conquered, for he was the only one lacking crude implants rewiring his brain. Several of the World Eaters had attacked him in the disorientation of fighting while Nails-Lost. Each time he'd beaten them back, forcing them to recognise him, taking another wound or three in the process.

Now they ran with Audax, converging on the vast form of the *Corinthian* as it took its first two steps to get clear of the coffin-ship. He crouched atop a Rhino tank with one damaged tread, straining its engine to push through the floodwaters. He'd wrenched his claws into the armour plating to hold on; World Eaters filled the hull and hung from the outside, gunning their chainaxes in readiness. Khârn was with him, released from the Nails and looking no better than his brother. A sick desperation flavoured the whole fight – warriors on both sides were throwing everything they had into the conflict, as though it were the only war that ever mattered.

The World Eater and Word Bearer crouched together, both looking up at the Imperator rising above.

'I've lost contact with the *Conqueror*,' Khârn admitted.

Argel Tal tried to make the link himself. Bolter fire answered; bolters and shouts of anger and pain. Lotara had a fight on her hands.

'They were boarded,' said the Word Bearer.

Khârn nodded. 'I'm not worried. Delvarus stayed this time.'

There was an ugly pause between them, then Khârn turned. 'What are you doing?'

'Fighting,' Argel Tal replied.

'No. You're fighting with *us* over your own men. Erebus's prophecy is meaningless. I won't die here, brother. Go lead your Word Bearers.'

Argel Tal shook his head. 'Do you have any idea how close you've come to death this morning? How many times I've turned aside a spear or broken a blade?'

'Many, I'm sure,' said Khârn. 'But no more than usual.'

'You're wrong.' The daemonic deathmask, haunting in its perfect beauty, melted into a smile. Even that was damaged, showing cracks like tears down one cheek, splitting the fine lips. 'And you're a fool.' He gripped Khârn's forearm, forcing the World Eater to pay attention. 'You are one of the last remaining warriors of the Twelfth Legion that can be relied upon.'

Kargos was hanging onto the tank's side rails, and looked up at both officers as he heard Argel Tal's words.

'Not very complimentary,' he ventured.

Khârn chuckled, but Argel Tal ignored the Apothecary completely.

'The others are degenerating faster,' the Word Bearer insisted, 'or suffering much worse. The Legion needs you, Khârn. The rebellion needs you.'

'I'm flattered,' he said, though in truth he felt chilled by what sounded grievously close to a threat.

'Enough jests,' Argel Tal growled. 'Times are changing, brother. Great changes are coming to the Imperium and the Legions fighting to rule it. Warriors like you and I, at the right hands of the primarchs, will be the Lords of the New Empire. It doesn't matter if we have no ambition, or if we've no desire to serve in such roles. Circumstance will decide for us. The rebel Legions are growing stronger with enlightenment, but not all will survive the trials of ascension.'

Khârn wasn't sure what this meant. It bordered on typical Word Bearers zealotry, but that was something Argel Tal was rarely guilty of spreading.

'Are you sermonising?' he asked.

Argel Tal's deathmask gave him an irritated look. 'I'm warning you.' The Rhino jerked as it crashed through a jury-rigged barricade, but the Word Bearer paid no heed. 'We need the World Eaters in order to win this war. It's why Lorgar is sweating blood to save Angron's life.'

'And why you're fighting to save mine.'

'Don't make light of this.'

Insight struck with his brother's annoyed tone. 'You're doing this just to prove Erebus wrong,' Khârn stated.

'Not *just* to do that,' Argel Tal replied, and nodded to the *Corinthian* now towering above them. 'Be ready. This will not be easy.'

'Wrong.' Khârn was grinning now. 'Watch and learn how hounds bring down a bear.'

* * *

The Corinthian couldn't be allowed to fire. Nothing else mattered. It had taken one monumental step to come free of its bindings, and a second to reach the very edge of the city. Below, racing through the streets of the burning city, thirty Warhounds came on in a rush of crude mechanical precision. World Eaters and Word Bearers units raced with them, as did skitarii troop transports and skimmers in the Legio Audax's dark red and black.

Ultramarines met the oncoming horde. Oberon skitarii, recently spilled from landers, joined their Macraggian allies. Enemy Warhounds lurched at *Corinthian*'s heels, raising weapons of their own.

But Lotara's efforts left the forces making planetfall a fraction of what Guilliman's armada had hoped to land. Without knowing the fate of their flagship above – beyond sporadic vox-transmissions of screaming and bolter fire – the World Eaters crashed through the thin lines of defence at the Imperator's clawed feet. The defence towers that served as the Titan's legs spat turret fire down in a ceaseless barrage. Audax Titans went down, crushing their infantry escorts as they toppled; setting fire to them as their plasma cores went critical in crowded streets. Every Audax Warhound poured fire upwards, their vulcan bolters glowing red-hot, then white-hot, still spinning and still spitting. Spent shells rained onto the streets below with foundry crashes. Warriors on the roads beneath the Titans fought shin-deep in steaming, empty shell cases.

Such was the force of the firepower turned against *Corinthian* that its void shields caught fire. Flames washed over the tormented energy screens, each bolt shell's igniting impact flare blending with the others to bathe the entire kinetic barrier in orange fire. The force bubble shielding *Corinthian* – which wouldn't have been out of place on a small space frigate – burst, the boom heavy and resonant enough to shatter every remaining window in a five-kilometre radius and adding a rain of glass to the tempest of shell-fall.

In the midst of this, as Khârn and Argel Tal fought back to back with blade and claw, *Syrgalah* sounded her war-horn. Alone, it was a pale blare against the roar of *Corinthian*'s deafening voice.

But a second Titan took up the cry. And a third. Soon, all eighteen remaining Warhounds were howling up at their prey. Each of them was as tall as the Titan's knee, but together they roared loud enough to eclipse its cry of freedom.

The Imperator took another step into the city – a great stride of protesting metal and straining servos, bringing down a low-rise habitation block and flattening a World Eaters Bloodhammer tank beneath its tread. Under way now, *Corinthian* brought its hellstorm cannon to bear, panning across the cityscape in a slow arc. Every warrior's teeth itched in the sky-shaking whine of accruing power.

Syrgalah fired first, and *Audax* followed. Ursus claws loosed skywards, harpoons punching home in *Corinthian*'s weapon-arms, drilling and magna-locking in place. The Warhounds back-pedalled, withdrawing in straining union, their reinforced chains lashing taut at once.

'They'll bring it down,' Argel Tal called to the World Eaters around him. His deathmask was awash with skitarii blood. 'They'll bring it down on top of us.'

Khârn incinerated an Ultramarine with a kicking burst from his plasma pistol.

'Wrong again,' he called back.

Yet more harpoons fired, ramming home with leaden *clangs*, their chains whipping tight alongside those cables first to land. With the sound of almost divine protest, *Corinthian*'s massive arms – each the size of a hab-spire – began to lower. The great god-machine's war-horn sounded again, sounding more furious than triumphant this time. Argel Tal doubted such inflection of emotion was possible, yet the impression stuck all the same. He found himself laughing through the pain, the cursing, and the grind of armour against armour.

The immense guns came lower, lower, forced down to aim at the ground – at the flooded streets beneath the Titan's own feet. If it fired to destroy the closest Warhounds, it would annihilate its own infantry as well as its own legs. And still it struggled. Despite the incremental strength of so many smaller Titans leashing its arms in place, the *Corinthian* kept trying to turn and bring its fortress guns to bear. All recognised it for what it was: a move of desperate futility.

She was shackled. They'd bound an Emperor-class Titan.

The voice that came across the vox was wickedly assured, and every warrior heard the smile in the woman's words.

'This is Moderati Keeda Bly of the *Syrgalah* to all infantry forces. Everybody into the water, begin boarding-siege at once. Repeat: lay siege to the *Corinthian*. Try to remember that we want her alive.'

LHORKE FOUGHT ALONGSIDE Vorias's cabal of Librarians, killing the Ultramarines that battled like lions in the doomed hope of helping their primarch. His combi-bolters were almost dry; caution left him killing with his energised claws. That suited him fine, he'd fought the same way in life, and his ironform was built to wade through enemy units rather than hold back and fire from afar.

He'd tried several times to raise Lotara, or even that runt Kejic, but the *Conqueror* had taken to transmitting gunfire instead of language. Lhorke wished the captain well, and focused on what he could do something about.

He admired Lord Guilliman's plan. Although it suffered from the unexpected presence of the Word Bearers king-ship, and Lotara's tactical refusal to give ground unless she had no other choice, this was the Ultramarines' best chance to kill both rebel primarchs before they fled Ultramar's borders once and for all. Lhorke couldn't begin to guess what intelligence Lord Guilliman was using in his operations, but given the Ultramarines commander's reputation for tactical acuity across the length and breadth of the Imperium, he knew this was no thoughtless raid. At best, it was a strike that had gone at least partly awry due to the World Eaters' fierce resistance. Much likelier, it was the vanguard assault of a much larger fleet action about to break open across the Nucerian System.

Lhorke suspected the Lord of the Five Hundred Worlds had gathered what vessels he could spare after Kor Phaeron's ambush, drawn additional numbers from the first relief fleet bound for Calth after the massacre, and chased Lorgar directly through the XIII Legion's own astropathic choirs. He was certain of it because it was exactly what he would have done in Guilliman's place.

Perhaps other psykers could hear the Word Bearers' mythical 'song'. Perhaps they could sense the disruption of Lorgar's sixth sense. Lhorke knew nothing of it, and cared even less. But Guilliman was here, and forcing them to fight. Courage and honour.

Vorias, Esca and the few Librarians still living among the XII Legion made valuable battle-brothers. They'd come together as a coterie-squad, sharing power and silent words between their linked minds, forming among themselves the very brotherhood they were denied by the rest of the Legion. He considered them War Hounds rather than World Eaters – that piece of positive prejudice offered on account of them lacking the Butcher's Nails.

When the fighting allowed it, Lhorke would turn his attention to the primarchs, seeing their furious three-way battle playing out atop a mound of the dead. Even there, Guilliman had been holding his own against both of them, until Lorgar ceased his attack and started his achingly resonant chant. Angron and Roboute still fought, with the Lord of the Ultramarines giving ground each time Angron landed a blow. For all Lhorke's disgust, he had to grant a shade of respect to his gene-sire. Guilliman had no hope against Angron. The former Legion Master wasn't sure anyone would have had.

Despite his emotion-dulled existence in a walking coffin of cold amniotic fluid, the temptation to join that fight burned fierce in whatever withered husk remained of Lhorke's heart. Several times, he found himself on the edge of doing it. How easy it would be to tear himself from this battle, with all the memories it dredged up of the Night of the Wolf, and pit his ironform against the genetic divinity of the warring primarchs.

What stopped him wasn't the pull of good tactical sense, or fear of being destroyed. No, what stopped him was that of the two duelling primarchs, he wasn't sure which one he'd really aid once he took that fateful first step closer.

Angron plunged his chainsword up under Lord Guilliman's breastplate – a shallow stab, but a telling one. The Ultramarine crushed the impaling sword in one fist and staggered back, truly bleeding now.

Lorgar's alien chanting continued unabated. Despite the tepid dawn, the sky was slowly growing darker.

+Something's wrong,+ said Vorias's voice in the Dreadnought's mind. +Lorgar is dealing in power beyond mortal tolerance. Legion Master, if we call, will you stand with us?+

+Master? Do you feel that?+

+I'd feel that even were I back on Terra,+ Vorias answered over their telepathic bond. Psychic fire was streaming from Esca's axes, the energy of his soul manifest as flame. Each chop that crunched home into cobalt-blue armour set the ceramite aflame, incinerating its way through any open wounds to boil the blood in his enemies' veins.

+It's Lorgar.+ Esca thundered a boot into another Ultramarine's chest, hurling the legionary back into his brethren. +The power's coming from Lorgar.+

Vorias fought with staff and blade, spinning both in arcs of lightning-wrapped metal.

+No. The power is coming from the warp. Lorgar is bringing it through.+ A bolt shell took the Lectio Primus in the back of the leg, driving him down to one knee. Vorias's cry of pain was a silent sigh, pulsed across the link. Esca and another Codicier, Damarkien, fought their way to their wounded lord and mentor, fighting to protect him as he rose.

Esca risked a glance to the sky. The clouds themselves were lost in a slow swirl, darkening to form the un-colours seen only in the warp. With no place on this side of reality, they manifested as a hundred impossible shades of black, each one swarming with the thrashing suggestions of trapped, shrieking souls.

+What is he doing?+ Esca asked. +What's happening?+

+I cannot breach Lorgar's barrier of will,+ Vorias sent to them. +His strength is immense.+

Esca reached out with his senses. The moment he drew near the Bearer of the Word, a hurricane's force repelled him back.

+The Communion,+ he said.

+We'll die,+ Ralakas whipped the thought back. +There are hundreds of our Legion here, and not one of them will defend us while we leave our bodies prone.+

Esca wouldn't be swayed. +The Communion could break through,+ he insisted.

Vorias's face, aged but strong, was lined by effort. 'Perhaps,' he admitted aloud.

That was the moment the sky tore open. Stormclouds formed from the ghosts of a hundred murdered worlds began to rain blood on the dead city below.

Lorgar lifted his head to face the bleeding, weeping sky. The sanguine rain washed over him, warming his skin, filling his mouth. He didn't stop chanting, speaking the true names of countless Neverborn in a breathless stream, demanding that they devote their energies to his will.

So much power. Power defying description, defying comprehension. Reality mangling itself to his desire, the power wielded as easily as opening one's eyes, or lifting a hand. This was the game of the Four gods. They dealt with power on this scale each second of their existences, but they lacked the corporeal presence to carry out their designs in the material realm. Metaphysics was an unkind master, even to the Powers Behind All.

A beam of screaming sunlight lanced from the tortured heavens, casting its poisoned luminescence across Angron and Guilliman.

Shadows lengthened beneath every warrior, beneath every building and tank, twisting into the flickering images of writhing, reaching human silhouettes. The screaming came from everywhere: every shadow-soul across the city was wailing in the rain of blood. They danced like smoke and fire, crawling and cavorting in their hunger to reach the Eater of Worlds.

The crescendo of the warp's song, played through an instrument of perfect, depthless fury. *No purer emotion than rage.* Angron himself had said those words. Once the pain had passed, perhaps he'd even agree with them once again.

Angron himself still fought Guilliman, standing above the kneeling Ultramarine. Had he even noticed the storm of blood streaming from the sky in a red torrent? Sparks sprayed from Roboute's raised gauntlets as he struggled to ward off blow after blow. He was beaten. He was down. Wounds painted him, a palette of proud defeat. Even now, his warriors were fighting to retrieve him. With the scarring across his armour and the sense of pain bleeding from his mind, Lorgar reckoned his brother would be lucky to ever walk again.

Angron looked little better. Already an icon of mutilated majesty, huge rents and gashes marked his flesh from the knuckles of Guilliman's gauntlets.

Now. It has to be now.

Lorgar focused his concentration on the triumphant form of his mutilated brother, calling for the Neverborn to answer in kind. He locked Angron's muscles, setting fire to the synapses in his brain. He stole the chance at a killing blow, fuelling the World Eater's rage even higher. The screaming began: a melody of murdered worlds, finally singing in the material realm.

History repeated itself. Another primarch crawled away from Angron's wrath – another brother who'd come into an inheritance without being cursed, without being torn from his roots and left to mourn what might have been. There was no pleasure in beating them. The rage never faded. It only deepened, turned rancid by bitterness. The hoped-for serenity of battle fled from him, deserting him with the hollow promises of a false lover.

Hatred offered no victory. Nothing did.

Even those he defied and destroyed... even they pitied him.

Forgive me. I tried to tell you. All of us dance to the warp's tune. Even you, Angron.

This time, as Guilliman – rather than Russ – dragged himself clear, the World Eater staggered back himself, clawing at the ruin of his face and chest. He was tearing at his own armour and flesh, ripping it away in fistfuls, screaming a sound that no living thing should be able to make.

Flesh and bone, blood and soul, his body vibrated with the warp's tidal rhythm. It rang through every atom – every subatomic particle – of his divinely-wrought form. Billions and billions of screaming souls.

And with their cries came the pain.

The first spasms wracked their way through Angron's sinews, turning his blood to quicksilver, then to lava and at last to holy fire. His cries of thwarted rage were tainted by an agony beyond comprehension. His body started tearing itself apart, growing, rising. Perfecting, after a lifetime of broken torture.

Lorgar stared at his brother's agony with guilty joy.

You were always the conduit, No one else hates the way you do, with the same depthless strength. No one else feels such pain, violated by life's treacheries. It had to be you, in the deepest moment of rage and sorrow. There could be no other conduit.

Guilliman was escaping into his sons' defiant phalanxes, retreating in enviable unity as they waded down the flooded roads. Lorgar saw the expression of disgusted awe on his brother's face as the wounded Ultramarine stared at Angron atop the mound of dead sons from all three bloodlines. The XIII Legion still fired even in retreat – their shells crashed against Angron's bared muscle-meat, staining his skinless flesh black, bursting gouts of blood into the air.

A drumbeat. The gunfire was just a drumbeat, adding to the great song's crescendo. Bolts thudded into him, blasting viscera free in sloppy arcs. They did nothing at all. Angron had transcended corporeal pain, in the grip of heavenly torment.

Lightning struck him. Even Lorgar hadn't expected that.

Thunder pealed, forming another part of the great song, and more bolts of lightning snapped down from the bleeding sky, igniting the World Eaters primarch, the corpses at his boots and the very earth around him. The fire burned red, formed of flickering, writhing ghosts. The lives of those lost, in exchange for his.

The blood rain fell harder, hotter now – hot enough to fog and bleach the paint from the cracked ceramite of countless warring warriors. Lorgar never ceased his chanting, naming the Names, calling upon them to obey as they'd promised. He'd given them oceans of blood and worlds aflame. Now they owed him. He'd sold trillions of lives in exchange for one. Let it never be said that Lorgar Aurelian wasn't a loyal brother.

The inferno that had been Angron of the World Eaters raged unchecked. Doubt's first kiss touched Lorgar in that moment; he couldn't make out anything through the sanguine blaze. Was Angron even within that conflagration? Had the gods annihilated him, in reparation for some flaw in the great song? He reached out with his psychic sense, questing towards the bale-flame. All he could hear was the wailing of the unfairly slain – their rage, their agony. This was the song he'd composed from fire and genocide, playing now for his brother's salvation.

He felt another presence in that moment: something inhuman and vastly more powerful than any mere psychic soul or ghost of Ultramar. This was a voice he couldn't tune out, and for a moment of absolute ecstasy, he believed one of the Four had come to bless his efforts.

I am no god. The voice was softened by amazement, but nothing could conceal the power in its sepulchral tones. **I am the Communion.**

The name meant nothing to Lorgar. *Aid me!* he demanded of the presence.

Sadness preceded the reply. **I see now. I see everything. You are killing our father.**

I am saving him! Ascension! That is how worthy he is in the eyes of the Four!

Lorgar Aurelian, said the voice, **we will not allow this.**

And just as they'd let themselves drift from their bodies, they pulled Lorgar from his.

He was falling.

He was falling into the tides behind the veil, into the song itself. The melody was a much harsher, acidic tune on this side of reality. It washed over his flesh, burning and boiling, running into his mouth and filling his lungs. He rejected this invasion, channelling his concentration into a repelling force. It did nothing. If anything, it made the fire-water sear hotter against his body.

Lorgar raked his hands against the un-colours of the warp, forcing sense to the senselessness. Vision resolved into something a flesh and blood mind could process in a realm of the unreal.

He wasn't falling. He was being pulled down, deep under the blackest tides. He was drowning, with his crozius in his hands.

And then, light. Something that blazed with its own inner light dived after him, chasing him down.

A World Eater.

No. A War Hound. The armour was a serene pale blue marked with white. On its shoulders reared the red dog of war: that old, abandoned symbol, consigned to the vaults of memory.

The War Hound matched the primarch in size, even without its corona of cauterising light. The two figures met as they fell together, axe against maul, the sound of psychic iron on psychic iron sending ripples through the tides of unreality.

'You are an echo,' Lorgar told the ghostly warrior. 'A revenant. A nothing.'

The warrior turned in the swirling black. 'I am the Communion.'

Their weapons met again and again, sending the same ripples out into the Sea of Souls. Each time they crashed together, the warp itself screamed in answer: faces melted out of the fire-water to deliver their shrieks, then sank back into the primal matter from whence they came.

The War Hound's helmet was an older design, calling back to more innocent, easier days when the Imperium's ignorance allowed its people to feel safe. The sight of it made Lorgar laugh.

'You are a relic,' he told the warrior.

'Our Legion has suffered more than any other, Lorgar Aurelian.' The low voice was a knight's cold and righteous threat. 'Enough. Enough. You will not corrupt our lord.'

'I am saving him!' Lorgar spoke through clenched teeth. He was weakening in the tides, still falling, knowing his body lay motionless back on Nuceria. He could imagine its armour and skin being inked dark by blood from the storm.

This battle was a contest of wills, perceived as the mortal mind allowed it. Their weapons clashed again. The War Hound pushed against him, but the dissipation of strength was an affliction they both had to bear. Clawed hands reached out from the turbulent water. Lorgar repelled them with a snarl and psychic shove of concentration. The War Hound suffered their assault, his whole being focused solely on Lorgar. Trails of smoking white blood streamed away from the wounds clawed in the Communion's antique armour.

'You tried to drown me in the warp.' Lorgar was smiling now. 'But I am just as strong here. I am the archpriest of these powers, little ghost.'

The War Hound sagged, its shoulders straining against the locked weapons. Weaker, weaker. A growl left its throat.

Then it struck faster than even a primarch could follow. It came apart, discorporating into the black water. Lorgar's maul sliced the tides, all resistance gone. The War Hound reformed in Illuminarum's wake, its hands at the Word Bearer's throat.

The psychic manifestation of his crozius slipped from his hands, vanishing the moment it left his fingers. Lorgar wrapped his own hands around the War Hound's neck, struggling to breathe despite neither of them needing to do so in this place. Instincts died hard.

As they fell in that killing embrace, tumbling through the tides, Lorgar looked into the War Hound's eye lenses and saw just what he was fighting. It wasn't one spirit beneath that helm. It was a gestalt of souls.

Another smile creased his lips, more an amused grimace than a grin.

'Boldly done, though,' Lorgar hissed. 'Very clever.'

He released his grip, ramming his hand into the War Hound's breastplate, right through and into the psychic meat beneath. The warrior tensed, stunned, its grip slackening but not falling free.

Lorgar closed his hand into a fist. Something burst within the warrior's body.

'Who was that?' Lorgar shouted over the roaring sea. The War Hound's corona of light faded, no longer throwing back the gloom with such intensity. 'Was that you, Esca? Ralakas? No, I still sense you both in there...'

Lorgar punched his other fist home in the warrior's chest. The corona dimmed further as he burst another sphere of searing liquid in his grip.

'Lhorke...' The War Hound struggled feebly, almost shaken loose by the current. More hands were clawing for him now. 'Lhorke...'

Lorgar opened his eyes to the slick rainfall, hauling himself to his feet. The inferno still blazed – had any time passed at all? – and he still saw nothing of his brother within its blazing core. Weakness seemed to follow him back through from the warp, sinking into his flesh and binding there. He was wearier than he'd ever been in his life.

The Communion died in his mind. The primarch felt it quite literally crumble apart in some untouchable psychic diminishment, and in its place, the bolter fire began.

There was a grinding snarl of powerful iron joints, and the jagged stabs of shells bursting against his armour. Something eclipsed the shaft of spectral sunlight. Something taller than a primarch and twice as broad.

'My Legion has suffered enough,' boomed a mechanical vox-voice.

A huge claw crashed against Lorgar's breastplate, throwing him from his feet. 'Now we must endure corruption as well? Was madness not enough of a curse?'

TWENTY-THREE

Destiny's Hand
From the Fire
Blood for the Blood God

Khârn fought in the blood rain, butchering skitarii along the battlements. The fortress on *Corinthian*'s back was already drenched in the downpour, with blood sluicing from the gargoyles and rain gutters to fall to the city below. Looking over the edge revealed blood waterfalls streaming in cascades, as well as the packs of Audax Warhounds now moving free from their ambush. With the Imperator Titan's bridge crew dead – Kargos swore he'd be keeping the princeps's skull as a trophy for his tally – nothing remained bar purging the skitarii castle on the god-machine's shoulders. After the leg-towers and the savagely outnumbered defenders on the command deck, the fighting was thickest here in the fortress. The defenders mustered from their barracks for a last stand, despite the fact they'd already lost the battle for their Titan.

Skitarii cybernetics ran the gamut of contextual usefulness and lethality. The Legio Oberon's fleshsmiths and mechnicians had a penchant for augmenting their war-slaves' arms with heavy rotary cannons, which gave off the powdery reek of fyceline as they chattered with the bloom of muzzle flares.

Khârn cleaved his way through them, his retinal display lighting up with damage warnings and runes marking his left knee-joint as compromised to the point of instability. Smoke trailed up from the egregious gunfire pockmarks covering most of his armour. These rotary cannons lacked penetration, but they made up for it by sheer volume of fire.

The battlements were wide, more like gantries and iron bridges than anything like a fortress from a feudal world. The bloody downpour left the metal platforms slick and treacherous.

With the last of the skitarii slain, the World Eaters went through the cowering slaves and brain-dead servitors lingering in the habitation quarters. While the Legio's indentured servants begged and cried out as they were butchered, the cyborged slaves simply stared in slack-jawed apathy.

Lacking any more enemies, the World Eaters took to the battlements, raising their axes and yelling their triumph to the blood-red sky.

The colour of that sky was all Argel Tal could focus on. Red. Not grey. Lorgar was working his will across the city, and Erebus had been proven wrong.

Khârn dies at sunrise on a world of grey skies. In every future I've seen, he dies as dawn lightens the sky. And he dies with a blade in his back.

But Khârn lived. He'd not died during Nuceria's infinitely protracted dawn, and the skies were no longer grey. There'd been no blade in the back.

Argel Tal's armour had been left as beaten and worthless as that of the World Eaters he was with – but where theirs required maintenance and repair, his was already healing in slow, scabby regeneration. Raum had fallen quiet the very moment the last slave had wheezed his final breath. With no one to slay, the daemon coiled up in irritated respite.

He made his slow, bleeding way to the battlements, where Khârn was looking over the city. The blood-storm was filling the flooded streets, turning the invading waters red. The entire city seemed to be drowning in blood.

'Gunships inbound,' said the centurion. His helmet was a cracked ruin, and Khârn pulled it free, blinking in the blood rain. His pale face was a mess of bruises, in every colour it was possible for a bruise to be. 'What's happening?' he asked. 'What is this storm?'

'Lorgar,' Argel Tal replied. 'This is the Ruinstorm, finally released.'

'It's horrific. It isn't what I expected.'

The Word Bearer lifted his shoulder guard in a shrug. 'It's exactly what *I* expected.'

Khârn wiped his face and replaced his helm, masking his features in the grille-maw and slanted eye lenses that the Imperium was already coming to dread.

'Erebus was wrong,' the World Eater pointed out. 'And I saved you seven times on the way up this beautiful war machine.'

'Only seven? You're still alive because I saved you at least a dozen times.'

The brothers shared a smile neither of them could see and thudded their bracers together. Once-white gunships, now stained red by the storm, came in low over the fortress and burned their engines hot to hover above the battlements. Crew ropes dropped from open hatches, and the World Eaters abandoned their towering prize to redeploy elsewhere.

Argel Tal turned to move with Khârn, but Raum stirred in a weary slither.

The Deceiver comes.

He didn't deceive us, the Word Bearer replied. *He was merely wrong.*

I want to kill him. I want his blood.

He brought back Cyrene. He warned me about Khârn. I owe him.

All we owe him is pain. Cyrene is dead, her Second Breath taken for nothing. Now the Deceiver comes to speak more falsehood and ape emotions he cannot truly feel. Kill him, brother.

I cannot kill everyone in the galaxy purely for the sin of being despised. There would be no one left.

Khârn was tilting his head, staring through his helm's eye lenses. 'You're speaking to the daemon, aren't you?'

'Yes.'

'I can almost hear it. It makes my gums ache.' Khârn shook his head as if dislodging an unwanted thought. 'The Nails are biting. I can't stay.'

Argel Tal spread his raked and bleeding wings. They rose high from his shoulder blades, chiropteran and thick-veined, rattling in the rain.

'Go ahead,' he said. 'I'll rejoin my Legion and see you at the muster.'

'So be it. Good hunting, brother.'

The centurion jumped from the battlements, catching a hanging crew rope and hauling himself up into the last gunship. As its engines flared and carried it away, Argel Tal closed his wings back against his shoulders again. He heard the bootsteps he'd known were coming.

'You look weak, my son,' said Erebus from behind him. Argel Tal leaned on the battlements, the blood rain washing his armour.

'I feel weak. I spent several hours on the front lines, being stabbed and cut and shot, trying to defy your prophecy.'

Kill him, or yield control of our body, so I may kill him.

No, I have to hear this.

Erebus walked out from a tower onto the battlements to join his former pupil. His crozius was pristine, unmarked by gore, as was his armour. Argel Tal noted it with a disgusted shake of his head and looked back over the warring city, beginning to drown in blood.

'Khârn lives,' Erebus said. 'That's good, my boy. He has to live. The Powers have so much hope for the Eighth Captain, you know.'

Kill him, Argel Tal. Kill him now.

Be silent, Raum.

'What do you mean?' Argel Tal asked aloud. Erebus's scholarly face, so solemn and stern, softened for a moment as he met the other Word Bearer's gaze.

'Khârn has been chosen.'

'By the gods?'

'Of course,' Erebus replied. 'Who else?' He took a breath, pushing away from the battlements and pacing the wall. Argel Tal's wings twitched and itched as Erebus walked away. He watched the Legions fighting in the city below, driving back the Ultramarines, pushing them through the streets back to their landing sites.

'Argel Tal,' Erebus said quietly. The inflection was strange; despite saying the name, it didn't sound as if he was speaking to the other warrior.

'Wh–'

KILL HIM. HE FORCED US TO FIGHT FOR THE SLAYER'S LIFE SO WE WOULD BE WEAK N–

The ritual dagger slid into Argel Tal's spine, gentle as a lover's touch. Raum's furious cry trailed away, faded, and not even an echo remained.

For the first few seconds, there was nothing. When pain blossomed from the wound, it did so like something unfolding cold inside him, wrapping around his bones. He staggered, claws scraping over the metal battlements, all strength sucked from him. Claws? Hands. His hands scratched at the battlements. A legionary's hands. A legionary's weakness.

Raum. Raum!

There was no Raum. The daemon's absence was a shock many times more painful than the knife.

Argel Tal's helmet slipped clear, baring his too-human face to the downpour. He tasted the blood of countless innocents slaughtered in the Shadow Crusade. It stung his eyes, and he couldn't summon the strength to wipe his face clean.

The knife came free with a jerk and the crunch of violated meat. It took the pain with it, flooding his muscles with a hatefully pleasant numbness.

Erebus stood patiently, watching Argel Tal collapse. In his hands he held a knife the length of his forearm, bone-handled and engraved in Colchisian runic script.

'It was always you,' the Chaplain said. 'In every one of the Ten Thousand Paths, your erratic, emotional foolishness leads us to lose the war. You had one last chance to turn away from this fate, if you could just overcome the death of that worthless whore-priestess. But no. You begged me to bring her back, and in doing so proved you were as worthless as she was. You cannot be relied upon. You cannot be trusted. You cannot, for want of a better word, be *controlled*. And we need control if we are to win this war, my boy.'

Argel Tal coughed blood, reaching a trembling hand out to drag himself closer to his killer.

'Don't fight it.' Erebus shook his head. 'I confess I'm amazed you can move at all. No one else has been able to move after the killing stroke. What a saddening moment to discover you're stronger than I thought.'

Argel Tal crawled another metre closer. Erebus smiled, resting a boot on the Vakrah Jal's hand. Ceramite started to split and crack, but there was still no pain.

'Khârn has been chosen,' the Chaplain stated. 'And in every future I saw, the one thing that altered his fate… was you. *You*, my boy, would have saved him. I am Destiny's Hand, Argel Tal. Can you even conceive of my role and responsibility? You would break my path and change Khârn's fate. I cannot allow it. Let him carve his destiny free of your fraternity. Immortality awaits him this way.'

Argel Tal lifted his head, speaking through clenched teeth. 'I die,' he breathed, 'in the shadow of great wings. Not here. *Not here.*'

Erebus stepped aside. Behind him, the fortress tower was marked by the Imperial aquila, streaked with blood from the hellish storm. The two-headed eagle stared into the rain, its wings wide and proud.

'So you do,' Erebus agreed, and the Chaplain turned away. 'Goodbye, my son.'

* * *

The Contemptor was relentless, reaching for him, clawing at him, driving him back. Lorgar parried every blow with Illuminarum, each cathedral-bell clang meshing with the great song. His muscles ached from the Communion's cunning assault. Even his bones hurt from their insipid little ambush. Concentration was a poor jest.

Behind Lhorke came the coven of Librarians – their survivors at least – bolters high and force weapons raised. He could feel their weakness, their hesitation after being so cruelly torn apart as the Communion. But they still came. The fire and lightning bathing their blades flew forth in a hybrid of elemental rage. Lorgar willed a protective barrier into being, but his focus was shattered. The barrier shattered with it, leaving him open to the fire.

But it was weak. As weak as he felt, they were even weaker. The flames gusting towards him paled and dispersed, sucked into the red inferno where Angron had been. The lightning veered with it, whip-cracking away to join the conflagration. What blasted against Lorgar's armour was a thin remnant of their rage, scorching his flesh, igniting his cloak, and met with a telekinetic wave in reply. Lorgar poured his sapped strength into it, literally shouting them from their feet with a sonic bellow.

Iluminarum came up, warding back another of Lhorke's sweeping blows. Vorias's wretched coven refused to face their defeat, clambering back to their feet and opening fire again. Several of their bolts struck Lhorke himself – the Contemptor didn't even notice.

One of them took the Word Bearers primarch in the thigh, blasting his armour open to the bone. He staggered, lifting the crozius only to have it knocked from his hand by the Dreadnought's claws. He didn't see where it flew, only that it spun away over the surrounding bodies, hopelessly lost.

Lorgar raised his hand to hurl secret fire of his own, but his hand burst in a bolt shell detonation, exploding in fragments of meat and bone. Before the pain even took hold, he powered the other fist through Lhorke's carapace, digging for the corpse-pilot within.

The Dreadnought howled, falling back, leaving Lorgar with one remaining hand clutching a fistful of iron and wire.

He saw Esca, Vorias and the others. Haskal died the moment Lorgar turned his eyes on the warrior, and as the primarch clawed the Librarian's soul from his skin, he sensed that Haskal had been the one to land the bolt shell that blew off his hand.

The others kept coming. They threw fire, lightning, wind... Lorgar battered it all aside, staggered but still standing.

The Ruinstorm. Angron. The great song. The Communion. The Dreadnought and the coven. He was tired enough to lie down and die. No living being had channelled so much psychic power in the history of life itself.

Another Librarian died – this one speared through the throat by a fallen sword. Lorgar lifted it telekinetically with his violated arm and hurled it home, straight and true.

He staggered again, and this time he went to his knees. The whine of gunships fighting the storm's wind howled above him, but they were too late, too late. He couldn't beat back Lhorke and the coven while defending against their unleashed energies.

Salvation came from the unlikeliest place.

'*My brother!*'

The primarch butchered another of the advancing Librarians, repelling the warrior's fire and forcing it to wash back over the War Hound. Despite everything, Lorgar laughed as Angron roared and came to his aid.

Khârn hit the ground running. With nowhere to land in the inferno raging across the hilltop, their gunship hovered at the bottom, letting the World Eaters leap down into the blood-flooded street.

He had no idea what was happening up there. Even so, it pulled at him, making the Nails bite deep, turning the chemicals in his brain to acid. Every step closer made the pain fade a little more. Each metre brought him closer to serenity. He would have killed anyone, even his own primarch, to banish that pain and chase that peace.

Kargos was with him, keeping pace as they half-ran, half-hauled themselves up the desecrated hill. Legionaries from across the city were streaming closer, scrambling up the hill, chasing the same promise of peace. Their primarch was calling, though they knew not how. All that mattered was flocking to his side, among the red fire and the blood rain.

They saw Lorgar, driven back and bleeding. They saw the last living members of their forgotten Librarius standing with Lhorke, ringing the wounded primarch. They saw the fire alive with the shadows of the dead.

And they saw Angron.

Every World Eater stood frozen before the fire. The reflection of a god's son played across their eye lenses as it rose from the flames of a Hell the Emperor had sworn didn't exist.

Even Lhorke turned to face his gene-sire.

'*My brother!*' Angron roared again. '*Hnngh.* Traitors, traitors, seeking my brother's blood.'

'Sire,' the war machine rumbled, but all sense of what to say died when he saw what Angron was becoming. The Change wasn't finished – red flame still blazed in the primarch's flesh, and where the flames receded, they roared higher elsewhere on his abused form. Blood shook from him with every movement. Beneath the fire, Lhorke saw a sliver of what was coming to be.

The primarch's scarred flesh was the inhuman red of bare meat, armoured in bone fused with blackened bronze. He saw impressions only: a colossal molten thing, an avatar of volcanic anger, its flesh steaming in the foul rain and its clawed boots boiling the puddles of blood littering the earth. He was still growing, still rising, his entire form rippling to the warp's music. The great song was more than a harmony to rewrite the void; it was the tune destined to rewrite a primarch's genetic coding while immolating his very soul. Through the fire, something *purer* would emerge into the material realm. Something immortal, composed wholly of rage, not subject to pain or the mortal prickings given by the Butcher's

Nails. Lorgar had composed the warp to perfection.

Lhorke never saw the metamorphosis end.

The claw that crashed against his ironform tore the Contemptor-shell apart, sending wreckage tumbling across the ground. The biological revenant that was Lhorke himself – a crippled and withered corpse – broke against the rough earth, still trailing its life support cables and milky with amniotic fluid. It gave one breath, a sudden, sharp inhalation, and moved no more. Blood filled its open mouth and washed over its wide eyes.

The primarch-beast turned to the Librarians. The creatures that had pained him for decades. The warriors that had made the Nails sing and his brain bleed just for the sin of standing near them. Now they moved against his brother, hurling their foulness at Lorgar, who crouched one-handed and wounded, down on his knees.

'Traitors,' the thing breathed. Its maw cracked and stretched, iron teeth lengthening into rusted sword-fangs. The Butcher's Nails were a thrashing, dreadlocked crest, hissing and buzzing in the rain.

Each of them tasted a different doom. Vorias, eldest of all, was struck blind by his eyes bursting in their sockets. He died in a strange peace, not hearing his gene-sire at all, hearing nothing in fact except for Lorgar's exultant chanting. He thought the Word Bearers lord was laughing – and indeed, he was right.

Several of the others died from embolisms, brain haemorrhages, and in one case, Ralakas's skull detonated as though struck by a bolt shell, showering bone fragments and bloody-grey ooze across his last living brothers.

Those who sought to escape met the implacable forms of their armoured kindred standing vigil on the other side of the flames. Kheyan crashed headlong into a centurion, lifting his bleeding gaze to the officer's visage.

'Khârn…'

Hands gripped the fleeing Librarian – his throat, his wrists, his shoulder guards. Kargos and the others hurled him back through the shrieking fire. He crashed onto the corpse-mound, to lie before his primarch's mercy. Angron's stormcloud-shadow fell over him, but the last thing Kheyan saw was Khârn watching in silence through the flames.

Esca was the last to die. He didn't know which of his brothers threw him back across the fire, but he picked himself up and held his broken axe at the ready. Angron towered above him – Angron, who was eating Kheyan's corpse. An armoured torso and one arm rattled down the primarch's monstrous gullet. He even heard the muted hiss of digestive acid doing its corrosive work, deep inside the great beast's body.

It was the roar that hurled him from his feet. Angron's eyes ignited in the sockets of that malforming skull, triggering a roar that shook the sky. It sent Esca crashing back to the ground, weaponless and aching from too many torn muscles for his retinal display to track in one scan.

Esca rose again, scrambling to his knees, looking up at the face of Lorgar Aurelian, Lord of the XVII Legion. Viscous lifeblood bathed the Word Bearer's serene features.

'You should thank me,' Lorgar said. 'Your whole Legion should thank me.'

Esca snarled up at the primarch, all words failing him. A shadow draped over him from behind: Angron – or whatever Angron was becoming – was drawing close.

'Blood,' said Lorgar, lifting his crozius, 'for the Blood God.'

'They're running.'

Feyd Hallerthan had been accused of arrogance in the past, and was accordingly proud of his appearance. As he looked into a sliver of glass in his hands, he had to confess he'd never be handsome again. Not without extensive facial reconstruction.

He dropped the knife of glass, letting it smash on the deck, and stared into the hololith with his remaining eye.

'They're running,' he said again, then realised there were no higher-ranking officers to speak to. The only souls still alive on the *Conqueror*'s ravaged bridge were thralls, menials and servitors. Lehralla was a corpse hanging by the Medusa-cables of her augmetic links. Tobin was in similar health, impaled by a fallen ceiling girder-beam pinning him to the deck, right through his chest.

Dead Ultramarines lined the deck. Dead World Eaters populated the floor alongside them, along with a number of crew Feyd almost feared to count.

A few World Eaters walked here and there, their chainaxes idling. They seemed disorientated, but with their helmets on, Feyd had no way to be sure.

He recognised one of them, crested as a captain and anointed with enemy gore. 'Delvarus,' he called. 'Where's the captain's body?'

Delvarus crouched, lifting wreckage aside and offering his hand down. Feyd saw Lotara take the gauntlet, and she was heaved to her feet by the massive legionary. Soot marked her face, and blood had crusted darkly down one side of her face.

'Thank you, Del,' she said. 'I take back everything I've ever said about you.'

The Triarii smiled. She never saw it beneath his helmet. Hesitantly, the captain reached a hand to the split in her skull, where her hair was matted and grimy around the gash. 'I have a headache,' she said. 'Feyd, you look terrible.'

Feyd's smile was a guilty and childish thing. 'They're running, captain.'

She limped her way to the hololithic table. 'The Ultramarines never run. They engage in fighting withdrawals and tactical retreats. And in this case, they're right to do both.' She gestured at the *Trisagion*'s rune, still pulsing with healthy vigour. 'It galls me to thank the Word Bearers for anything, but that ship is a killer.'

She turned her gaze back to the retreating runes of the Ultramarines survivors. 'They almost had us, though. Engines?'

'Dead, ma'am.'

'Weapons?'

'Dead.'

'Navigation?'

'Dead.'

Lotara snorted. 'Lucky for us they're running, then.'

'Agreed, ma'am.'

She turned to the oculus, which was marred by several vicious, smoking bolt shell holes, like craters in the reinforced glass. Nuceria's image wavered, flawed by visual corruption, but the red tempest above Meahor was visible from orbit.

'What am I looking at?' she asked anyone near enough to hear.

'No idea, ma'am,' Feyd replied.

Lotara kept staring, and finally cleared her throat. She spoke in a calm, clear voice, as if nothing untoward had happened recently, or indeed ever before.

'Someone get me a link to the surface,' she said. 'I need to speak with Angron.'

EPILOGUE

I

'What have you done?'

It didn't matter how softly Khârn asked the question, anger was still the emotion that drove it. A cold anger though, rather than the heat of rage. This wasn't born of the Nails. It was much more personal.

Lorgar's newly-claimed reflection chamber aboard the *Trisagion* was a humble space of bare iron and naked steel, untouched as yet by the personal touches of a soul at home. Khârn knew that in time it would become another library-temple, housing whatever scrolls and tomes the primarch chose to devote himself to. For now, its emptiness made it much less inviting, yet strangely more tolerable. The chamber had no windows, no portals looking out into the warp. Khârn couldn't tell if that change was significant or not. The primarch was mercurial; guessing his moods and methods was a trial at the best of times.

Lorgar was robed as he usually was when away from battle. He worked at a writing desk, the scratching of his quill a continuous whisper.

'I did what needed to be done, Khârn.'

The former equerry stepped forwards. 'There's a… a daemon shackled in the *Conqueror*'s hold.'

Lorgar still didn't look up. 'It is Angron. Nothing more, nothing less.'

'*Nothing more?*' Disbelief made him bold. 'It butchered hundreds of my men before you bound it. It does *nothing more* than roar down there in the dark, breeding shipquakes. Lotara wants to jettison it into space – several decks around it have turned to human flesh, Lord Aurelian. The walls have started shrieking at us with moving mouths. Our water supplies are turning to blood as soon as they're reprocessed. Whatever is down there is not "Angron and *nothing more*". What did you do?'

'Go down there.' Lorgar still wrote; *scratch-scratch* went the quill. 'See for yourself.'

'What did you do? Answer me.'

Lorgar raised his head with threatening slowness. His eyes blazed with warp light. Looking into them was like staring into the Sea of Souls itself.

'I saved him, Khârn. It was the only way. I alone sought to save him from the Nails that were killing him by degrees. I alone looked into the ways to free him from an existence of unrivalled agony. And I alone acted to save him.'

'But…'

Lorgar's glare silenced him. 'Go down there and see for yourself. Angron is the future, *our* future. Humanity's future. Immortal strength, and an eternity to learn the universe's secret metaphysics. He didn't die, Khârn. He ascended.'

'But he's trapped.'

'For all our safety,' Lorgar agreed. 'Ultramar is blighted by the Ruinstorm, cut off from the Imperium. But I know the way back through the fire. We will gather our fleets spread across the Five Hundred Worlds, then we shall rejoin Horus. Has Vel-Kheredar finished forging the blade?'

'He has.'

'Is it all I asked?' Lorgar asked calmly.

'Its blade is black. It burns with god-runes.'

'Bring it to me, Khârn. I will deliver it to Angron, just as I will release him when the time is right.'

'When will that be?'

'Can't you guess? When we next reach a world that must bleed like never before.' He smiled, though it was a sad thing to see. 'Is that so different from how Angron has lived his life these last decades? Summoned only for slaughter?'

Khârn had no answer to that. No sense arguing with the truth.

'Is he in pain?'

'Yes.' The primarch went back to his writing. 'But nothing compared to what has wracked him since his gestation pod first crashed on Nuceria, and the Desh'eans hammered the Nails into his skull.'

Another silence stretched out between them. Khârn broke it by bowing; his armour joints snarled at the movement.

'I'll see with my own eyes, then.' He turned to take his leave, but stopped when Lorgar said his name once more.

'*Khârn.*'

The captain glanced back, expecting Lorgar to be occupied with his parchment. Instead, the primarch's gaze was raw and pained; a dignified, restrained fury.

'Lord?'

'Would you like to know,' Lorgar asked softly, 'who killed Argel Tal?'

II

Erebus bowed to the crowd, facing the applause of fists thudding against bare chests. The deactivated crozius in his hand was flecked with blood – first blood – and ever the dignified victor, Erebus offered a hand to help Skane up from the deck. The sergeant took the proferred hand, gripping it with his new augmetic limb.

'A fine bout,' the First Chaplain said.

The World Eater still hadn't had his throat mechanics repaired, leaving him speechless, but he grinned and nodded in place of words, and moved back into the crowd.

Delvarus stepped forwards. So did Khârn. The crowd, on the edge of cheering at the first warrior, fell silent at the sight of the second. The captain said two words to the Triarii centurion.

'Let me.'

Delvarus saluted and backed away.

'First blood?' Erebus asked.

The axe in Khârn's hand was Gorechild, toothed by mica-dragons and once thrown from the hands of a primarch. He'd chained it to his bare wrist in imitation of the Nucerian gladiators, whose bones he'd seen and honoured mere days before at Desh'elika Ridge.

The captain was stripped to the waist, as were all the warriors present.

'*Sanguis extremis*,' Khârn said. Some of the crowd breathed in, showing their shock as the humans they once were. Others laughed or cheered. More fists beat against chests.

Erebus regarded Khârn with cold, composed eyes. Several seconds beat in silence, before the Word Bearer's lips curled in a soft, indulgent smile.

'Bold, Khârn. Are you s–'

Gorechild revved for the first time since its rebirth, eating air with the throaty snarl of an apex predator. That interruption was the only answer Khârn would give, and Erebus raised his crozius in reply.

'Come then.'

Three blows. The first: Khârn smashed the maul aside with the flat of his new axe. The second: he cannoned a headbutt into Erebus's nose, breaking cartilage with a wet crunch. The third: Gorechild tasted first blood, ripping across the Chaplain's chest, carving a canyon of flesh over the dense subdermal armour of the warrior's black carapace torso implant.

All of this happened in the time it took Erebus to blink. No one could move as fast as Khârn moved. No one human, and nothing mortal. The Chaplain threw himself backwards, crozius up high to guard.

Khârn walked forwards, gunning Gorechild's trigger. The crowd was silent now. This was a Khârn they'd never seen – not even on the field of battle.

Another three blows, delivered with the same blinding speed. Erebus's maul clang-skidded across the deck; he took a fist to the throat and a boot to the stomach, knocking him back with enough force to send him crashing onto the bloodstained iron grillework.

He looked up at Khârn from the ground and saw his death in the World Eater's eyes. He'd never seen this before, not in any of the paths of possibility. It couldn't be happening. It couldn't end like this. He was Destiny's Hand.

Khârn looked down at him, clearly allowing time for the Chaplain to recover his crozius.

'Get up.'

Erebus rose, his mace in his hands again. He attacked this time, showing the speed and skill that had allowed him to hold his own against Lucius of the Emperor's Children, and Loken of the old Luna Wolves. His crozius trailed killing lightning, buzzing furiously as it thrummed through empty air again and again. Khârn weaved aside from every blow, quicker than a blink, surely quicker than muscles could ever allow.

Their weapons crashed together. Khârn had parried the last blow. Erebus expected accusation in the World Eater's eyes, or surely anger. He saw neither. Worse, he saw a bored indulgence. The captain even sighed.

Three more blows. Erebus was on the deck before he knew how. Pain flared across his chest, hot and urgent, matching the thick throb of his smashed face. He reached to touch the wound with a hand that was no longer there.

His hand. His hand was on the deck, several metres away. Blood leaked from the chewed veins nestled in the meat of his severed limb. Turning unbelieving eyes downwards, he saw where his arm now ended at the wrist.

'Going to need an augmetic for that,' Kargos said from the crowd. Several warriors laughed, but few with any real relish. They were too fascinated by what was unfolding.

Erebus looked up at Khârn again. He was just waiting.

'Get up.'

The Chaplain rose. Khârn didn't wait this time – the blows were bloody blurs of whining motors and tearing chain-teeth. Pain bloomed across Erebus's body, and he was face-down on the deck again before he'd managed to fully rise from the last time. Even without his armour's pain nullifiers and chemical stimulants, Erebus suppressed the pain by whisper-chanting a sacred mandala. Khârn interrupted it.

'Get up.'

Erebus actually tried, but he froze when he felt Gorechild's teeth against his spine. The idling chainblade was purring and breathing out its promethium fuel-stink, the axe's stilled teeth kissing Erebus's vertebrae.

Never, not even in fragmentary glimpses, had he foreseen this duel.

It couldn't end like this. *He couldn't die here.* There was so much to do. Signus Prime. Terra herself. In all the Ten Thousand Futures, Erebus had seen himself fighting the Long War to the very last.

The very same second Erebus reached for the ritual knife at his belt with his remaining hand, Khârn pulled the chainaxe's trigger.

There should have been a scream. Everyone expected it. Every warrior present waited to hear the First Chaplain of the Word Bearers shriek as Gorechild bit into his flesh. But there was nothing beyond the rotating whine of an axe blade chewing empty air.

No one seemed surprised at the display of Word Bearers sorcery.

Even fewer were surprised at the cowardice. Khârn turned from the blood marking the deck, leaving the circle without a word.

III

An hour later, armed and armoured, Khârn stood ready once more.

'You don't have to do this.'

Khârn looked at Kargos by the console. 'Yes, I do. I've done it before. Open up.'

The Apothecary worked the key controls and the doors swung silently outwards. Beyond them, sticky with drying blood, a set of bone steps went down into the shadows. Another roar, wordless and deep-throated, came echoing up from the gloom.

Khârn walked forwards and let the darkness fold over him as Kargos swung the doors closed behind him. The first thing he heard was the dead whispering in the dark. The second thing was the beast's breathing. Even his genhanced eyes couldn't pierce the absolute lack of light. He walked slowly, drawing no weapon despite the temptation, listening to a daemon breathing in the black.

'*Khârn,*' said something unseen, from everywhere and nowhere. Whatever it was, it smelled of fresh graves and funeral pyres, and its teeth were wet.

'Lord?'

Slow thunder answered. No, a laugh. A chuckle. '*I am no one's lord. I never was. Even less so now.*'

Khârn swallowed, still edging through the dark. He heard the thing that had once been his gene-sire licking its maw.

'*I want something from you, Khârn.*'

'Name it.'

'Hnnh. *Take your axe. Take your brothers. Kill three hundred souls on the thrall decks.*'

Khârn stared in the direction where he was sure the monster was at rest. 'Why, sire? To what purpose?'

'Three hundred of them. Take their skulls.'

Khârn heard the thing smile, heard the wet peeling of its fanged maw curling into a grin. Something huge, winged, and wreathed in the smoke of dead souls tried to move closer to him, and strained against the rune-etched chains that bound it. He saw its eyes burning in the dark, orbs of ember-fire, the colour of boiling blood.

'Take their skulls, Khârn. Build me a throne.'

ACKNOWLEDGEMENTS

THANKS AS EVER to Dan, Jim, Gav, Nick, Graham and especially Laurie Goulding for all the backup: research, ideas, encouragement, various whip cracks and the unlicensed street barbering.

Thanks also to Alan Merrett, Alan Bligh, and John French for use of their third eyes, seeing into the warp of the IP, and to Matt Farrer for paving the way with the inspiring 'After Desh'ea' in *Tales of Heresy*. Extra special thanks to my draft readers: Rachel, Nikki and Marijan, who pulled out all the stops this time.

Gemma Noon's loan of a laptop in Canada was the difference between this book hitting its deadline and never seeing the light of day, so 'thanks' seems a bit weak, but it's sincere all the same.

And last but far from least: thanks to Jon O'Sullivan and GW Dublin, for helping me get my killer gaming table together (read: for doing all the work); and to Cathy and GW Belfast for the coolest offer of all time (still gutted I couldn't take you up on it, but I was really honoured you offered).

A portion of this book's proceeds will go to Cancer Research UK, and the SOS Children's Villages charity, to help orphans in Bangladesh.

ABOUT THE AUTHOR

Aaron Dembski-Bowden has written many novels for Black Library, including the Night Lords series, the Space Marine Battles book *Helsreach*, *The Emperor's Gift* and the *New York Times* bestselling *The First Heretic* for the Horus Heresy. He lives and works in Northern Ireland with his wife Katie, hiding from the world in the middle of nowhere.

THE HORUS HERESY

MARK OF CALTH

Edited by Laurie Goulding

The next instalment in the *New York Times* bestselling series

An extract from Mark of Calth
Edited by Laurie Goulding

From 'The Traveller' by David Annandale

On sale April 2013

Jassiq Blanchot was on digging duty. He was nearing the end of his shift. The ache in his limbs from hauling collapsed rock was so constant, so enveloping, that his arms and legs didn't seem to belong to him anymore. For six hours, his work detail had chipped at the cave-in, dragging away hundreds of kilos of stone. The large chamber to the rear was filling up with debris, but the collapse was as intractable as ever. He could easily believe that the barrier went on forever. Still, he kept working. He loaded up a makeshift sled – just a plasteel door and rope – and began dragging it away from the dig. The rope worked deeper grooves into his neck and shoulders.

He leaned forward into his burden. As he was reaching the storage chamber, he crossed paths with Narya Mellisen. The lieutenant from the Numinus 61st Infantry was taking her empty sled back for another load.

'You lead a charmed life,' she said.

He stopped, brought up short. He'd just been thinking dark thoughts about eternity.

He was trapped in an underground arcology along with hundreds of other refugees. Over half the system had collapsed, hammered by the earth-shaking blows of the war on the surface, except 'war' was really too weak a word. Could a simple war turn the universe upside down, and shatter his every taken-for-granted conception of how reality worked? He didn't think so. That was what cataclysms did.

There had been no communication from the outside world since the warning voxed by Captain Ventanus of the Ultramarines. The surface of Calth was now being scoured by its agonised sun. Survival meant staying underground indefinitely – underground was where the war now raged – but it also meant escaping this particular arcology by somehow digging through who-knew-how-many thousands of metres of blocked tunnel.

A charmed life? Was Mellisen trying to be funny?

'I'm not sure what you mean,' Blanchot said. He ran a ragged sleeve over his brow. The cloth came away soaked.

'I heard that you were on Veridius Maxim.'

Yes, he had been there. He had been there to see the Word Bearers cruisers *Annunciation* and *Gospel of Steel*, and the heavier *Vox Finalis*, move up to bracket the fort. They unleashed an interlacing web of destructor-cannon fire so dense, so continuous, that it was as if the star fort were caught in the birth of a star. Precious few shuttles and salvation pods were launched before the end. Many of them were vaporised by the fort's destruction. XVII Legion fighters descended upon the others, predators striking at weak prey.

Blanchot's shuttle had made it through. His impression of the flight from the star fort was a smear of end-times fragments. He had no memory of conscious, rational thought from the moment of the attack to the terrible arrival on the surface of Calth. What he retained, instead, were jagged shards of sense impressions. The bone-rattling shaking of the craft that tested the limits of the g-force webbing's strength. The shriek of threat klaxons. The light and flame of the terrible revelation that so modestly called itself 'war.'

He saw, through a viewing block, the shuttle's port wing sheared off by cannon shells. For a moment, the craft had continued its controlled descent. Then it tumbled into a crazy, cartwheeling spin. The terror of that plunge was so absolute that it flooded all of his senses with white noise. There were no concrete images he could grasp until after the impact.

He had become self-aware again when he was standing on a rocky plain a dozen metres from the smouldering wreckage of the shuttle. He was surrounded by blackened, twisted remains – some from the craft, many from his fellow passengers. He was the only survivor.

He'd been thrown clear, he supposed, by the providence of blind luck. Before him was a storm of black smoke, fire, and a monster's skeleton big as a mountain range. It was a sight so colossal, so hideous in its contortions of ruin, that it defied comprehension. It was simply destruction, the concept given form, and it made him scream. It would not be until much later that he would learn that he had been looking at the infernal grave of Kalkas Fortalice.

He had stumbled away, then, through a shattered landscape, beneath a flaming sky. There had been no purpose to his steps, no direction, and no hope. He had moved through vistas of devastation that he revisited now every time he closed his eyes. He doubted that he would every truly escape them.

So yes, he had been on the Veridius Maxim.

'That's right,' he said, simply.

'And you're alive.'

With that simple statement, she brought home the immensity of his good fortune. He felt ashamed of his despair. He had experienced horrors, but survived them all. He was, to his knowledge, the one remaining soul who could bear witness to the star fort's tragedy. His continued existence was so improbable, it could be nothing less than a miracle. He should be grateful.

With a swelling heart, he realised that he was.

'I don't know if "charmed" is the right word,' he said, then caught himself, hoping he had sounded casual, nervous that he had not. He glanced around, but they were alone. No one other than Mellisen would have heard him over the din of improvised digging tools.

The lieutenant's gaze was serious, unwavering. 'Blessed, then?' she asked, reading him easily and reassuring him at the same time.

So she too followed the *Lectitio Divinitatus*. He nodded. 'Blessed,' he agreed.

Mellisen nodded. 'Then if you were spared, you are here for a reason,' she said. 'Why would you be saved only to die a slow, futile death here?'

'There would be no point in that.'

'Exactly. You have a destiny that must exist beyond this blocked tunnel. And if you do, then I must believe that so do the rest of us. Your presence here gives us hope.'

Exclusively available
from *blacklibrary.com*
and

Hobby Centres